**"I'VE WANTED YOU FOR SO LONG,"
HEATH SAID, AND PRESSED HIS
MOUTH IN THE FRAGRANT VALLEY
BETWEEN HER BREASTS**

Lucy moaned with pleasure, then gasped
as his lips probed her willing flesh. Writhing with desire, she could feel a maddeningly wild sensation pulsing through her
body, causing her to shake uncontrollably.

"Just relax." His tone was caressing and
low in her ear. "Let me love you . . ."

As Lucy looked up at Heath's tawny features, lit by his fierce hunger, she couldn't
imagine sharing this closeness with anyone else, and she knew that after tonight
nothing would ever be the same. . . .

LOVE, COME TO ME

Love, Come to Me

Lisa Kleypas

AN ONYX BOOK

NEW AMERICAN LIBRARY

NAL BOOKS ARE AVAILABLE AT QUANTITY DISCOUNTS WHEN USED TO PROMOTE PRODUCTS OR SERVICES. FOR INFORMATION PLEASE WRITE TO PREMIUM MARKETING DIVISION, NEW AMERICAN LIBRARY, 1633 BROADWAY, NEW YORK, NEW YORK 10019.

SIGNET, SIGNET CLASSIC, MENTOR, ONYX, PLUME, MERIDIAN and NAL BOOKS are published by NAL PENGUIN INC., 1633 Broadway, New York, New York 10019

First Printing, June, 1988

1 2 3 4 5 6 7 8 9

PRINTED IN THE UNITED STATES OF AMERICA

Dedicated to Helene and Grant Wilson with love
. . . and special thanks to Phil Kenyon for the title!

Chapter One

HEATH TURNED UP the collar of his overcoat, cursing through his teeth as he felt an icy draft of wind slip down his neck. It was his first winter here, and he was discovering that New England was not kind to misplaced Southerners. His booted feet crunched through hardened layers of snow that had accumulated over many recent storms. It had snowed and frozen over so many times that he suspected it would take until June to melt completely away.

Although he was dressed in heavy wool garments like a native Northeasterner, it would have been clear to anyone that he hadn't lived here long. His skin was dark with the permanent bronze of someone accustomed to the heat of the Southern sun. He was six feet tall, which wasn't all that remarkable in Kentucky or Virginia. Here he towered over most of the slender, compact New Englanders, and he looked at them with a blue-eyed directness that seemed to make them uneasy. At home strangers greeted each other as they passed in the street; here, it seemed you weren't privileged to look someone in the eye unless you were kin, old friends, or business associates. He wondered why people in Massachusetts didn't realize how odd they were. There was no explaining why they were so stiff and cold, and how they came by such a damned strange sense of humor. Maybe the weather had done it to them.

He smiled at his thoughts—a warm, flashing smile that had once set every female heart in Henrico County aflutter—and his gloved hand tightened around the ax handle as he set out for more stove wood. He used up wood and coal fast, trying to keep the small house he had bought last spring warm enough. It was so chilly outside that it was hard to whistle, but as he walked he occupied himself with producing a passable rendition of ''All Quiet along the Potomac Tonight,'' one of the most popular tunes of the war. It had been composed by a Northerner, but a catchy tune was a catchy tune.

Slowly his footsteps came to a halt and his whistling stopped as he became aware of a muffled noise from the direction of the river. He lived on high ground near the river, and the quiet sound floated up to him, borne on the steady breeze, dispersed by the trees until it was difficult to hear. But it almost sounded like a woman's voice.

It could not be possible that she would actually die now, in this way, in this place. Crossing the frozen river here instead of walking the extra quarter mile to the bridge had been foolhardy, but she did not deserve *this*—no one did. After the first shock of falling through the surface, Lucy had struggled violently among the chunks and shards of ice that floated around her, flailing her arms until she had grasped the edge of the hole. It had taken less than five seconds for the bite of the water to sink through her clothes into her flesh, down to her bones. All of it had happened so quickly, in less than a heartbeat. Her breath shuddered from deep in her lungs as she tried to pull herself out, but her cashmere mittens slipped on the ice, over and over again. Each time she slipped, she sank in the water almost up to her mouth.

"Someone help me! S-someone . . ." Her voice cracked as she looked toward the snow-blurred landscape of the river bank, which was punctuated with the drifts of smoke from the chimneys of nearby houses. She could not help crying, even though she knew it was draining her strength, and she called out in a wavering voice with words that intermingled with sobs. "I'm in . . . the w-water . . . someone . . . help . . ." Someone had to hear her. Someone would help.

None of this could be happening to her. Not to Lucy Caldwell, who had been safe and protected all her life. In a burst of panic, she managed to get her mittens off and scrabbled wildly at the ice, coughing on a mouthful of water. The weight of her skirts and petticoats dragged her down like lead, and for one terrifying moment she slipped completely under. Surrounded by chilling darkness, she fought the weight that tried to pull her deeper. Reaching for the surface, the air, she somehow rose back up again, and she was able to breathe. Weeping helplessly, she clutched at the edge of the ice and rested her cheek on it. Unable to move any longer, she would not let go.

Lucy closed her eyes, and dug the tips of her bare fingers into the frozen surface. No one knew she was here. Her father thought she was still in Connecticut with Aunt Elizabeth and Uncle Josiah . . . and she had not sent a message to Daniel about coming back early . . . because of their last argument . . . because she had forced him into the quarrel that she had been spoiling for. *I'm so sorry,* she thought, no longer able to feel the tears dripping down her cheeks. *I always make you argue with me . . . Daniel . . .*

Slowly the coldness of the water turned into a

dry burn, and she floated motionlessly, her fear fading into numbness. The river seemed to be talking to her, and its silent voice—insistent, lulling—penetrated her mind.

A girl had drowned here once before, many years ago. Had the river taken her as easily, as gently as this? Had it seemed like a dream to her?

Let it all disappear, the darkness urged.

Sunlight, springtime, Daniel . . . love . . . all a dream . . . all nothing.

Suddenly one of her wrists was seized in a cruel grip hard enough to send pain piercing through her numbness. She stirred in protest and her eyes fluttered open. Through the wet strands of her hair, she saw that a man was lying on his stomach near her. His unearthly blue eyes moved to the pale mask of her face, and his relentless hold on her tightened as he began to pull her out of the river. Her lips came together to form a word, but the only sound she could produce was a faint gasp.

He seemed to be saying something to her, but to her ears his voice was indistinct. She felt him pull harder on her arm, and then she sank swiftly into darkness.

She was being carried through the woods. Her head rested on a wool-covered shoulder. Her forehead was nestled intimately in the crook of a man's neck. Her legs swung gently, bumping against the stranger's side. The man who carried her trudged through the gathering drifts of snow with the steady, dependable stride of a workhorse, his feet moving in an unbroken rhythm. Sensing that she was conscious, he spoke softly, in a pronounced Southern accent.

"I was going out for stove wood when I heard you. I don't know what you were doing out there,

honey, but you should've had better sense than to set
foot on that river. Couldn't you tell it wasn't frozen
all the way?''

Opening her mouth was like prying apart
rusted iron. Lucy tried to say something and heard a
funny shuddering sound. She was too cold to talk, too
cold even to think.

''Don't worry. You're going to be fine,'' he
said lightly, and in her misery and shock, his voice
sounded immeasurably callous. Her clothes were
heavy and icy, clinging to her body and making her
limbs ache. All of her life, her cuts and scrapes and
miseries had been attended to quickly, and with plenty
of sympathy. She had never felt pain like this before,
all-consuming, enveloping, unrelenting. This was *suffering,* and she found that she had no tolerance for it.
She began to cry weakly, and with a soft oath, Heath
lifted her higher in his arms until her head was settled
more firmly on his shoulder. His lips were right by her
ear, and he murmured to her quietly. ''Such a cold
little ear. Listen to me, honey. It won't be long, and
you're going to be all better. I'm taking you to a nice,
warm room with a hot fire. We're almost there. Don't
cry. Hold on for just another minute, and we'll see
what we can do about thawing you out.''

He was talking to her as if she were a little
girl, and although he sounded outrageously patronizing, she was comforted by his soothing. Despite his
assurances that they were ''almost there,'' it seemed
to take hours before they reached a small, well-lit
house, and Lucy was nearly panicked by the realization that she couldn't feel anything from the neck
down. Wild fears ran through her mind. Was she paralyzed? Had she lost any fingers or toes? Fear kept her
quiet as the stranger carried her into the house. After
closing the door and shutting out the billowing gusts

of snow, he deposited her carefully on a sofa. He seemed heedless of the way her water-soaked clothes and hair dampened the furniture. The room was lit by the cheerful blaze of an open-grate wood stove. Lucy could see its warmth but could not feel it. Her teeth chattered audibly, complementing the animated crackle of the flames.

"You'll warm up in a minute," Heath said, fueling the blaze with more wood.

"N-n-Never," she managed to say, shaking violently.

He smiled slightly, dropping an armload of quilts into a nearby chair. "Yes, you will. I'll have you so warm in a little while that you'll be asking for a fan and a glass of iced tea."

"I c-can't f-feel anything." Fresh tears welled up in her eyes, and he knelt by the sofa, pulling the sodden tresses of hair off her face.

"I told you not to cry . . . Miss Lucinda Caldwell. That's your name, isn't it?"

She nodded, shivering fitfully.

"I've seen you working at your father's store," he continued, unwinding the limp, dripping cashmere scarf from around her neck. "My name is Heath Rayne . . . and you should know, Lucinda, that for a long time I've planned on meeting you. The circumstances are not of my choosing, but we'll just have to make the best of them." He unbuttoned her cloak with quick, impersonal efficiency, while her eyes rounded and her teeth chattered harder. "Lucinda. You're all curled up like a little snail. I need you to help me. Let me turn you onto your back."

"N-No—"

"I won't hurt you. I'm going to help. Make this easier for me, Lucy, and turn over. Yes, just like that . . ." Quickly his fingers moved to the basque of her drenched walking dress, unfastening the garment and spreading it open. She cringed away from him as she realized what he was doing. No man had ever undressed her before. But it had to be done, and she couldn't do it herself. With an effort, she tampered down the instinct to struggle against him. "It's a good thing the river had such a weak current," he remarked matter-of-factly. "If it didn't, this bunch of petticoats and all these . . . ruffles . . . would have dragged you down fast."

Lucy closed her eyes, unaware that tears were still rolling down her temples until he dried them with the corner of a quilt. Deftly her dress, the fashionable bustle, the collapsible crinoline, and all of her petticoats were removed. Several buttons popped off her boots, making Heath swear under his breath as they rattled across the floor. The laces of her stays were soaked and impossible to untie. Grimacing, he drew a bowie knife with a clipped point from his vest and cut the cords. The boned material gave way and the corset expanded, causing Lucy to gasp feebly as knifelike pains seemed to slide through her ribs. Heath paused only a split second before hooking his fingers underneath the straps of her dripping camisole. Her body went even more rigid, which hardly seemed possible. This had to be a nightmare. That was the only explanation for what was happening to her.

"I'm sorry," he whispered, stripping her of the flimsy camisole and pantalets. She thought she heard a soft intake of breath, but the sound might have been the rustle of the quilts that he proceeded to wrap her in. He cocooned her in them tightly, so that nothing except her head was visible. The cold was settling in at her joints, causing her to groan in agony and harden her knees and elbows against it. Picking up her swaddled form easily, Heath sat down in a chair by the fire, cradling her in a solid grip. Even through the blankets she could feel that his arms were rock-hard.

"Daniel. I want Daniel," she said as icicle tears rolled down her face. She was forgetting that he didn't know who Daniel was.

"Let me help you." A huge, warm hand moved over her forehead, pushing the tangled hair away, sliding down to soothe her prickling cheeks with a gentle palm.

"My l-legs hurt. My knees are *aching*—"

"I know. I've been through the same thing before."

"Not like th-this—"

"I sure as hell have." He smiled down at her. "And lived to tell about it. So there's hope for you yet."

"When . . . ?"

"In sixty-four, during the siege on Richmond. I was ducking some sharpshooters and landed myself in an iced-over pond. Hell isn't a hot place at all, honey. It's very, very cold."

"You fought against . . . us."

As she lifted her eyelashes, she saw that he was staring at her intently, his startlingly blue eyes filled with pity and something that she didn't understand. "Yes. I'm from Virginia."

"Why are you . . . here?"

He didn't say anything, just looked away from her and into the fire. His arms tightened around her quivering body, holding her still. Lucy thought that if her circumstances had been a little less dire, she would have died of shock. She had never been touched by a Southerner before, much less been wrapped in one's arms. But no matter who or what he was, it felt good to be held so tightly, anchored, and protected from the cold.

"Better yet?" he asked eventually.

"No. I'm . . . frozen on the inside . . . in my bones."

Heath shifted her slightly and reached inside his vest for a battered silver flask, which gleamed dully in the firelight. "Some of this will help."

"What is it?"

He twisted the top off the flask, and instantly she could smell the pungent fumes of strong liquor. "Ever hear of forty rod?"

"I can't!" Her eyes rounded with horror. She had been raised strictly on the doctrine that drinking was evil and led to all kinds of immoral behavior, especially in women. Her father and the reverend of the First Parish Church, Grindall Reynolds, had always said so.

"This is going to sink right down to your bones, Lucinda. Open your mouth."

"No, don't!" She would have struggled away from him had the quilts not been wrapped around her so well. Easily he wedged the neck of the flask between her lips and tilted it upwards, filling her mouth with a noxious flood of whiskey. She swallowed and choked, then swallowed again, until the pit of her stomach was burning with the fire of it. He took the flask away. Coughing, Lucy glared up at him and fought to catch her breath. As soon as she had recovered, she opened her mouth to say something and found the flask pushed between her lips again. This time the liquor went down easier, and she drank helplessly, her head caught in the hard crook of his arm. With a discomfited sound, she turned her face into his shoulder as soon as he took the flask away. No one had ever treated her so rudely before. She was going to tell her father about this, just as soon as she was able. Heath must have had a good idea of what her thoughts were, because he grinned suddenly. As he looked down at her cheek and saw the trace of whiskey on it, he removed the droplets with the tip of a long finger.

"For shame, sweet . . . turning your nose up at good Southern corn liquor. A sight better than what they drink up here—"

"Don't," she said, shrinking away from his touch. To her surprise, he was not put off or disconcerted by her rebuff. He only laughed softly.

"To ease your mind—no, I'm not going to take advantage of your helpless condition, despite the fact that you're as cute as a bug's ear."

"I am not," she contradicted groggily. "I look like something you . . . dragged up from the river . . . which is exactly . . . what I am."

"You're the most adorable thing I've ever held in my arms. I can see you don't believe me. Can't you bring yourself to trust me?"

"You're a Southerner," Lucy said thickly, her head spinning from the whiskey. Its warmth was burning deep inside her.

"Before the war started I was a Unionist," he offered in a conciliatory manner. "I'm sure that makes me a little more appealing, doesn't it?"

"No."

He smiled at her tipsiness and at the returning color in her cheeks. "You are adorable," he said huskily. "Poor little Yankee."

She was both irritated and fascinated by the way he spoke to her in that soft drawl, as if she were someone to be coddled and cherished. She had never been babied so outrageously by a man, not even by Daniel. Closing her eyes against the dancing firelight that filled the room, she sighed tiredly into Heath's neck. The dull ache was bearable now, and it was slipping away bit by bit.

"Take me home soon," she whispered, slumping against him.

"Go to sleep, honey, I'll take care of you."

As Lucy fell into an exhausted slumber, she was confronted by confused images and tumbled dreams: the memories of growing up with Daniel; their antagonism turning to friendship, their friendship turning into a far deeper affection; Daniel going off to war, sharp and neat in a uniform of red-trimmed indigo, his brown eyes twinkling and his face so attractively divided by a smooth crescent mustache. Daniel—her love, but not her lover.

She remembered Daniel's homecoming after the South had surrendered. Through her joy she had noticed that he seemed tired and so much older, his gaze dark and warm, but no longer twinkling.

"*Daniel!*" She called his name eagerly as he stepped off the train. She had loved him for years with the adoration a child would have given him, but now she was seventeen, and she wanted him with all the warmth and passion of a woman. And though his family and all his friends were there to greet him, he turned to her first.

"*Lucy, is it really you?*" he asked, opening his arms, and she ran to him with an exuberant smile of happiness.

"*Did you get my letters? Did you read them? Did—*"

"I read every one of them." He bent down and kissed her swiftly. "*I kept every single one.*"

* * *

She remembered Daniel as he had proposed to her, his arms warm and firm around her, the softness of his mouth on hers.

"It won't be right away," he said. *"We'll have to wait a year or two while I get established at the railroad company."*

"But I want you now—"

"There are too many things I want to give you. Wait for me, Lucy. Give me your promise that I won't lose you to someone else."

"I'll wait forever," she told him, with tears shining in her hazel eyes. *"You'll never lose me . . . I'll be yours as long as you want me . . . as long as you love me."*

Three years, three frustrating years of belonging and not belonging. He was not ready to marry her yet, and there was no sign that he would be ready soon. In the meantime, she would have given him anything he wanted of her, everything she had to offer him, but they had never made love. A gentleman to the core, he would not take her before their wedding night. He was a man of honor, and honor had a stronger hold on him than passion. Restless and troubled, she clung to him in supplication.

"Daniel . . . tell me you love me. Stay with me tonight . . . stay."

He brushed warm, questioning kisses on her forehead, his mouth pressing at her temple, caressing her cheeks and the fragile skin underneath her eyes. She sighed, quieting against the warmth of his body. *"Shhhh . . . ,"* he whispered, cradling her head with his hand and pressing her face against his shoulder. *"Go to sleep . . . sleep . . ."*

Heath's turquoise gaze traveled over her features slowly. Lucinda Caldwell, slumbering in his arms. He shook his head in wonder. By a stroke of fate, all his well-thought-out plans had just been rendered unnecessary. Who would have thought she would have landed in his grasp so easily? He cradled her helpless form, testing the feel of her in his arms. She fit perfectly. So small, so deliciously small, and surprisingly voluptuous.

He had wondered about how she would look this close—what her skin was like, what shape her eyebrows followed, how long her eyelashes were. Now the answers were right in front of him, and his curiosity was more than satisfied. He had seen her before, often enough to know that her smile was merry and full of charm, and that she walked across the street with a lively step. Now he knew details that he suspected no one else had been privileged to know—the natural shape of her body, the smooth, perfect paleness of her skin, the freckle on her left breast.

She looked impossibly young, with tear-marked cheeks and baby-fine skin. Her mouth was inviting; for all that, it was too wide and too strongly set. Her eyebrows were dark and slanting. The combination of those uncompromising features and a round face gave her the appearance of a determined child. The more Heath looked at her, the more fascinated he was. How could any man resist the vulnerability, the sweetness, the contrasts of that face?

Lucy turned over and moaned, aware of a terrible ache in her head as she endeavored to open her eyes. Squinting, she peered through the dimly lit bedroom to the closed window curtains. A streak of daylight peered around the edge of the curtains, betraying the fact that it was morning.

"Father?" she asked thickly, aware that

someone was entering the room. "Am I . . ." Her voice died away as she realized that the intruder was not her father, and she remembered what had happened the day before. Her face went white. "Oh! You are . . . Mr.—"

"Heath Rayne," he said, approaching the bed with a light tread. She shrank away from him immediately, jerking the covers high under her chin and looking so much like the caricature of an outraged virgin that the corners of Heath's mouth twitched.

"Don't tell me you don't trust me, Lucinda. For the way I exercised such commendable restraint last night, I deserve a medal, not suspicion." Before she could move or protest, his hand curved over her forehead, nearly engulfing her skull as he measured her temperature. The tip of his thumb lightly grazed the throbbing pulse at her temple before he removed his hand. She didn't like the way he touched her, as if he owned her. "A fever. No surprise in that, considering all that happened yesterday." Comfortably he settled his long-limbed body into a nearby chair.

It took her a few minutes to pull together her scattered thoughts. "You pulled me out of the river—"

"That's right."

"I . . . I didn't even thank you."

"Wasn't much trouble to pull a little thing like you out."

"But you're a Southerner. And I'm a—"

He looked at her with mock dismay. "And you think that a Southerner wouldn't extend a hand to someone who needs it, even if that person's a Yankee?"

"Well . . ."

"Don't even answer," he said, smiling ruefully. "I'll tell you one thing, Lucinda, it's clear even to a degenerated enemy of the Union that you're much too precious to be used as food for a few miserable little perch and bass.''

She was reasonably certain that he was teasing her, but she didn't know how to respond. It was alarming to have a stranger treat her so familiarly and casually, as if he already knew her. No matter what he had done for her or what restraint he had exercised last night, he made her uneasy.

''I would like to go home now,'' she said uncertainly.

''I know what you would like to do. Unfortunately, Lucinda, you have a fever, and I might as well stuff you back down that hole in the river as let you go out. Also, it's impossible for either of us to go anywhere. It's still snowing. One of your famed Northern snowstorms has decided to pay a nice long call.''

''Oh, no. I can't stay here. I can't!''

''Is someone going to be looking for you? Your father?''

''No, he thinks I'm still visiting with my aunt and uncle in Connecticut. He doesn't know that I decided to come back two days early. I took the train and then tried to walk back from the depot—''

''And landed yourself in the middle of the river. Honey, don't you have someone to look out for you?''

''My father. And my fiancé, Daniel Collier. And neither of them would like it if they knew you were calling me that . . . that *name*—''

''But it suits you, honey.'' He emphasized the word as if to irritate her, and his blue eyes sparkled as he gave her a lazy smile. ''I suppose they wouldn't be pleased to know that you were in my bed, either.''

"They can't find out that any of this happened. I must leave. There must be some way—"

"Do you actually think you can keep what happened yesterday a secret?"

"I have to. I'll be in terrible trouble with father . . . and Daniel . . . Daniel will start a terrible brawl with you!"

"Think he'd get the best of me?" Heath asked thoughtfully.

It was doubtful. But that was hardly something she would admit. "I know he would. He was a hero in the war, and he was a sharpshooter, and he has closets full of medals."

"Oh." He paused thoughtfully. "Well, I suppose we could try to keep all of this a secret."

"You're not worried about my reputation at all. You're worried about your own hide!"

"I'm afraid so. I've spent the last few years trying to keep it in one piece." Lifting up his hands and forearms, he inspected them idly, then quirked the side of his mouth at her. Hesitantly she smiled back at him, really looking at him for the first time. How different he was from the men she was accustomed to. He was handsome, but it was a different kind of handsomeness than she was used to. There was something earthy and untamed about him, a quality that was unaltered by the fact that his clothes were perfectly made and obviously expensive. He was one of the largest men she had ever met. His shoulders were broad underneath his tailored white shirt. Gray trousers made without a cuff or crease were fitted to a lean waist. Deeply muscled thighs were spread slightly as he slouched in the chair.

Flushing guiltily, Lucy darted her eyes past his thighs, the buttoned fly front of his trousers, his chest and shoulders, back up to his face. To her dismay, he smiled at her in a way that indicated he knew that she had been looking at his body in a way that no properly raised young woman should have. At least, not so indiscreetly.

His eyes were so blue, so vivid against his burnt-in tan that they were the color of pure turquoise. There was a thin scar that slashed across his temple, almost reaching the outward corner of his eye. It disappeared into a tracing of laugh-lines that deepened when he smiled. A rakish touch, that scar; it lent character to his handsomeness and accentuated his riverboat-gambler appearance. Turning her face away, she shifted around on the goosefeather mattress, trying to get comfortable. Immediately Heath stood up and reached across her for the pillow on the other side of the bed. "Here, I'll put this behind your back—"

"No, I can do it—"

"I don't want you lifting a finger, do you hear?"

Sliding an arm behind her shoulders, he lifted her up enough to tuck the pillow in place. For a few seconds Lucy was aware of nothing but the power of his body, and how ridiculously easy it was for him to support her weight. There was an attractive scent that clung to his skin and clothes, a fragrance of cleanliness, health, and vitality. It was the nicest thing she had ever breathed. Of course, she corrected herself loyally, he didn't smell as good as Daniel, who wore fancy cologne that came all the way from New York.

As Heath let her down and resumed his lounging in the chair, she suddenly realized what it was about him that was so different from the men up North; he was completely clean-shaven. She was used to seeing men with sideburns and beards or mustaches. A crescent mustache like Daniel's, or a handlebar with waxed tips, a horseshoe, or the kind of neatly trimmed vedette that most of the military men wore. But there was no such refinement about this man's appearance. The line of his jaw was almost startling in its cleanness, as were the contours of his straight mouth. She wondered for one traitorous second what it would be like to kiss a man without a tickling mustache. *You should be ashamed, Lucy Caldwell!* she berated herself instantly.

"Anything you like in particular?" Heath inquired lazily.

Suddenly she wasn't afraid of him anymore. "You look like any ordinary overgrown Southerner, as far as I can see."

"They do grow us taller down South. You scrawny New Englanders spend too much time indoors, and the Lord knows you don't eat well—"

"We most certainly do!"

"If you call fish and chowder good eating. In Virginia we fill a plate right to the edge with real food, not with the dabs of colored paste you call a meal. A little here, a little there . . . a man could eat for days and not get full."

"How long have you been up here?"

"Almost a year."

"You don't look like you've suffered too much from our cooking—even if we don't serve peach cobbler or fried chicken too often—"

"Fried chicken," he said wistfully. "Or good smoked ham. Or black-eye peas and bacon . . . or buttered yams . . ."

Lucy couldn't help smiling. He possessed an artless charm that was difficult to resist. Suddenly she wanted to fix him a good dinner: corned beef and cabbage, brown bread flavored with blackstrap molasses and steamed in a pail for hours, apple pie for dessert.

That would show him that Northern cooking could satisfy him just as much as whatever it was they ate down South.

"Why did you move to Concord?" she asked, and the sparkle left his turquoise eyes abruptly. "It hardly seems to make sense. Now that the war is over and Reconstruction—"

"Reconstruction. Like most everyone else around here, you have no idea what it is."

"Yes I do. It's to help the South get on its feet—"

"And brace us up with hollow crutches. I've never understood why people here seem to expect us to be grateful to you for taking over our newspapers and our right to vote, and denying us the chance to say a word about it—"

"Obviously it will take some time for the South to restore itself," Lucy countered in a dignified manner, "but eventually—"

"Eventually? Never."

"What do you mean? Of course it will."

He looked at her with disturbing concentration and quoted softly, " '. . . how thy ways have changed, and thy sweet, smiling summer face altered its expression. But those times are gone . . . The soldiers have left thee little but the past and thy loneliness.' "

She stared at him, hypnotized by the rise and fall of his voice, the subtle cadences that fell so gently on her ears. "I . . . I don't understand . . ."

"Of course you don't. How could you?" He stood up and gave her a careless smile. "It was written by a very weary war correspondent . . . a Southern one, as a matter of fact. Are you hungry?"

"Yes, but I'd like you to explain—"

"I can make tolerable sourmilk biscuits."

"Why did you—"

"And coffee."

"Oh, alright! I won't ask you any more questions."

"You do like to ask a lot of them, don't you?"

"Actually . . . there is one more thing."

"Yes? What?"

Lucy hesitated and looked down at the clean, faded quilt, her face turning progressively brighter shades of red. It took several seconds of concentrated thought before she could phrase the question. "I . . . I need to . . . is there a water c-closet, or—"

"Of course. I don't have a robe for you. Would you mind wearing one of my shirts?"

"No, I wouldn't mind . . . thank you."

Mercifully, he was sensitive to her mortification, his attitude completely matter-of-fact. Or was it just that after having been through the privations of a five-year war, he had forgotten that the functions of the human body were something that most people were embarrassed by?

As she watched him stride over to the chest of drawers, Lucy blushed even deeper, aware that underneath the covers she was wearing nothing but her corset cover and pantalets. He must have put them back on her last night after they had dried. It was a disturbing thought, that he was the only man who had ever seen her naked. Except for Dr. Miller, who had delivered her twenty years ago. All sorts of thoughts occurred to her, thoughts that she should have put away immediately, but she couldn't help wondering what Heath had thought of her looks. In contrast to the fashionable ideal, she was dark-haired and petite, the owner of a lively tongue and feet that tended to move too quickly for the rest of her body to follow. Ever since the age of sixteen, her figure had taken on a generously curved shape that made her appear shorter than she really was. For years Lucy had wanted to be tall, slim, and elegant. Still, she had been told often that she was pleasing to the eye. Did Heath Rayne think she was?

Impassively Heath laid a soft white shirt and a pair of woolen socks across her knees, then turned his back. Since it didn't appear that he was going to leave, she blushed deeply and dressed with record haste. Lucy discovered as she slid her arms into the silken garment that it had the same scent she had noticed about him before—clean and fresh, faintly dry. The shirt was hopelessly big for her. She rolled up each sleeve several turns to shorten it to her wrists. The hem of it would fall to her knees when she stood up. Wincing at the bruised and battered feel of her body, she pulled her legs out from under the covers and began pulling on the socks, the heels of which reached well past her own feet. Risking a glance upwards, Lucy saw that Heath had turned his dark golden head to the side, just enough to glance at her out of the corner of his eye. Instantly he moved his eyes back to the wall and lifted his shoulders in a slight shrug. She should have been terribly offended by his sneaky glance, as well as afraid and mistrustful of him. Strangely, her instincts told her not to be.

"Mr. Rayne," she said crisply, "you're not behaving like a gentleman."

"Miss Caldwell," he replied over his shoulder. "A long time ago I had high hopes of becoming a gentleman. I was raised to be one. Unfortunately, the events of the past few years forced me to make a choice . . . between remaining a gentleman or staying alive. War is the best way there is to weed out the gentlemen . . . very few of them manage to survive it. The scoundrels, on the other hand—"

"Oh, stop it!" she cried, staring at him in a

mixture of horror and confusion, wondering if he was actually sincere. "There are some things you shouldn't joke about."

"I agree. However, I don't think war is one of them. Or are you of the opinion that it should be remembered as a righteous undertaking? If so, you're one of many. The winning side always remembers war fondly, and justifies it quite adeptly."

She didn't know what to think of him. Warily she followed him to the second-floor bathroom, taking care not to touch him, even accidentally. The oblong bathtub was shining clean, made of tinned iron. In the corner a water closet stood like a stalwart sentinel. How cunning and modern the little room was!

"I would like to take a bath," Lucy said, eyeing the brass faucets that glistened at her invitingly.

"Not while you have a fever."

"The house is warm, and I feel just f—"

"In five minutes you'll be as weak as a baby, and I doubt you'd like it if I had to charge in here and save you from drowning . . . although I certainly wouldn't *mind* rescuing you from your bath—"

"I'm not going to take a bath," Lucy informed him shortly, closing the door in his face. What a big, shameless scamp he was. It was indecent of him to tease her as he just had, even more reprehensible than undressing her last night. After all, he had undressed her in order to keep her from getting pneumonia, but he teased her merely because . . . because he was a devil!

After relieving her more urgent needs, she splashed water on her face and smoothed her long, gnarled hair with her hands. It didn't take long for her to discover that Heath had been right—she was exhausted. She opened the door, and he appeared in the hall immediately. Flashing blue eyes swept over her, taking in the sight of her small feet in the floppy socks, the lace trim of her pantalets, the ridiculous length of his shirt on her.

"Please don't look at me like that," Lucy murmured. "I know I'm a sight."

"Before I met you, I'd heard you were the prettiest girl in town. I had no idea you would be one of the most beautiful women I'd ever seen."

Self-consciously she lowered her eyes, disliking his empty flattery. "You're an outrageous liar."

The comment would have frozen Daniel up, would have made him coldly quiet. Heath Rayne merely grinned. "I might stretch the truth about some things, yes. About you, no." He followed her back to the bedroom with a long and indolent stride. She could feel his eyes on her back, a fact that hurried her pace considerably.

"I'm going to sleep now—" she began.

"Not until after I bring you something to eat."

"I'm not hungry."

"There are some books by the bed that you might like to look through while I fix breakfast."

There was no arguing with him. Resignedly Lucy got into bed, wrapping her arms about her middle and staring at him with round hazel eyes as he tucked the covers around her. "Thank you, but there's no need for you to—"

"In some ways you remind me of the women I used to know in Virginia." Heath paused after straightening the quilt, his turquoise eyes glowing with amusement. "Sweet. And maybe a little spoiled . . . and so very well-behaved. Are you really as prim and proper as you pretend to be, Lucy?"

She floundered for a response to his disrespectful question. Finding none, she settled for giving him a withering look. He chuckled and left the room, not at all bothered by her disdain.

The touch of fever was gone after a day's sleep, but still Heath wouldn't let her get out of bed. He brought soup and bread up to her for dinner. He sat in the chair by the bed while she ate, crossing his well-muscled legs in front of him and studying the scuffed surface of his blunt-toed boots. "You said you came back two days early?"

"Yes," Lucy replied in between spoonfuls of delicious broth. "But Father doesn't know that, and he won't be expecting me until the day after tomorrow."

"Good. The train won't be running until then anyway. I'll take you home and we'll say that I was driving by as you were walking home from the depot—what about your luggage?"

"I lost my bag when . . . when I fell in. I'll make up some story about leaving it on the train." She sighed despondently. "Now it's at the bottom of the river."

"Don't frown so much, honey. Why don't they teach the women up here to smile more?"

"We're raised to economize," she said, and her eyes sparkled as she laughed. "We don't waste our smiles on just anything."

"Or anyone," Heath added, staring at her intently. He seemed to be fascinated by the sight of her as she bent her attention once more to her dinner tray. "Why did you decide to come back early?"

Lucy looked up at him quickly, her mouth full. In just a fraction of a second his mood had changed. Although his question was casual, the interest in his eyes was not, and the new realization made it difficult for her to swallow. There were several ways in which he could make this entire situation very difficult. She just hoped that he wasn't the type to take advantage. "I had to apologize to someone," she said shortly.

"Daniel Collier?"

"Yes. I had an argument with him, and then I left to stay with some relatives in Connecticut without making up to him." How strange. After thinking about him for days without end, she had actually forgotten about Daniel for the last hour or two. "I just had to tell him I was sorry for arguing with him, and I couldn't wait."

"It takes two to argue. Why don't you wait for him to apologize first?"

"Oh, but it's only fair that I apologize first. I've always been the one to start the arguments. Ever since we were children."

"Oh. I should have guessed that," Heath said, grinning at her. "Well, I guess it wouldn't take long for him to forgive you for just about anything. Not if you put those big brown eyes of yours to good use."

"It takes a few days," Lucy said gravely. "He's a very serious man. Things mean a lot to him. But after we talk and I tell him I'm sorry, and we come to an understanding, I know he's forgiven me when he reaches over and takes my hand, and I know that in a day or two he'll have forgotten all about—"

"Takes your hand?" He seemed to be amazed. "That kind of making up is hardly worth the trouble of getting into an argument. What exactly is it that you two fight about?"

"That's none of your business," Lucy said, affronted by his criticism of her relationship with Daniel. "If you'd ever met Daniel, you would understand what an honorable man he is. He's quiet and thoughtful, and that means he cares far more deeply than someone who is loud and brags about his own feelings!''

"Yes, yes. I know . . . still waters run deep. Tell me, are you planning on getting married soon?''

"Yes. Soon. We haven't set the date yet, but we've been engaged for three years, and we both agree that it's time for—''

"Three years? You've been engaged since the war ended?''

"You don't have to repeat everything I say!''

"Incredible,'' Heath muttered. "I'll say one thing. You Northerners are a different breed alright. Don't know which is worse, him wanting to wait that long or you being willing to wait.''

"We're waiting until Daniel has enough money to buy a nice house and support a family. He doesn't like to leave things up to chance. He wants the best for me.''

"He's not afraid some other man will come along and take you for himself?''

"No man could.'' Her voice rang with sincerity. "No one could ever take me from Daniel.''

"I'm sure both you and he believe that . . . but the odds don't look good on it, not when you've been dragging it out for three—''

"I'm finished with this soup,'' Lucy said sharply, handing the tray to him. "You may take it now.''

He closed his mouth and took the tray from her, his eyes brimming with quiet laughter. Just before he left the room, he glanced at her and winked, and Lucy realized ruefully that he had been enjoying himself immensely at her expense, teasing her and laughing at her stiff-backed pride.

The next day Lucy looked outside the window

and found to her relief that the day was clear and bright.

"Mornin'."

She spun around and then smiled at Heath. He was leaning against the door frame, his eyes traveling over her until they reached her slim ankles and bare feet. Then he threw her a dark, irritated look, and she made the discovery that he was handsome even when he was scowling.

"Good morning," she said.

"Hell's afire, what are you doing out of bed with nothing on your feet?"

She scampered back to the bed, hunting for the wool socks and yanking them on hurriedly. "There's no need to use such language with me."

"Are you trying to make yourself sick?"

She smiled at him, ignoring his testy mood. "I'm not going to get sick. I'm perfectly healthy, and I'm going home tomorrow. Just look outside."

"So that's why you're so happy. Can't wait to go back and apologize to your fiancé. How does humble pie taste, Lucinda . . . sweet or tart?"

"A big slice of it wouldn't hurt you any."

Reluctantly he grinned back at her. "Probably wouldn't."

"And a nice, long bath," Lucy continued hopefully, "wouldn't hurt me any."

"Probably right about that, too." He got her a fresh shirt and handed it to her, conspicuously careful not to brush her fingers with his.

"Just think," Lucy said brightly. "Tomorrow night you won't have to sleep in the parlor again. You'll have your bedroom back."

"But I don't mind you sleeping in my bedroom."

After giving him a reproving glance, she

turned away from his innocent smile and left the room. Heath went downstairs to build the fires up and make sure that the rooms were extra warm, while Lucy luxuriated in the bathtub, vigorously plying the cake of soap on her skin and hair. When she appeared in the parlor, pink and flushed and damp, he spared her not even a cursory glance, as he became preoccupied with bundling her in a chair by the fire and weighting her down with quilts. The room was filled with light and a curious sense of companionship. Lucy separated the tangles in her hair with her fingers and then ran a comb through the drying chestnut tresses while Heath pored over a stack of tattered newspapers.

Lucy didn't notice the frequency with which his bright blue eyes flickered to her. Heath studied her unobtrusively, appreciating the picture she made with her hair tumbling loose and her skin gleaming in the light. She presented no small temptation to him, for although he had known many women, there had been none quite as sweet, as vulnerable, as unawakened as Lucy Caldwell. She had a strange combination of sweetness and spirit, and an innocence that both attracted and repelled him. All of her dreams were intact. And his dreams—what remained of them—were lying around him in bits and pieces, captured in the words and the lines of print of the old newspapers he had saved. He kept them and read them every now and then, to remember. He would never forget the lessons of the past five years, had never allowed himself to make the same mistake twice.

"What are you reading?" Lucy's curious voice interrupted his thoughts, and he answered readily.

"An old edition of the Atlanta *Intelligencer*. About the campaign of Atlanta."

"Why in the world would you want to read that?"

Heath smiled wryly. "For its mistakes. This account of Johnston's retreat across the Chattahoochee, for example. The reporter states that the troops 'retired in good order.'" He shook his head and snorted. "I was there. I served under Johnston. We didn't retire in good order—we ran like hell, stepping all over each other in an effort to save our skins."

"You were with Johnston? Why, Daniel served under Sherman in that campaign!"

"We probably came nose to nose. In fact, I'll bet he was one of the bas—the soldiers who battered us with their flanking operations."

"Why are you reading those papers for their mistakes?"

"It's a hobby of mine to look them over . . . to see how they cover things, to see what the editorial policies were. Most of the time you get more information from looking at something that's been done wrong than when it's been done right. And everyone knows a lot was done wrong by the press during the war—on both sides." He settled himself on the rug before the fire and handed the paper to her. "Look on any page—rhetoric. Rhetoric instead of facts. Now if I were an editor . . ."

"Yes?" Lucy prompted when he didn't continue. "If you were in charge of a newspaper, what would you do to fix things? You might start it off doing things your own way, but sooner or later you'd probably bow down to the politicians, and start writing what they told you to write, and—"

"So hard-bitten," Heath said, his eyes glinting with sudden amusement.

"Not at all . . . that's just the way we do things in Massachusetts."

He threw back his head and laughed. "I wouldn't, no matter what everyone else did. If I were in charge of a paper, I wouldn't let it be anyone's puppet, and I'd steer my own course instead of following fashions. Most editors let anyone and everyone manipulate their newspapers, especially the politicians. And the papers up here are just as bad as anywhere else—they're too soft, too partisan, too . . . timid. Hardly anyone has the backbone to step on a few toes, print the truth without using a lot of fancy words to soften it up—''

"But would *you* always print the truth if you were in the editor's shoes? Even if you didn't like it?"

"Damn right I would."

"I don't think so. Maybe you would at first, but eventually you'd start printing your own *version* of the truth, just like all of the other editors do."

"Ah, but I'm different from all of them," he said, smiling at her animated expression. "I wouldn't be so eager to sweet-talk the subscribers that I couldn't call a spade a spade. I have few biases—"

"Except that you hate Northerners."

"Oh, that's a little strong. When you get right down to it, I don't. In fact, there are some I could get to be quite fond of." He chuckled as she stared into the fire with renewed absorption.

"Tell me," she said, still not looking at him, "have you ever worked for a newspaper? It seems like you have."

"I was a journalist for the Mobile *Register* during the war. I reported for a few other papers, too. I tended to switch around, usually when the editors were too heavy-handed. Nothing makes a writer mad quicker than seeing one of his reports cut almost in half—"

"But surely they had good reasons for cutting your work."

Heath laughed softly, shaking his head as if

the world didn't make sense and any man who tried to find reason in it was a fool. "Yes. They felt that a reporter should try to keep the public's morale high. The editors didn't like my battle reporting—said I was faultfinding, glum, that I didn't look on the bright side of things. Problem was, I couldn't find much cause for optimism in the middle of a battle—especially since I was on the losing side."

As he smiled again, Lucy regarded him curiously, unable to share his amusement. The firelight turned his hair into a brilliant blaze of coppery gold, filtered through his dark eyelashes and cast long shadows over his tanned cheeks. He looked so carefree and handsome, as if he had never known the hardship of battles and gunfire. With all the horror and bloodshed he had undoubtedly seen, she could not understand why he could smile and talk so easily about the war. It seemed utterly heartless of him to be so comfortable about it all. Every other man she had ever heard talk about the war got all riled up, bitter, excited, proud. Frowning slightly, she sought another direction for the conversation.

"The *Register* was a big paper, wasn't it? You must have gotten published often."

"Often enough."

"Do you have any copies of what you've written?"

"Actually, I don't."

"That's too bad. I'd like to read something of yours. Did you use your initials or—"

"Rebel. That was my pseudonym. I couldn't use my initials, since I occasionally took unpopular stands. My . . . associates . . . wouldn't have appreciated the fact that I could never see angels and golden banners flying over the battlefield. All I could see were wounds and indignity. Even when we won the battle,

I couldn't see triumph in all that wretchedness . . . but then, maybe I lacked imagination.''

Wearing a stricken expression, she stared at him. ''Your pseudonym wasn't really Rebel, was it?''

''You don't like it?''

''That's not what . . . I mean . . . I have read something of yours. They reprinted them in some of the newspapers up here. You wrote about the fall of Atlanta better than anyone—''

''Well, I really was walking down the center of the road if something I wrote was printed in a Yankee paper.''

''Don't make light of it. I read what Rebel— what you wrote, over and over again . . . the refugees, and the children in the street, and the deserters. You're not teasing me, are you? I would never, never forgive you if you weren't telling me the truth about this—''

''I'm not teasing you, Lucy.'' Suddenly Heath's face was grave and hard.

''You wrote a book about the war after it ended . . . or at least someone using the name Rebel did—''

''I wrote it.''

''Everyone's read it . . . well, I haven't yet— but I will.''

''Please do. My royalties have been diminishing lately.''

Lucy didn't smile. She sat there, staring down at the paper in her hands without seeing a word. That article about Atlanta was one of her few vivid memories of the war. Concord had been so far away from the actual fighting that she had felt removed from all of it, reminded of it mostly by the fact of Daniel's absence and her own work in the Ladies' Soldiers' Aid Society. And then, the reporter named Rebel had written about the battles in Georgia, the people fleeing

Marietta in droves, the weariness and desperation of the besieged city of Atlanta. His words had been so bleak and dismal that she had finally understood just a little of the horror it had been for all those people to see their world being torn up. It was difficult to believe that the man in front of her was that reporter.

"We all looked for more articles by you," she said. "We were sure that whatever you wrote about the surrender would be printed. But there wasn't anything."

"I wasn't at the surrender. Wounded at Harpeth Creek. We were sent on a suicidal charge. A noble, last-ditch effort to win the war. At that time, we figured there wasn't much to lose. Most of the regiment was killed."

"I'm so glad you weren't," Lucy said, her eyes moistening with tears despite her will to hold them off. He looked up in surprise at the quaver in her tone, then shook his head and smiled ruefully.

"You're too soft-hearted, girl."

"I know. Daniel says I shouldn't cry so easily, but sometimes I—"

"Daniel again. I don't believe I've ever known a man so well and disliked him so much without ever having met him."

She chuckled at that and swallowed hard against the biting tears.

His hand slid over hers, enclosing her fingers in the warmth and strength of his. Though she did nothing to encourage him, not even daring to look at him, her pulse became light and rapid, and an almost pleasant sensation of nervousness took hold of her. Slowly, she turned her palm up to meet his, and their fingers laced together. A strange and unfamiliar sweetness seemed to drift through her body. *There's nothing wrong in holding hands,* she told herself defensively.

Yet somehow, this felt disloyal to Daniel, finding such pleasure in the touch of another man. The gentle clasp tightened briefly; then, Heath pulled away, leaving Lucy with a feeling of deprivation.

"I'm going to see about splitting some wood," he said, and she nodded silently, suddenly confused and eager to be away from him, and reluctant to let him go.

Chapter Two

THE DUNKING IN the river had been even more of a disaster for Lucy's walking dress than for Lucy. The garment was shrunken in some places and oddly misshapen in others. Futilely she fussed with the velvet plaits that looped the sides of the overskirt up. She retied the brown satin ribbons several times, but it was impossible to disguise the damage. She was thankful that her cloak would cover everything until she could find a way to dispose of the clothes secretly. Even though her father was meticulous about the details of his store, he was absent-minded about most matters concerning his daughter, and he would never notice the absence of a few garments.

This morning there was a thoughtful silence between Lucy and Heath, a silence that was puzzling in light of the easiness of their earlier conversations. He took her to the village in a small carriage drawn by a dappled gray gelding, and as they neared Concord green, the pace of the horse seemed to slow down.

"Almost there," Lucy said reluctantly, realizing that her strange adventure of the past two days was coming to an end. Suddenly it occurred to her that there were things she had not talked about with him, things that should have been discussed. "Heath, wait. Could you stop the carriage?" His eyes, shining cool and blue-green in the daylight, flickered to her as he pulled on the reins, easing the horse to a halt. "There is something we have to decide," Lucy continued, her voice subdued. "About how we're going to behave if we see each other in public. I don't want to treat you as if you're a stranger to me, not after what you've done for me . . . but I can't let on that I know you!"

His face was blank, the thin scar on his temple uncamouflaged by any laugh lines. "Because I'm a Reb?"

"No. No, of course not. Because we haven't been introduced . . . and I can't ever talk to you like the other night, never again. I'm engaged. And you're not the kind of man that an engaged woman could be friends with. No one would understand, especially not Daniel."

"Of course he wouldn't," Heath said, and the quiet sound of his voice comforted her slightly. He did understand. She raised her eyes to his face, her gaze alighting on the tawny color of his skin and the rich gold of his hair. How out of place he was, up here amid the snow and the icy air. He had been born to live where there was plenty of sun and green land. His lazy smiles and his foreign drawl would never be accepted here. *Why has he decided to settle so far away from home?* she wondered. *What could his reasons possibly be?* She couldn't bring herself to ask him. For the first time, she saw that there was a thin, almost unnoticeable scar on the side of his neck which seemed to extend past the collar of his shirt. How far down did it go? How had he gotten it? It looked like the one on his temple.

She wondered what kind of man he was. She only knew enough about him to recognize that there were depths of experience and emotion locked inside him that no one would ever be able to understand. Unlike Daniel and the others she knew who were basically uncomplicated, Heath Rayne was too complex, too . . . deceptive. She was grateful for what he had done, but she would not delude herself into thinking that there was any basis for a friendship between them. They had nothing in common. They were worlds apart.

"I'll never forget what you did for me," Lucy said gravely. "Nothing I could do would ever repay—"

"I don't want your everlasting gratitude," he interrupted, a wry smile spreading slowly across his face. "Don't look so woebegone, honey. This isn't goodbye."

"But it is. That's what I'm trying to tell you."

"Ah, I see. Forgive me. It's just that in Virginia we have a different way of saying goodbye."

There was deviltry dancing in his blue eyes, and Lucy smiled in response as she turned her face away from him. "Don't tease," she said, turning coquettish, knowing that now he was going to try to cajole her into allowing him a liberty; and certainly she would refuse, no matter how persuasive he was. She was an engaged woman.

"I'm not teasing. This is a serious matter. Don't you think you owe me at least one kiss? As you just pointed out, I saved your life. Would Daniel begrudge just one of your kisses to the man who rescued you? Would Daniel ever know? God knows *I* would never tell him. A kiss is such a little thing to ask, Lucy."

"I've never kissed anyone but Daniel," she said primly, finding an irresistible delight in flirting with him.

"Yes, but I'll bet he doesn't know where your birthmark is," Heath said, and smiled as she blushed.

"Sorry, honey. You were right before—I'm not much of a gentleman, am I?"

"No, you're not."

"Are you telling me the truth about never kissing anyone but Daniel?"

What a conversation for her to be having with him! She felt her cheeks go hot as she avoided his gaze. "It's basically true. Before we were engaged, I . . . tried kissing with a boy or two . . . but they weren't real kisses like they are with Daniel."

"Real kisses," he repeated thoughtfully. "I didn't know there was any other kind except real ones."

"You know what I'm talking about. Some kisses don't mean anything at all. But a real kiss is one that means something."

"No, I didn't know anything about these interesting distinctions. Look at me, Lucy."

Aware of a mixture of confusion and excitement, she obeyed for a reason that she didn't understand. Yes, he was going to kiss her, and she shouldn't let him, but she couldn't find it in herself to tell him not to. Deliberately he removed his gloves, his eyes holding hers. Then one of his brown hands was clasped around the back of her neck, his fingers sliding into her chestnut hair. The other had lightly gripped the nipped-in curve of her waist. The way he held her was very different from Daniel's undemanding embrace.

"Tell me if this is real or not, Lucy."

His head lowered over hers, and she closed her eyes, inhaling quickly. The first touch of his mouth was dry and warm and urging, demanding something that she didn't know how to give. She clutched the edge of the seat and offered her lips to him cautiously. Long after she thought that he would stop, the pressure of his mouth was still on hers, and then it slanted harder, forcing her lips apart. Gasping, she put her hands on his chest to push him away, her palms flat on the broad surface. The kiss was now hot and intimately moist, making her tremble in a funny combination of repulsion and pleasure. Bewildered, startled, she felt the velvet stroke of his tongue against hers, tasting her in a way that she had never dreamed of. His mouth was blazing and hungry. There was a magic about him that wound around her senses and tugged delicately. She was shaking, just as she had the first time he had held her, only this time it was not from cold but a heat that burgeoned from deep inside her.

With a muffled sound, Heath ended the kiss, and there was a disturbed expression on his face. Dazed, she met his eyes; her heart was throbbing and her stomach jumping. He had just tasted the inside of her mouth. The thought that anyone would want to do that was absolutely astonishing. And yet . . . it hadn't been unpleasant.

"Don't do that with your fiancé," Heath said. "He'll be asking where you learned it."

Lucy pulled away from him with a hasty jerk, sliding to the corner of the seat and averting her face. Her lips felt soft and swollen, and she could still feel the brush of his tongue against hers. Every time she thought about it, she felt limp and shaky. How could she have let him do that to her? Guiltily she thought about Daniel, who had never attempted to do such a thing. She and Daniel would probably never kiss with their mouths open, not even after they were married. As Daniel had told her, a man held one kind of woman in a way that meant lust, and the other kind of woman in a way that meant love, and he had said that *she* was the kind who was meant to be held with love.

"In your opinion, was that a real one?" Heath

smiled wryly as Lucy refused to look at him. "Alright, honey . . . I'll take you home now."

In the evening Daniel came to call. Conveniently, it was only a short walk from his house to the general store on Main Street. Lucy and her father had lived above the store on the second floor ever since Lucy's mother Anne had died of consumption years ago.

"I'm going to be downstairs taking inventory," Lucas Caldwell said, checking absently to make certain that the ends of his snowy white mustache were twirled into neat points. Lucy smiled gratefully at him, knowing that he was giving her a few minutes alone with Daniel, and her eyes followed the immaculately clad form of her father until he closed the door with careful precision. Then she flew to Daniel's arms. How perfect they were together. He was just the right height, tall enough for her to feel protected, yet not so tall that she felt overpowered by him. They fit together so comfortably, like two hands clasped together. They even thought the same way. Daniel was her dearest friend, and she knew that that would never change, even after he had become her husband.

"Oh, how I missed you," Lucy said fervently, lifting her mouth for his kiss. The familiar brush of his mustache feathered across her upper lip. Inexplicably, a new impulse swept over her, and Lucy started to let her lips drift apart, wanting more than just the pressure of his mouth. She wanted to taste him. She wanted him to kiss her harder, like she had been kissed that afternoon. Maybe in the past Daniel had been afraid to try that with her because he hadn't wanted to upset her. But even as her mouth softened with yearning, he lifted his head away from hers.

"I missed you too," Daniel said, his brown

eyes traveling fondly over her face. "I've thought about what we talked about before you left—"

"I've done some thinking too. I'm so sorry that I have been pushing you so hard."

"Of course you're anxious to get married. I understand that, my dear . . . I want to be married just as much as you do. We'll set a date soon. I promise."

"But you've said that for the past three years."

"We can't get married until I can afford to get you what you deserve—"

"You have enough to get a small place. I don't want a big house. I just want for us to be together. I don't see why you won't even consider us living here with Father or with your family, just until we have enough money to get our own place."

"It's a matter of pride, and that's my final word—"

"Can't you put aside your pride for a minute and listen to me? Other men live with their family or their wife's family. Other men start off with smaller houses and build bigger ones later. Can't you decide on doing one of those things? I don't want to go on like this anymore." Her voice caught in her throat as she added softly, "I'm lonely."

Astonishment crossed his sternly handsome face, and his hands came to rest on her shoulders. "How could you be lonely? You're surrounded by people all the time. And I see you every day, sometimes more that once a day. We go to the dances and lectures—"

"A person can be surrounded by people and still be lonely. I feel as if no one needs me. I don't *belong* to anyone."

"Your father—"

"Father has his store. That's what means the

most to him. His whole world is the store and his customers, and that's all he really wants. Oh, I know he loves me, but it's not the same. And you have your family, a big family with too many brothers and sisters to count. You are all so close, you support each other, you all belong in that family.''

"But you belong in my family—"

"I'm an outsider," she insisted stubbornly. "And *I* need a family too. I'm a woman, and there's so much I want to give to you—so much that you won't let me give you. I . . ." She hesitated before rushing on. "I want to be close to you and love you in the way that a woman loves her husband. I'm tired of kisses on the porch and holding hands when no one's looking."

Daniel's ears became red as he understood what she was saying. "Lucy, hush. You don't know what you're asking."

"I want to be *yours,* in a way that I can never be anyone else's. I don't want to wait anymore, not if we're going to put off the wedding for another few years—"

"My Lord." Daniel let go of her, laughing nervously. "I never guessed you would have thought about such things, Lucy."

"Of course I do. All women do, whether they say them or not."

"But we can't. I want you to be unspoiled on our wedding night. Like a bride should be."

"You're always so concerned about the way things should be," Lucy said hollowly, the passionate desperation dying in her eyes. "What about the way things are right now . . . what about the way I feel?"

"You won't have to wait much longer. We'll set a date—"

"Soon. I know."

"I promise." He bent to kiss her on the fore-head. Suddenly Lucy wrapped her arms around his neck and pressed his lips hard against his, her young, ardent body molding to him. He froze in surprise, then slid his arms around her, beginning to respond to her feverish kisses. Lucy quivered in triumph, tilting her head back and clinging more tightly to him. She felt his masculine body, firm and well-exercised, tauten against hers. Against her abdomen there was a rising pressure and throbbing that she knew was the physical evidence of his desire for her.

Daniel pulled his hips away instantly. His face was flushed and uncomfortable. "Not now," he said hoarsely. "I told you, Lucy, we're going to wait."

Some part of her rejoiced in the fact that she had affected him so strongly—at least she knew now that she wasn't alone in her frustrated need—but another part of her sank in disappointment. When Daniel made a decision, he stuck by it no matter what. "Al-right," she murmured, looking down at the floor. Shame was beginning to wash over her as she sensed his disapproval.

"You've got to learn not to be so impulsive. It's difficult enough in moments like that to keep from taking advantage of you. But I respect you, Lucy, and in the end you'll be glad for it."

"I guess I will."

"Of course you will."

The snow from the February storm melted a little. The snowdrifts became solid and compacted around the stripped elm trees that lined Main Street. Lucy worked with her father in the store, which was unusually busy as people bought supplies to restock what they had used while being snowed in, everything from coffee and tea to beeswax and milled soap. There

was little time to think about Heath Rayne and the
small house on the other side of the river, where she
had lived for two days in secret. But occasionally Lucy
would pause while some detail of the Southern stranger
would pop into her mind, like the exotic turquoise
color of his eyes, or the way he had called her
"honey," and his sense of humor, sometimes dry,
sometimes whimsical. It bothered her that she sometimes thought of Heath while Daniel was nearby, for
then she had to think up various explanations for her
blushes or her quietness.

Saturday morning in the store, Daniel and his
friends were gathered as usual around the Seavey stove,
talking, smoking the cigars that General Grant had
brought into vogue, reliving battles they had been
through. Lucas Caldwell was polishing the glass case
where the knives were kept, while Lucy helped Mrs.
Brooks select material for an everyday dress. As Mrs.
Brooks left and the bell above the door swung back
and forth jauntily, another customer came in. Folding
a length of linen, Lucy paid no attention to the new-
comer until she realized that Daniel and his friends
had grown strangely quiet. Glancing at the doorway,
she saw the flash of gold-shaded hair and the glow of
deeply tanned skin, and she dropped her eyes to the
counter hurriedly. Her hands shook as she picked up
the linen and stacked it on top of other bolts of cloth.

"Good morning, Mr. Rayne," Lucas Caldwell said easily. "Come to check on your order? It
came in yesterday."

"That and the mail," came the distinctively
accented reply. The sound of his voice, as warm and
drawling as she had remembered, caused a silky ripple
down Lucy's spine. Unobtrusively her hands went to
the sash of her Irish poplin dress, neatening the large
bow that tied in back and straightening the ribbons so

that they trailed properly over the plain overskirt and striped underskirt.

"Lucy, will you take care of that?" Lucas asked.

"Mornin', Miss Caldwell."

She forced herself to meet his gaze and saw a smile in the blue-green depths. Had he seen her checking her sash? And if he had, did he think that it was for his benefit? Conceited scamp! "Mr. Rayne," she acknowledged him coolly. Her fingers were all thumbs, but she managed to go through the glass-partitioned boxes near the front door. There were two letters for him, one addressed in feminine handwriting. Resisting the urge to look at it more closely, she handed it to him. Their eyes locked again, and her heart beat faster at the fact that he was there, that the two days they had spent together had not been a dream, that he and she and Daniel were all standing in one room together.

"Thank you, Miss Caldwell."

"Mr. Rayne," Daniel suddenly said—his voice so different from usual, so filled with contempt, that for a second Lucy didn't recognize it—"is our resident Confederate, Lucy."

"My fiancé, Mr. Daniel Collier," Lucy said to Heath, who fixed Daniel with an interested look, then turned back to her.

"Really," Heath murmured dryly. It was all Lucy could do to keep her lips from curving into a smile, because she knew exactly what he thought of Daniel. She felt as if they were sharing a private joke. The amusement was wiped from her expression abruptly as Daniel walked over to her and stood side by side with her.

"Look close, Lucy." A sneer pulled at his lips. "You're always asking questions about the war and the Rebs we fought. This is one of those men who wounded and killed so many of our friends, and kept boys like Johnny Sheffield in filthy prisons until they died of smallpox.''

"Daniel!'' Lucy looked at him in amazement. Surely this couldn't be her gentle, polite Daniel—a man who hated to argue—trying to pick a fight! All of the softness in his brown eyes had disappeared, and he looked so cold and angry that she instinctively took a step back from him. His shoulder had brushed against hers, and it had been as rigid as steel.

"I wouldn't have thought a Southerner would pick up his own order,'' Daniel said, staring hard at Heath. "Why don't you have one of your niggers do it?''

"Because I've never believed in slavery,'' Heath replied softly.

Two of the men lounging in chairs by the stove stood up quickly. "You can say that,'' one of them said tightly, "but you fought for it, didn't you? You believed in it enough to slaughter thousands of good men in order to keep it.''

"I had my own reasons for fightin'.'' The Virginian accent became more pronounced, contrasting sharply with the flat Northeastern voices. "Mostly I didn't like a bunch of Yankees tellin' me what to do, when they didn't know what the hell—''

"Lucy, why don't you take Mr. Rayne to the downstairs shelves to get the glass pane he ordered?'' Lucas Caldwell suggested, his face set in a way that promised a lecture for the men gathered around the scene. A businessman first and foremost, he would never tolerate this kind of upset in his store. His words would be listened to and respected by the men there. Lucas was a trusted and popular figure in Concord, and almost everyone owed him a favor or two. He wasn't above reminding them of that, either. Lucy looked into her father's eyes, read his intentions, and nodded slightly.

"I don't want her going anywhere alone with a Reb," Daniel said.

"I believe my daughter is safe enough with him. Isn't she, Rayne?"

"Yes, sir."

"Then go on with him, Lucy."

Lucy led Heath to the back of the store and down a narrow flight of stairs. As they left, she heard her father's voice—"Now in my store, boys, a customer is treated with respect, whether he's a Northerner, a Southerner, a Frenchman, or an Eskimo, and if you don't like the way I run my business—"

They reached the cellar and stopped in front of the wooden shelves, piled with paper-wrapped packages. Lucy's nostrils flared slightly as she fumed with agitation. "I'm sorry. I apologize for Daniel—for all of them. Daniel isn't usually such a . . . such a . . ."

"Intolerant, high-minded jackass?" he suggested politely.

"I've known all of them since I was little. None of them would have said anything to you if it was just one-to-one, but when they're in a group—"

"I know that. And I won't try to tell you that the same thing wouldn't have happened had one of them been in the same situation down South. Except down there, he would have been lynched before he got to answer back."

She looked up at him and some of her anger faded. Apparently Heath was not upset. He didn't even seem bothered by the scene upstairs, while *she* was the one carrying on! Taking a deep breath, she forced herself to calm down. It wasn't seemly for her to take up for another man against Daniel, especially when the other man was a stranger.

"How are you?" he asked.

"I'm fine. I didn't even have a cold after . . . after you-know-what."

He smiled at her vague reference to the misadventure at the river. "Good. Wouldn't want Daniel to catch anything from you."

"No."

"Did you and he settle whatever it was you argued about?"

"Well . . . not really."

"What a shame."

"Please," Lucy said, starting to laugh. "So much sympathy just overwhelms me."

"I'll admit something—he's about what I expected. But you didn't mention anything about his mustache."

"Very distinguished, isn't it?"

"Maybe I'll grow one."

"No!" Lucy said quickly, her face all sincerity, and then her cheeks colored as he laughed.

"Whatever you say. So you're not particularly fond of mustaches—"

"Except on Daniel."

"He's put quite a spell on you, hasn't he? Or is it just that he's had a while to work at it? Maybe . . . given a little time . . . someone else could make you care just as much."

"Absolutely not. Daniel and I have been together forever. We've . . . well, we've grown into each other. Nothing could break that kind of bond."

"*Nothing* could break it? If there's one thing I've learned in the past few years, honey, it's that you can't be certain of anything."

She gave him a long, expressive glance, effec-

ively warning him that the conversation was becom-
ng much too personal. "I would rather you didn't call
me that anymore."

He grinned at her. "Would you hazard a guess
as to which one of those is my package, Miss Caldwell?"

Silently she turned to the shelves and reached
up for one of the parcels on the end, rising on her
toes. Getting a hold on the edges, she started to pull
it down. His hands nearly covered hers as he reached
from behind her and lifted the wrapped pane away
from her faltering grasp. For one shattering moment,
she felt the hard, lean length of his body press against
her back, and Lucy whirled around instantly. "Don't,"
she said fiercely. "You leave me alone, do you understand?"

"It wasn't intentional. Seeing you wobble on
your toes while holding a window pane that I've had
on order for almost a month was more than I could
stand."

"I wasn't wobbling!"

"I see. You would prefer to think that I was
so enthralled by your charms that I would use any convenient excuse to—"

"No, I wouldn't! . . . I . . . oh, get out of
here!"

He indicated the stairway with a gesture that
was at once mocking and deferential, his eyes shining
with amusement. "After you, Miss Caldwell."

She preceded him regally, walking back into
the main part of the store and stopping at her usual
spot behind the counter. Accepting his money without
bothering to count it, Lucy went over to the cash
drawer.

"Now if you'd like to wait for one more minute," Lucas Caldwell said to Heath, "while I write out your receipt—"

"Obliged, but I don't need a receipt."

They all watched in silence as the tall Southerner strode towards the doorway. George Peabody, a hotheaded boy who couldn't resist making one remark from the safety of the corner, muttered an insult under his breath.

Heath stopped and turned around, giving him a measuring glance, but before he could make a reply, Lucy rounded fiercely on the boy. "George Peabody, you button your mouth!"

"He'd better see to his britches first," Heath said, and touched the brim of his hat respectfully to Lucy before slipping out the door.

Automatically they all looked at George's trousers, discovering that one of the buttons did indeed need to be fastened. The tension broke, and as the flushed boy spun around to restore his injured dignity, they all chuckled. Even Daniel had to smile. "Impudent Reb," he said ruefully, and no one disagreed.

The purpose of the latest series of intellectual meetings, which were held in various parlors in Concord, was to talk about Reconstruction with objectivity, sensibility, and a lack of prejudice. As everyone had expected, the meetings were far from objective, seldom sensible, and never unprejudiced. Still, the highly-charged discussions were well attended and interesting. The parlor debates were solely the province of the men, though the women who wished to listen were allowed to sit quietly along the sides of the room. Men like the long-winded, methodical Bronson Alcott and the insightful Ralph Waldo Emerson traded observations about the war and Reconstruction with other townspeople. This time the meeting was being held in the Caldwell parlor, which was scarcely large enough to hold the gathering that had accumulated this week.

Lucy surveyed the kitchen while the meeting was in progress. Quickly, she filled the urn of water on top of the shining cast-iron stove, so that moisture would disperse through the dry air, and then she cast a glance at the trays of tea cakes that would be brought out to the parlor later. Satisfied that everything was in order, she smoothed down the muslin and lace apron-front of her dress and tiptoed towards the sound of voices. At this moment Bronson Alcott was standing at the front of the circle of people, his gray hair flowing to his shoulders, his broad hands making moderate gestures as he spoke with the attitude of a man who loved the art of oration.

Cautiously Lucy stood in the shadowy doorway and looked around the room. There was her father at the back, checking his pocket-watch and no doubt wondering when the tea cakes would be served. Daniel, his legs crossed and his hands resting on one knee, was in the innermost circle of the group, gazing raptly at the speaker. In the far corner of the room, Heath Rayne sat in a patch of darkness, the shadows dimming his hair to a muted wheat color. His legs were crossed ankle over the knee, his arms folded casually across his chest—the perfect picture of boredom—but Lucy knew somehow that he was listening intently to everything that was being said.

She wondered why he would want to come to the meetings on Reconstruction, when he was the only Southern contingent. True, in Concord there were occasional traces of pro-Southern sentiment when it came to the issue of Reconstruction. But Heath Rayne was an outsider here—he and everyone else knew it. His

presence had definitely inhibited the first few meetings
or so. Everyone kept looking at him, wondering when
he was going to jump up with the Rebel yell and start
brawling, yet he had been gratifyingly quiet during
every discussion so far. Now they had almost forgotten
that he was at the meetings at all. He arrived, made
pleasant small talk with those who dared to approach
him, listened quietly to the lecture, and then left, as
if he were a disinterested observer and had had no
experience with the war! Lucy didn't understand him
at all. She comforted herself with the fact that no one
else did either.

"And to those that say the conflict should not,
in retrospect, be viewed as a confrontation between
the absolute wrong and the absolute right," Alcott was
saying, "my reply is for them to examine in the cold
light of objectivity the evil of slavery. A sympathy for
those who supported slavery and a wish to grant them
leniency . . . must be considered in terms of the highest treason . . ."

Having heard the speech countless times before, Lucy had to fight back a betraying yawn. Delicately she raised a hand to her mouth and stifled it,
blinking to clear away her weariness. Glancing at
Heath again, she saw that this time his blue eyes were
resting on her steadily. She held his glance for a long
moment, unable to look away, and as his mouth curved
in the faintest of smiles, she felt one coming to her
own lips. Then Mr. Emerson was adding to what had
just been said, his green-gray eyes cast with a dark
sheen. His words, as always, gained the attention of
everyone in the room. "Leniency to the Southerners
should not and cannot be given, not if we wish to
uphold the ideals for which the war was fought. Rebels
should be pounded and not negotiated into a peace, if
we are finally to realize our aspirations. War is not a

game. It should be conducted without mercy to the opponent, if any moral inspiration is to be gained by the men who fight it.''

"Without mercy?'' Lucas Caldwell echoed humbly. ''But shouldn't we try to—''

"Man is made pure by war, scourged of shift-iness and putridness,'' Emerson stated flatly. ''In some ways, war is good for man. That—and the rightness of our beliefs—is why I encouraged our young men to fight.''

Suddenly a new voice cut through the air with deceptive softness. ''You're wrong . . . sir. Man is robbed by war . . . of his humanity.'' All eyes turned to the corner, where Heath Rayne still sat with decep-tive laziness threaded through his posture. One side of his mouth lifted in a mocking echo of his usual smile. ''Easy,'' he continued even more gently than before, ''easy for a man like you to tell the young ones to fight, when you're too old to tote a rifle and your son is just a babe. Easy to throw them into the lions' den when they'll believe anything that's wrapped up in the flag.''

A low rumbling of voices grew after the initial shock had faded away. Lucy twisted her hands in her apron, clenching the folds of it tightly as she stared at Heath. She was filled with sympathy and acute fear for him. She understood why he couldn't keep quiet any longer, but she was afraid that he had just bought him-self trouble at doubled value. No one dared to tell Emerson, one of Concord's most beloved and re-spected men, that he was wrong. And no one, least of all a Southerner, implied that Emerson was a coward. *Oh, what have you done to yourself?* she wailed si-lently, wishing she could turn back time and stuff a handkerchief in the stubborn Confederate's mouth be-fore the words had been said.

"War is a test of man's integrity." Emerson said, his elderly visage pale with what could have been either anger or upset. "An apprenticeship. By subjugating the Rebels, the North proved its moral integrity. It was worth the loss of our men, every one of them."

"That's right, Mr. Rayne." Daniel plunged into the fray, his mustache barely moving as he spoke stiffly. "Good men, who died because of Southern arrogance, starting with the secession of South Carolina and going right on through—"

"South Carolina seceded," Heath interrupted, "because you toed a line and dared us to step across it."

"As I said," Daniel cut in with a small half-smile, "Southern arrogance. The fact is, South Carolina did step across that line, with the full support of the rest of your people, even though you all knew what would happen if you did. And now we have good Northern men lying in graves—"

"Yes, and twice as many Southern graves—" came the swift rejoinder.

"Graves of uneducated Rebels. As Mr. Emerson once said, the whole State of South Carolina is not worth the death of one Harvardian," Daniel sneered, and then fell silent.

Heath's face paled. His eyes glittered with a full draught of the pride that had kept his people fighting long after their cause had been lost. But his hands, formerly clenched into hard fists, relaxed and loosened. "Lot of good men in South Carolina," he pointed out, and then he smiled oddly. "Even a few who were Harvardians . . . Mr. Collier."

And with that, he left amid an uproar of raised voices, the orderly discussion becoming a tumult of people wanting to be heard. Lucy fled through the kitchen and out the back entrance of the building, nearly tripping over a cement dismounting block as she crossed over to the side of the street. "Heath . . . stop. Wait, please . . ." He stopped and then turned slowly to face her, his expression wiped clean of emotion. The branches of the bare elm trees cast streaks of shadow across his face. "You were right," Lucy said breathlessly, her eyes dark and troubled. "A lot of what you said was right—but you've got to be careful about what you say. You *know* how they feel up here about the war, and how they feel about Mr. Emerson. No one ever tells Mr. Emerson outright that he is wrong."

"Someone needs to."

"You've only seen one side of him tonight. You don't understand what a good, kind man he is. You should see him stopping to talk to little children, and pitching in to help whenever it's needed, and doing so much to benefit the town. He is kind and benevolent, and the most loyal—"

"Please," Heath snapped, holding up his hands in a defensive gesture. "No lectures on him."

"The point is, he is the most beloved citizen of Concord. My Lord, if you sat and thought for hours, you couldn't have come up with a better plan for making them want to run you out of Concord—why, Daniel and his friends—"

"If they do, it's nothin' to you, honey," he said, his voice light and unconcerned, his jaw rigid. Suddenly he seemed so alone, so terribly alone that Lucy felt a sharp ache of compassion she couldn't hold back. She reached out and laid her small hand on his upper arm in a soothing gesture. Under her fingertips the muscled surface was smooth and hard as steel, shaking slightly with the force he exerted over it.

"What are you doing here?" she asked softly,

the sound of her words a sweet hum in the stillness of
the night. "Why have you come so far away from
where you belong? You should be at home with your
family, with people who care for you—"

"No," he interrupted suddenly, jerking away
from her touch. A laugh caught in his throat. "Don't
playact with me, Cinda. It's not helping."

"I'm not playacting. You helped me once. I
wish I could help you."

She stared up at him with reluctant concern,
her skin pale and translucent in the cold light of the
moon. Suddenly, Heath looked at her in a new way,
without tenderness or friendly amusement. No one in
the limited scope of Lucy's experience had ever
switched from one mood to another with such ease.
The lazy, laughing stranger had turned into quite a
different man, whose expression was bitter and his eyes
sharp. Bewildered, she let her hand drop from his arm.

"You can," he said roughly. "You damn well
can." In a swift movement he caught her wrists in his
and dragged her to the space between two buildings,
pulling her into a space of frightening darkness. The
peaceful, familiar street seemed to disappear, and she
went rigid with fear.

"Don't!"

His arms were tight around her, his breath hot
against her neck. "Go ahead," he muttered. "Scream
and kick . . . that would bring the whole lot of them
down here, won't it? I don't give a goddamn, honey.
I don't care . . . I don't . . ."

His mouth, ferocious and greedy, bore down
on hers so hard that it hurt, and Lucy struggled against
him wildly. The night surrounded them in a flood of
velvet, suffocating her with blackness. Desperately she
took a handful of hair, grasping the close-shorn thickness at the back of his neck, and then his kiss gentled,

the painful pressure of it changing into the sweet, searching warmth that she remembered from before. He was using her to soothe a hurt, she realized, and gradually she stopped fighting him, her gasps changing into sporadic sobs.

She stilled and began to lean against him, out of pity—yes, out of sympathy and nothing else. Then his arms loosened and slid around her in a different way, protective, sheltering. His head bent deeper, his mouth beginning to play on hers expertly. Lucy moaned in her throat as she succumbed to the pleasure of it, responding to every touch and stroke of his tongue, her mind going blank as she became a stranger to herself. Her hands clenched in the silken hair, and the ends of it curled around her fingers. Gently—oh, so gently—he curved her body to his, and his warm hand slid down the line of her back with a caressing touch before coming to rest on the upper rise of her buttocks. Her body was wedged into his as if they had been made for each other. Her breasts thrust against his chest. Her hips fitted snugly into his, so closely that she could feel the powerful outline of his arousal. He pulled her even harder against his body, his anger changing into pure desire.

"This is wrong . . ." she gasped as his mouth left hers and slid down the fragile outline of her throat. She tilted her head back and let it fall to his shoulder. While his lips marauded the delicate skin of her neck and the shallow depression underneath her jaw, she began to realize that he knew things about her she had not been aware of. He knew how to make her feel things she had never felt before, and all of it was forbidden. He had no right to do this to her, just as she had no right to encourage it. "Stop," she whispered, her nostrils filled with the scent of him, her body clamoring for her to let him do whatever he wanted.

His mouth returned to hers, both of his hands cupping around her head as he took one last, devouring kiss. Then his chest rose and fell with an unsteady sigh, and he let go of her.

"It's not my fault," Heath muttered, while Lucy retreated until her back was against the wall of the building. Her heart was hammering almost audibly. His voice was thick and heavy, the sound of it curling around her in the darkness. "I can't help it any more than you can. So don't follow me again, or you know what to expect."

Motionless, she stood there, her palms pressed to her racing heart.

"Go back to your father," he said harshly. "And to Daniel. Go on."

She stumbled back to the street, her feet moving faster and faster as she fled back to safety.

Lucy could not understand or get rid of her secret fascination with Heath Rayne, who was now known around town simply as "the Confederate." The less she saw of him, the more she thought and wondered about him. She thought that he deliberately tried to avoid her, for he never came into the store during the hours when she was helping her father, and he never even looked at her when they happened to be in the same area. Perhaps it was better that way.

Rumors spread around Concord very quickly about him, for the subject of Heath Rayne was a continual source of interest. He was reputed to keep fast company. Mrs. Brooks said that she and her husband had seen the Southerner in Boston escorting a well-dressed woman, while some of the more reckless and younger Concord men reputedly went with him to a dance hall in Lowell and came back reeking of spirits and cheap perfume. The general opinion was that

Heath Rayne was a hot-headed hell-raiser who had come up North to stir up trouble. No one knew the answers to the two most important questions about him: who was he and what did he *do* for a living? He didn't seem to have any sort of occupation, but he seemed to have quite an adequate amount of money, for he was always superbly dressed and generous with a dollar.

Then there came a long silence about Heath, for the simple reason that he went to Boston for undisclosed purposes and stayed there for more than two months. The weeks passed by slowly while the talk about him burned out for want of fuel. Although his gray horse was being kept in the centrally located livery stables, which surely meant that Heath would return, Lucy began to think that she would never see him again. Putting him out of her mind, she devoted herself to concentrating on her duties as Lucas Caldwell's daughter and Daniel's fiancée, keeping busy with her involvement with the Ladies' Tuesday Club and the Concord Female Charitable Society as well as her literary clubs and meetings. Whenever it was possible Daniel took her to a dance, since there was a new one held nearly every week by a different organization.

The Charitable Society sponsored its annual dance to raise funds for the poor and needy. They asked for ten cents from everyone who attended; twenty-five cents was the family rate. Having been elected as a member of the organizing committee, Lucy found much of her time taken up with planning meetings. The dance was to be held in the town hall—its theme, of course, was the advent of spring—and she spent an entire Saturday with the other women on the committee, decorating the second floor, the large balcony, and the main staircase.

The women helped each other to get ready in

the dressing rooms, and Lucy felt pleasurable pangs of excitement in her stomach as she took out her dress from the box in which it had been carefully packed. It was a brand new dress, one she had never worn before, and she knew that Daniel would be stunned by the sight of her in it. Perhaps tonight he would be so enchanted that he might even want to set the date of their wedding.

"Lace me extra tight," she said breathlessly to Sally Hudson, a bubbly girl of nineteen who had been one of Lucy's closest friends since childhood— mainly because Lucy had always been sweet on Daniel and had never competed against Sally when it came to men.

"Nineteen inches?" Sally asked, wrapping the laces around her fists and pulling firmly.

"It's got to be eighteen . . . for the dress . . . I'm going to wear . . . ," Lucy gasped, holding her breath and closing her eyes.

"I don't think it's going to work," Sally said, yanking harder. "Why did you have a dress made with an eighteen-inch waist? You never get past nineteen—"

"I thought I . . . was going to be *thinner.*"

After a mighty tug, Sally knotted the laces and surveyed her handiwork admiringly. "Eighteen and a half . . . almost. A perfect hourglass." She angled her blonde head in a considering attitude. "But the next time you want to lace this tight, you should try the Swanbill. What's the kind you're wearing?"

"Thompson's Glove-Fitting Corset. It's new—"

"Oh, yes. I saw it advertised in *Godey's*. But I'd never use anything except the Swanbill—it's much stiffer."

Industriously Lucy struggled into a bustle and

petticoats, then lifted her arms as Sally dropped the new dress over her head. As it settled into place, there were several sighs of admiration heard around the room. The dress was made of white silk that glistened as pristinely as a new snowfall. The skirt was adorned with deep flounces of silk and huge puffs of transparent illusion, while the waist was trimmed with sprays of heartsease and leaves. The neckline of the bodice was almost indecently low and trimmed with silk rosettes, while the puffed sleeves were fastened with more rosettes. Sally fastened the gown and then gave Lucy an envious stare.

"Don't ever speak to me again, Lucy Caldwell." Sally held up a handmirror for her and mock-scowled over the top of it. "You look exactly like an engraving in *Godey's*."

Lucy smiled and checked her hair in the mirror. Her chestnut locks had been crimped and fastened into a chignon. Several curls had been allowed to escape, and they bobbed enticingly against the back of her neck. Her malachite earrings and necklace emphasized the green in her hazel eyes, while her cheeks burned with a glow of anticipation. She knew she had never looked more attractive. "I wonder what Daniel will say," she wondered aloud.

"He already loves you madly. I suppose he'll do nothing more than fall to his knees and recite an ode to your beauty." Sally smiled wickedly. "If I were you, Lucy, I'd be careful of Daniel trying to pull you into one of those empty offices downstairs."

If only that were the problem, Lucy thought, and twisted her mouth ruefully. "I just hope he isn't dreadfully late for the dance," she said, fluffing out the petals of a silk rosette.

"Late?" Sally echoed. "Why? Does he have

another one of those meetings with the other law-yers?''

"I'm afraid so."

"I don't know how you stand it, with Daniel so busy all the time—"

"I'm very proud of him. Daniel is the young-est railroad attorney at Boston and Lowell, and it's taken a lot of dedication to get there. Now that the war is over, all sorts of new plans are being devel-oped, and that means that he has to work that much harder—"

"Oh, well," Sally interrupted, looking bored, "I guess you can get used to just about anything—even his long Friday meetings. I mean, at least *you* have a fiancé, which is more than most of us can say. With the shortage of men, it's getting so that I can't afford to be as selective as I once was. Just think—I'm al-ready twenty and still not engaged—"

"You're talking as if you're some old spin-ster," Lucy said, laughing.

"No—that's one thing I'll never be," Sally stated with utter conviction. "I couldn't bear to be like Daniel's sister Abigail, thirty-three and never been kissed—oh, look, she's heading over this way."

Lucy smiled engagingly at Abigail, who was prim and tight-mouthed, a woman with an iron dis-position and a complete lack of humor. Had she ever wanted to be kissed? It didn't seem likely. Few people presented such an unapproachable front. Her eyes were dark brown, the same eyes that Daniel had, and her face seldom revealed whatever it was that she thought about. Abigail doted on Daniel, just as the rest of his family did. In fact, the Colliers doted on him so much that Lucy felt privately that in some ways they didn't think she was good enough for him.

"Good evening, Lucy," Abigail said politely.

"I wanted to tell you that we got word from Daniel earlier today. He said to tell you that he would be in Lowell until late this evening."

"You mean he won't be coming to . . ."

"That's right," Abigail said, her sharp eyes almost daring the younger woman to complain. "You know how important his work is, Lucy. He can't fall behind just for the sake of a little dance."

"Of course not," Lucy replied, flushing, and she felt her heart sink. To her dismay, her disappointment was so sharp and immediate that tears pricked at her eyes. *Don't you dare cry!* she commanded herself, and managed to will them away. Sally and Abigail looked at each other frostily, and then Abigail left.

"That was a mean trick," Sally declared indignantly, "to wait until you were dressed and ready before telling you. Without Daniel here—"

"Everyone seems to think that my life should center around Daniel," Lucy said in a low voice. "I guess now I'm supposed to go home, or mope around here and look lost because he's not here with me. Well, I'm not going to do either of those things. I'm going to have a good time, and . . . and dance with other men, and . . . and laugh . . . and maybe even flirt a little!"

"Lucy!" Sally looked shocked and delighted. "You couldn't. What will everybody say?"

"I'm not Daniel's property . . . not yet. There's no reason to put me on a shelf. We're engaged, but we haven't even set the date of the wedding. And I'm young and unmarried—and I want to enjoy myself tonight."

Determinedly Lucy lifted her chin and swept out of the room, clutching her silk fan as if it were a small hatchet. True to her word, she swept through the evening as if she had no attachment to any man, chat-

tering in an animated fashion and dancing uninhibit-
edly. Lucy knew that she was not behaving like her
usual self, and she knew that she was attracting much
attention with her quick laughter and fast manner.
Good, she thought grimly, plying her gleaming smile
on any man who happened to catch her eye. *When
Daniel hears about this, he won't be so eager to work
so many extra hours instead of being with me.* Maybe
he would get angry and demand an explanation from
her, or insist that from now on she talk to no other
men. All she knew was that she would gladly welcome
any attention from him. Ignoring her father's reproving glances from across the room, Lucy whirled
around the dance floor with partner after partner.
Gradually, as the music rang through the room and the
windows were partially opened to let some cool air in,
the hard knot of frustration inside her loosened.

"Daniel's going to be sorry he missed seeing
you tonight," David Fraser, her current partner, said
as they waltzed to a popular new melody. Lucy beamed
up at him in pleasure, because that was what she had
most wanted to hear.

"Do you really think so?" she asked, and as
David launched into a series of prettily phrased compliments, Lucy giggled unrestrainedly. But just a few
seconds later her laughter stopped abruptly as she
looked over his shoulder and caught a glimpse of the
small group of men by the refreshment table. Heath
was there, saying something that made his companions
chuckle, and his smile was startlingly white against
his tan.

So he had returned.

Chapter Three

LUCY STUMBLED SLIGHTLY as she stared at Heath. David Fraser slowed the pace of their waltz. Following the direction of her eyes, he noticed the object of her attention. "That's Heath Rayne, the Confederate who—"

"I know who he is." Lucy tore her gaze away from Heath and looked up at David with a smile. "I'm just surprised to see him with those people in the corner," she said lightly. "I thought everyone hated him."

"Not everyone. He's the type that you either admire or you hate—and I guess his style is something that some of the men around here want to imitate."

"Style . . . do you mean the style of his clothes?"

"That and everything else . . . the way he does things." David smiled wryly. "Some men are just that kind. It's hard to explain, and I certainly don't understand the admiration he attracts, not when he was trading shots with us just three years ago."

"Well, there's going to come a time when everyone's going to have to stop remembering who was trading shots with whom, and start learning to get along with each other," Lucy said absently, peering over David's shoulder again as they did a slow turn.

It was rare, even in Concord, to see a man as

stylishly dressed as Heath was. Who nowadays could afford to wear such clothes? His vest was superbly fitted and made of white piqué, cut low on the waist of his black trousers. Unlike the baggy Prince Albert coat that everyone else had on, his was less bulky, the sleeves more tapered, the wrists narrowed. And instead of the false-front shirts fastened with wide ribbons, which were just beginning to go out of style, Heath wore a crisp tailored shirt and a narrow white necktie. His sunstreaked hair shone with a rich gleam, cut short at the temples and the back of the neck in a new style that made the full curls at the temples of the other men look outdated. *Big, vain peacock,* Lucy thought, irritated by the fact that hers were not the only female eyes fastened on him. *He knows that every woman in the room is stealing glances at him . . . and he certainly seems to be enjoying it!* Not a shred of shame or modesty in him.

She continued to dance with David, but now she had lost her flirtatious mood and her movements were purely mechanical. After a few minutes she took another quick look at the refreshment table and saw that Heath was gone. Her eyes made a survey of the room, and then Lucy realized that he was dancing with *Sally,* of all people—Sally, who was flushed and giggling, reveling in the attention she was getting by waltzing with a Confederate. Heath was staring down at her with a smooth, blank face, his lips curved in a slight smile. People were watching the pair with clicking tongues and disapproving faces, while Sally's mother fidgeted uneasily in the corner. Lucy saw the two blond heads draw closer together as they talked. She wondered what Sally and Heath were saying to each other.

"It's getting very stuffy in here, isn't it?" she murmured to David, feeling suddenly that the glitter and the brightness of the evening had faded. He understood her hint immediately.

"Would you like to finish the dance some other time?"

"Please."

Solicitously he led her to the side of the room, and Lucy promptly escaped into one of the ladies' dressing rooms. Pressing a handkerchief to the sheen of dampness on her forehead and cheeks, she strove to regain her composure. She checked in a mirror to repair her hair, which was escaping its pins in straight wisps, and stared into a pair of fretful hazel eyes.

"What's the matter with me tonight?" she whispered, and set down the mirror jerkily. Innate honesty compelled her to admit the truth. She wanted to be the one dancing with Heath Rayne. She was jealous of Sally.

Why, that can't be, Lucy told herself, astounded. *I've got Daniel. I can't possibly be in love with one man and jealous over another one. Why on earth am I behaving like this?*

It was because Daniel wasn't here, that was all. And she just couldn't seem to dismiss her confusing feelings for the Southerner. There were secrets between her and Heath Rayne: the secret of those two days they had spent together in the warm, intimate confines of his home, the secret of those private conversations, and those kisses. But that didn't mean she had any claim to him or his attentions. For heaven's sake, she didn't want that at all! Sighing, Lucy straightened her puffed sleeves and went out to the main room again, heading towards the refreshments. A glass of punch would help to cool her down.

She lifted the ladle out of the half-filled bowl, preparing to fill a cup with the pink liquid.

"Allow me . . . please."

The ladle clattered in the punch bowl, and Lucy cursed herself for having let it slip through her fingers. She looked up and met Heath's turquoise eyes, which were dancing with amusement. He took the cup from her and ladled a small amount of punch in it, aware that filling it too full would make it difficult for a woman to handle without spilling a few drops on her dress. He seemed to have an unusual sensitivity about such things, about all the intricate details of handling a woman.

"Did you enjoy your stay in Boston?" Lucy asked demurely, accepting the punch without looking at him.

"Yes, thank you," he replied with mocking politeness, his eyes traveling over her slowly. He had been oddly moved by the sight of her tonight, so young and defiantly animated, and somehow forlorn, and he would have gone to hell for any excuse to hold her.

"Did you go there for business reasons?" Lucy failed utterly in her attempt to keep from seeming too curious.

"Hardly for a vacation. The scenery was unremarkable."

"Of course. Boston in wintertime is not very—"

"I didn't mean Boston. I was referring to the Yankee women." He made a slight face and then grinned at her indignant expression.

"And what exactly do you think is wrong with Yankee . . . I mean, with women up here?" she demanded with a scowl.

"None of them look like you."

As she saw the roguish light in his gaze and the mischievous smile that tugged at one corner of his mouth, she laughed. "You are a scoundrel."

"And you're still the most beautiful woman

I've ever seen." He said it in an easy manner that robbed the words of any seriousness; still, Lucy felt a twinge of pleasure and was exasperated with herself. Was she so in need of reassurance that she was going to start jumping at meaningless compliments like a fish after bait? "In fact, you're the reason why I came back," Heath continued. "I kept on remembering you—usually at the times when I wanted to forget you the most."

"You came back because your horse is stabled here," she said pertly.

"Panama? Ah, yes. I left him here because of you."

"Because of . . . what do you mean?"

"Someday I'm going to throw you across his back and ride off west with you . . . and you'll learn to make coffee in a tin pot over a fire, and we'll sleep underneath a wagon and peer out at the stars—"

What did he think of her, that he would make such brazen comments to her? She didn't know how to react. If she laughed, that might encourage him to embarrass her with further teasing, but if she got mad, he would probably laugh at her. She decided on a mild threat.

"My fiancé might have something to say about that."

"Really? Where is he?" Heath inquired innocently.

"Stop looking around the room as if you expect to see him. You know perfectly well he's not here, or else you wouldn't have dared to approach me."

"Where you're concerned, I tend to dare a great deal . . . as you might recall, Miss Caldwell."

She couldn't believe that he had the gall to remind her of the last time they had met, when his golden head had bent over hers and his mouth, to her trembling response, had been so hot and crushing. His teasing remark seemed to defile the memory of it. How could he make light of it, she thought with sudden anger, and all of her amusement fled as she looked away from him, her cheeks burning. "You coarse, mannerless . . . get away from me," she muttered, and he laughed softly.

"What a quick temper you have, honey. Is Daniel aware of it?"

"Yes . . . no . . . he—oh, leave me alone!"

"After I dance with you—or did I mistake those longing stares you kept sending me from the middle of the dance floor?"

"Leave, or I'm going to make a scene!"

"Go ahead. It'll mean nothing to me, since my reputation's already far gone . . . but yours . . . well, after your behavior tonight, it won't take much more to finish yours off. Now set down your punch, Cinda, and take my arm."

Reluctantly she took his arm, wishing she had it in her to call his bluff. But she did want to dance with him, and she wasn't sure why—except that it felt good to know that she was doing something that Daniel would have forbidden. "Everyone's looking," she whispered, letting him lead her to the center of the waltzing couples, several of which moved to allow them plenty of room.

"Everyone's been looking at you all night," he said wryly. "Especially me." His eyes slipped down to the low-cut bodice of her dress, touching on the generous swell of her breasts, then moved back up to her face. Lucy felt a warm tingle in her midriff at the bold appreciation in his gaze. Though he was the same age as Daniel and the other men she had grown up with, he seemed to be so much older than they were, so thoroughly confident. In an odd way she trusted him, but at the same time he made her a little bit afraid. Heavens, she didn't like being so unsure of a man!

They began to waltz, and Lucy's thoughts were diverted from her worries as she relaxed and enjoyed the dance. His arms were around her again, and they were as hard and supportive as she remembered. Dancing with him was pure pleasure. The steps of their feet were wonderfully synchronized, his strong arm fit around her waist snugly, and he swept her around the floor with unfaltering authority. She knew exactly where he was going to lead her and where she was going to follow. Lucy felt as if she were flying, yet at the same time she felt vaguely dominated, and that wasn't something that she liked at all.

"Why are you looking at me like that?" she demanded, aware that his turquoise eyes were locked on her face with unbearable intensity. He smiled and became the lazy scamp once more, a change that caused her to relax.

"Just thinking that Daniel Collier is a fool."

"Unlike others," Lucy reproved, gaining a measure of her self-confidence back, "he devotes most of his time to hard work and dedication to others—"

"Leaving you alone a good deal of the time . . . leaving you open to all sorts of demoralizing influences."

"Like you?"

"Exactly like me." Heath eyed her assessingly. "Now, judging from the way you played your cards tonight, he ought to whale the devil out of you when he finds out about how you've been kicking up your heels. At least that's what you're hoping. But I'll bet he doesn't. No, he'll fuss and frown for a few days while you apologize to him, and then he'll finally relent, taking your little hand in his forgivingly—"

"What makes you think you know enough about me," Lucy asked, stiff-backed with dignity, "*or* Daniel, to presume anything about what I want or what he wants, or what will happen between us, you overbearing, rude—"

"I'll bet he doesn't lay a hand on you," Heath said matter-of-factly, "even though he should, and would if he was half the man he ought to be."

"How can you say that to me? No gentleman would ever—"

"Ah . . . don't be angry, Cinda," he entreated. "It's the way I was raised. I just don't know any better."

"Why did you call me that?"

"Cinda? Because no one else does."

Lucy scowled at him, knowing that for the rest of the dance he was going to bend his efforts toward charming her into good humor again. And furthermore, that she probably wouldn't be able to resist.

Contrary to Lucy's expectations, Daniel's reaction to the rumors about the dance was not anger but something far worse. He came to visit the next afternoon, his eyes full of bewilderment and hurt. As they sat in the parlor, their hands clasped tightly, Lucy was wracked with guilt. She warded off his every question with fervent reassurances.

"Does it make you unhappy to be betrothed to me?" Daniel asked quietly, his thumbs stroking over the backs of her hands. "Is there someone else you would rather—"

"Oh, no . . . no, Daniel," Lucy said in a rush, her heart nearly breaking at the sight of the defeated slump of his shoulders. His manner was so calm and serious that her lighthearted rebellion of last night took on a new magnitude of importance. How wrong

she had been to try to get back at him in such a way!
She had not thought that it would hurt him so deeply.
The more she thought about what she had done, the
more childish her own actions seemed. In fact, she
was becoming acutely embarrassed by the recollection
of her shameless flirting and loud laughter. "You're
the only one I'll ever want or love," she said, holding
onto his hands with a desperate grip. "I was just so
disappointed that you weren't there."

"We've talked about this before, Lucy. I am
working very hard in order to make our wedding take
place that much sooner. You've told me so often that you
want to be married as soon as possible, but that can't be
if I interrupt important work in order to go to dances and
parties all of the time. I can't spend the days working and
the weekends socializing without finding time to rest. A
man needs sleep every now and then!"

"I know that. I do," she said, her eyes shining with tears. "I'm so very selfish sometimes, but it's
just that I care for you so much—"

"Don't cry, Lucy. You cry too easily. Only
children . . . Lucy, don't."

He broke the clasp of their hands to fish in his
pockets for a handkerchief, and she put her palms to
her eyes, biting her lip. "I'm sorry," she sniffled,
heaving a great sigh. Daniel finally found the handkerchief, handed it to her, and winced as Lucy blew
her nose with unladylike vigor. "I'll die if I ever hurt
you again," she said in a muffled voice. "I just wish
I had your strength and your patience."

"I understand. Women just aren't very patient
creatures," Daniel said, patting her back and then rubbing her shoulders gently. "It's not in their nature."

Lucy smiled a little into her handkerchief,
making a wry face. But instead of arguing the point,

she blew her nose again. "Well, it's certainly not in *my* nature," she said. "But I'm going to work at it. From now on I'm going to be the most perfect—"

"You're already perfect," Daniel interrupted, pulling her into his arms and laying his cheek on her hair. "You're perfect for me."

She snuggled closer to him, sighing in relief. Only with Daniel did she feel this safe and secure. "I don't know why you put up with me sometimes," she said, hugging him more tightly.

"I have for years. I'm not about to stop now."

After having known him for so long, Lucy couldn't imagine turning to anyone else for love and comfort, for peace and protection. Tenderly she pressed her face against his chest.

"I've adored you my whole life," she whispered, with all the ardent emotion of youth. "Ever since I was born."

"Lucy." His arms tightened, and she felt him kiss her hair. "I can't hold out against you any longer. Alright. We'll make the wedding in September. We'll get married this fall."

Since nearly every family in Concord kept at least one small boat at the old or the new stone bridge, paddling up and down the river was the most popular warm weather activity. It was impossible to row along the Sudbury branch of the river, which paralleled Main Street, without passing several friends along the way. On this particular day, the Fourth of July, the river was especially congested with traffic. Lucy laughed and called out to many of her friends as Daniel rowed her past the boat houses that flanked the river banks. She and Daniel were in the middle of a large group of canoes and boats that drifted lazily in the direction of the Old North Bridge.

"How lovely this is," Lucy said, trailing the finger of one hand in the cool water while using the other to maintain a grip on the ivory handle of her frothy parasol. The day was hot and humid, putting everyone in a mood of idle contentment. They had all heard the Fourth of July speeches at the town hall and were heading to numerous spots on the river for picnics. Tonight there would be a carnival, in which specially decorated boats would float down the river while fireworks burst in the air overhead.

"Someday I want a portrait done of you in that hat," Daniel remarked, and she smiled at him. Her hat was small and perched on the front of her head flirtatiously. A spray of coral-colored flowers curled over its plaited straw brim, reaching down to her temple and mingling with her chestnut curls.

"Why, you told me when I bought it that you thought this was a silly hat."

"Did I? Well, not very practical . . . but charming nonetheless."

"Me or the hat?"

"You know which one I mean," Daniel said, looking out over the water as he pulled on the oars.

Lucy wished that he would have taken the trouble to give her reassurance. She took her hand out of the water and shook the droplets from it; a tiny frown drew her dark brows closer together. Lately she had become aware of things that she had never taken serious notice of before, including the fact that Daniel often treated her as if she were a difficult child. In his own words, "not practical but very charming." She suspected that like many men, he tended to think that a woman's head was mainly used for holding up a hat. There were certain subjects that he refused to discuss with her in anything but a superficial sense. Politics, for example, was something they never talked about.

And when she approached him with ideas or questions, he listened with only half an ear and a complete lack of flexibility, as he had when they had been talking about the recent election of Elizabeth Cady Stanton as the president of the National Woman Suffrage Association. "The whole issue is a waste of time," he had said flatly, as if that was supposed to end the discussion then and there.

"But I don't think it's a waste of time for people to talk about it and listen to others' opinions on it." Lucy had persisted. "There's a lecture about it next week that I'd—"

"Women will never be allowed to vote. In the first place, they don't need it. They belong in the home, taking care of their husbands and children, making the home a comfortable and restful haven. And in the second place, when a man votes he speaks not only for himself but for his whole family, so women are well represented in the voting booth."

"But what if—"

"Lucy, it's a waste of time."

She wondered if Daniel would respect her opinions more as they got older. It wasn't that he wasn't interested in what she thought. He just hadn't been brought up to have much tolerance for women's ideas about things he considered to be men's business. Well, most men were like that to some degree. The only difference was that some were a little worse and some were a little better. The only exception she could think of was Heath Rayne. She thought of the brief exchanges she'd had with him at a few sociables and dances—stolen moments, for the most part. For the sake of her reputation, she had to be careful that no one would notice her talking to him. But she couldn't help being fascinated by him. While Daniel always had an absolute opinion about everything, Heath seldom seemed convinced of the absoluteness of anything. He always paid full attention to what she said, and while he sometimes liked to argue with her and twist her words around to annoy her, he never told her that what she thought or did was silly.

"You're the most terribly manipulative man I've ever met," she had told him at another dance, when he had goaded her into waltzing with him. She hadn't wanted to accept, since Daniel had been working that night and would undoubtedly hear about it the next day. But somehow Heath knew just how to tease her into doing what he wanted, a fact that sometimes irritated her when she thought about it later on.

"Me? Manipulate you?" Heath's blue eyes had been guileless.

"Whenever I'm happy, you become maddeningly provoking. And when you finally manage to rile me to your satisfaction, you smooth everything all over with wagonloads of compliments. When I'm pleased with myself, you puncture my vanity, and when I'm already up to my hairline in trouble, you manage to get me to do and say the most shocking things. And always, always you get your own way—"

"Now wait, honey. You're not some little puppet. No matter what I do, you're the one who decides what to do and say. And even if I corner you into doing something, like dancing with me when you'll probably catch hell for it tomorrow, I always give you a chance to escape. Fact is, Cinda, you don't ever have to do anything you don't want to do."

"Yes I do. Sooner or later, everyone does. Even you. I mean, you didn't want to have to fight in the war, but you enlisted because you had to, and because—"

"What gave you the idea that I didn't want to fight in the war?"

"But . . . ," she stammered, suddenly flustered, ". . . you said it robs men of humanity."

"Yes. Eventually it does. But much as I hate to admit it, Emerson was right about one thing—it does have a way of purifying things. It makes real life seem downright dull. On the battlefield you see the most spectacular extremes that a man can experience—death, bravery, cowardice, heroism—more vivid than anything you can imagine. I've been through every emotion there is and felt it deeper, stronger than I ever knew it could be felt." His reflective mood had disappeared instantly as he looked down at her with a provoking grin. "Every emotion except love."

"Then you haven't met the right woman."

"I don't know about that."

"Maybe you just haven't been looking hard enough."

"Oh, I've been looking."

Lucy thought about that now as the rowboat made its way down the river, and she smiled slowly.

"What are you thinking about?" Daniel asked, and she shrugged.

"Nothing in particular."

"You've been smiling to yourself very often during the past few months."

"Is there anything wrong with that? Smiling's usually a sign that someone is happy."

"No. I don't mind it," he said, looking mildly perturbed.

As the congregation of boats approached a bend in the river, a turtle perched on the end of a fallen log to watch them. It plopped in the water when they came closer, attracting the interest of some ducks who floated near the grassy riverbank. Watching the scene, Lucy could hardly believe that the warm, fresh river, filled with the green leaves of water lilies and bordered by willows, had been the same icy, barren place in which she had nearly drowned. More than once she had wanted to tell everyone that she had Heath to thank for her very life. It would have done much for his standing in the town and probably would have opened many a door that was not opened to him now. But neither of them had ever told a soul because of the irreversible damage it would do to her reputation. No one would ever believe that her two-day stay with him had been innocent, not in a small town where rumors stirred up trouble so easily.

"Luuucy!" came a high, excited voice from the riverbank, where many of the boats and canoes were stopping. It was Sally, who was dressed in white, red, and blue, in honor of the day.

"Tell her later not to call out and attract attention to you like this," Daniel said under his breath. "It's undignified."

"Daniel, no one minds. Everyone here is our friend."

"Lucy, I thought we had agreed to wear the colors of the flag!" Sally exclaimed. "How *unpatriotic* it was of you to renege!"

"I'm not short on patriotism," Lucy shouted back, her voice dusted with laughter, "I just have a smaller wardrobe than you do."

"Never mind. Just tell Daniel to bring you over here."

"I dislike being ordered around by a female," Daniel muttered darkly, causing Lucy to chuckle.

"Poor darling. Please try to be nice for my sake. She's my very best friend, and I promised her we would spread our blanket next to hers."

"As we do every year . . . so that she can dip into our picnic basket. Everyone knows she can't cook.

Who is she with this time? That no-account farmer? Or Fred Rothford, or that mumbling—''

''I don't know. But I'm sure that whoever it is . . .'' Lucy's voice disappeared somewhere in the back of her throat as she saw a tall figure leaning negligently against a tree trunk while Sally hovered nearby. His broad-shouldered, narrow-hipped form was clad in a white shirt with a soft collar and roomy sleeves, buff-colored trousers, and well-worn boots.

''For God's sake,'' Daniel hissed, ''*that's* who Sally's with? Don't tell me that I'm going to have to eat lunch with that Confederate!''

''Daniel,'' Lucy said, wondering somewhere in the back of her mind why it took so much effort to produce a mere whisper, ''please don't embarrass me. Don't embarrass both of us. You can get through forty-five minutes of being civil to him. You don't have to be friendly, just don't start a fight.''

''If he starts one, I'm going to give him what he's looking for!''

''He doesn't want a fight. I'm sure of it. He's here to enjoy the picnic, just like you are.''

''Don't compare the two of us,'' Daniel said harshly. ''I'm nothing like him.''

''I agree,'' Lucy said feelingly, closing her parasol and breathing a quick prayer for mercy. This was the kind of situation that nightmares were made of.

After Daniel landed the boat and helped her ashore, she lifted the hem of her skirt and went up the slight incline alone. Daniel rummaged in the rowboat for the picnic basket, taking his time and dawdling with the reluctance of a man who faces an unpleasant task. Sally and Heath met her at the edge of the clearing where the picnic blankets were being spread.

''You two have met before, so I guess there's

no need for introductions.'' Sally's voice seemed like nothing more than a superfluous drone in the background as Lucy stared into spellbinding blue eyes and felt her pulse accelerate with alarming speed.

"Miss Caldwell," Heath said politely, "what an unexpected pleasure."

"Is it really an 'unexpected pleasure?' " Lucy asked as Sally went to help Daniel with the boat.

"No and yes."

"What does that mean?"

"No . . . it's not unexpected. And yes, it is a pleasure."

"You planned this. You're with Sally because you knew she and I are friends and that the two of you would probably be sitting near Daniel and me at the picnic."

"Such modesty. You think that I would be so devious, to go to such lengths for the sake of watching you chew on a beat-up sandwich?"

Lucy blushed, embarrassed by his light mockery and aware of how conceited she had sounded. "No, I don't really think that."

"Well, I just might have."

She looked up at him and saw that his smile was full of friendly teasing. Sternly she held an answering smile at bay. She was troubled by the feeling that had suddenly come over her, this combination of gladness and nervousness and excitement. As he spoke his voice touched something inside her, as if his fingers brushed well-tuned strings.

"Mr. Rayne, I hope our New England humidity doesn't spoil the picnic for you," she managed to say.

"Not at all, Miss Caldwell. I'm used to warmer climates."

"Convenient on a day like today." She was

aware that his eyes had made a quick journey from her
head to her toes and back again. She was glad that she
had chosen one of her prettiest dresses to wear today,
made of glowing peach muslin with a sash that tied at
the side. It was fastened up the front with buttons made
of coral shells, with one pearl peeking out of each
shell. As Daniel approached from behind her, Lucy
fingered one of the little buttons agitatedly and sent
Heath a guarded look.

"Good afternoon, Mr. Rayne," Daniel said
grimly, his mustache twitching with the irritation he
felt at having to be cordial to a man he disliked so
intensely.

"Afternoon, Mr. Collier."

Lucy was thankful to see that for once there
was no taunting smile on Heath's face. She looked
from one man to the other, surprised at how stiff and
staid Daniel looked in his rigid collar, plaid vest and
trousers—dear Daniel, so dependable and proper, so
entirely different from the stylish Southerner. Daniel
would always take care of her, and while he may not
have been as dashing and exciting as some men, he
was solid gold. She suspected that Heath, on the other
hand, was about as stable as quicksilver.

Lucy and Sally managed to fill the hour that
it took to eat with vivacious chatter, regaling Heath
with stories about what it had been like for all of them
to grow up together in Concord. Even Daniel had to
smile at some of the tales, especially the ones about
the amateur theatricals they and their friends had per-
formed.

"The best one we ever did," Sally said, holding back a fit of giggles, "was *The Dog Will Have Its
Day,* a comedy of errors from beginning to end. Written in honor of a stray mutt that Lucy had taken in."

Heath smiled. "He must have been a remarkable canine."

"Not an ounce of talent," Lucy said, her eyes sparkling with laughter. "Or discipline. He didn't interpret his part in the way the author had originally intended."

"Who was the author?"

"Lucy, of course," Sally said. "When we were little, she was always writing theatricals and stories. Some of them were absolutely nifty."

"Nifty?" Daniel repeated the unfamiliar word with distaste.

"Short for *magnificent,"* Sally translated for him, and giggled.

Heath looked at Lucy, his eyes warm and speculative. "You like to write. I didn't know that."

"Is there any reason you should have?" Daniel interrupted shortly.

Heath regarded him expressionlessly. "Not at all."

"Whatever happened to that dog?" Sally asked of Lucy, breaking into the conversation hurriedly. "You never really told me. I went to visit relatives one summer, and when I came back he was gone."

"I couldn't talk about it then." Lucy smiled reminiscently. "Do you remember how he used to run out into the street, yapping at anything that moved? He got caught under a carriage wheel."

"How awful," Sally said sympathetically.

"Oh, it took me weeks to recover," Lucy replied lightly. "Ridiculous, to be attached to such a scraggly little thing. He wasn't very handsome."

"He was ugly," Daniel corrected.

"I guess he was," she conceded. "Poor thing. I found him near the milldam when he was no bigger

than a fist. Someone had abandoned a litter of pup-
pies, and he was the only one still alive. Father was
appalled when I brought the puppy home, but he let
me keep it. That dog was a lot of trouble, always getting into things, but you can't imagine how sweet he
was. I never had another pet after that.'' Suddenly
Lucy's eyes watered, and she laughed self-consciously
while searching for the handkerchief. ''I'm sorry. I
don't know what brought this on.''

''It doesn't take our Lucy much to boo-hoo.''
Sally smiled affectionately and patted her on the back.

''That's something that's going to change,''
Daniel said, looking embarrassed and annoyed as he
watched Lucy dab at the corners of her eyes. ''No one
should be so emotional over a dog that died years
ago!''

Lucy flushed at the reprimand and didn't know
where to look. There was a second or two of silence.

''Well, now,'' Heath said gently, ''I don't see
anything wrong with a woman having a tender heart.''

''A woman is supposed to set an example to
her children,'' Daniel contradicted. ''If she doesn't
learn to control her emotions, her children will turn
out to be a bunch of mollycoddles who'll cry as easily
as she does.''

Heath said nothing, his eyes flickering to
Lucy's pinkened face. The depths of his gaze were
bright with exasperation. Lucy knew that he was wondering why she didn't talk back to Daniel, the way she
usually did with him. But there was no way that she
could make Heath understand how it was between her
and Daniel. *I don't need defending from him,* she
wanted to tell him, *and especially not by you!* She had
to content herself with giving him a ''don't make trouble'' look. Heath turned his eyes to the river. The

sharp, clean edge of his jaw took on a stubborn slant as he clamped his teeth together.

"Does anyone want more almond cake?" Lucy asked.

"At least a dozen pieces," Sally said, grateful for the change of subject. But the two men were strangely silent, as if neither of them had heard a word.

Lunch dissolved into leisurely socializing. While the women cleared away the food, repacked the baskets, and folded the blankets, the men gathered together to exchange bits of masculine talk and jokes that were not considered fit for the ears of ladies. Lucy and Sally sat together, talking with shared relief after Heath and Daniel separated and went to different groups.

"I never dreamed there'd be a problem with putting those two together," Sally said, shaking her head in dismay. "Daniel's always been so . . . so sweet, so friendly to everyone, so gentlemanly. And Mr. Rayne—why he's one of the most charming men I've ever met, even if he is a traitor and a Rebel."

"For Daniel it's still too soon after the war to be friends with a Southerner," Lucy explained quietly. "Daniel can't forget what the Confederates did to some of his friends. Even though Hea . . . Mr. Rayne didn't do anything against him personally, the fact is they both fought on opposite sides and neither of them can forget it."

"I always thought the Confederates were mean and wild," Sally remarked thoughtfully. "He doesn't seem to be—"

"Of course not. He's a man just like Daniel or any of the rest of our friends."

"No, I wouldn't say that," Sally began, and then she was interrupted by the volley of rifle shots and masculine whoops that came from a meadow far beyond the picnic ground. "A shooting match," she said, her voice rising in pitch with her excitement. "So that's where they all went. Daniel and his friends are at it again."

"I'll be glad when they grow out of it," Lucy said, standing up and arranging her dress properly before going with Sally to the clearing. Several of the couples and groups they passed on the way were grumbling about the noise that disrupted the formerly peaceful picnic—the boys setting off firecrackers, the men aiming rifle shots at cans, the girls giggling loudly with each other. None of the complaints were serious, however, since they all knew that such things were to be expected on the Fourth of July.

Lucy and Sally gossiped and laughed as they made their way across the small clearing to the meadow where the men had gone. They weren't hesitant about invading the privacy of the shooting match because the men were always pleased to be watched and admired by a female audience. Lucy felt immense pride and pleasure in Daniel's performance at the matches. He was the best marksman in Concord— maybe the best in Massachusetts. During the war, sharpshooters had been valued highly, since the average marksman had used up more than two hundred pounds of powder and almost nine hundred pounds of lead to shoot just one Confederate.

Daniel had received many medals and a great deal of recognition in the war, a fact that was never forgotten by the people of Concord. They were all proud of him for having fought so well for them and the Union. Many people had joked to Lucy that Daniel no longer belonged just to her but to all of them. Of course she never failed to agree, but what no one seemed to understand was that she wasn't always happy about it. It would have been nice, she reflected wistfully, if Daniel didn't care quite so much about what other people thought—if he belonged not to all of them but to her alone.

At the edge of the meadow David Fraser was standing about 150 yards away from a fallen log that had been braced up on two stumps. Carefully he lifted a Spencer rifle and took his time aiming at one of the seven tin cans lined up on top of the log. He fired, and the empty cartridge case fell to the ground. Several of the men chuckled and ribbed David good-naturedly, for the seven cans continued to sit placidly in their perfect row.

"I surrender. Your turn," David said to Daniel, who chuckled and took the rifle.

Pausing to fill the empty chamber with another rimfire cartridge, Daniel glanced in Lucy's direction and saw the two young women sitting on a large boulder. Lucy gave him an impish little wave and arranged her skirts as she settled further up on the flat-topped rock.

"You're the luckiest woman in the world," Sally whispered. "Daniel adores you. And he's so gentlemanly and handsome—"

"Yes, he is," Lucy said, her eyes resting on Daniel's dark hair and wiry form. He had the lean, slim build of an aristocrat, and his hands were beautiful and sensitive as he lifted the rifle and held it. Gently he pulled the trigger. One shot, and the first tin can jumped off of the log. Two, three, four—the next cans were picked off in rapid succession. Five. Six, seven. Daniel had hit them all flawlessly. They all cheered and whistled while Daniel smiled modestly and looked over at Lucy. She clapped her hands in delight, her face glowing.

"Now I want a chance!" Hiram Damon, a towheaded boy of seventeen declared, causing the group to chuckle indulgently. Hiram had been too young to fight in the war, a fact he was forever lamenting.

"Alright, Hiram, you've got a chance now," Daniel said, overseeing the process of loading the rifle as the boy fumbled inexpertly with the new cartridges.

"Bet a quarter he can't hit more than one," someone said.

"I'll bet a quarter he can," Daniel replied, giving Hiram a firm pat on the back. "Aim a hair to the left, Hiram, and take your time."

"Daniel's going to make a good father," Sally whispered. "He's so good with children."

Laboriously Hiram aimed and fired, managing to hit two of the cans. Sally and Lucy applauded loudly, even managing to give close approximations of unladylike whistles.

"Anyone care to take me on?" Daniel asked. "I'll take a disadvantage to even things up. I'll stand back farther, or—"

"Put a blindfold on him," Sally suggested, and they all cheered.

"I'm feeling lucky today," David Fraser said amid the noise and laughter. "I'll take you on, Daniel, if you let me stay here and you go back to two hundred yards."

"I'll give a quarter to anyone who can beat him!" Sally declared loudly.

"And what'll you pledge, Lucy?" Daniel asked, his mustache lifting up at the corners as he smiled at her.

"A kiss to the winner," she said, and the whole group laughed, because they all knew that Daniel always won.

"Now that is an interesting offer." A new voice entered the conversation. Everyone looked to the right, where Heath Rayne half-leaned, half-sat on a slanting boulder. His drawl was soft but pronounced as he added, "This competition open to anyone?"

Lucy felt her cheeks go cold. She looked down at her hands and clenched her fingers together while Sally murmured, "That Southerner's got a mouth on him."

"You should save yourself the trouble, Mr. Rayne," Daniel said stiffly, all the warmth and enjoyment fading from his expression. "I was a sharpshooter—as more than a few Johnny Rebs can testify."

Heath's glinting eyes were startling against the background of the golden meadow as he smiled, seemingly unperturbed by the taunt. "Fine. I'll watch. Don't let me disturb you."

But he had disturbed the entire afternoon, and they all knew it. The shooting match, which had been filled with a spirit of lighthearted fun, had taken on the atmosphere of a battlefield.

"No. Join us. Please," Daniel invited, his face twisted with an expression of bitterness that was entirely unfamiliar to Lucy.

"Don't. Don't do it," Lucy whispered, even as David handed over the gun to Daniel and backed away respectfully. Now the group of men, which had been so boisterous and friendly, was quiet, watchful, eager, and tense. Lucy wasn't aware that she had taken Sally's arm, or that her fingers were biting down into it, until Sally jerked it away with a squeak and looked at her reproachfully. Lucy, her face white, was too absorbed in the scene before them to apologize. She couldn't believe Heath had dared Daniel so boldly, and that Daniel had decided to take him up on it.

"Practice shots?" Daniel asked Heath with overdone politeness.

"No, thanks."

The cans were set up as Daniel loaded the rifle
and glanced over at Heath. "You know how to handle
a Spencer? It's quite different from the muzzle-loaders
you Rebs are used to." Spencer rifles were more modern than anything the Confederates had been able to
use, so modern and fast that the federal ordnance men
had been afraid the Union troops would waste am-
munition by firing too quickly and not taking careful
aim.

"I think I can manage." Heath stood up and
walked over to the spot where they had been shooting
from, his eyes narrowing as they focused on the row
of tin cans. "Why don't we take it back to two hundred," he suggested, causing them all to murmur
amongst themselves. Whatever else could be said about
the Confederate, he didn't lack brass.

With low exclamations, the group backed up
several paces, so that Lucy and Sally found themselves
almost in the middle of the gathering. Some of the
men braced their hands against the boulder and leaned
against it as they watched. Lucy sat with every muscle
clenched as Daniel raised the rifle and took aim. His
back was rigid and set tightly as he pulled the trigger.
Shot after shot, he hit every can, making them bounce
off the log cleanly. When he was through, they all
released their breaths and congratulated him warmly,
more than a little amazed at his skill.

Lucy was torn between a sensation of pride on
Daniel's account and a feeling of pity for Heath. There
was no one who could shoot as well as Daniel, and
Heath had just set himself up to look like a fool in
front of the group. She wished that she wasn't here to
watch, and a feeling of protectiveness surged through
her as she watched Heath take the reloaded Spencer
and run his fingers lightly over the butt of the gun.
Why did he feel obligated to take the world on alone?

His feet splayed apart slightly as he turned his left shoulder towards the fallen log and lifted the rifle. Lucy was surprised by the looseness of his posture. He looked as if he weren't taking any of this seriously. She was startled by the sound of the first shot—he had barely taken time to aim! The sharp cracks of the rifle sounded off so quickly that Lucy wondered how the gun was keeping up with him. After the seventh shot Heath turned his head and looked at Lucy, their eyes locking in a lightning-hot stare.

"Holy Jesus," Lucy heard someone whisper, and with an effort she tore her eyes away to look at the log. All the cans had been knocked off. There was dead silence in the meadow.

"A tie," Lucy said, so unnerved by the incredible demonstration that her voice wavered.

Heath's eyes hadn't moved from her face. "Does that mean we both get a kiss?" he asked interestedly, and Lucy wondered where he got his nerve from.

"It means neither of you do," she replied, wishing that she could give him a piece of her mind for putting her and Daniel through this.

"It means the contest isn't over," Daniel snapped. "We'll take it back to 225. First one who misses, loses."

In the next few seconds there was a great deal of scurrying. The battered cans were set up once again, the Spencer was loaded. Shot after shot rang through the meadow as Daniel hit all of the cans. His brown eyes were alight with cold satisfaction.

Then it was Heath's turn, and he shot all the cans cleanly off the log with alarming dispatch. Oh, he was good. They all knew it, and no one more than he. He wore a slight smile on his face as the match continued, and his casual attitude made it clear that this was all ridiculously easy for him.

Daniel, on the other hand, was irritated nearly beyond endurance. He looked more and more strained as each round was completed. Lucy watched in silent agony as Daniel's face became red and perspiring. She had never seem him look so angry, and silently she cursed Heath and his predatory ways. To think that she had felt sorry for him before! He was taunting them all with his skill, and he couldn't help but know that instead of admiring him they were coming to dislike him intensely, but he continued to draw the game out.

Lucy glared at Heath's broad back and then looked at Daniel, who was fighting against a threat to his masculine pride. Her gaze softened with concern, for she knew that Daniel had never been bested at a shooting match by anyone, and it would hurt him terribly to lose.

And somehow, they all knew he was going to lose.

She felt Heath's eyes on her. She looked over at him, unable to keep the anxiety and outrage out of her gaze. Her lips trembled with the words that she wanted to speak but had to keep inside. Suddenly the hint of savage enjoyment left Heath's face, and he raked a hand through the ruffled thickness of his hair. When he took the rifle this time, his hands were more deliberate on the weapon and his movements were slower. He threw a quick glance at Lucy and then swerved his eyes to the target. One, two, three . . . four, five . . . six. There was a slight hesitation before he fired the last shot.

The seventh can was left standing.

Sally squealed and jumped down from the boulder to run towards Daniel. Loud enthusiasm erupted from the gathering as they all crowded around

Daniel, thumping him on the back and congratulating him vigorously. Lucy remained sitting, staring at Heath as he gave her fiancé a cocky salute. Daniel nodded coolly and then turned back to his friends, grinning as they overwhelmed him with cheers.

Heath walked over to Lucy, his brown, clean-shaven face as inscrutable as that of a statue. With the absence of a smile, the scar on his temple was more noticeable than usual. She wanted to trace that healed-over line and lay her palm against his cheek in comfort—until she suddenly realized what he had done. Though none of them knew it, he had allowed Daniel to win! Missing that last shot had been a gesture of contempt for them, for the game that had meant so much to them and so little to him. She wondered if he held her in contempt as well.

"You did it on purpose," she said in a low voice. He stared at her without making any effort to wipe the hunger from his gaze.

"I did it for you," he answered huskily. "Though God knows it's damned irritating to have to admit." There was a self-mocking edge to his voice. "You seem to be a weakness of mine."

"Don't think I owe you anything!" Hurriedly she turned away and scooted down the side of the rock. He caught her beneath the elbows, helping her down, and she was shocked by the feelings that rushed over at the simple touch of his hands on her bare arms. Even though all these people were near and Daniel was just a few feet away, she wanted, against her own will, to be held by Heath Rayne. For one explosive moment she felt the urge to cling to him, bury her face against his copper skin and inhale his scent. Though she fought against the craving, Lucy couldn't deny that he had a power over her that no one else had, not Daniel or anyone else. The absoluteness of it frightened her. Wrenching herself away from him, she ran blindly to the group that surrounded Daniel, fighting her way in until she reached Daniel's side. When she looked over at the boulder, Heath was no longer there.

"What did you say to him?"

"Nothing. I hardly remember," Lucy murmured, squinting against the brightness of the sunlight, which glinted off the sides of the train. They walked by the milk car while farmers from the edge of town were stacking the last of their produce on board. Daniel's face remained stony as Lucy accompanied him to the passenger car. After a good fifteen minutes of badgering, she was wishing heartily that she had not promised to see Daniel off on the train headed for Boston. "What time is your railroad meeting going to be?" she asked. "I hope the train will be on time."

"Sally said you and he were looking at each other during the shooting match."

"I was looking at *you!*"

"I don't want you talking to him anymore. Not one word, ever again, unless I'm there."

"Daniel, that's silly. What if we pass each other in the street? Should I just ignore him? That's bad manners!"

Her protest seemed to incense him ten times over. "Lucy, I won't tolerate any argument from you on this. If we're going through with this wedding, and if we're going to become man and wife—"

"What do you mean, *if?*"

"Then we're going to have to come to an understanding. You've been different the past few months than I've ever known you to be, wild and argumentative, trying to push me to the edge of my limits. But no more. I don't want you talking to that . . . that

Southerner any more. I want you to cool your friendship with Sally down. Maybe she's having a bad influence on you. I don't want you going to socials or gatherings without me, since your father obviously doesn't keep a close eye on you.''

''I'm not a child to be watched over!''

''If you want to be my wife, there are some rules we're going to establish right now.''

''Daniel . . .'' Lucy's cheeks turned red as she trembled with frustration. Ever since the shooting match a few days ago, he had worn an austere, troubled expression that suited his slim features far too well and showed no signs of leaving soon. The dark brown eyes had been cold, his mouth tight-lipped underneath the immaculately groomed mustache.

''The train's going to leave soon,'' he said, hardly looking at her. ''I'm getting on board. We'll talk more this evening.''

As he climbed aboard the train, Lucy watched him and folded her arms across her chest, her jaw mutinously stiff. Daniel thought that she had changed. Well, there was no doubt in her mind that he had changed as well!

The train pulled laboriously away from the depot and started down the iron tracks. Lucy watched the lumbering bulk of it turn into a small blotch in the distance before she sighed moodily and turned around to head back home.

''You two have such interesting conversations.''

Startled, she looked up in the direction of the voice. Her eyes narrowed on Heath Rayne's handsome, rascally smile.

''Are you spying on me?'' she asked gruffly, glancing around to make sure that no one was near enough to overhear them. Heath shrugged, slipping his hands in the pockets of his trousers. The action made the well-fitted trousers almost indecently tight, outlining the powerful shape of his thighs. Lucy berated herself for noticing such things about him. But there was an aura about him that few men possessed, of full-blooded maleness and confidence, that she'd have to be blind not to notice.

"No, I'm not spying." The corners of his wide mouth tilted in an irrepressible smile. "I have a few things to take care of in town, and I happened to catch a glimpse of that charming hat."

Defensively she raised a hand to check the position of her dainty white hat, which was festooned with a pearl butterfly and a bouquet of marabou feathers and pearl drops.

"Don't touch it. It's perfect," he said, and her eyes fell before his frankly appreciative glance.

"If you overheard anything—"

"I did," he assured her.

"We were discussing private matters—"

"I know." Heath seemed to take a great deal of enjoyment in enumerating the list of rules Daniel had given her. "Don't be friends with Sally, don't be seen with me, don't go to meetings or dances without him at your shoulder. Even after you're married, he'll still be telling you what to do and who to talk to—"

"That's a husband's right, isn't it?"

"Is it?"

The conventional answer would be a simple yes. Lucy was silent for several seconds. Her lips parted and closed several times as she sought a suitable reply. She couldn't think of one.

"Things change after people are married," she finally said, talking more to herself than to him. "People change."

"Yes, but not usually for the better."

"How would you know? Are you an authority on marriage . . . or on me, for that matter? You act just like Daniel, as if you know what's best for me Well, maybe I should start deciding what I want!"

His eyes gleamed like a cat's. "Maybe you should. What do you want?"

She wanted Daniel. But she wanted Daniel to be different. "That's none of your concern."

"But it is. I'm afraid I've already invested a lot in you."

"Invested what? A lot of what?"

"A lot of worry and vexation, honey." His casual tone of voice belied his words. "About the fact that he's bent on changing you. He's not good for you."

"Stop it. I'm not listening."

"He's trying to change you into the kind of obedient little creature he wants, and all that's going to wind up doing is making you miserable. And it's not because he means to—he's just made that way, the opposite of everything you are."

"*Opposite!* That's laughable. That's ridiculous. I've never met anyone more like me than Daniel. He and I are the same kind of person."

"Is that how you see yourself?" he demanded, and suddenly there was a scowl riding between his eyes. "The kind of woman who'll be happy with a husband who wants to make her into a reflection of himself? Do you really believe . . ." He stopped and looked at her, and the spark left his eyes as he wiped the expression off of his face, leaving it smooth and unreadable. "Stubborn little hardnose. With every word I say, you dig your heels in deeper, don't you? Well, I won't let you use me to whip up your determination. If you want him, you decide on your own. I'm not going to waste another word on it."

"But . . . but we aren't done with the conversation. I want to know what you were going to say."

"I'd rather talk about something else."

"But Heath, won't you just tell me—"

"No."

Lucy couldn't remember the last time someone had used that word to her, all by itself, ringing with finality. Flat-out, no. She discovered that it irritated her to no end, as if he had just closed a door in her face. "Why not?" she asked, her voice subdued and, though she wouldn't have liked to admit it, rather sullen-sounding.

"Because you're spoiling for an argument and I'm not. And you should be having this discussion with Daniel. You should have given him an argument five minutes ago instead of waiting for me to show up."

"I wasn't waiting for . . . oh, I don't want to talk about this anymore. You make me feel like—"

"Like what?" he prompted in a swift pounce.

"Like when I was little, and I would do something that made Father mad . . . before I could explain anything, he'd already made up his mind about *why* I had done it. There's no way to fight that, and it's not fair!"

Heath laughed, shaking his head ruefully. "No, it's not. But with a daughter like you it's no wonder your father had to resort to such tactics. Most of the time you have him wrapped around your finger, and he and everyone else knows it."

"He's a good man. He's steady, straightforward, he knows exactly what he wants—"

"Yes. You must favor your mother."

She smiled reluctantly at the gentle taunt. "I don't really know. I was too young to remember much about her. But I know that she was very beautiful."

"I'm certain she was," he said, giving one of

the curls clustered at the back of her head a playful tug. The gesture was much too familiar, but she was to intent on her own thoughts to notice or reprove him for it.

"Father never says a word about her. But Mrs. Morgan . . . one of the women who used to belong to some of the same groups and clubs, told me that my mother liked to make speeches at all the ladies' charity clubs and social meetings. One time she burst into one of those town council sessions and made a fifteen-minute speech about letting girls go on through higher grades at the town school. They make them leave, you see, whenever there's not enough room for all the boys. I think that Father had a hard time keeping her quiet."

"That I can believe."

"Were there women like that in Virginia when you were growing up?"

"Making speeches? Not exactly."

"Is your mother—"

"No, honey. She passed away when I was a boy."

Surprised and fascinated by the revelation, Lucy suddenly wanted to know other things about him.

"What about your father? Does he—"

"He died during the war." Heath's indulgent mood seemed to drain away like water out of a tub. Apparently he didn't like to answer personal questions.

"Any family at all?"

"A half-sister, a half-brother . . . and a step-mother. Who fulfills all of the clichés about stepmothers that you've ever heard."

"Do they ever—"

"Look at the sky . . . rain's on the way. You'd better get back home before your hat gets ruined. Would you like me to take you in the barouche?"

"Oh, but people will see."

"Yes, you must follow Daniel's orders to the letter. I forgot."

"I'm going to walk," Lucy said stubbornly. "It isn't far."

He grinned and caught one of her hands in his, lifting it to brush a kiss across the tender skin below her knuckles. She went still, a strange, hushed feeling suffusing her at the merest touch of his mouth on her skin. "It's been a pleasure, Cinda," he murmured, and walked away with that distinctively lazy stride, as if he had all the time in the world to get wherever he was going.

Chapter Four

THE FIRST PARISH bell was ringing.

Lucy threw off the lace-trimmed sheet that was tangled around her legs and staggered out of bed to the window, staring at the scene outside before she was fully awake. The sky was filled with thick, low clouds that showered a gentle mist over the sleepy town. Despite the threat of rain, the clouds glowed a dull red, especially over the section of Concord around Lexington Road.

Red clouds, she thought, and her eyes widened as the street began to fill with people, vehicles, and horses. The wind drifted to her in a moist, warm surge, bringing with it the faint scent of smoke. She ran to the closet and hastily pulled out one of her oldest dresses, her movements awkward from haste and sleepiness. Everyone went to help when there was a fire; there were tasks that even the women and some of the older children could do.

Ignoring the corset that lay across the embroidered seat of a chair, Lucy squeezed herself into the powder-blue dress and buttoned it hurriedly. Stays would have made it fit much better, but there was no time to waste. She tied her hair back with a ribbon and slipped on a pair of worn shoes that made little sound as she scurried downstairs.

Lucas Caldwell was already there, coiling a

length of rope. He tucked the rope into a bucket that he had carried as a member of the bucket brigade, which had operated in the days before professional, paid fire departments and steam-pump engines. His white hair and show-white mustache, usually so neatly groomed, were ruffled in comical disorder.

"Father, I'm ready," Lucy said breathlessly, her flurry lessening in the face of his calmness. He was always so practical, so patient about everything, even in the face of disaster.

"The Hosmers have stopped their barouche outside. We're going with them," he replied, patting her on the shoulder briefly as they went to the front door.

"Father, please don't take any chances tonight—you always take on the riskier tasks instead of letting the younger men do them! Remember, you're all I've got, and if anything happens to you—"

"I'll only do what's needed, nothing more," he assured her. "No heroics. But a Caldwell never avoids his duty, Lucy."

"Yes, I know," she said, and as she glanced at him she realized for the first time how quickly he was aging. A fine network of lines had dug into his cheeks and spread down to his neck, while pale brown age spots dotted his skin. She hated to think of how easy it would be for him to get hurt. "Please be careful," she repeated softly, urgently. Lucas nodded absently, his attention caught and held by the sight of the thickening clouds in the distance. There would not be enough rain to quench the blaze or hinder its progress.

There was little talk between them and the Hosmers as the carriage raced in the direction that all the others were going. The Hosmer's three sons perched eagerly in their seats; all of them were in their teens and filled with excitement untempered by the

worries that the adults had to face. Lucy gripped the
edge of a cushion in tension, her long chestnut hair
threatening to escape its fastenings as the wind
whipped over her. She let out a brief, surprised sound
as they approached the blaze.

It was the Emersons' home. The roof and the
upper floor were already consumed by fire, which
seemed to rise higher with each second, until it seemed
to brush against the clouds. Hordes of people bustled
around the ground, some daring to make brief forays
into the bottom floor to rescue furniture and clothing.
The members of the fire department were hard at work
to control the flames, but it looked like it was too late
for them to do much good. In front of the house, the
huge white horses that had pulled the steam-pump en-
gine stomped impatiently. The black boiler of the en-
gine emitted large gusts of smoke as it labored to pump
water through the thick suction hose, while water
dripped down the shiny brasswork and gold-striped
wheels. Slowly the barouche was brought to a halt in
front of the yard, which was littered with personal
articles and papers that had been brought out of the
house.

"That poor man," murmured Mrs. Hosmer,
a graying redhead with keen blue eyes undimmed by
fifty years of hard living. She was a brisk but kindly
woman. Lucy followed her gaze to see Mr. Emerson
standing before the burning house, his pale hair lank
against his cheeks, his bent shoulders covered with a
sodden coat. "He's set in his ways, he is, likes everything in its proper place. This is harder on him than it
would be on most."

"He's got many friends," Lucas Caldwell observed mildly, helping Lucy out of the carriage. "The
Emersons will get through this just fine."

"I hope so," Lucy said, and gave her father

a quick kiss before dashing off to the line of women and children next to one of the downstairs windows. They were passing armloads of clothes and pieces of china from the house to the end of the line, out of harm's way. The men were busy taking the best pieces of furniture outside, grunting with effort and sweating from the incredible heat of the fire. From several feet away Lucy could feel it scorching her cheeks. It was like standing in front of a hot oven in the middle of August.

"Has someone seen Mrs. Emerson's document box?" Daniel's sister Abigail asked loudly, coming over from the spot where the Emerson family was gathered. "It was in the library. She said she put some important papers there, some bonds and contracts." They all searched the yard quickly, but no box could be found. There was a moment of silence and indecision, and Lucy looked from face to face, realizing that they were all afraid to go in the house.

"I'll do it," she said, tightening the ribbon around her hair to make sure that it stayed tied back.

"But it's dangerous—"

"Not yet. The men and boys are still inside, getting the furniture. The fire hasn't made it downstairs." Lucy dashed to the half-open window before anyone could offer any further objections, hoisting herself up and clambering over the sill. She closed the window most of the way before venturing further into the room, which looked like the parlor. It was so hot and smoke-hazed in there that she could barely see. An unearthly stillness settled in the room while the sound of fire roared all around.

The doorknob was still pretty cool. Cautiously she opened the door and went into the hallway, where men rushed back and forth in the last efforts to rescue valuables. In the frantic, traffic-ridden hallway no one seemed to take notice of her, and she sidled along the wall to the next doorway. It was the library, she saw with relief, and slipped inside. The smoke stung her eyes and seemed to sear the inside of her nose. Coughing, Lucy felt her way around a huge, solid table and bumped into a chair, knocking something to the ground. A pang of triumph quivered in her chest as she squinted down at the square metal object. The document box.

Grabbing the box, which was already warm to the touch, she stowed it under one arm and ventured gamely out into the hallway, where the shouted warnings and crashing sounds were deafening. She was coughing so hard that she could barely breathe. As a boy carrying a heavy chair rushed by, he bumped her accidentally, causing her to stumble against the wall. Suddenly a burning timber fell down from the ceiling, narrowly missing her, and she stared at the splintering, blazing hunk of wood in shock. The ceiling was beginning to crumble in! Lucy's hasty courage fled as her face paled with the beginnings of real fear. Her pulse raced as quick as lightning. Irrational though it was, her first instinct was to head for a corner to hide in. She had to get out of here! Afraid that her skirts would catch on fire, she started to edge around the timber carefully. Just then a booted foot kicked aside the timber in one swipe and her shoulders were seized in a grip so brutal that she dropped the document box.

"What the hell are you doing in here?" a hoarse masculine voice demanded, and she looked up into Heath Rayne's hard eyes. She was so startled by the vicious bite of his hands and his savage appearance that she couldn't have said one word to save her life. His coppery skin was gleaming with sweat and smudged with soot, his eyes narrowed and reddened from smoke. The shirt he wore was rolled up at the sleeves, revealing heavy muscles that strained tightly against the damp linen; the shirt parted down his chest to a midriff that was taut and patterned like a washboard. He looked so angry that he seemed about ready to cuff her, and for just a second she was afraid that he would. "I want you to get your little rear end out of here!" he snapped. "Why hasn't your father or your damned fiancé kept an eye on you? If neither of them is going to bust your backside for this, I sure as hell am!"

"I came in here for an important reason!" Lucy interrupted indignantly, wriggling free of his painful grip and bending to scoop up the box. She paused as a spasm of coughing shook her.

Heath muttered a curse and took the heavy object from her as soon as she straightened up. He hooked an arm around her waist and rapidly half-dragged, half-carried her through the hallway. The front door was edged on either side with long tongues of flames. Lucy stopped struggling as he sheltered her with his body and carried her through. Her nose and cheek brushed against his wheat-gold hair, which was darkened with sweat. She could feel the cruel, limitless power of his arms around her, as secure and unyielding as the jaws of a lion. His lack of fear made her feel like the kind of woman she most despised, the kind that acted clinging and helpless in the presence of a strong man. Breathing deeply, she hung onto her wits and lifted her head from his shoulder. She started to pull away from him as soon as they got through the door. He let her feet drop to the front porch, steadied her, and handed her the metal box. It felt much heavier than before, and she took it with trembling arms.

"First you almost drown, then you're almost burned to a cinder," Heath said, turning her around and giving her a firm push in the direction of the steps leading to the street. He still sounded angry, but not quite as much as before. "God knows what you'll get into next."

"I would have been fine without you!"

"Like hell. Now stay away from here."

She didn't dare talk back to him as she watched his broad-shouldered frame disappear through the doorway again. Going down the steps, Lucy was surprised to find that her knees were weak as she made her way to the pile of furniture in the yard. After setting the document box down carefully on a sofa, she watched as the men carried the last pieces of furniture out of the house. None of them could go back in now. The fire had destroyed the top floor and was spreading to the downstairs; it had eaten at the ceilings and crumbling walls until the house was a deathtrap.

She made her way over to her father, who was standing near the Emersons and watching the magnificent blaze. Mr. Emerson was clearly suffering from shock, his eyes traveling slowly over the crackling flames and seeming to take none of it in. Filled with pity, Lucy averted her eyes, unable to look on the face of such open grief. Several yards away she saw Daniel's wiry figure as he and some others took inventory of what had been saved. Guiltily she realized that she hadn't even given a thought to Daniel or worried about whether he was alright or not. Clenching her hands together, she made up her mind to go over to him as soon as the scene calmed down a little.

"My manuscript," Emerson suddenly said, his voice so soft at first that it was difficult to hear. "My last manuscript. There is no copy of it aside from the one in the house. My manuscript!"

"Don't worry, Mr. Emerson," someone said soothingly. "I'm sure someone's got it—"

"Who? Where is it?" Emerson latched onto

the idea with new energy, his voice rising in agitation. "It was kept in a white box in the library. Where is it?"

There was a brief scuffle around the yard as they all tried to find the manuscript, but it didn't turn up. "My manuscript," Emerson said, his voice shaking. His face was papery white as he stumbled away from the people who tried to surround him and offer their comfort. He nearly tripped over Heath, who was seated on the ground with his forearms propped on his knees in a weary posture. Heath, his blue eyes narrowing, lifted his head and looked up at the other man. There was a world of difference between them, one man elderly and frail, filled with the knowledge of a lifetime of experience, the other strong and so very young, with a whole life stretching out before him. One from the North, one from the South. But there were similarities between them. If nothing else, they both shared an uncommon respect for the written word, and Heath understood exactly what the loss of the manuscript meant to the old man. As they stared at each other silently, Heath got to his feet, and then he muttered an explicit oath, taking off for the house.

Paralyzed, Lucy watched as he snatched up a soaked quilt from the ground and loped up the front steps. No one made a move to stop him. "No," she said, too quietly for him to hear, and as he got nearer to the inferno, she cried out in panic. *"Don't!"*

If Heath heard her, he ignored her, and he disappeared into the blazing house. As she tried to take a step forward, her father held her back, whispering that everyone was looking at them. Her breath came harshly through her throat; her heart pounded until it hurt. Her eyes were fastened on the doorway as she stood like a statue, her muscles as rigid as iron. From somewhere in the house there came a thundering

crash, the sound of another section of the roof falling
in. Her father put a hand on her arm and she flinched
away, staring at the doorway as if that alone would
make Heath appear. It seemed that hours passed by,
and still there was no sign of him.

"Lucy, what's the matter?" She heard Dan-
iel's voice, and she turned to him. He looked tired as
he sighed and stretched his shoulder muscles.

"The . . . I . . . Mr. Rayne is in there," she
said tightly. "Don't you even care?"

"Care?" Daniel repeated, catching her by the
elbows and staring down into her face. Confusion and
then irritation shone in his dark brown eyes. "I suppose we all do . . . but no one quite as much as you.
Why is that, Lucy?"

"He's a human being! Why doesn't anyone
seem to care about what's happening? Why doesn't
anyone understand?"

Daniel's voice was sharp and steady as he answered her. "You were just a child during the war—
you are the one who doesn't understand. His kind
would just as soon shoot us as let us live. My God,
do you know what the Rebs did to us during the war?
Some of them were no better than Indians, scalping
Union soldiers, skinning them! Do you know what they
did to us in those stinking prisons? They treated us
like animals, letting us die for want of food and medicine—oh no, I won't forget, and I won't forgive. And
as for this particular Confederate—he may be handsome and as charming as the devil, but underneath
he's as dirty and rotten as the rest of his kind. He isn't
worth caring about."

"But they weren't the only ones. I heard about
what Union soldiers did to the Southerners," Lucy
said, wiping at the tears that fell down her cheeks.

"About burning their homes and land, about what they did to the women . . ."

Daniel went very still. "What are you saying?" he demanded, his face harsh and his eyes piercing.

"I don't think either side was all good or bad—"

"You're upset by all the excitement," he interrupted coldly, "which is why I'm going to forget this conversation. Don't try to think about things that are beyond your understanding, Lucy. If you had been in the war you would know what kind of people Southerners are, and you would know enough to hate them. And if I were you, I'd stop worrying about your stinking Rebel, because the only thing that's going to get him out of that house now is a miracle."

Lucy bit her lip as Daniel strode away. Why did everyone suddenly seem like strangers to her? Daniel, her father, the townspeople—it was like she had never known them before, like she was standing on the edge of a stage and watching them take part in something she didn't understand. All she knew was that Heath was somewhere inside the burning house and that she cared about what happened to him, cared desperately. No matter what he was or what he might have done in the past, she didn't want him to die. She pressed her hands against her temples to quiet her raging headache and stared at the fire until her eyes were blinded by the brightness.

There was a movement in the doorway. Heath staggered out, dropping the quilt and clutching a white box. He was silhouetted against a backdrop of yellow flames as he took the steps two at a time, while more of the roof and upper walls crumbled inward. The crowd stared at him wordlessly, and some people fell back as he walked past them. His face, chest, and

arms were covered with soot. His once-white shirt was
singed and gray as it gaped open to reveal a body that
was tanned and slick with sweat, a body crisscrossed
with scars from wounds that had healed a long time
ago. He was limping slightly, but instead of detracting
from his fearsome appearance, the limp seemed to
make him more threatening, like a wounded animal
ready to spring in self-defense. Eyeing them all warily,
he approached Mr. Emerson and handed him the manuscript.

"Thank you," Emerson said, bowing his head
and accepting the box with the tender hands of a parent holding a child. "I am indebted—"

"Don't be. This doesn't mean I like you or
your politics any better," Heath said gruffly, and he
limped away, heading to the woods near the back of
the house. Lucy stared at the ground to hide her feelings, almost sick with relief.

As the morning approached, the townspeople
all set to organizing the contents of the yard and chas-
ing after the papers, letters, and notes that the wind
had scattered around the grass. The fire finally died
down, leaving nothing in its wake except a few blackened walls and several feet of rubble and coals. Covertly Lucy glanced in the direction that Heath had gone
and followed him when no one was looking. She knew
she should have stayed with her father or Daniel, but
she was driven to find the Southerner and would not
breathe easy until she did.

Heath was sitting on a long, flat rock, his back
propped against the trunk of an old white-shelled birch
tree. His knees were bent, his elbows rested on them,
and his head was buried in his hands. He heard the
crackle of her feet on the pine needles and leaves that
carpeted the ground, but he didn't move.

"You shouldn't have done it," Lucy said vehemently, handing him a dipper of water. He took it and drank thirstily; the sweet coolness of it spilled onto his chest and shirt. She sank to her heels beside him and folded one of several damp handkerchiefs she had found in the pile of clothes in the yard, hesitating only a second before using the corner of it to wipe some of the dirt off his jaw. Heath rested his head against the trunk of the tree, watching her warily. "A pile of papers isn't worth your life," Lucy continued in that same tight-lipped way, "no matter what's written on them."

"Some would argue . . . ," he said, his voice rasping, and then he began to cough.

"That's ridiculous," she said sharply, her hazel eyes flashing. She dabbed at his face with increasing confidence. Heath would have smiled at her take-charge manner had he not been so exhausted. He wondered if she knew how proprietary she looked as she sat there and cleaned his dirt-grazed cheeks.

"It's been a long time since anyone's done that," he said huskily.

"How long?"

"About twenty years ago. My mother pretty near wore my face off for scrubbing at it."

She paused in her ministrations. "Close your eyes," she said quietly, and wiped away most of the irritating soot that encircled them. "Why are you risking your life up here when you should be at home?" she asked, and he caught her wrist in one large hand.

"That's enough." They both knew he wasn't talking about the handkerchief. Still, she let the cloth drop and let her wrist remain unresisting in his hand until he released it.

"Why does everything have to be such a mystery about you?"

"There's no mystery—"

"You won't tell me *anything* about yourself."

"What do you want to know?" he demanded with a quick frown.

Immediately they were both quiet. Lucy knew that she was treading on forbidden ground. She shouldn't want to know anything more about him than she already did. She shouldn't ask him any questions; she shouldn't even be here with him. But she would never have this opportunity again.

"Where exactly do you come from in Virginia? And what did your father do?"

"I come from Richmond. My father was an attorney; then, he had to quit his practice and run the family plantation in Henrico County."

"Plantation? But you once said you didn't have slaves—"

"I didn't."

"But if the Raynes had a plantation, then how—"

"No. Not the Raynes," Heath said, looking at her expressionlessly. "The Prices. My father's name was Haiden Price. I never lived with the Prices on the plantation. I was brought up in a hotel in Richmond by my mother, Elizabeth Rayne."

"Your mother and father were . . . never married?" Lucy felt her ears turn red. She wished that he wouldn't stare at her so closely, as if to measure her every reaction to his words.

"No. She was a distant cousin who met my father during a family visit. He was already married. He installed her in Richmond after she discovered that she was expecting. Understandably, no one in the family wanted anything to do with us."

Lucy wondered what it had been like for him as a little boy, raised in a hotel, disgraced through no fault of his own. "Did your father come to visit you?"

"Occasionally. He saw to it that I was dressed well and educated . . . no more and no less what he did for his legitimate offspring. I was sent abroad when I was eighteen, but a month after I left, South Carolina seceded, and . . . well, you know the rest."

"And after the war . . . ?"

"I went to the plantation like a damn fool, thinking that they might need another pair of hands to help around the place. And they did. But not my hands."

No home. No family. Lucy felt like weeping at her own tactless questions about his home when he'd had none to go to. "How . . . how did he die?" she asked, and he shook his head silently, refusing to answer. He looked at her with weary challenge in his eyes. "Why did you come up here?" she asked.

"I can't tell you that."

"Why not? Because you don't know?"

"Because I don't want to tell you."

She smiled suddenly. "That's because you're so contrary."

He relaxed and closed his eyes. "I suppose you're right."

"You scared the wits out of me when you went back into the house," she said reprovingly. "Why did you do it? To prove something?"

"To preserve Emerson's manuscript for posterity," Heath said, imitating Bronson Alcott's ponderous way of speaking so perfectly that she almost laughed.

"Horsefeathers."

"And I'm not afraid of fire, while it was clear that everyone else capable of going after the manuscript was."

"Why weren't you afraid?"

"When the worst happens, there's nothing to fear anymore."

The words, said so matter-of-factly, struck at her heart. Lucy could not stop herself from smoothing the tumbled, smoke-scented hair off his forehead. He made no response to the gentle touch of her hand. "The worst? What was the worst that happened to you?"

"When I was in my teens, the hotel caught on fire. I came back late, after a night of . . . ah, what should I call it? . . . ungentlemanly behavior, and I saw the smoke from a few miles off. My mother was sleeping upstairs. No one got to her in time."

She murmured something soft and indistinguishable. Her fingertips drifted lightly through his golden hair in a repeated stroke.

"Cinda?" he said after a long while, his voice drowsy from the effects of exhaustion and her stroking.

"Hmmn?"

"I'm still going to raise hell with you for going in that goddamned house."

"I can take chances if I want to. You did."

"There's a difference," he said, his dark lashes lifting as he looked at her. She took her hand away as if she had been burned. "I've had more experience at taking care of myself."

She frowned in a troubled way, her forehead creasing. "Heath . . . do you think I'm a child?"

"No. I wish to hell I did."

"Why?"

"Because I wouldn't feel this way about a child."

He reached out and stroked the curve of her throat with his fingertips. The lines of his mouth gentled as he looked at her. His stare was so concentrated and intimate that she couldn't move, not even when he sat up and wrapped his hand around the back of her neck. Before she knew it, she was leaning against his chest, surrounded by the scent of his bare skin. "Cinda," he whispered, and she shivered at the purring sound of his voice. "You shouldn't have come out here."

"I had to see if you were alright."

"You shouldn't have."

When had she been held so carefully, so possessively? He seemed to relish the feel of her against him. It was a heady sensation to be desired like this. His touch was different, special, and for a despairing moment she wondered why it couldn't be this way with Daniel. Daniel's embraces were familiar and comfortable, but they never caused sweet, summer-hot joy to surge through her.

Did she want Heath because he was forbidden? Because he was a Southerner? Her fingers curled into the tattered remains of his shirt as she clenched her fists.

"What is the matter with me?" she whispered.

"Nothing. You're a woman . . . and you want to be needed." He smiled slightly. "And need to be wanted."

"But Daniel feels that way about me."

"Then why is he so set on changing the best things about you?"

"The best things?" she repeated incredulously. "You call my temper—"

"I like your temper."

"And my crying—"

"You're tenderhearted."

"And my useless daydreaming—"

"Your imagination," he corrected softly. "I

wouldn't change any of it. Except for one thing. You don't look well-loved, Lucy . . . you don't look satisfied.''

Heartsick, she looked away from him. "Don't say any more. You're right, I shouldn't have come here to find you—''

"But you did. And we both know why. You want to be rescued again.''

She was startled by his words. "W-what?''

"Pretend you're mine,'' he urged, his arms closing around her. "Just for a minute. Pretend there's never been anyone but me, that I'm the one you're promised to. Do it for me . . . I'll never ask again.''

It was her secret fantasy. How had he known? He knew her well enough to tempt her when he knew she couldn't refuse. She tried to think of Daniel, but his image fled from her grasp, and something she had no control over was urging her to tilt her head and surrender her mouth to his. Heath kissed her slowly, hotly, making the rest of the world seem to fade away. He was so warm, so gentle. She forgot she didn't belong to him, forgot that there was anything wrong with wanting him. Drugged by the magic of his kiss, she let reality slip through her fingers.

Heath bent over her and pressed her down on the flat surface of the rock, his forearm supporting the back of her neck. She caught a glimpse of the beginnings of sunrise lightening the sky, and aware of what their closeness would lead to if she didn't stop him, she tried to struggle away.

"Don't. It's alright. Don't be afraid,'' he murmured against her throat, savoring the taste of her fragile skin against his lips. His body eased over hers, and his mouth muffled what she had been about to say. Through their clothes she felt his thigh intrude between hers, riding against the vulnerable softness of her. It was surprisingly natural to be fitted against his body like this. Lucy slid her hands underneath his shirt and across his wide back, exploring the silken surface of it until she reached a long diagonal scar. Slowly she raised her hand to touch the scar at this temple, pulling her mouth away from his. His eyes burned with a steady blue flame as he looked down at her.

"Where?" she asked breathlessly. "Where did you get this?"

"The war."

"All of them?"

"Yes. Do they offend you?"

"No . . . I . . . don't like to think of someone trying to hurt you."

He smiled slightly. "I wasn't enthusiastic about it myself."

"Heath, let me go."

He couldn't. His willpower had vanished. "One more minute. Just one more."

She closed her eyes and shivered as he kissed her throat. His lips searched out the most vulnerable places and lingered over them. "Why did you move up North?" she asked, trying to divert his attention. Her hands pushed at his chest.

"Because you're here."

She laughed shakily. "No that's not why . . . that's not . . . oh, Heath . . ."

His lips were at the highest slope of her breast, and she could feel his fingers tugging at the buttons of her basque. "Please, you can't—"

"I'm just going to kiss you."

"No, I don't want . . ."

But his lips had slid down an inch, and then another, and then his mouth was on the tender peak. She felt her nipple contract inside his mouth, responding to the feathery strokes of his tongue, and she moaned deep in her throat. A terrible struggle raged inside her—it was wrong, she shouldn't encourage him—but what he was doing felt so good that soon she didn't care. Her fingers twined in his hair, tightening as she felt his hand skimming the surface of her bodice. Boldly his hand slipped inside her dress, cupping her breast and stroking the tip of it with his thumb.

She was dissolving in a warm, heavy rain of feeling: the weight of his body on top of hers; the tickling hotness of his mouth on her skin; the hard strength of his muscles, able to crush her but imprisoning her so gently; his low, unsteady breathing; the pulse that beat so feverishly.

"This is what it's like," he said huskily, "to have a man want you, Cin, want you more than anything else . . . who would kill to have you—"

"You've got to stop—"

"Not yet." He took her mouth in a scalding kiss, and she thought dizzily that after this she would make him stop—after one more kiss. Her slender hands slid across his shoulders, holding him closer as he bent his head to whisper her name. "Lucy . . . my Lucy . . . God, how I want you . . ." His hand covered her breast again, massaging gently. Her toes curling, she went boneless, lying helplessly underneath him and groaning his name. Her heart pleaded silently for it to last forever. But just as she writhed closer to him, she heard a woman's sharp cry.

Startled out of the haze of pleasure, Lucy opened her eyes. Her lips red and swollen, she looked groggily to the side where the sound had come from. Standing only a few feet away were Daniel and Sally, both of them white-faced.

Heath cursed viciously, sitting up and pulling Lucy behind him in one swift movement.

"We . . . we were looking for you . . . Lucy,"

Sally stuttered, her hands going to her mouth; then she turned and ran off, her feet crashing noisily through the leaves.

Daniel did nothing except look at the pair of them, his expression of shock gradually changing into hate. The forest was still except for the sound of rustling leaves. His bitter brown eyes met taunting blue ones; then Daniel smiled faintly.

"I would put a bullet right between your eyes," he said to Heath in a thin voice, "but you're not worth the trouble."

Lucy buried her face in her hands, listening to the sound of Daniel walking away. The heat of passion faded from her body and left her with a cold, sick feeling.

Lucy would never forget the misery of the ride back home, during which every one of the Hosmers stared at her wordlessly. Mrs. Hosmer drew her youngest son under her wing and watched Lucy balefully, as if she thought Lucy was a threat to the moral health of her family. After they were dropped off, Lucy sat alone in the parlor while her father went downstairs and minded the store. She couldn't think straight. She merely stared at the wall and sorted through bits and pieces of what had happened, over and over again. She prepared lunch mechanically and set the table, wiping the endless stream of tears from her cheeks. Lucas Caldwell's feet were unusually light on the steps, as if he dreaded having to face her as much as she dreaded it.

"How was business?" Lucy asked in a quavering voice. There was a feeling of unreality about the whole situation. How could they talk about commonplace things when her whole life was upside-down?

"Slow," her father answered, and sat down to the table with a long sigh. She watched him while he ate, knowing that if she touched even a morsel of the food on her plate she would be sick. Finally Lucas set his fork down and met her swollen eyes with a resolute stare. "Knowing how you feel about Daniel, I would have believed it of any girl in town except you. Not only that, but . . ." His expression was bewildered and severely troubled, "doing what you were doing, with the whole of Concord a few yards away." Lucy nodded, putting a shaking hand to her brow, unable to meet his gaze any longer. "I'm surprised at your actions, not his," her father continued, sounding unbearably tired. "Everyone knows what Southerners think of Northern women. Of course he would take advantage of you, given half a chance. Mind you, he's not a bad man for a Southerner, but he's got the same faults as the rest of them."

"Why are you talking about *him?*" Lucy demanded, her nerves strung to the breaking point. "I'm the one who's in trouble—"

"Let me talk," Lucas interrupted, his expression turning harsh even though his voice remained calm. She subsided quickly, staring down at her plate and wrapping her arms around her middle. "Mr. Brooks stopped by the store this morning. He told me that his wife and little girl wouldn't do business here as long as you were working behind the counter, because of the kind of influence you might have on them. Other people feel the same way, Lucy—"

"Then I simply won't work in the store anymore."

"They'll still hold it against me. Business is going to stay slow until you get married and become respectable again."

"They have no right to judge me!"

"That's true. But they're going to, just the same. And what you've done, Lucy, has hurt me and my store just as much as it's hurt your reputation."

"You must hate me now," she whispered, wishing that she was a little girl again, wishing he could make her troubles disappear as he once had been able to. Oh, for the times when her problems could be solved with a few words of advice, or a dollar bill, or a piece of candy!

"I don't hate you. I'm disappointed in you. And mostly I'm concerned about what you're going to do now. Even if Daniel still wants you, his family will never accept you. They set a big store by reputations."

"That's fine," Lucy said dully. "I'll just be an old maid like Abigail Collier. I'll just live here with you."

"Lucy." For a second he didn't seem to know what to say. Then he cleared his throat quietly. "If you stay here with me, my business will get worse. I can't afford that kind of loss."

"Are you serious?" she demanded, shooting up from the table with new energy and wiping her eyes angrily. "Has what I've done been that bad? That terrible?" He said nothing. His expression closed. The lines around his mouth and nose cut deeply. Lucy sat down slowly. Her face felt stiff and cold, as if it had been chiseled out of stone. He was using the store as an excuse. His disapproval of her was so great that he didn't want her with him anymore. He did not want to have to stand by a daughter with a blackened reputation. She had never felt so alone. "You're saying I can't stay here with you," she said slowly. "Then where . . . what . . . what will I do?"

"We can try to find someone from your mother's family in New York to take you in, though I doubt we'll be able to. She cut herself off from all of them when she married me instead of her cousin. Or you could live with your aunt and uncle in Connecticut.''

"Oh no," Lucy breathed, shaking her head. "Their house is so tiny, and they can't afford . . . oh, that wouldn't work at all. And I'm fond of them, but they're so . . . strict . . .'' She trailed off as her father looked at her regretfully.

"You could have done with a stricter upbringing," he said. "I've done wrong by spoiling you so much. I see that now. But you're my only child, and for your mother's sake I didn't want to deny you anything—''

"Please don't talk about her," Lucy choked, turning her back to him and burying her face in a handkerchief.

"There's one more choice," Lucas said, and hesitated a long time before continuing. "You could marry Mr. Rayne.''

Lucy spun around and stared at him, stunned. "What did you say?''

"He came by to see me not two hours ago and offered to make you his wife.''

"You'd . . . you'd marry me off to a Confederate?''

"He said he could provide for you. I believe him.''

The breath left her body. For a moment all the rich promise, all the happy anticipation of being Daniel Collier's wife hung before her. They would have been the most handsome young people in town, popular and admired, with just enough money to go to dinners and plays in Boston; invited to the nicest parties; accepted in the oldest and most respected circles in Concord. All of that would never be hers now. And as Heath Rayne's wife? They would all look down on her, and Sally would be *so* sympathetic and sorry for

her, and she would have to be humble and self-effacing
for years before she was forgiven for having defiled
herself with a Southerner.

"No, I won't," she said in a near panic. "You
can't make me marry him, you can't force me to—"

"Of course I won't force you," Lucas said.

"Then tell him no. I don't ever want to talk
to him again. Tell him that I don't want to be his wife,
and I would never—"

"I told him we'd wait a few days before giving
him an answer. Wait, Lucy, and think about what
you're going to do. I don't think you realize yet what
things are going to be like for you from now on."

It took less than twelve hours for the news to
spread all over town. Best friend or not, it seemed that
Sally hadn't been able to keep her mouth closed about
it. Lucy took to hiding in the house, for every time
she ventured outside she was met with cold stares, or
avidly curious ones, or worst of all, pitying ones. She
was snubbed so many times that she started to expect
it instead of being surprised by it. People who had
known her all of her life and had always been friendly
and kind to her now ignored her, as if she had com-
mitted some hideous crime. She had never dreamed
how awful it would be.

From Daniel there was no word, and Lucy was
tormented by sleepless nights of wondering what he
thought of her. It wasn't possible, she told herself, that
he felt nothing for her, not if he had once loved her
so much. Perhaps she could make him understand, as
no one else seemed to want to understand, that she
was still untouched; but was that really what the scandal was about? She came to realize during the next
few days that people weren't stirred up about the question of whether or not she was still innocent. No, it

was the fact that she had been caught with a man from the South. Old wounds had not begun to heal, and it was too soon after the war for Lucy to be forgiven for what she had done. No one dared to come out and say it, but they all felt that she was a traitor, and that was why they treated her like one.

After nearly a week had gone by, her father treated her to a long lecture about making a decision. Even though it was an unusually cool night, Lucy ran out of the house without a bonnet or a shawl, her face distraught and pale. Before she had time to think about what she was doing, she found herself on the doorstep of the Collier home.

Nancy, an Irish maid with bright green eyes and black hair, let her into the house and showed her to the parlor. Lucy sat alone in the serene room, surrounded by stately mahogany furniture. Her eyes were fixed on the closed door; behind which she could hear the subdued murmurings of the Collier family. Finally Daniel came in, closing the door firmly behind him. It was of some comfort to Lucy to see that he looked as white and strained as she was. His brown eyes, so dear, so familiar, were dark and opaque.

"I had to come here," she said, her voice trembling. "I had to talk to you."

He sat down on the other end of the sofa, his body stiffly set. "You've always known me pretty well," he murmured. "I think you know how I feel about all of this."

"Daniel," she whispered, rigid with fear, "it's easy to love someone in good times, when everything is alright and there aren't any problems . . . but real love . . . what I thought we had . . . real love is there when you really need it, when everything is so . . . horrible, and . . ." Suddenly she broke down and burst into violent tears. Daniel did not move. "Please don't

punish me any longer," she cried. "It was a terrible
mistake, but I'm so sorry for what I've done. I'll do
anything you say, whatever you say, for the rest of my
life . . . oh God, I need you so much . . . I need you
to hold me . . . please, please forgive me . . ." She
begged in that unfamiliar, broken voice until she felt
his hands on her shoulders. At his touch she sobbed
and tried to hurl herself against his body in overwhelmed relief—but his arms locked and he held her
apart from himself.

    "I'm sorry for you," he said. There was
something dead in his gaze. His voice was terribly
cool. "I'm sorry for what you did to us, and what
you've done to yourself. But I won't marry you out of
pity alone, and that's all I feel for you now. I wanted
you before, when I thought you were . . . a certain
kind of person. But I don't want the woman you've
become. I'm sorry."

    Even through her agony she heard the finality
in his tone. There would be no arguing. There would
be no forgiveness. Slowly Lucy pulled away from him
and stood up on trembling legs. He stood up as well,
reaching out automatically as she swayed. "Don't
touch me," she said. They were both shocked at the
thin, feral sound of her voice. "Keep your pity. I don't
need it." Unsteadily she backed away from him, then
fled the house as if possessed by demons. There was
only one place to go now. Her mind was filled with
silent, feverish chattering as she focused on her des-
tination.

    Heath appeared at the doorway of the small
house as she rode up on Dapper, a small mare her
father had given her a long time ago. Heath didn't show
a bit of surprise at the fact that she was there, and he
made no comment about her being alone. There was
a certain freedom in her position of disgrace, Lucy

realized. No matter what she did now, eyebrows could not raise any higher and tongues couldn't wag any faster. As she walked into the house and sat down in a chair before the fire, her desperation fled, leaving behind a blessed, numbing coldness that served to douse the shame and torment that had burned so steadily for a week. Wordlessly Heath sat across from her. She felt his eyes, assessing and calm, on her; and she lifted her face defiantly.

A mere week had wrought tremendous changes in her, more changes than she would have gone through in her whole lifetime had she never met him. She had lost weight and the soft splendor of her figure was reduced to a more compact slenderness. Despite the puffiness from crying, her face was noticeably thinner. The sweetly rounded cheeks were gone, making her stubborn jawline more noticeable and her cheekbones more prominent. Her hazel eyes now gleamed with a hardness that was a far cry from their former vulnerability. The slanting determination of her eyebrows was more striking than ever, and the childish look had left her forever, to be replaced by something far more arresting.

"I'd like something to drink," she said, noticing abstractedly that her voice was no longer so choked and tight. She felt better already, as if coming here had given her the control she had lacked before. Knowing exactly what kind of drink she meant, Heath rose to his feet and returned shortly with a small draft of whiskey. Lucy took a sip and tightened her fingers around the glass as the liquid seared down her insides. Strange—how she could feel it burning, even though the ice inside her had not melted. "I've been frozen out by the entire town this week," she said bitterly, taking another sip and coughing from the sharpness of it. "Everyone I know has managed to get a cut in one way or the other. My father told me that I couldn't live with him any longer. The business . . . you understand.'' She didn't mention Daniel. The fact that she was here made what had transpired with Daniel obvious. "You told me once that hell was a cold place. You were right.''

Heath remained silent, picking up a poker and shifting a log in the fire to fit over the blaze more comfortably. The light shone on one side of his face, leaving the other side with the scar in darkness. He kept his expression blank, unwilling to reveal his thoughts to her. He knew that somewhere under Lucy's defeated exterior there had to be a huge load of anger, and probably no small amount of it was directed at him. That being the case, he knew it galled her to have to accept his help. But the two of them and everyone else knew that he was the only way out for her, unless she wanted to turn her back and leave her town, her people, her whole life. He knew from experience how hard *that* was. God, he had wanted her, but not this way—not with her hate, not with the gratitude and sense of duty she might come to feel later. He swallowed hard, finding it difficult to accept the fact that once more he would not have what he wanted without a handful of bitters thrown in.

"I've thought about your offer to marry me,'' Lucy continued, hearing her own voice as if it were someone else speaking. "It's funny, isn't it, that you're the only one in this town who can save the last shreds of my respectability, seeing that you contributed so much to ruining it. If the offer still stands, I accept. If not, I'll go to Connecticut to live with my aunt and uncle. Truly, I don't care which it is, so don't martyr yourself on my account—''

"No. It sounds like there's enough martyring

going on already,'' Heath said, but she refused to respond to the gentle sting.

"Then you'll still go through with it?'' she asked.

He paused, and it seemed like forever before she heard him speak. "Only if you wear a white wedding dress.''

"Oh, I intend to,'' she said grimly. "It's my right . . . though everyone in town will say that blood red would be more appropriate.''

"Cinda . . .'' he said slowly, his eyes searching. "You're giving yourself to the man who ruined you.''

"You don't deserve all the blame,'' Lucy said after a long hesitation. Then she finished off the whiskey, which had helped a little to soften the hard lump in her throat, and added coldly, "After all, I wasn't exactly kicking and screaming, was I? That's *my* burden . . . you can carry the rest.''

"I don't believe in lifelong burdens . . . or martyrdom,'' Heath said, his eyes gleaming with mockery. "But since you do, I hope I'm heavy enough penance for you.''

Lucy felt a stab of uneasiness. She stared into the empty bottom of her glass. So he knew that she was marrying him to punish herself. She wondered why he was going through with this. There had been no pity in his expression, just a hard sort of amusement and maybe a trace of understanding. She tried to envision her future with him, an entire lifetime with no escape, but she couldn't see anything except hazy darkness. And then she told herself that the future didn't matter any longer.

"I'd like another drink,'' she said.

"No, honey. I'm taking you home now, before

you get too liquored up to remember what we talked about.''

"I'm a full-grown woman. I can decide what I want to do and what I don't want, and if you don't want that in a wife, then just forget that our discussion tonight ever took place, because I'm through with being told what—''

"Shhhh.'' He took the glass from her and helped her up, his touch light and strangely reassuring. She had the strangest feeling that he understood exactly what was going through her mind. "Don't throw away all the rules at once, honey . . . do it one by one. You can do whatever you damn well want after we're married. For now, I'm taking you home.''

"Because I want to,'' she corrected fuzzily, now utterly exhausted, "not because you're telling me to.''

"Yes, I know,'' he said gently, guiding her towards the door. She would have told him not to humor her, except that just now it felt good to be humored and helped and talked to softly. Heath was the only one in the entire world who wasn't looking at her with the cutting gleam of judgment in his eyes, the only one who wasn't smirking or gloating over her downfall. Whether or not he was the cause of it didn't matter at the moment. The fact was, he *knew* the truth, and it was comforting to have someone believe her.

"Oh, good Lord . . . ,'' Lucy murmured wearily, shaking her head. "I'm going to be the wife of a Confederate. None of the Caldwells will ever accept it.''

"Honey,'' Heath said quietly, and his white teeth flashed in a wry smile, "that ain't half as bad as me marrying a Yankee.''

"You aren't planning on ever going back, are you? I won't. One of my reasons for marrying you is

that I want to stay here, and you might as well know
it.''

          ''No. I'm never going back.'' His fingers
closed on her arm in a brutally tight hold. ''And that's
a promise I'll never break.''

          ''You're hurting me,'' she said, tugging at her
arm, and he released it instantly. Lucy rubbed the sore
spot and looked at his shoulder, so near her face. Suddenly she wanted to rest against the inviting strength
of that shoulder, perhaps let herself cry some more,
rest her cheek against his steady heartbeat, and hide
from the rest of the world in the circle of his arms.
But somewhere inside her there was a hard knot of
pride that would not let her seek comfort from him,
and she clung to that pride desperately, finding that it
lent her its own kind of strength. She was beginning
to understand for the first time she did not need other
people half as much as she had always thought she did.

Chapter Five

THE DRESS LUCY had intended to wear for her wedding with Daniel was only half-done. She went to the dressmaker's home and viewed the unfinished garment regretfully. They had planned it to be the most exquisite creation a bride had ever worn down the aisle of the First Parish, but now Lucy's dream of the perfect bridal gown was only a "would have been." She could still picture every detail of it clearly. It would have been made of white silk, pulled tightly in front to outline her figure, drawn into a huge bustle in the back and ornamented with cascading bunches of orange-blossom sprays. It would have had crystal-dotted tulle at the hem, while the overskirt would have been trimmed with a luscious drop fringe of satin and crystal. The veil would have been of white tulle, fastened in her hair with her mother's gold combs. Oh, how heartbreakingly beautiful it would have been, and how admiring and envious everyone in Concord would have been!

But if she wore something like that to her wedding with the Southerner, people would have laughed and talked even more about her scalded reputation and how ridiculous it was for her to be festooned like an untouched maiden. It galled Lucy to have to sit down with the dressmaker and figure out a new design, one that could be made quickly and efficiently. But she

would die before wearing one of her old gowns to her own wedding. She still had her pride, no matter whom she was marrying.

They finally decided to take the foundation of white satin that had already been sewn and finish it off with pink crepe de chine and morning glories—white funnel-shaped flowers, which Lucy privately dubbed "mourning glories." Since her father had insisted that the marriage take place as soon as possible, the dress was finished and delivered to her in a week, just in time for the ceremony.

It was all happening so quickly that Lucy had no time to sit down and think about everything. There was the packing to be done, a small, conservative trousseau to be ordered, things to be bought. She did it all without any help, stubbornly refusing the tentative overtures of friendship from Sally and her former friends, feeling that the only way to get through all of this was to stand alone and pit herself against the world. She didn't want to forgive Sally for her gossiping or the others for their snubs—no, it felt much better to grind her resentment between her teeth and chew on it a while.

On her last day spent in the home she grew up in, Lucy walked around aimlessly from room to room, her eyes alighting on the things that were the most familiar and precious to her. Most of what she would take with her had already been packed in trunks and boxes, which at this moment were being taken to Heath's place by her father. The rooms looked empty without her knick-knacks and possessions strewn about, and she wondered if her father would see that. If he did notice how bare the house was without her, he would never say so. It was not in his nature to say things like that.

She stopped in front of the mantelpiece, looking at all the odds and ends lined up on it. A little china figurine was perched on the edge, nearly ready to topple off. The faded figurine was a woman wearing an old-fashioned, high-waisted dress, her slippers and sash painted a shade of gold that had almost been rubbed away by age and handling. It had belonged to her mother. Lucy realized that she had nothing of her mother's to take with her. She reached out hesitantly, rescuing the figurine from the uncertain balance and clasping it firmly in a small fist. Feeling as if she were stealing something she had no right to, Lucy wrapped it in a handkerchief and closed it in her handbag. What would Anne Caldwell have thought about all of this? Would she have been heartbroken that her daughter was marrying a Southerner? Maybe not. Anne had gone against her own family and married a man they hadn't approved of. Maybe she would have understood.

Lucy sat down at her father's rolltop desk, toying absently with a stack of letter paper as she allowed herself to think about Heath for the first time in days. She hadn't seen nor heard from him personally since that crazy, disjointed night a week ago when she had accepted his proposal. She wondered what his reaction would be as he helped her father unload her boxes and trunks from the wagon. The small house would be improved a good deal by the things she had sent over— the blue and white china, the bright patchwork quilts, the expertly stitched sheets and embroidered cloths that she had made for her hope chest in the expectation that they were for her home with Daniel. A misguided hope chest. She did hope that she hadn't embroidered a big *C* for *Collier* on anything.

A sudden thought struck her, and she pulled a sheet of paper off the top of the stack. Carefully she wrote *Lucy Caldwell* across the center, then right below it, *Lucy Rayne*. Perhaps Lucy Caldwell-Rayne? No, the shorter version was better, more dashing. It wasn't a bad name, she thought, staring at the piece of paper intently. It wasn't bad at all. As she crumpled the paper in a closing fist, she dropped her head in her arms and cried.

On the afternoon of her wedding Lucy stood in front of the mirror in her pink and white dress, twisting and turning to see herself from every angle. She had taken all morning to get dressed and arrange her hair, but no amount of pinching could bring color to her pale cheeks. There was nothing she could do to make herself appear radiant or joyful, not when her heart was numb and her whole body filled with dread. She heard her father's knock on the door—he always knocked timidly with just one knuckle of his hand. "Come in," she said tautly, her nerves already in shreds. Lucas was dressed in a light tan sack suit, his white mustache freshly groomed and waxed.

"You look very attractive," he said.

"I look more like a bridesmaid than a bride."

He made no comment about Lucy's sharp tone, choosing instead to rock back on his heels and give her another appraising glance. "Are you going to wear a veil?"

"I decided not to." It had been a decision that she now regretted fiercely. It would have been nice to have her face covered, to look out at everyone else and know that they couldn't see her.

"It's better this way," Lucas agreed mildly, then turned to leave the room. "We must leave in five minutes."

"That's fine, I'm ready," she heard herself say, while that little nagging voice in her head chimed in: *I'm not ready! I'm not!*

She was trapped. There was nothing she could

think of to do except follow the course she had set for herself. But other people had done this very same thing. Others had married people they didn't love, and if she wasn't going to have Daniel, she might as well have anyone.

As they went in a small carriage to the church, Lucas cleared his throat and spoke to her with unusual awkwardness. "Lucy . . . when a girl is married, it falls to her mother or some female relative to speak to her about the . . . the marital relationship. Notwithstanding what you may have already . . . experienced . . . there are things that a bride should be aware of. I trust you took my advice and spoke to the reverend about any questions you may have had?"

Lucy noticed that her father's face was even redder than hers. *Now* he asked her such a question, ten minutes before her wedding ceremony, when he knew there was no time for her to ask the kind of personal questions he would have hated to answer. "I did speak to him," he said, her eyes falling to the small bouquet of flowers in her hand. "He gave me a list of Bible quotations to read. I looked them up last night, and . . . I think I know everything . . . mostly."

"That's good," he said with obvious relief, and the subject was promptly dropped.

Lucy frowned down at her flowers. In truth, the Scriptures had not been as enlightening as the reverend had said they would be. There had been a lot of passages with advice to "be obedient" and "be fruitful" and, of course, "be faithful''; but the material was sadly lacking in the specifics she would have liked to know.

She had drawn her own conclusions about marriage from her own experiences, some common sense, and some gleanings from *Godey's Lady's Book.*

The novelettes wedged between the "chitchat" section and the fashion columns had given a clue here and there about what to expect. There was, for instance, that thrilling paragraph in "Philomena's Dilemma," in which the hero had kissed Philomena with ardent vigor and "clasped her to his breast," thereafter "bringing Philomena to the true realization of womanhood." Lucy had a fair idea of what had happened to Philomena after the hero had clasped her in his arms. After all, it was impossible for men to hide what happened to them when they held you too close for too long. And thanks to Heath Rayne, she also knew without a doubt what happened at the beginning of the wedding night, if not the middle and end. Picturing the two of them alone in his bed, she felt her insides clench up.

The reverend, his plump, smile-bedecked wife, and his little girl were waiting with Heath just inside the front door of the church. Lucy preceded her father through the doorway and stopped in front of her husband-to-be, looking up at him with trepidation. He was very handsome in a fawn linen suit that had the look, as all of his clothes did, of being unspeakably expensive. The suit was superbly cut and fitted; it was flat collared and had stylishly made sleeves without cuffs. Everything was perfect from the top of his dark blond head to the polished side-buttoned shoes on his feet. More annoying than his flawless appearance was his relaxed manner—he was as casual as if they were at a picnic! The way he looked at her gave the impression that he knew how anxious she was and that he was silently daring her to go through with the wedding. *I'll bet he thinks I'm going to back out like a coward,* she thought, and set her jaw determinedly.

As they all walked to the front of the empty

church and took their places, it was clear that everyone except Heath was nervous. Even the Reverend Mr. Reynolds, who had done this hundreds of times, had to take off his glasses and wipe the perspiration from the foggy lenses.

"Is there something wrong, sir?" Heath inquired politely.

"I've . . . never married a Southerner before," came the apologetic answer, which suddenly infuriated Lucy. For heaven's sake, why did everyone keep saying *Southerner* as if she were marrying some different species of man?

"That's alright," Lucy said acidly. "I assume they use the same vows as we do, Reverend, even if they don't pronounce the words right."

It took all of Heath's concentration to smother a grin. For a spoiled and pampered New England girl, Lucy Caldwell had done pretty well at raising her back up and showing signs of a fine temper. He was more than a little relieved to see that she hadn't let them all humble her spirit, for he couldn't stand the thought of a meek and submissive wife. On the other hand, it amused him to a certain extent to know how it galled her to marry him instead of her fine Northern beau from a well-respected family. She was a little hypocrite, he thought with a grim smile. If he had been from an old Boston family with an established name, she would have dropped Daniel Collier and leapt on him in a minute. The attraction between them had been there from the first moment they had met, though it would take some doing to get her to admit it.

Now Lucy was looking up at him, challenging him to say something about her shrewish manner, but he merely smiled and shrugged, as if he had already resigned himself to the odd ways of Yankees.

Lucy clung to her irritation for the next several

minutes, finding that it helped to take her mind off
what was happening. Just as her grand wedding dress
had been reduced to a far simpler and modest garment, her grand wedding had been reduced to a short
and businesslike ceremony. The vows were taken;
then, the rings were exchanged during an enthusiastic
bout of organ music provided by the reverend's wife.
Lucy barely had time to register the rich gold band
around her finger before she felt Heath's fingers under
her chin, tilting her face upwards. He kissed her
lightly.

There. It was done. Her dreams of Daniel
were forever gone. Her pledge was give to another
man, and her hand was placed in a stranger's keeping. While Heath accepted the reverend's congratu-
lations, Lucas Caldwell left the church to bring round
the carriage. Lucy bent to the little Reynolds girl to
give her the bouquet, and her fingers brushed against
the tiny, warm hands that clutched the flower stems.
Then she straightened and looked at Mrs. Reynolds,
whose round face was touched with gentle pity as
she saw what was written in Lucy's eyes. ''A bride
shouldn't wear such a frown, dear,'' she whispered
kindly. ''He seems like a fine man who'll do well by
you.''

Lucy nodded mutely, a lump of misery rising
in her throat as the woman continued.

''Life isn't always what we expect it to—''

''I understand. Thank you, Mrs. Reynolds.''
Lucy interrupted more harshly than she had intended,
her rudeness freezing the other woman into silence.
Suddenly she felt the warning bite of Heath's hand,
closing like a vise on her upper arm. Wincing slightly,
she glanced up at him in protest, but he was directing
a charming smile to Mrs. Reynolds. ''We both appreciate your kindness to us this afternoon, ma'am,'' he

said in that beguiling drawl, smoothing down the older woman's ruffled feathers. Lucy didn't understand why he took the trouble—it didn't really matter to him what Mrs. Reynolds thought, did it? "We'll never forget what you've done to make this occasion a beautiful memory that we'll always cherish."

"Why, Mr. Rayne," fluttered the reverend's wife, her expression self-preening and pleased, "all I did was play a hymn and witness the ceremony—"

"And bless us with your presence." Heath gave her a slow, appreciative smile, which no doubt established a storehouse of good will in Mrs. Reynold's ample bosom. Then he turned Lucy with a twist of his wrist and steered her down the aisle.

"You're going to bruise my arm!" she hissed under her breath, prying at his fingers until they loosened. He did not miss a stride, continuing to pull her out of the church.

"I'm going to bruise more than your arm if you don't calm your temper down. If you've got a crow to pluck with me, Daniel, or your father, that's one thing, but you don't have to spite some nice old woman who was trying to coax you into a better mood—"

"Crow to pluck?" she repeated disdainfully. "You mean *bone to pick.*"

"You Yankees might pick bones, but south of the Mason-Dixon we pluck crows."

"At the moment we're not south of the Mason-Dixon!"

They paused in front of the carriage, and blue eyes met brown in one nerve-jarring moment. Gradually Lucy's gaze dropped. "Are we going home now?" she asked in a low voice.

"I thought it would be best to go to the Wayside Inn for dinner."

"I'm not hungry."

Heath sighed, his patience worn thin. He raked a hand through his golden hair, causing it to fall over his forehead in attractive disarray. "Cinda . . . since this is the only wedding day that either of us is likely to have, let's try to make the best of it. We'll go to the Wayside, have a relaxing dinner with a glass or two of wine, and by the time we come back to Concord everything will be unpacked—"

"By who?"

"A woman named Colleen Flannery and her daughter Molly—I pay them to do the washing and cooking a few times a week. They'll come by tomorrow to meet you."

She nodded slowly and let him help her into the carriage. Now that the ceremony was over, Lucy was tired, strung out, and even more tense than she had been this morning. She tried to do her best to carry on a conversation, but after a while they both lapsed into wordlessness. The next part of the evening went by in a blur while the silence between them lasted all through dinner, broken only by the necessities of ordering from the menu and passing the salt. After a second glass of wine, however, Lucy's tongue was loosened sufficiently for her to ask some questions that had been bothering her.

"Are you going to write another book?" she asked.

"Hadn't planned on it. Why do you ask?"

"Well . . . money for us to live on. I mean, the money from your first book can't last forever, and I thought to make more, you'd have to—"

"Oh." His turquoise eyes gleamed with sudden amusement. "Cin, a man should try to make a living as an author only if he doesn't value the luxury of eating three meals a day."

"But your book was a success—"

"Yes, but the total amount of money I got for it wouldn't last us a week."

Her jaw dropped open in amazement. Her father had said Heath could provide for her! It had never entered her mind to doubt that, not when Heath's clothes were so handsome and his expression always so free of worry.

"But I had always assumed . . . then how do you make a living?"

"After the war ended I sold some of the more valuable tracts of land that my father left to me and made some investments. One in particular promises to pay off very well, more than enough to keep us in a comfortable style. Have you ever heard of refrigerated railroad cars?"

"No," she said, relaxing with sudden relief. Land. Investments. Those words meant money.

"It's a way for the big shippers to increase their business ten times over, packing their fruit and vegetables in low-temperature cars and sending them on down the line to the larger retailers, bypassing the small merchants along the tracks—"

"But wouldn't that put a lot of people out of business?"

"Yes. But that can't be helped . . . especially when they're standing in the way of progress."

"How callous you sound! Don't you feel guilty about it? Responsible for those people you put out of work?"

"I should have known you'd moralize about it," Heath said, and smiled slightly. But as she continued to stare at him in that half-appalled manner, his smile disappeared and his expression became at once sober and ruthless. He was utterly remorseless, Lucy realized, and for a split second she was almost afraid of him. What kinds of things was he capable of? "No, I don't feel guilty," he said. "I don't like putting people out of work, but I have a strange fondness for sleeping with a roof over my head."

"But those people—"

"That's what war does . . . it shakes the established order up. Some of us float to the top while others sink to the bottom. And no matter what I've had to do to keep from going under, it's better than drowning."

"Some men would rather drown than lose their integrity," Lucy said, Censure threaded thickly through her voice.

Heath's blue eyes turned to ice, sending a shiver down her spine. "You'd be surprised, Mrs. Rayne, about the amount of things you don't know about men and their integrity. Including the fact that during the war your beloved Daniel probably did things to survive that would make you sick to your stomach."

"I didn't say a word about Daniel!" she said hotly, but they both knew she had been thinking about him.

"I'll tolerate a lot from you," Heath said, staring her down effortlessly, "but I won't have you sitting in judgment on me—or making comparisons."

After that they didn't talk at all, but this silence, cold and unbreakable, was worse than the one before.

After supper was over, they returned to Concord late in the evening. Lucy had a few minutes alone before they retired to bed. Carefully she took off her dress and put it away. All her movements were slow, as if she were in the middle of a dream. Clumsily she undid her corset and swayed as a deep breath of air rushed to the bottom of her lungs. Clinging to the bedpost, she rested her cheek against it and closed her eyes until the dizziness passed.

"Cinda?" She started in response to Heath's voice and her eyes flew open. "Are you alright?" he asked, walking from the doorway to the bed. His handsome face was touched with concern. Letting go of the bedpost, she backed away a step or two, her bare toes digging into the pliant braided rug.

"I'm fine," she said defensively, wrapping her trembling arms around her waist. She was unbearably aware of the fact that he was still fully clothed while she was dressed only in her pantalets and the wrinkled camisole that had been crushed underneath the corset all day. "I didn't know you'd be up here so soon. I haven't had time to . . . get ready."

"I didn't know how much time you'd need."

"Well," she said uncomfortably, "why don't you leave and come back in a few minutes, and by then I'll have found my nightgown and—"

"Why don't I stay?" he suggested softly, already shrugging out of his coat. She watched hypnotized as he took off his shoes. "It might be easier, Cin, if we didn't make such a production out of this."

"I can hardly be . . . casual . . . about it—"

"There's no need to be so jumpy. Remember, I've seen you wearing a lot less than that."

Turning away, Lucy avoided the sight of him as he continued to undress. Her hands went to the straps of her camisole, but then she froze—no, she couldn't take it off in front of him. Did he expect her to strip naked right now, with him watching? Or worse was *he* stripping naked right now? And if he was, where would she look, what would she say? This was a hundred times worse than she had imagined it would be. Oh why, *why* hadn't someone told her what she was supposed to do? Surely there had to be a proper way to do things, yet no one had warned her of the terrible awkwardness of this moment. Mute, frozen, and shivering, she stood there while her mind raced for some plan of action. Ah—she hadn't taken the pins out of her hair. That would give her something to do for a minute or two. Fumbling with the pins that fastened the coil of hair at the top of her head, she heard two or three of them drop to the floor at the same time that she heard Heath's bare feet approaching her.

"Here. Let me."

His fingers, sliding possessively through the long chestnut locks, brushed over her silky hair and removed the pins leisurely. Reluctantly Lucy turned to face him. He was still wearing his trousers, thank God, but without a shirt he seemed so much larger, so much more intimidating than she had expected. She had never seen so much bare skin at once, and all of it tanned that swarthy shade of brown, marked in many places with scars. The tapered line of his waist gradually broadened upwards into a powerful chest and shoulders. One corner of his mouth lifted in the beginnings of a half-smile as he looked down at her.

Without the heeled slippers she was fond of, Lucy only came up to his shoulder. She hated feeling so dwarfed by him, hated having to tilt her head so far back when she tried to meet his eyes. She wished that he was closer to Daniel's height. Oh, big men and small women weren't meant to be together! If Heath took her in his arms right now and held her like Daniel might have, her nose would be flattened in the middle of his chest. His large hands settled on her shoulders; his thumbs stroked the line of her collarbone. Lucy fixed her eyes on the base of his throat as she forced herself to stay still, but his nearness was stifling. She wanted to fling off his hands and jerk away from him, run away. Her tension gathered in a big, choking knot, which became more and more unendurable. As his hands moved down to her waist, she pulled away from him with a gasp, spinning around and hiding her face in her hands. Her whole body was tensed in shrinking anticipation of his touch.

"I can't," she said wretchedly. "I can't stand this. Not now—please, I need a few days, a week or two, to get used to everything—just leave me alone! I don't want you to touch me. I shouldn't have married you, I don't even know you. I shouldn't have, but I didn't think . . ." She stopped in midsentence, gasping with the effort it took to control herself.

When Heath broke the silence, his voice was very low and quiet. "Oh, Cin." He sighed. "We both have a lot to learn. Come here."

Step by step she went back to him, her eyes glued to the floor. Automatically she flinched as he reached out for her. His arms closed around her and he pulled her right against his body, which was astonishingly warm against the iciness of hers. Lucy thought that she would never be able to stop shaking. As he felt her rigid unwillingness, he murmured to her quietly, as if he were soothing a skittish animal. "Easy, easy . . . it's alright, my sweet girl . . . there's nothing to be afraid of." He did nothing more than hold her, and gradually she relaxed against him as his warmth seeped through her skin, flowed through her in a slow current. She put her palms on his hard, bare chest and pressed her cheek against it so that the steady rhythm of his heartbeat was against her face. She felt his lips brush against her hair. It felt good to be enveloped and swallowed up in his arms, to rest her weight against him and know that he had the strength to support her easily. "I know how difficult it's been for you," he whispered, stroking her back underneath the long fall of chestnut hair. "But the worst is over."

"No, it isn't," she said in a muffled voice. "Maybe for you, but not for me."

"The last thing I intend to do is frighten or hurt you—"

"Then give me some time," she begged. "A week, maybe a month, just so I can—"

"Do you think it'll get any easier if we wait a month?" he asked gently. "You'll dread it more each day."

Illogically she clung to him in her confusion. Heath waited until it was clear that she was not going to reply. His arms loosened, his hands went to the hem of her camisole, and giving her no chance to resist, he pulled it over her head in one decisive motion.

"The lamp—," she started, excruciatingly aware of the golden light that bathed her bare breasts.

"I want to see you," he said, his blue-green eyes suddenly flaring with heat. "And I want you to see me." He braced one knee on the bed and pulled her across the mattress, his fingers splaying over her midriff as lightly as a ray of sunshine. His lips touched hers—just the briefest caress—settled more firmly, and coaxed her mouth to open to his. The taste of him filled her senses. She felt the slow, sensual stroke of his tongue against hers, and she wound her arms around his neck, finding a welcome escape in the pure physical sensation. His fingers caught in the waist of her pantalets, urgently pulling them down over her hips and legs.

Her mind was pleasantly clouded, focusing only on his mouth and his hands. He kissed her patiently, without urgency, and it seemed that the more

eager she became to deepen the contact, the lazier he
got, making her work, making her seek his elusive
kisses until she thrilled with frustration and tangled
her fingers in his hair to hold his head still. Chuckling
softly, Heath rewarded her efforts with a long, thorough kiss, his tongue plunging deep in her mouth.
Somewhere in the back of Lucy's mind was the surprised realization that not only did she want him to go
on kissing her but she was hungry for the touch of his
hands. Those things he had done before—she wanted
them again. She wanted *him* again.

Drawing away reluctantly, Heath left her in order to shed the rest of his clothes. Flushing, Lucy
started to pull at the light quilt at the foot of the bed,
wanting instinctively to cover her nakedness. She heard
his trousers drop to the floor, and she closed her eyes
tightly as he joined her on the bed. His voice was very
near her ear.

"Cin . . . look at me. Aren't you the least bit
curious?"

Her long lashes fluttered open as she met his
eyes, which were glinting with wicked amusement.
"Not really, no."

He grinned suddenly. "You are," he insisted.
"You're just too muleheaded to admit it."

"Muleheaded? I'm—"

"Don't glare at me like that, honey . . . it
cools a man off quicker than ice water."

"Good!" she said, trying to twist away from
him, annoyed at the way he had dispelled the mood of
soft dreaminess. "And stop smiling at me like that—
there's nothing funny about this at all!"

"Be still." He pinned her down and dropped
a kiss on her nose, forcing his smile away even though
his eyes were still twinkling. "You don't like to laugh

at yourself," he observed more quietly. "You should learn to."

"Why?" she demanded in a muffled voice. "You laugh at me enough for the both of us."

He kissed each corner of her mouth, then nibbled on the lobes of her ears and the hollows behind them, whispering to her so softly that she only caught bits and pieces of what he was saying. He whispered that she was beautiful and that he wanted her, and he was so flattering and seductive that Lucy's temper was mollified in no time at all, and she curled up to him, mesmerized by his gentleness. He cupped her breast in a light stroking motion, and his fingertips began to toy with the hardening peak. Pleasure seemed to stream from his hands through her entire body, pleasure so heady and rippling that she was floating in it. "So very shy," Heath murmured at the side of her neck. "You have such beautiful hands . . . I want to feel them on me."

"Where?" she breathed, touching his shoulders hesitantly.

"Everywhere."

"I don't know how—"

"Do anything you want," he coaxed, keeping rein on his urgent passion with stupendous effort. Gamely she ventured down his chest and around his back; her fingers learned the symmetry of his muscles, as solid as bolted steel, and the long curve and the sensitive hollows of his spine. She stopped when she reached his lean hips, coloring in a mixture of apprehension and uncertainty. Murmuring encouragement, Heath took her hand in his, fitting the back of her hand into his palm.

"Heath—"

"Don't pull away from me."

"I can't—"

"No barriers between us," he said. "Not in this room, not now. No walls . . . nothing forbidden . . . nothing to fear, nothing to hide . . . nothing to lose."

The sound of her own heartbeat was in her ears like the thunder of waves against the shore. Trembling, she let him guide her hand downward. First the brush of thick hair against her fingertips, then the incredible heat and hardness of him against her palm. Heath caught his breath, held it and then released a taut sigh. Her slender fingers traveled over the length of him, exploring delicately, pausing as she sensed the leaping fire and tumult she was causing in him, resuming more slowly as her awkward shyness was replaced by curiosity. She was vaguely amazed at the discovery that she didn't mind touching him in this way. It was unfamiliar and intimate but strangely exciting. She caressed him more boldly.

"Am I doing it right?" she asked, her breath warm on his neck, and he shivered.

"God, yes." He gave a laugh that was little more than a catch in his throat. "You're disproving all those stories I've heard about Yankee women." He caught her wrist and pulled her seeking fingers away from the source of his blistering desire. "Just a minute," he said breathlessly, rolling on his back as his hand retained possession of hers.

"What's wrong?"

Heath lifted her hand to his lips, kissing each knuckle. "Nothing. But if you keep doing that, tonight's going to be over much sooner than I had planned."

She raised herself on one elbow and looked down at him. Her reserve began to unravel rapidly as she felt the warmth of his stare go through her. The tenderness of his touch soothed her fraught emotions like a balm. "What do you mean?"

"Around you I have no control. None whatsoever."

"That . . . that's good, isn't it?" she whispered.

"Oh, don't smile like that," he groaned. "You're making it worse."

In an unexpected move he took hold of her and rolled over like a stretching cat. His legs settled between hers as he braced his forearms on either side of her. Lucy gasped at the feel of his masculinity wedged so intimately against her. She could feel the heaviness and driving power of him, only barely restrained and trammeled. Uneasily she tried to wriggle away from him, but was pinned so securely by his weight that she resorted to shrinking deeper into the mattress.

"None of that . . ." His arms slid beneath her back, forcing her to arch so that her breasts were thrust upward, her body vulnerable to his pleasure. He nuzzled the warm underside of her breast, his lips moving upwards until her nipples tightened in eager anticipation. His tongue touched the contracted flesh, circled the pinkening aureole with a stunning awareness of its sensitivity, danced lightly upon the tingling peak until Lucy was shivering. Desire, searing, shattering, irresistible, swept from her head to her toes, and left her helpless with need.

Unconsciously she stroked his hair in a silent entreaty not to stop. The tip of her middle finger found the scar on his temple and traced along it tenderly, but then she accidentally brushed her palm against her breast and felt it round and warm, pulsing with life. She jerked her hand away as if burned. Heath lifted his head and stared at her with glowing turquoise eyes.

"What's the matter?" he asked huskily. "I don't mind if you touch yourself."

She went crimson with embarrassment, her desire fading quickly. "I didn't meant to. It was an accident . . . oh, don't look at me like that!"

He started to smile. "There's nothing wrong with what you just did," he insisted, taking her hand, his fingers tightening as she tried to pull it away.

"Oh, *please* stop talking about it!"

"Not yet. I want to show you something first."

"What?" she asked, and he couldn't help grinning at the apprehension in her voice.

Heath drew her hand to her breast, cupping underneath it and lifting its weight upwards. Flushing red with embarrassment, Lucy tried to tug her hand free, but he would not let her. Bending his head, he used his teeth gently on her nipple.

"If I let you be shy about your own body," he said, pausing to savor her with the tugging warmth of his mouth, "then you're going to be shy about mine . . . and I don't want that." He dragged her resisting hand down her body, down the planes of her stomach and over the curling softness of her hair until she stiffened in shock. Her fingers were pressed between her own legs, against a hot dampness that was quivering slightly. "See how good you feel? That's why I can't get enough of you."

Lucy pulled away from him with a muffled sound, her chest rising and falling rapidly. The back of her hand came to rest on the pillow beside her head, and she shivered as she felt the cool air against the moisture on her fingers.

"How could you?" she whispered, overcome with such a strange mixture of emotions that she could barely think.

"Nothing forbidden," he reminded her, and as if to prove his point, he lowered his mouth to her fingers, licking them one by one.

"But you're not . . . supposed to do things like that," she stammered, her eyes wide.

"How do *you* know?" he said, his voice soft and teasing. "For all you know, all husbands may do this to their wives."

No. Innately she knew that Daniel would never have wanted to be this intimate with her, would never have dreamed of making her do something she didn't want to do. Daniel would have made this a romantic experience, full of dignity and tenderness, not the kind of lusty, pagan ritual her husband seemed bent on performing.

Heath froze, his smile vanishing. Only a fool couldn't see what she was thinking about—*who* she was thinking about—and it wasn't him. How long, he wondered bleakly, was he going to be faced with the shadow of the man she had wanted for so long? "Little prude," he said softly. "You'd rather have a cold New Englander in your bed, wouldn't you, with his fancy manners intact . . . someone who'd lift the hem of your nightgown oh, so respectfully, and ask your permission for every move he made—"

"Don't talk like that to me."

"Admit it. You'd give anything if I were Daniel Collier right now. You'd sell your soul to be in bed with him instead of someone who dares to laugh at you and makes you *feel* instead of letting you lie there like a wax doll—"

"Yes!" she cried, angered by his sarcasm. "I wish you were him! I do!"

His handsome face darkened with a sneer. "Misguided little fool. You only want him because he doesn't want a thing to do with you. And do you know why he doesn't?''

His taunting was more than she could bear. She tried to jerk away from him, but he held her wrists and pinned them over her head. ''Because of you,'' she gasped.

He showed no reaction to her words except for the paling of his face and the faint curl to his lower lip. ''Ah . . . you finally admit it.'' His voice was silky, mocking. ''You would prefer to blame me for everything despite what you said to the contrary the other night. How dishonest of you to accept my proposal when you felt that way. You're a little cheat, Mrs. Rayne.''

''I've loved Daniel for years,'' she said, trembling with rage. ''How dare you think that a few months could change that? You don't understand loyalty or real love . . . you think everything can be solved in bed—''

''Real love,'' he repeated scornfully. ''I'll tell you the truth, Lucy, the truth about why he doesn't want you now, and it hasn't got a damned thing to do with me. He finally realized that you were going to be too demanding for a man like him to satisfy. You're starving for things he could never give you—and yes, that includes several good tumbles in bed. He would never be able to satisfy all of those needs. You wanted too much from him and the only way he could think of to deal with that was to keep putting you in your place. But it became obvious to him that it wasn't going to work—''

''I was satisfied by him,'' Lucy said hoarsely. ''None of that is true.''

''The hell it isn't. Why do you think you turned to me so eagerly whenever he wasn't there? Because you were so satisfied?''

"Because I felt sorry for you!"

"Pity? Oh. I wasn't aware that it was pity that motivated you to respond to me that morning after Emerson's fire."

"You did it on purpose—you planned to seduce me so that someone would see."

"I'm surprised you're not accusing me of setting the fire to lure you there. It certainly is easy to blame everyone else but Lucy, isn't it? But what if it was your fault too? What if Lucy was encouraging another man to make love to her so that Daniel would find out and become jealous?"

"I wasn't!" she said, spluttering with fury. "And there was no need to make him jealous! Everything was fine until you came along."

"Yes, I'm sure everything was just dandy, all during your three-year engagement with him. Three years! And you were still as clean and untouched as a new-minted penny. I'll bet you begged him to make love to you. I'll bet you nagged him to death about it while he put you off with mouthings of honor and respectability. What held him back, Lucy? Why didn't he make you his?"

"He loved me. He *respected* me!"

Heath let go of her with a gesture of distaste and reached for his trousers on the floor. "Respect had nothing to do with it," he said savagely, buttoning up the trousers and scooping up the rest of his clothes as he headed towards the door. "He finally understood that he couldn't handle you. He realized he didn't have the strength, the time, and God help me, the patience to deal with you. But you'll never accept that. You're planning to keep on hankering after him and dreaming about how it all could have been, instead of trying to find out how good things could be between us."

"I didn't do anything to stop you from . . .

from taking me tonight. You were the one who started the argument.''

"Don't be such a martyr. Poor, sinned-against Lucy. I'd sooner fight the war over single-handed than try to change your mind about your pure-minded ex-fiancé.''

Lucy said nothing, clutching the quilt over her naked body; her fingers whitened with the pressure she exerted on the patchworked edge.

"Let me know when you've decided to grow up,'' Heath added from the doorway, sounding a few degrees more controlled than before, and then he closed the door with unnatural quietness. She would have preferred a slam.

Lucy awoke reluctantly, dreading the crushing guilt that would face her as soon as she opened her eyes. Sliding lower under the warm covers, she tried to avoid the morning sunlight, which glared malevolently through the window. Her mouth tasted like it was stuffed full of chalk. He eyes were mere slits as she peered around the empty room and clasped a hand to her head. She doubted that she could have had a worse headache had a train run right between her ears. Groaning, she burrowed her face under a pillow and thought over what had happened the night before. There were so many things that she had said, things she longed to take back and would never be able to. Blinded by anger, she had said them without thinking.

It seemed as if another person had been speaking and acting in her place. Surely she, who had always hated to hurt anyone, had not turned into the vindictive shrew of the night before. Her pride was stung by the recollection of the nasty things Heath had said to her, but still, remorse attacked her vigorously. His bad behavior didn't justify hers.

Lucy wished she had ignored the whole sub-ject of Daniel. Of course she still cared for him. That kind of love didn't die easy, and she was still besieged with all the tender memories she had shared with Dan-iel: the times they had laughed together and held each other; the times he had walked with her by the river when the scent of golden willows was heavy in the air; their gentle kisses and long, romantic embraces. Even now that she was married to another man it was hard to believe that all of that was over. But she didn't want to make Heath miserable, and she didn't want to be a bad wife. It was just that he had an uncanny power to stir her up in a greater rage than she had ever felt before.

She wondered if he was still angry with her—how could he not be? *I don't want to face him,* she thought miserably. But only a child would stay up here hiding in her bed when she could hear him up and around in the kitchen. She had to go downstairs and face him, no matter what dreadful things he might say to her, no matter how icy his blue eyes might be. Slowly she crept out of bed and hunted through the closet for her robe. The rich fragrance of strong-brewed coffee floated to her nostrils. The realization that Heath had made it made her feel doubly worse. *I'm his wife,* she thought guiltily. *I should be doing that now.*

Heath sat alone in the kitchen, his brown hands curled around a thick mug of coffee. His tousled blond head rested against the high-backed chair as he experienced the indescribable numbness that follows a sleepless night. He had always been one to accept the truth for what it was. A man never had control over his own destiny until he learned not to lie to himself. Only during the war had he let his idealism mask the truth. Like the rest of his people he had been too bullheaded to accept that they were beaten. Not until they were crushed and humiliated, not until disillusionment had eaten down to his very bones.

Now he had stolen another chance for himself—a chance to enjoy life again, a chance to care for someone—and he was throwing it away without meaning to. Lucy was going to come to hate him, and that was the last thing he wanted. He walked out to the small porch outside, taking a deep, hot swallow of coffee and looking down the road that led to town.

There were too many differences between them, with little ground to meet in between. She had never known hardship or want; she had never known the fear that drove ambition; she had never known what it was like to have everything and then lose it all; she knew nothing about any of the things that had gone into making him what he was. No wonder she didn't understand him. No wonder he understood so little about her. But he understood her more than Daniel Collier ever had. He understood her enough to hurt her, and he had to keep his temper in check. If it killed him, he would keep it in check.

"Heath?" He heard her timid voice from the kitchen. Strolling leisurely to the kitchen doorway, he leaned one shoulder against the doorjamb and regarded her silently.

Lucy found that the sight of her disheveled husband had a strange effect on her sensibilities. She had never seen any grown man in such a state. Her father always dressed and shaved before appearing for breakfast each morning. But there was a shadow of a beard on Heath's face, and his hair was uncombed, and she was overwhelmingly conscious of the lazy grace of his tanned body, clad in gray trousers and an unbuttoned shirt. He smiled slightly, seeming to be cool and utterly in control, but there was a fire smoldering right under the surface that she could sense without any difficulty.

"You . . . made the coffee this morning," she said in a low voice, not quite meeting his eyes. "I'll do it from now on. A wife is supposed to do things like that."

It took all of Heath's self-possession to keep from pointing out that there were more significant things a wife was supposed to do for her husband. "Fine. As long as it gets made, I don't care who does it," he replied in a monotone.

"You're using a mug," she said nervously, going over to the cabinets and searching until she found the blue-and-white china all neatly stacked. "Do you prefer that over a cup and saucer?"

"Doesn't matter."

She pulled out a china cup and saucer for herself, poured some coffee, and sat down at the table with a faint sigh of weariness.

"Sleep well?" Heath asked.

Her eyes shot to him sharply as she tried to figure out if his question was jeering or not. His face, however, was expressionless. "Yes. I was very tired after yesterday."

"So was I."

Lucy drank her coffee while he watched her thoughtfully. She knew he was looking at her, and she could hardly sit still under such quiet watchfulness. "I'm going through the house today," she said in order to break the silence. "I'm going to find out where everything is, especially the pots and pans and cooking—"

"There's no need. The Flannerys take care of the cooking and cleaning. You can put together a meal now and then whenever you feel like it, but I didn't marry you in order to make a housekeeper and cook out of you.''

Lucy stared at him in confusion. For the first time she wondered why he *had* married her. If he didn't need someone to take care of him, then had it merely been out of pity? The thought didn't leave a pleasant taste in her mouth. ''But . . . how am I going to spend my time?''

''Any way you want to. You can go into town or stay here. You can do nothing or everything, whatever you wish. I won't expect your schedule to revolve around mine, since mine will be erratic during the next few months.''

''That's fine, as long as you're home by dinner so we can—''

''To be blunt, we won't be eating many meals together. I won't be coming home at regular hours. I've got . . . business . . . to attend to in different areas, mostly Lowell and Boston.''

Business? Lucy had been long accustomed to that word, and she hated it passionately. What a convenient term for men to be able to use, a perfectly acceptable way to explain or disguise anything they wanted to hide. *''That's just the way a business is run,''* her father had told her when she had resented the long hours he spent running the store instead of spending time with her. ''Business reasons,'' ''business demands,'' ''business problems''—her father and Daniel and every other man she had ever known used the mysterious world of business as an excuse for their faults, their unfulfilled promises, their absentmindedness. And it seemed that her husband knew how to use that word as well.

''What kind of business?'' she asked suspiciously.

''Something to do with publishing. Any objections?'' Heath asked, now sounding sardonic, and though a multitude of protests trembled on her tongue—*yes, I object . . . I'll never see you . . . we'll never be a real husband and wife . . . you don't even care about how I feel about it*—she couldn't tell him any of that.

    ''Of course not,'' she said coolly.

Chapter Six

THERE WAS MORE freedom in being married than Lucy had ever dreamed of. She had never had so much money to spend on herself, so much leisure time and so few responsibilities. Her reputation had been mended somewhat by her marriage to Heath, though it remained slightly fractured. There were still some people who sniffed and raised their noses as Lucy walked by, but there were very, very few these days whose opinion she cared about. Her money and her new status had made her popular with the kind of people she had never known before. Spending most of her time in and around town, she made new friends and kicked up her heels in a way that caused her father and her old friends to shake their heads silently at her.

She was hardly ever with her husband. In fact, Lucy saw Heath so seldom that during the day it was almost difficult for her to remember that she was married. At night things were slightly different—they did share the same bed—but they had never made love, and the distance between them was so wide that they might as well have been on different continents. Many nights he arrived home very late, and she would already be asleep, alone on her side of the mattress. She would stir drowsily as she felt him get into bed beside her, and then they would lie there, side by side, not touching, until sleep claimed them both. They were both careful not to venture on each other's territory: the left side was hers; the right side was his, and not even in sleep did an arm or a leg cross the invisible line that separated them. But in spite of their lack of closeness, their lack of communication, sharing a bed with Heath became a habit that Lucy would have hated to give up. Even though she could doze off without him there, it seemed that her sleep was never deep or complete until she knew that he was beside her. There was something strangely comforting about knowing that he was next to her, hearing the deep, even rhythm of his breathing, waking up in the middle of the night and seeing the dark outline of him nearby.

On the nights when he got home early, Lucy would turn the lamp down low and get into bed first. She always kept her eyes closed as Heath stripped off his clothes and stretched out beside her, but often when he was asleep, she would open her eyes and let her gaze wander over him. Even though the graceful, pantherish lines of his body became familiar to her eyes, she would always become a little bit breathless. He was an uncommonly handsome man. And since their wedding night, he hadn't made one move toward her.

At first she had been relieved by his lack of attention to her, and then curious, and gradually even a little resentful. Now she spent a lot of her time wondering how to make herself more attractive to him. Once he had seemed to want her very much. What had happened to change his feelings so radically? Was he ignoring her out of consideration or actual disinterest? She couldn't bring herself to talk to him openly about it, and since he didn't seem inclined to broach the subject, it seemed likely that she would end up like

Abigail Collier after all—a sharp-tempered, immaculate old maid.

A few weeks after her marriage, Lucy became a part of a young and fashionable set in Concord, called the Thursday Circle. It consisted of several beautifully groomed women who had too much time on their hands. They had servants to do their work and busy husbands who were away too often. The wives volunteered their money for charities and musical organizations in order to get their names publicly acknowledged, and they took on many cultural and social projects that Lucy joined eagerly.

She was welcomed readily into the circle, since she had all of the qualifications to be a member—she was young, fashionable, and as bored as the rest of them were. They, too, had husbands that they hardly ever saw. They spent their excessive amounts of free time just as she did, shopping, talking, and leafing through fashion magazines. Their meetings always seemed to end in gossip, gossip about intimate and personal matters that Lucy had never heard anyone talk about so openly before. Privately she was sometimes embarrassed by their frank discussions of lovers and sexual exploits and affairs, and yet for all their careless chatter, she could see that many of them were lonely underneath, as lonely as she was. And they were great fun to be around, priding themselves on being shocking and sophisticated, filling the room to the ceiling with their brittle laughter and tobacco smoke. Many of them liked to smoke factory-made cigarettes, a habit of popular actresses and daring society women.

"Dixie," Olinda Morrison, a local banker's wife, drawled smoothly at one Thursday evening meeting, "you must tell me about something."

"Dixie?" Lucy repeated, lifting her dark winged eyebrows quizzically.

"Yes, that's what I'm going to call you from now on—I had no idea until yesterday that you were married to a Confederate. I think it's absolutely delicious."

"What exactly do you want to know?" Lucy inquired, smiling at the avid curiosity that shone in Olinda's velvet black eyes. The brash possessor of striking beauty, Olinda had the confidence to ask anyone anything. Only the truly beautiful could dare to be as rude as she was.

"What is it like with him?" Olinda demanded.

"Do you mean—"

"Oh, don't give me that little-lost-lamb expression . . . you know what I mean! Is he very charming in bed? Are Southerners as soft-spoken as they say, or does he give the Rebel yell at the crucial moment?"

They all howled with laughter. Even Lucy, who had turned bright red, couldn't help joining in. As they all waited expectantly for her answer, she lifted a crystal glass of ice water to her lips in the hope that it would cool her burning cheeks. She had to maintain their impression of her as a woman who was as knowledgeable and familiar as they were with the subject of lovemaking.

"I'll tell you one thing," she said, ignoring a twinge of guilt at leading them all to believe something that wasn't true, "he told me that I disproved all the things he had heard about Yankee women."

That set off another gale of laughter and scattered applause.

"In the South they think Northern women are

all blocks of ice," Alice Gregson, the pretty wife of one of the town councilmen, said dryly.

"We are, compared to them," Betta Hampton replied. Betta was salty and witty; at forty-two she was the oldest one of the group, as well as the most experienced. She often disconcerted Lucy because her knowing smiles and ribald revelations always seemed to contain an unrelieved disenchantment with life. Betta didn't seem to care for anyone or anything. "It's the climate. I'm not talking about the weather, you ninnies—it's the social climate. Here the men are all hardheaded and coldblooded. They only care about one thing. I'll tell you how to make a Northerner stand to attention . . . just rustle a wad of greenbacks near his ear. But Southerners . . . that's a different matter altogether. I had a Southern paramour once, and I can tell you that no matter how many men she's known, a woman is never truly awakened until she's had a Southerner."

"Why? Why is that?" Olinda demanded.

Betta smiled wickedly. "They all have a special secret. Ask Lucy what it is."

But Lucy would not, could not answer, despite the avalanche of entreaties and playful demands for her to reveal the secret. Secret? She had no idea what it could be. She had never made love with Heath—she barely knew her own husband! She looked up silently and met Betta's mocking gray eyes, feeling like a fraud.

"I'll tell you," Betta said smugly. "Southerners do everything—*everything*—very slowly. Isn't that right, Lucy?"

When Lucy returned home that night she was mildly surprised to find Heath already there. It was still early enough in the evening for them to have dinner together, something they almost never did. Lucy dreaded times like this. It was becoming unbearably difficult to sit across the table from him, exchanging stilted conversation and finding very little to say to each other. Sharing a meal was something that was supposed to be warm and cozy and intimate, but instead it made Lucy uncomfortable and cold. He was not the same man who had once teased her and made her laugh, who had provoked her and made her blush with his seductive smile. The man who sat across the table from her became more of a stranger to her every day, a stranger who had hard blue eyes that revealed no trace of desire for her. He did not seem to want her at all, and his indifference was much, much worse than anger.

Lucy figured that the only reason for such a complete lack of interest in her meant that he was seeing another woman. Perhaps he kept a mistress in Boston—she wasn't sure—but it did hurt to think about it. She had no idea how things had deteriorated so far, but it seemed too late to change or fix anything between them.

"How was your day in Boston?" she murmured, spearing a tender bit of asparagus with her fork and lifting it to her mouth.

"A few difficulties with the investment I want to make. I'll have to go back tomorrow."

"Of course," she said, tight-lipped as one suspicious thought after another went through her mind. Did he make all those trips into the city for business reasons, or was he visiting some woman?

Heath's blue gaze sharpened on her. "What about you? A profitable meeting with the good ladies of Concord? What exactly were you discussing tonight—orphans or veterans, the art students' fund or—"

"We were discussing plans for a benefit,"

Lucy said with dignity, stung by his sarcasm. He had made it clear many times before that he didn't hold a high opinion of the women she had chosen to associate with lately. "A benefit for the musical society."

"Ah. I had no idea you were such a patron of the arts."

"I am!" she snapped, slamming down her knife and fork. Her anger gave her temporary bravery. "Why are you always ridiculing my clubs and meetings and my friends? You told me I could do whatever I wanted to do—you have no right to criticize me. You don't really care about any of it, you just want to irritate me!"

"I am interested. I'm fascinated, in fact, that given complete freedom you've made such uninspired choices. I should have expected that it would be that particular crowd to draw you in, but I had hoped that by now your taste would have been developed enough to avoid them."

"They're my friends."

"Are they? What about your old friends . . . the respectable elements in town, the ones whose invitations and notes you refuse to answer? What about that little blond one you knew—"

"Her name is Sally. And you know the reason I don't accept invitations from her or the others I used to know. I told you about the week when—that week before we were married. They were all horrid to me. I'm not ever going to forget or forgive them for deserting me so quickly. I don't care how sorry they are—"

"Careful honey. As the saying goes, if you live in a glass house. . ."

"Why are you taking up for them?" she demanded, trying desperately to ignore an odd, almost painful thump of her heart. Casual and careless though his endearment had been, it had been so long since he had called her that. Oh, what she wouldn't give to know if he felt anything for her still! He sat there in such a self-possessed manner, unruffled by her temper or her useless attempts to get the better of him in an argument.

"I'm not taking up for anyone," he said smoothly. "But only a coward turns his back on someone who's trying to apologize to him. It'll take some spunk to forgive them, but that's one thing you're not short on."

"I don't give a fig about their friendship or their apologies. Betta Hampton says it's better just to forget all about them and go on to—"

"Betta Hampton? That aging. . ." Heath started to say, then stopped abruptly. Lucy was startled to see a hot glow in his turquoise eyes and the sudden hardness of his jaw. She felt chills of uneasiness and anticipation race down her back. For weeks he had been so cool, collected, and taunting. Now, for once, she had managed to drag a noticeable reaction from him. "What else does Betta tell you?" he asked, standing up and bracing his hands on the table, leaning over her. "How to lead me a merry dance just like she does with her husband? That woman is known as the most unfaithful bitch in town—yes, I've seen her prancing down Main Street with her false curls tucked under the brim of her hat and her two paid studs in tow—"

"Those are her footmen," Lucy said defensively. "Her husband is a very important banker and she needs those men to accompany and protect her in case someone tries to—"

"Explain, then, why she can't keep her hands off those fine, strapping *footmen* when she's out in public. She's nothing but a high-class whore. Her kind feeds off of people like you—she won't rest until she's managed to drag you through the mud she wallows in.''

Lucy shot up from her chair. ''You don't even have any friends,'' she said vehemently. ''Except for whoever it is you visit in Boston, whoever it is that fascinates you so much—''

''What the hell are you talking about?''

''And you don't want me to have any friends either. Well, I will! Nothing you do will stop me from seeing Betta and the rest of them!''

''So be it,'' he said, the softness of his voice making her shiver. He turned and strode out of the room while she called after him in impotent rage.

''And you can't ever make me leave here! You'd have to drag me away kicking and screaming, and then I'll leave *you* and come back!''

She heard nothing but his tight, padding steps as he went up to his bedroom. A few seconds later she was weak and tired, staring at the dirty dishes on the table, pondering the question of how her life, which had once been so good, had been ruined so completely. Was it her fault—had she done something so terribly wrong that she had deserved to have Daniel taken away from her and a hateful stranger put in his place?

Maybe Heath will leave me, she thought dully. Neither of them could last much longer like this. Maybe he would decide that he'd had enough and that he wanted to go back South where he belonged. It was ironic that that thought brought a terrible emptiness inside instead of comfort.

Why didn't she understand anything anymore?

The Country and the Cause. She had bought a copy of the book that Heath had written, and she had sneaked it home as guiltily as if she had been doing something forbidden. Thick and well-bound, the book made barely a crackle as she opened it. Alone in the parlor, Lucy turned each page as if seeking some elusive clue to the man she had married. The book outlined the story of a regiment from Virginia during the war, written in a clean, stripped style. Sometimes the writing was as casual as that of an unedited journal, while at other points it took the form of clear and precise prose.

Slowly the book caught her interest as she recognized bits and pieces of her husband winding through the pages with increasing frequency. There were odd notes of humor and descriptions that were sometimes moving, sometimes grotesque. There were stories set off by themselves without preface or conclusion, so cryptic and personal that she was embarrassed and startled by their frankness. The more she read of his book, the more hopeless a task it seemed to come to an understanding of him. The men she had known—Daniel and David Fraser, the boys she had gone to school with, the shy and polite men she had met at dances—had all seemed like such uncomplicated creatures. They liked to flirt with pretty women. They liked to talk among themselves about war and strike manly postures. They were so easy to flatter and cajole. Most of them couldn't stand a woman's tears, and none of them could bear a woman's frosty silence when they had displeased her.

But Heath was different from all of them. He only laughed when she was mad at him, or did his best to provoke her even more. Her silences didn't bother him a bit. And even when he looked relaxed and lazy, underneath the surface lurked the most biting sarcasm that she had ever been exposed to. Surely there was some key to him, something that would give her the

ability to know what to say to him. She would dearly
love to know how to make him wince uncomfortably
as he could make her wince. She would give her left
arm to know how to win an argument over him. But
trying to see into his heart was like trying to see
through a stone wall.

Something in this book, perhaps—there must
be something here that would help her find the answers. Staring at the pages intently, Lucy found that
she didn't have the objectivity necessary to see things
clearly. All she understood was that as chapter followed chapter, his scruples seemed fewer and farther
between, and his feelings more shadowy. He wrote
about the heroic deeds of his comrades in a way that
made them seem like vainglorious fools. Somewhere
in the middle of the book a chapter ended in the
middle of the description of a battle. The next chapter was headed with the words *Written at Governor's
Island* . . .

"Prison Camp," she whispered, feeling a chill
of shock at the revelation. Heath had never mentioned
anything about having been kept in such a place. On
both sides, North and South, the prison camps had
been known as the most disgusting, unsanitary, and
dangerous places on earth. Hundreds of men had been
crushed together without adequate shelter, forced to
survive on tiny quantities of unfit food. Disease had
swept through the camps unmercifully, unrelieved by
medicine. A few words jumped out of the next few
pages: . . . *captured in summer clothes . . . so cold
here . . . men dying of typhoid . . . new outbreak of
measles . . . exchange, exchange—the rumors lead to
the highest hopes and the worst depressions . . . no
water fit to drink* . . .

Lucy closed the book with fumbling hands,
curiously upset. She didn't want to know what Heath

had gone through during the war, how long he had been in prison camp or how he had gotten released.

You'd be surprised, Mrs. Rayne, about the amount of things you don't know about men and their integrity . . .

Did he ever think about the prison camp or had he buried it deeply in his mind? What had he done to survive? Why hadn't he ever told her about it?

She didn't want to know. She didn't want to feel sympathy for him. She didn't want to know this insistent urge to take him in her arms and offer comfort for things that had happened so long ago. It was all in the past, she reminded herself. He didn't need comfort or sympathy now, and he certainly didn't need any silly attempts of her to approach him.

As night approached and Mrs. Flannery arrived to prepare dinner, Lucy wandered into the parlor where Heath was settled on the sofa in a long-legged sprawl. Several newspapers were piled around him in neat, crackling stacks. Heath lowered the paper he was reading and watched her walk across the room, his eyes bright blue and unrevealing as they followed her every move intently.

"What are you reading?" she asked idly, glancing at one of the piles and bending to pick up the top sheets. A paper from Vicksburg, the *Citizen*. "Oh, these old things . . . oh, how strange—this one isn't the usual sort of paper, it's. . ."

"Printed on the back side of wallpaper," Heath said, one side of his mouth lifting in a half-smile.

"Why?"

"Supplies ran low near the end of the war, and the paper mills were burned. Some newspapers printed on wrapping paper, wallpaper, anything they could stick in the presses. And when they ran out of ink, they started using shoe-blacking.''

Lucy smiled, admiring the persistence and determination of the Southern publishers. ''I guess we Northerners don't have the market cornered on stubbornness, do we?'' She shuffled through a few more sheets. ''The Charleston *Mercury*. Why did you save this one?''

''Read the headline.''

''The Union is dissolved . . . oh, the announcement of South Carolina's secession—''

''That's right. At fifteen minutes past one, December 20. The moment everyone knew that there would be war.''

''And this other newspaper—why did you keep this?''

''That . . . ah, that one. . .'' Heath reached out a hand for it and settled back down on the sofa, his expression softening with distant memories. Lucy tilted her head as she looked at him, mesmerized by the bittersweet smile that played gently on his mouth. ''This is what my father died for.''

''What do you mean?'' Lucy asked, stricken by his words.

'' 'This paper,'' ' he read aloud, '' 'which has heretofore strayed from its former Unionist loyalties, is under new management which will seek to uphold the principles of the United States of America. . .' ''

''I don't understand.''

''It was a Richmond paper, run by one of my father's closest friends. My father was a loyal man as well as a firm believer in the Confederate press—he had a great respect for the printed word and swore that as long as the Southern press was alive, the South would never fall. He rushed over to the newspaper office where the editorial staff had started a battle to keep the paper from falling into the hands of the Union troops and becoming a Yankee mouthpiece. My father was killed in the fight and the paper was taken over. This Union edition came out the next day—the struggle to keep it from the Northerners had been useless. My father's fight had been in vain.''

"I'm sorry—"

"Don't be. There were worse ways to die. Slower ways. It was good that he never found out how the war ended.''

They looked at each other for a long moment. A soft and unexpected feeling of warmth swept through Lucy's chest as she found what she had been seeking all afternoon. Why, of course, she did understand much more about him now. It all made perfect sense. "Your father's feelings about writing . . . was that why you became a correspondent?'' she asked hesitantly. "Is that why you wrote that book, and why . . . why you're so interested in newspapers and publishing and things like that?''

Heath's gaze pulled away from hers. He shrugged slightly. "I would have been interested in it anyway.''

"Did you find out about his death before or after. . .''

"Before or after what?''

"Governor's Island," Lucy said, suddenly pinned by his narrow-eyed stare.

"So you got your hands on a copy of the book,'' he mused, raking a hand through his tawny hair. "What did you think about it?''

"I thought . . . ,'' she faltered, uncertain of exactly what she had thought about it. "Well, I was a little . . . revolted. . .''

"Yes?'' he prompted, seemingly fascinated by the shifting emotions on her face. What was he looking for? Why did he appear to be so absorbed by her expression?

"I was . . . sorry that you had been in prison camp. . ."

"A reassuring sentiment, coming from my wife. Anything else?"

"I . . . didn't really like it. I didn't expect it to be so . . . dark. There was no . . . kindness, no hope."

"No. I didn't have much hope then. Or kindness." As he saw that Lucy's forehead had become furrowed, he smothered a grin. "But that doesn't mean I didn't develop a little of each in the last few years. Don't look so anxious. Is Mrs. Flannery almost ready with dinner? I've been hungry for hours."

Instead of the regular Thursday Circle meeting this week, the club was sponsoring a special musical evening. A huge crowd of men and women filled the impressive drawing room of the Hampton's home, while several young musicians played selected works by German composers. Betta, Alice, Olinda, and the rest of the Thursday Circle were well-known for their quick, sharp tongues and the short work they could make of anyone who was targeted by their gossip. During the musical evening Lucy sat close to Betta and Olinda, whose presence would ward off the approaches that her old friends might have made to her.

Sally Hudson, usually so bubbly and friendly, dared not come near the acid-tongued matrons for fear of being ridiculed by them. Lucy glanced at Sally across the room occasionally, trying to ignore the guilt that the pretty blond's uncertain smile caused. They had once been such dear friends. They had once told each other everything, laughed about boys and parents, talked about dress patterns and candy recipes, cried for each other's heartaches. Now Lucy felt that they didn't know each other at all. *I've changed too much for us to be friends ever again,* she thought sadly, knowing that even if she and Sally made peace with each other, they would have nothing to talk about. Lucy had too much pride to confess to anyone that her relationship with Heath was practically nonexistent and that her marriage was a sham. Neither did she want to hear about Sally's problems, which were so little and insignificant that they made her own look that much more appalling.

Fidgeting absentmindedly, Lucy traced the black jet beads that glittered along the box-plaited ruffle of her rich blue evening dress. It was one of the most daring dresses she had ever worn, cut so deeply at the neck that her breasts appeared to be spilling out of the basque. She had worn it with the intention of attracting as much attention as possible, and she was aware of many men's eyes on her. Only one man in the room was not staring at her. He was looking at Sally, whose golden prettiness was accentuated by demure pink and white ruffles. Daniel, who looked much younger than she had remembered him, handsome, proper, starched and combed, and sitting up straight in his seat, staring at Sally as if . . . as if . . .

He had once looked at Lucy that way.

Noticing Lucy's sudden intake of breath, Betta Hampton leaned closer and followed the direction of her eyes. "Why do you keep looking back and forth between that puppy-eyed Daniel Collier and that blond twit?" she whispered.

"I think there's something between them," Lucy said stiffly, fixing her eyes on the musicians at the front of the room.

"Oh." Shrugging disinterestedly, Betta leaned the other way and began to talk to her husband.

Lucy, who had no husband there to talk to, heard not one note of music all through the rest of the evening as she sat and wondered. As the performance concluded and all agreed with pleasure that it had been a resounding success, wine was served and several toasts were made to the Thursday Circle. Lucy nodded and smiled with the others as the club was thanked repeatedly for sponsoring such a delightful evening. Before the crowd began to disperse, Mr. Hudson, Sally's father, stood in front of them all with a glass of wine and a red, beaming face. Somehow knowing what would come next, Lucy stared disbelievingly at Sally, who had blushed and modestly turned her face downward.

"My friends," Mr. Hudson said, gesturing expansively with his free hand, "I am certain that a more appropriate occasion could have been found for this announcement to be made . . . among a quieter and more private gathering, perhaps, as is the Concord way. After all, we know how to do things just as well as those cold-roast Bostonians." The crowd chuckled as a whole, while a few Concordians laughed outright. Mr. Hudson set his glass down and held out a hand to Sally, who went up to the front of the room to join him. "However, the joy of my family, and most especially my Sally, is something we feel should be shared with everyone here tonight. I wish to announce the engagement of my daughter to a fine young man from one of the most respected families in Concord— a young man whose intelligence and responsibility have impressed me many times over—Daniel Collier. To Daniel and Sally."

"To Daniel and Sally!" everyone took up the cry and lifted their glasses in a toast.

Daniel and Sally.

I don't believe it, Lucy thought as the dry,

acrid wine passed over her lips and trickled down her throat. *I'll wake up any minute now, and be Lucy Caldwell again, and Daniel will still be mine, and Heath Rayne will never have come to town . . . Emerson's house will still be standing . . . I'll be in my own little bed at home and hear Father shuffling around in his room . . .* She felt people staring at her, and their curious gazes caused cold, hard sense to enter her mind again. She would never be Lucy Caldwell again. She was Lucy Rayne. She paused in the act of sipping more wine, her eyes meeting with Sally's soft, doelike gaze. The first few rays of adult understanding burned inside her head as she thought, *It's not your fault, Sally. I lost him because of the things I did. I can't blame you for anything.* Her hand trembled slightly and her fingers clenched around the stem of the glass as she raised the wine to Sally in a private toast and smiled at her. Sally's eyes suddenly glistened with tears of gladness as she smiled back.

A prickle ran down the back of Lucy's neck. Her eyes flew to the doorway at the side of the room. Heath stood there, having arrived a few minutes early to pick her up and take her home. His legs were crossed negligently as he leaned against the doorjamb. Someone had given him a glass of wine, which was held carelessly between his long fingers. His mouth quirked in an ironic half-smile.

And he raised his glass to her.

It could have been a compliment. Or the most sarcastic gesture anyone had ever made to her. Lucy didn't know which. She stared at her husband in confusion, his name poised on her lips. His eyes slid down the slender line of her throat to the pale, generous curves of her bosom, lingered there boldly and traveled back up to her face. His stare was so warm and thorough that she flushed as if he had touched her intimately in public, and he kept on looking at her even while he drank from the delicate wine glass. Her heart raced wildly as an electric current of awareness raced over her skin.

"How remarkable," Betta murmured speculatively, and Lucy jerked her glance away from Heath in order to gather up her gloves and tiny blue handbag.

"What's remarkable?" she asked quietly, so thoroughly flustered that she dropped her program between the seats and couldn't retrieve it.

"Your husband. To look at him I wouldn't have thought he would be the marrying kind at all. I also find it remarkable that he should be staring at you in such a manner."

"He is the marrying kind," Lucy said, "I'm wearing a ring that proves it. And why shouldn't he be staring at me? I'm his wife."

"Husbands don't stare at their *wives* that way."

"Mine does," Lucy said with automatic defensiveness, casting a guarded look at her handsome, perplexing husband.

"As I said . . . remarkable."

Lucy turned away from Betta's well-preserved, worldy-wise face and murmured her goodbyes to the other women of the Thursday Circle. Heath took Lucy's black cape from the arms of a stout, white-aproned maid and pulled it around her shoulders. Her gloved hand rested on his arm as he took her out to the barouche.

"So it's over," he said when the barouche was on its way. The cheerful rhythm of the horse's trot steadily underlined their conversation.

"Yes. Tonight was a success."

"I wasn't referring to the Thursday Circle's musical evening."

Lucy hesitated uncertainly before replying. "Then I guess you're talking about Daniel and Sally."

"I saw what you did for Sally. It struck me as an odd gesture for you to make . . . but every now and then, you do show backbone."

"All I did was join in the toast—"

"A toast to the engagement of your former fiancé and your former best friend. Tell me, how hard did you have to grit your teeth?" As Lucy refused to answer, he laughed softly. "Forgive me. I don't mean to detract from your noble gesture. But I am curious . . . are you surprised by the match?"

"I . . . I've never thought of them together," Lucy said wonderingly, her gaze distant as she went over her recollections of the past. "The three of us were together many times, but Daniel never seemed to notice her."

"I'm sure he didn't. Not while you were around. You do tend to attract a man's complete attention."

"How quickly they . . . discovered each other. Just three months after I married you."

"Cheer up, honey. Daniel could have done much worse for himself. She's a little short on pluck, but she's a sweet enough creature—just what he needs."

"I suppose you think he's better off with her than he would have been with me."

"I suppose you don't."

"I could have been a good wife to him."

"If you say so."

She glared at his smooth, clean-cut profile. "And he would have been a good husband to me. At least he wouldn't have left me all the time to go to some other. . ." She caught herself just in time, her hand fluttering up to her throat to keep down the accusation. Wild impulses darted inside her chest like trapped birds seeking escape. All at once she wanted to throw all of her complaints and frustrations and fears at him. "Some other what?" Heath demanded, sliding her a narrow-eyed glance. "Courage, Cinda. Finish what you were going to say."

"Some other woman," she said bluntly, her breath coming faster as she gave into the relief of telling him exactly what she thought. "You're gone all the time, and you don't come back until late at night sometimes, and . . . that's what I think."

"What the hell . . . you think I've been gallivanting around Boston with another woman instead of working?" he asked roughly.

"Haven't you?" she countered in a small voice, while a flicker of hope was born inside her. For a second he had seemed so surprised, perhaps even a little hurt.

He was silent while she waited in agonized suspense for his answer. She had not expected that what he would say would matter so much, and yet she thought she would scream if he didn't say something soon. "Would it matter to you if I've been taking my pleasures where and when I've found them?"

"So it's true," she said, while sudden anger coursed through her body in quick pulses. "You have been with other women—"

"I didn't admit or deny that. I asked if it would matter to you."

"Why should I care? Of course it wouldn't matter to me," she said sharply, longing for the power to hurt him as she saw the cool smile that touched his mouth. "Why have you changed so much?" she burst out. "You used to be so much nicer . . . gentler—"

"You don't allow me to be gentle with you."

"I don't know what you want," Lucy said,

shaking with frustration. "I don't know why you're different now . . . I don't know why . . . I thought when we were first married that we might be able to . . . but now. . ."

"That we might be able to do what?" he prompted, his mood changing rapidly. The moment before he had looked jeering, but now he was staring at her with perfect seriousness. She couldn't answer. The words had jammed up in her throat, and she sat there looking at him mutely. Heath shook his head and returned his attention to the road while the tension between them leapt to an even higher pitch.

"I had hoped that we could find some way to get along with each other," Lucy heard herself blurt out awkwardly. "I didn't expect that you would want to see other women. I don't want that. I don't like it at all." She hung her head and froze in shame, unable to believe she had admitted it. Now he would ridicule her, now he *knew* that she had been jealous. She watched as his hands tightened on the reins, then the barouche pulled over to the side of the road and the horse nickered gently. "Heath? What are you doing?"

He caught her in a bruising grip, one large hand wrapped around the back of her slender neck while his other arm hauled her body right against his. His lips were urging hers apart, his mouth plundering hers with a violent eagerness that caused her to quiver in surprise. As he felt the pliancy of her body, the lack of struggle or fight in her, Heath eased the crushing pressure of his lips and kissed her slowly. She couldn't breathe, couldn't move away from the persuasive stroke of his tongue. His mouth was hot and sweet, drinking in the tenderness of hers, and his head bent further over hers until she collapsed weakly against his shoulder, her lips moving under his in response. His hand moved from her neck to her jaw, cradling the

side of her face as he devoured her with relentless
kisses. She clung to the lapels of his coat, surrender-
ing herself completely to his demands. The wildness
of it filled every pore until she was tingling with the
overflow. His arms trembled with strain as he lifted
his mouth from hers.

"Does that feel like the kiss of a man who's
recently been serviced by his mistress?" he asked
huskily, his breath caressing her moistened lips. Lucy
blinked drowsily, her arms creeping around his neck.
"I haven't had a woman in months," he continued in
that same rough whisper, "not since before I married
you. I haven't wanted anyone else, and I won't until
I've gotten enough of you, whenever the hell that may
be. Every night I promise myself you're going to pay
for the hours that I've wanted you and gone hungry.
By God, I won't go hungry anymore." He bent his
head again, his mouth seeking hers and absorbing her
soft moan. Suddenly Lucy could not separate sounds
and scents and textures from each other, she did not
know if the faint taste of wine came from her mouth
or his, she did not care if that rapid thudding was his
heartbeat or her own. The sky was falling around her
in brilliant ebony shards and little pinpoint stars, and
time was shuddering to a halt. Words and thoughts
vanished with lightning quickness while the only thing
that remained was the pleasure of his lips and the hard
strength of his body.

"There hasn't been any other woman," Heath
said against her mouth, making her tremble. "There
couldn't be. I'm too obsessed with my own wife.
There's only one thing you can give me that no one
else can . . . and heaven and hell be damned, I'll get
it from you no matter how long I have to wait, no
matter how hard I have to ride you. No, I'm not talking

solely about my husbandly rights, although that would be a good place to start.''

"Heath. . .'' She made a small movement to free herself, her eyes dark and clouded with confusion. His arms tightened on her.

"I've given you the time you asked for. But I didn't have too much patience to start with, Cin, and you've worn it threadbare. We've tried it your way and I've waited for you to come to me . . . and now there's a bigger distance between us than I ever should have allowed.''

But she had been waiting for him to come to her! Lucy looked up at him speechlessly.

"From now on we're going to do it my way,'' he continued, framing her small face with his hands. "In case you have any doubts left . . . starting tonight we're going to be husband and wife in every way. There are things we need to talk about . . . but they'll hold until tomorrow.'' His thumbs traced lightly over the dark, slanting lines of her eyebrows and rested at her temples. Unable to help himself, he lowered his mouth to hers again, the sensitive fire of his kiss penetrating down to her toes. She felt lightheaded, as if too much wine had suddenly gone to her head, and she pulled at his wrists feebly in a plea for respite. The pressure on her lips stopped. Heath looked down at her and traced his fingertips along the moonlit gleam of her skin. In an unexpected movement he dropped a kiss on the tip of her nose and deposited her back in her seat, where she curled up and eyed him with bewilderment.

When they reached the little circular drive in front of the house, Heath got out of the barouche and helped her down, his hands fitting neatly around either side of her waist. As soon as her feet touched the ground, she twisted around to pull down the folds and

draperies that flowed from the back of her dress. She
straightened up as his hands remained on her waist,
her heart jumping at the sight of him. In the darkness
his eyes were midnight blue and his perfectly honed
features were shadowed. He pulled her body up against
his, forcing her to stand on her toes and lean into him.
For all the differences in their respective sizes, they fit
together quite snugly. Her eyes closed as she felt the
warmth of his lips on hers, again and again, in light
kisses that caused a river of heat to flow through her.
The feelings were even stronger than before, drugging
her with sweetness. She swayed against him when he
stopped, and Heath stroked a tendril of hair away from
her temple as he stared down at her. ''Go and get
ready for bed while I see to the horse,'' he murmured.
''I won't be long.''

Lucy nodded jerkily. She turned after he released her and went into the house without a backward
glance, raising her hand to her mouth as soon as the
door was closed. Her lips felt tender and bruised. She
went up the stairs with a frown creasing her forehead
as different emotions pulled at her from every direction. Part of her was shaky and anxious; part of her
was relieved that soon the waiting was going to be
over, and there would no longer be anything to dread
or wonder about. Part of her was alive with anticipation. Finally, finally it was going to happen, and she
knew that it was right.

The light quilt and sheets seemed to resist her
efforts to pull them down, but she accomplished the
task with a determined tug. Then she turned the lamp
down almost all the way, so that it gave off a low,
inviting light. Heath would be up here soon, and this
time she wanted everything to be different from their
disastrous wedding night. Like a madwoman, she tore
at the fastenings of her dress and kicked off her slip-

pers, plucking pins out of her hair at the same time. Button after button—why did her dress seem to grow buttons faster than she could unfasten them? Yanking off her stiff silk petticoat, which was padded at the rear with a multitude of small ruffles, she let it drop to the floor in a billowing heap. Underneath the petticoat was a narrow crinoline, made of watchspring steel with a white cotton bustle attached. The whole affair collapsed into a huge, lumpy pancake, which she resolved to kick out of sight as soon as the rest of her things were off. Pins flew everywhere as she tugged more out of her hair. Oh, *where* was the hairbrush? She hopped on one foot, then the other as she stripped off her garters and stockings.

Flying to the mirror in her corset and pantalets, Lucy dragged a comb through her long hair until the chestnut locks fell thick and smooth over her shoulders. "Damn, damn, *damn*," she muttered as the clock seemed to tick faster. Heath would be here any minute. There was still her corset to take off, and that would take up a lot of time. It was made of thick white cloth that was starched, steam-molded over metal and whalebone stays, and laced tightly up the front. Usually she pulled the laces as tightly as she could by herself and tied them in a bow. This morning she had been in a hurry and had left them in a knot. Futilely she picked at the hard little knot with her fingernails, but it showed no signs of loosening. She could have wept with frustration as she heard Heath's footsteps on the stairs. Why was everything going wrong? "I'm not ready yet!" she called out, her voice tight and much higher than usual.

"Fine. I'm going to take a few minutes to wash up."

Lucy put her hands to her boned and stayed midriff, taking a deep, calming breath. Then she tore at the laces with renewed energy before giving up and hunting for a pair of nail scissors. The contents of a drawer rattled like thunder as she pulled it open and pawed through it frantically. Everything was there except the scissors.

"Anything in particular you're looking for?"

She whirled around, flustered and overwrought, her eyes bright with anxiety and exasperation. Heath stood before her in a dark blue robe, looking calm and collected, faintly amused by the sight of her flurry. "Don't make any jokes," she said tautly.

"I'm not about to."

She turned away and resumed her impatient search through the drawer, flinching as she felt the touch of his hand on her bare shoulders. "What is it?" he asked quietly. She gave up her search for the scissors and sighed tremulously, knowing that she was far more agitated than a pair of knotted corset laces should have warranted.

"I . . . oh, I knew something was going to go wrong . . . it's this corset, this horrible . . . thing . . . I can't undo the knot, and I was looking for something to cut the laces—"

"Is that all? Turn around. Well, you do know how to tie an impressive knot, but it's nothing to stew over." His fingers went to the laces, and he began to work at the tangle.

"It's impossible. You might as well help me find the scissors," she said, biting her lower lip, and he smiled.

"Give me a few minutes. We have a long night ahead of us." His head bent lower as he concentrated on the knot. The fragrances of soap and his skin combined in a subtly attractive scent that drifted to her nostrils. Lucy felt a light fluttering in her stomach at his nearness. "Why are you wearing a rough coutil corset? I thought that along with your new clothes you must have ordered new underclothes—''

"My old ones are just fine—"

"I beg to differ. Plain white doesn't suit you. And besides, I have a fancy to see you in colored satin and silk. I can see I'll have to take care of it.''

"Colored satin underthings?'' Lucy had never heard of well-bred women wearing anything but white, gray, or tan underneath their dresses. "You wouldn't dare buy me any of those . . . would you?''

"Dozens . . . including black pantalets with frilly ruffles and pink bows.'' He grinned down at her, and despite all of her jitters she felt a responsive smile tugging at her lips. Just then the knot came undone, and Heath unwound the laces from the metal studs of the corset. Lucy closed her eyes and breathed deeply with relief. As her ribcage expanded and her lungs filled with oxygen, familiar tendrils of dizziness curled through her head. "Feel better?'' he murmured. She nodded, raising her eyes to his as he peeled the corset away from her. The tip of her bare breasts brushed against the soft blue material of his robe. How oddly exciting it was to have him undress her so slowly, treating her like a precious object that would shatter from rough handling.

His fingertips traced her spine in one stroke, skimming over invisible, downy hairs, and his touch sent a sensual chill through her. Swallowing tightly, she reached around to the back of her pantalets to unfasten them. As she fumbled with the button, he slid his arms around her and took her hands, squeezing them briefly before moving them aside and freeing the button with a twist of his fingers. The pantalets dropped to the floor.

Heath lifted her up in his arms and carried her to the bed effortlessly. As she hooked her arms around his neck and was clasped against the hard sinew of his body, she began to relish the feeling that had once frightened her. It was actually pleasant to feel so disarmed and vulnerable, exciting to be held by a man who could throw her off balance so easily, a man who didn't shy away from arguments, a man so far above embarrassment or prudishness that she knew nothing she did could ever shock him.

He lowered her down to the bed and shed his robe. His tanned skin seemed to trap the glow of the light as he bent over her, his gaze moving from her toes all the way up to her face. Hungry blue eyes met hers, shining with dark fire. "You're beautiful, Lucy," he whispered.

They were words that he had said to her before, but in this moment of discovery it seemed that this was the first time she had ever heard them. Her gaze faltered and her eyelashes lowered as he kissed her, his hand sliding beneath her head to cradle it possessively. His mouth demanded that she respond to him, his stroking hand insisted on venturing to the most secret places of her body. All of the hesitation and the shyness that Lucy had expected to feel crumbled and burnt to ashes in the face of his passion. Were those really her arms, pulling his head down to make his kisses deeper? Were those muted, smothered sounds coming from her throat? Oh, she had never dreamed, never thought, never imagined how good his naked skin would feel against hers. She wanted to know what every inch of him felt like. Her hands slid up his back to his heavy, powerful shoulders, her palms smoothing over the faint edges of scars and back down to his lean waist. Boldly she let her fingertips drift to the hard surface of his buttocks and he groaned against her lips.

"It's been such a long time. I've wanted you

for so long. . .'' Heath slid down her body and pressed his mouth in the fragrant valley between her breasts. His thoughts careened into a haphazard jumble. The needs and the forceful demands of his body took the place of caution. His hands were filled with the softness of her; his mouth parched for the taste of her skin. She had fought him and denied him, turned his world upside down, set countless obstacles in his way, and suddenly here she was in his arms, yielding to him freely. All his frustrated desire was aroused to an acute pitch, and he was too far gone now to stop, think, or slow down. It seemed that his whole life was balanced on the outcome of this moment, and he knew that he had to have her or die of hunger.

Lucy gasped as his probing mouth found her nipple and surrounded the sensitive peak. His tongue stroked wetly over the very tip; then, his teeth caught at the contracting flesh and pulled at it delicately. Writhing, she felt the sensation extending to the pulsing softness between her thighs. Helplessly she let him spread her legs with his hands. She was so consumed by desire that she was shaking. He was kissing her everywhere. His hands caressed her thighs, and his body moved further down the mattress. His lips were on the inside of her thigh and they were sliding upwards. Suddenly she knew what he was going to do.

''Heath, wait—''

''Shhh.'' He nipped the tender skin at the top of her leg and nuzzled into the soft, dark triangle of curls. ''Let me . . . you're my wife.'' As he reached the burning flesh between her legs and his tongue flickered over the tiny, well-hidden cache of nerves, Lucy's knees drew up and her toes curled into the bed. Heath's hands cupped her buttocks, raising her up to the sensitive exploration of his lips.

Catching a sob back in her throat, she clenched

her teeth and turned her face to the side, aware of every subtle, dancing touch of his mouth, conscious of nothing else but what he was doing to her. Her buttocks tensed in his palms as she was overwhelmed by pleasure. Suddenly his tongue flickered inside her, and she arched involuntarily, her senses expanding until she was hurtled through an explosion of feeling.

Gasping heavily, she floated in a warm sea of weakness, her eyes heavy-lidded with passion as she saw Heath's face above her. She was too exhausted, too limp to protest as the weight of his hard-muscled body settled over hers. "Just relax." His tone was caressing and low in her ear. "I won't be rough. Let me love you. . ." There was an intrusion between her thighs, and somehow she was shifting her legs to make it easier for him, and then she gasped at the powerful invasion as he pushed into her. There was pain and the shocking realization that he was inside her. Responding to the gentle encouragements he whispered to her, she moved her legs further apart and he slid even deeper, huge and scalding as he moved within her. She flinched at the unfamiliar sensation and the discomfort, but his hands were there to soothe her quivering body, and his voice was soft and strangely broken. "You're so sweet . . . Cinda . . . I knew you would feel like this . . . I knew it would be this way. Put your arms around me . . . ah, Cin. . ."

Thrusting with a controlled rhythm, he gathered her more closely against him and showed her how to follow him. He was uninhibited and utterly abandoned, just as she had known he would be, ruthlessly stripping away her privacy and demanding with his hands and mouth for her to tell him what gave her pleasure. As Lucy looked up at the tawny features of the man she had married, she couldn't imagine sharing this closeness with anyone else, and she knew that after tonight nothing would ever be the same. Confused, she turned her face into his gleaming shoulder and felt a wash of heat inside her; she felt his body driving in and staying there as he stilled and buried his face against her neck. His hands clenched into fists that depressed the pillow on either side of her head.

Blindly she raised her mouth to his, her lips parted and eager. The hours drifted by as their two forms entwined and touched, sometimes urgently and sometimes at a languorous pace. Lucy matched his desire with her own, returning his passion with an equal measure and giving no heed to thoughts of yesterday or tomorrow. She didn't notice when the lamp burned out. She only knew that as the night deepened she became part of the darkness, part of a dream that was now long past innocence, wrapped in a sensual spell that would be broken as soon as morning arrived. With every touch Heath made her more a part of him, and in the hours beyond midnight she began to fear that he had taken more from her than just her innocence.

Chapter Seven

DISTURBED BY QUESTIONS that had no obvious answers, Lucy busied herself with small tasks all day as she pondered the intricacies of her situation. It had been disappointing to wake up and find that Heath had already left, but it had also been a relief to be alone with her thoughts. Everything seemed to have changed since last night. Heath had taken away many of her illusions. It would be a lie to say that she had not found pleasure with him—and that was puzzling when she had believed for so long that the only man she wanted was Daniel. But had her feelings for Daniel been merely a habit? Had she shared an "understanding" with him for so long because it was safer and easier than opening her heart to someone else? *I cared for him sincerely,* she told herself, confused by doubts that she had never allowed herself to consider before. *I still care for him.* But had it really been love, or just something she had mistaken for love?

Now she was starting to care for her husband in a way that she hadn't expected, though he was the most exasperating, unpredictable, and complicated man she had ever met. Despite his claims to the contrary, he almost always managed to get his own way, and he had no qualms about shedding gentlemanly scruples when they prevented him from getting what he wanted. There were two sides to him. He could be

a scoundrel just as easily as he could be a gentleman,
and the art of dealing with him in either case was
something she just hadn't been able to learn yet.

Heath arrived home well after dinner. As he
walked in the front door, Lucy took his coat, her fingers curling into the smooth, dark cloth before she
hung it up. There was a strange expression on his face.
He looked strained and a little tired, but there was a
barely suppressed energy about him, an air of triumph. Something had happened today—she knew it
just by looking at him. She had a premonition that she
was not going to like what he had to tell her.

"We have to talk, Lucy."

"Is is good news or bad news?"

"That depends on how you look at it."

"That doesn't sound very promising."

Heath smiled briefly and then gestured to the
sofa. "You'd better sit down. It's going to be a long
conversation." The way he looked, the exaggerated
calmness of his tone—all of it indicated without a
doubt that he was going to say something important.

"A conversation about what?"

"About all those meetings I've had in Boston.
I should have talked to you about them sooner. But the
longer I let it go, the harder it was to approach you
. . . and with things between us the way they were, it
was easier to keep putting it off—"

"I understand," Lucy said, sitting down suddenly, wondering if her earlier suspicions had been
right after all. What if he *had* been visiting some
woman in Boston? Oh, it was too awful to think about!

Heath sat down beside her and picked up a
glass she had been drinking out of earlier. It was
empty, and he turned it idly in his hands as he spoke.
"I wasn't sure about how things were going to turn
out, so I've been biding my time. Now the moment is

right, and we've got to take care of everything quickly.''

She nodded slowly. Was he trying to tell her about another woman? Would he be so cruel as to tell her something like that after last night? No, no, even if it was true, there was no reason for him to tell her about someone else . . . was there?

"Have you ever read the Boston *Examiner?*" he asked.

The question was so far off from what she had expected that she looked at him in blank surprise. "What? I . . . no, I don't think so . . ."

"I've done research on all the papers in the area. The *Herald* has the highest circulation, about ninety thousand . . . and the *Journal* has about half that many subscribers. Then come all the rest, none of them any higher than seventeen thousand subscribers each. The *Examiner* could be called the best contender for third place—a very weak third place."

Newspapers. He was talking to her about newspapers. What did they have to do with anything? "That's very interesting," she said dutifully, and he grinned at her lack of enthusiasm.

"The *Examiner* is being killed off by the combined efforts of the *Herald* and the *Journal*. They're stealing away advertisers and subscribers, and pulling all kinds of underhanded—"

"Heath," she interrupted impatiently, "I don't want to hear about all of that right now. I just want to know what you were going to tell me."

"Alright." The reckless sparkle in his eyes intensified. "The paper has been put up for sale. After approaching the publisher and looking through the books, I decided it could be made into a competitive enterprise. As of today, we're the new owners of the *Examiner.*"

Lucy stared at him in dawning amazement. "The whole thing? The whole newspaper? A *Boston* newspaper, Heath . . ."

"Actually, not the whole thing . . . just a little over half. The rest of it belongs to Damon Redmond—he's from a family in Boston that—"

"*Redmond?* As in the Lowells, the Saltonstalls, and the Redmonds?"

"Yes. That family. Third son of John Redmond, III. I met Damon when I was abroad, just before the war started."

"But . . . do either of you have enough experience to make the newspaper successful?" Lucy asked, too taken aback to be tactful.

Heath smiled wryly. "In this case, I'm not sure experience has much to do with it. The more experience a man has, the more inclined he is to stick to what's been done in the past . . . follow tradition . . . and that's exactly what I don't plan to do. The business is changing, and the way things were done ten years ago won't survive much longer. Some papers are keeping up with the times—like the New York *Tribune*—and the ones that don't are going out of business. Now is the perfect time to take advantage of that. I want to develop a new kind of journalist and a new kind of newspaper—"

"It sounds like a gamble. What if it doesn't work? What if we lose all our money?"

"We could always stay with your father above the store."

"Don't even joke about that!"

"Don't worry, Cin. I wouldn't let you starve."

"What about this . . . this Redmond person? Are you certain you can trust him as a business partner?"

"I have no doubt about it. He's ambitious, intelligent, and he'll pull his own weight—in fact, I suspect I'll have to find some way of reminding him that this is going to be an ensemble effort. He's the kind who likes to go his own way.''

"Surely it will take a long time to start turning a profit.''

"That depends on several things . . . if you're really curious, I'll go over the numbers and estimates with you in a day or two.''

"No, thank you.'' Lucy had never entertained an interest in numbers of any kind. Still, she was surprised by his apparent willingness to talk with her about such things. Usually men didn't care to discuss business with their wives, or with any woman at all . . . just as women didn't tell men about their private discussions and activities. "All I want to know is if we're going to have enough money to live on.''

"We will. Enough, at any rate, to keep you well supplied with hats and hair ribbons.''

"Running such a large newspaper . . . that will take so much work,'' she said, frowning.

"More than a few late nights,'' he admitted.

"And all that traveling back and forth . . . how are you going to manage it?''

There was a long pause, and then Heath looked up from the glass he held in his hand, his blue-green eyes locking with hers. "It would be impossible,'' he said quietly. "I can't live in Concord and run the paper.''

The implications of that hit her as soundly as a physical blow. If he couldn't run the paper from Concord, he would want to move.

"If you want to own a paper,'' she said rapidly, "you can buy a local one, or start one yourself. You don't have to get one in Boston—''

"I can't do what I want to do with just a local

paper. I don't want to report on how many eggs the Brooks' chickens laid on Thursday, and how Billy Martinson got the bee-sting on his knee—''

"But . . . but . . .''

"But what?'' Heath prompted, leaning forward to brace his elbows on his knees.

"Think of where you come from, and where you are. You don't know Boston. You haven't been here long enough to understand the people up here . . .'' As she faltered, he set the glass down and took one of her hands, holding it in a warm, electrifying clasp, his fingers pressing into her palms as if he would wring the truth out of her.

"Go on,'' he urged. "I don't want to have to guess at your thoughts about this, Cin. Not this time. Tell me.''

"You know better than I do that there's no sympathy for Southerners here. Bostonians want to punish them for the war . . . and you . . . you're thinking of taking over a big Northeastern newspaper? There won't be any support for you, not from any direction. There are so many obstacles in your way, and . . . and I can't begin to tell you how difficult, how *impossible* it's all going to be. They're not going to want to listen to what you have to say. There are so many intellectuals around here, with all their different ideas about Reconstruction, fighting it out right and left. I should know—I've been to enough political discussions and meetings in Concord to be certain that what I'm saying is the truth.''

"I know. And you're right, it won't be easy. But this is a battle that has to be fought, and it has to be here, in Boston. I can do more good for my people—and your people—here than anywhere else. This is where decisions are made. This is where the money and the education is . . . and God almighty, it's like stumbling around in a maze up here . . . they're all wandering in circles, caught in the middle of issues that are too complex to understand, and no one's taking a hard look at the truth. At the way things really are. The war is over, but nothing is solved—not states' rights, not the problems of the freed slaves, not the economy, or political policies—''

"But no matter what you say, you won't be heard," Lucy said, becoming increasingly worried as she saw how determined he was. "They won't listen—''

"Oh, I'll be heard," he assured her with a grim smile. "And they'll listen. Because I'm going to use Damon Redmond as my front. I'm going to make him my managing editor, and through him and his editorials, every point I want to make will be made. He has the support and influence of one of the oldest families in Boston, and I'll find a way to make use of that. I'm not going to hit anyone over the head with my beliefs—I won't have to. I'll sneak them in, here and there, and I'll make them damned easy to swallow. I intend to produce a newspaper like no one else has ever seen before, appealing . . . seductive . . . and if I have to turn the entire profession of journalism upside down to do it, then I will.''

Much of what he said went by her completely. No one had ever talked about a newspaper being *seductive* before, and she didn't understand how or in what way he planned to use Damon Redmond. All she focused on was the fire in his eyes, and the enthusiasm in his voice. His mind was firmly made up, and it would take a miracle to change it. "Can't you just wait a year or two before rushing ahead with this?" Lucy begged. "It's so soon. Wait until you get to know the area and—''

"I know enough to start now. The rest I'll

learn soon enough. I can't wait—there won't be an-other chance like this, not for a long time. The *Examiner* is a good newspaper with a small but established circulation, and the right kind of reputa-tion. It just needs new guidance. It needs to be shaken up—''

''Why?'' she demanded, jerking her hands out of his in a spurt of anger. ''Why do you always have to shake things up and turn everything upside down? What's the matter with leaving things alone like other people do?''

''Because 'things' don't leave people alone. A man either takes charge of life or lets it run over him, and I don't aim to be run over.''

''I'm happy with the way things are! I don't want anything to change!''

Heath was sensitive to the panic in her voice. ''Cinda, you're not happy—and don't try to tell me you are. I know you. I know you better than anyone else does.''

''That's not true—''

''How could you be happy? You were meant for more than living your whole life here. Your father and the rest of the town have tried to make you into something you could never be, and they've convinced you that it's what you want. But you've kept trying to resist in hundreds of small ways . . . crossing that damned river where you weren't supposed to, picking arguments with Daniel. Do you think I didn't know that your relationship with me was an act of defiance against all of them and what they were trying to do to you?''

''You don't know me at all.'' Lucy stood up and backed away from him.

''I know that you shouldn't be tucked away in some little house with only your embroidery and your club meetings to worry about, dreaming about things you'll never do or see. No one's ever asked anything of you before, except that you stay in your place. But I want more from you than that.''

"What you want is to take me away from my home and the people who care for me.''

"Good Lord, woman, I'm not talking about moving to the North Pole! Boston isn't so damned far away from here!''

"It's a world away from here! It's a city, a big one, full of strangers, and I don't know anyone there—''

"The fact is, you don't have a choice. We're moving to Boston . . . in two days.''

"Two days!'' she repeated in shock.

"The papers transferring ownership were signed today. The new edition of the *Examiner* goes to press on Monday. I'm looking at a house on Beacon Hill tomorrow, and if it's suitable, we'll move in right away. If not, we'll stay in a hotel until we can find the right place to live—''

"You can move to Boston,'' she said, glaring at him mutinously, her voice steady with determination. "You can live there and visit me on weekends . . . or don't visit me at all. But whatever you decide, I'll be staying here.''

He looked at her as if measuring the strength of her resolve, and his eyes flashed dangerously. "Like hell you will.''

"I told you once that you couldn't ever make me leave here.''

"Just why are you so hell-bent on staying here? Are you really that afraid? Or do you intend to shadow Sally and Daniel and make their lives miserable?''

"This has nothing to do with Daniel. I won't

go to Boston . . . I'll leave you if you try to make me go with you.'' In speaking hastily, Lucy made a serious error in judgment. As she confronted him and challenged him outright, she saw his jaw harden and his face become taut. In one sentence, she had managed to provoke him far beyond the point of reasoning with him.

"You're going if I have to tie you up and carry you there in the back of a wagon.''

"I'll turn right around and come back. You can't make me stay with you! You can't make me live with you!''

He crossed the space between them and seized her wrist, holding her hand up in front of her own face so that she could see the thick gold band on her finger. "Do you see that? I can damn well make you do a hell of a lot of things you don't feel like doing. That ring is proof of a contract we made with each other, and you can't back out of it.''

"A contract that can be broken,'' she said, flushing scarlet with anger.

"Oh, no it can't.'' His hand tightened around her wrist until it hurt. "You promised your loyalty to me. You're going with me.''

"I didn't give you the right to abuse me!'' she snapped, and the bruising grip lessened until she was able to twist away from him. They stared at each other, both breathing heavily.

"You're my wife. You made a vow to stand by me, and you're going to honor it.''

"I didn't vow to give everything up on some whim of yours!'' Lucy glanced at the stack of newspapers nearby, all of the old memories and pieces of history that he had saved, and she hated everything they represented. "All for a *newspaper*. My life is being ruined just so people can read four cents' worth of news while they drink their tea and coffee—''

"What life? Do you call it living, to be buried here for the next fifty years, hiding from the rest of the world?''

In a rage, Lucy picked up the stack of newspapers and flung them into the fireplace. Her chest was heaving with dry sobs as she watched the edges of the old and tattered pages glow bright orange. Suddenly it all burst into a dull roar of flames, and her face was illuminated by the blaze as she looked at Heath. He was not staring at the fire but at her. His eyes narrowed, and the thin, pale line of the scar at his temple stood out against the darkness of his skin.

"You should have done that long ago," she cried, at once furious and afraid. "You're so eager to tell me about my faults—well, what about yours? You said once that you didn't believe in carrying lifelong burdens, but you've carried your past around with you for eight years, reading it over and over, pretending you don't care about the war when you really do. Everyone else I know has let it go, but you're still mourning and letting it eat at you. *You're still trying to fight it!* Whoever heard of a Southerner trying to run a Boston newspaper? It's insane . . . and you're doing it in order to get your own against the—the *Yankees,* I *know* you are. I don't want to live with a man like that. I don't want to live with *you,* so go to the city and carry out your plans. I'm staying here.'' She picked up her skirts and flew up the stairs, intending to barricade herself in the bedroom. But he was there almost before she was, and his arm bit around her waist as he hauled her back against him and spoke harshly in her ear.

"During the next two days you're going to move your backside around this house and pack up whatever you want to take to Boston. I've already asked your father to help you while I'm gone. If you don't pack anything, you can wear the clothes on your back for the next six months. And if you don't haul your little body to where it's supposed to be when I tell you, I'll come and get you myself. Believe me when I tell you that you'd prefer to do it under your own steam.''

"I won't," she said hoarsely. He was holding her so tightly that it hurt, and he was so angry that she was afraid he would hurt her. His arms could crush her; they would if he tightened them just a little more, and fear leapt inside her, blazing higher and hotter than the burning newspapers downstairs.

His voice bit softly in her ear. "Not only are you going to live with me, Lucy, you're going to act so happy about it that the world will think there's no one else you'd rather be married to . . . even though we both know differently. And you're going to wait in bed for me every night with open arms and a smile on your face—"

"You're a *fool* if you think that."

"I don't think it. I expect it. I don't care if it comes naturally or if you have to force it, but you're going to play the part of Mrs. Rayne for me as well as for everyone else."

"You'll have to kill me first!"

"Don't be so melodramatic. You don't have the presence to carry it off, honey."

"I hate you. I wish I'd never let you touch me." She tried to think of the worst things she could say to him, something that would hurt. "Last night was the last time. I hate just being near you."

Heath froze. "That's going too far, Lucy."

"It's the truth!"

"No," he said quietly. "It's not. But let's see what is the truth."

She began to struggle against him as he dragged her to the bed, but his arms were like steel.

"My father will come after you if you lay a hand on me—"

"You'll never tell your father about what I'm going to do to you," he said, dropping her facedown on the mattress. He took hold of her upper arms in a grip that hurt. She tried to scramble away, but he straddled her easily, his muscular thighs clamping against either side of her hips to keep her from moving. As she felt him unfastening the back of her dress, she squirmed violently in fear and outrage.

"You have no right—"

"I have every right." He yanked at her corset laces until they came free from their hooks. The edges of the heavily boned garment parted, and Lucy gasped as she heard a tearing sound. He was ripping her underclothes off her as if they were tissue. Her protests were muffled as she fought to prevent the relentless exposure of her body, but nothing she did could stop him. "You're my wife, and from now on, you're not going to show the slightest desire to leave my side."

"Stop it!" She went rigid as she felt his warm hands settle on the rigid line of her spine, following it down until he was cupping her smooth buttocks. As his fingers curved over her and his palms circled across her tender flesh, she bit her lip, trying to quell the response that curled through her body. He continued to fondle her until she groaned involuntarily, shutting her eyes and pressing her damp forehead against the sheets.

"No matter how you feel about me," he said, slipping his hand between her legs, "you haven't begun to realize what you'll do for the sake of *this*. That's the truth, Lucy. Isn't it?" She swallowed hard and tried to answer him, but the only sound that escaped her throat was a deep moan. He pushed past the remnant of her clothes. His fingers massaged the softness of her femininity, searching the sensitive flesh with incredible skill. Leaning over her, he stroked her more intimately, his fingers gliding inside her while his mouth fastened onto the nape of her neck. The crescent of his teeth pressed against her skin as he bit down gently, and she lay there helplessly, unable to move as he aroused her without mercy.

Quivering, she felt his hand and his mouth leave her as he sat up and shed his coat and his shirt. When the garments dropped to the floor, he turned her over. The sight of his hard golden body, clad only in a pair of trousers, was branded across her mind in one searing moment. She struck out quickly, slapping his face, and he caught her hands before she could hit him again. Pinning her arms above her head with one hand, he pulled her skirts up and unfastened his trousers. The crushed padding of her bustle was wedged underneath her buttocks, raising her hips a few inches off the mattress. Lucy thrashed wildly, but as Heath stared down at her with taunting blue eyes, she realized the futility of fighting him. Clenching her teeth, she forced her body to go limp under his.

"I wouldn't have thought . . . you would force a woman . . . who doesn't want you," she said with pure loathing.

"You want me." Before she could answer, he drove into her with a powerful thrust, and she arched up to him with a thin cry. A wave of pleasure broke over her, spreading over every inch of her body, and she was paralyzed with astonishment as she felt him press deeper inside her. He moved within her just once and then pulled out, leaving her shaking with desire. Bending over her, he nuzzled past the sagging neckline of her dress to find the aching peak of her breast, and he pulled at it gently with his mouth. When Lucy finally breathed his name in protest and unwilling excitement, he turned his attentions to her other breast, circling her nipple with his tongue until her slender wrists were limp in his grasp.

"You're my wife," he said, widening the spread of her legs by pressing his knees against the inside of her thighs. "And from now on you're going to give me all that a wife is supposed to give her husband, without argument. Aren't you, Lucy?"

He had won—damn him. She wanted him, and she would promise anything, just as long as he didn't stop. "I'm your wife," she whispered obediently, and she nearly choked with relief as he pushed back into her. But just as she felt a surge of pleasure rise through her body in a swelling current, she felt him withdraw from her again.

"You're going with me," he insisted, and she kept silent, her body arching up to his.

"Please," she groaned.

"You're going with me."

"Yes," she gasped. "Yes, I'll go with you."

"And there are going to be no more lies."

"No."

"Then tell me the truth about last night." Slowly he circled his hips, and she felt the warm, heavy pressure of his loins against hers. "Tell me."

"I wanted you," she whispered.

"Like you do now."

"Yes."

He let go of her wrists and sat up, looking at her expressionlessly. Bewildered, Lucy met his eyes and realized that he intended to leave her now, in retaliation for all that she had said and done during their argument. He was rejecting her in the most intimate moment imaginable.

"Heath . . . no—"

"Now that that's all settled, you'd better try to get some sleep," he said coolly. "The next few days are going to be busy."

He stood up, and she understood that he really was going to leave her. She stared at him—her eyes dark and bright, her cheeks burning with feverish heat—while some barrier within her broke. "Don't do this," she whispered. "Don't leave me. Please." But as she saw that he was looking down at her with indifference, she closed her eyes in humiliation and curled up on her side, pressing her face into the pillow.

All at once Heath bowed his head as he fought for self-control. He tried to remember that he had to teach her a lesson, but somewhere it had all gone wrong. Swearing under his breath, he stripped off his trousers swiftly. Lucy felt his weight added to hers on the mattress, and then he was turning her onto her back, tugging off what remained of her clothes, running his hands down her shivering body.

"I'm sorry, Cin," he whispered, sliding his arms around her and hugging her remorsefully. "I'm sorry." He reached down to part her thighs, but they were already sliding open for him, and her loins were tilting hungrily up to his. He pressed into her slowly. She couldn't hold back a sob as he filled her with a low, smooth surge, giving her all the pleasure he knew how to give.

"Don't stop," she begged, and his heart seemed to break at the desperate plea.

"I won't," he whispered tenderly, sliding his hands underneath her buttocks. "I couldn't." He pulled her up hard against his loins, quickening his rhythm, concentrating solely on her satisfaction. His eyes shone into hers until her lashes fluttered down to hide her soul from his gaze.

Carefully, patiently, he reached past her inexperience to bring her to a new threshold. All he could give her now was a hint, a promise of all they would someday be able to share. He would make her understand all that he could not tell her out loud. She was made for him, she belonged to no other. He was a wanderer who had found her. He belonged nowhere but in her arms, a part of her flesh, claiming her, giving himself in return.

Wrapping her arms around his neck, she tangled her fingers in the golden fire of his hair, meeting his every movement. Gentle and fierce, tender and brutal, he took her in a storm of desperation. Her cheek pressed against his shoulder as she was consumed by a slow explosion of sensation. Sweet words were uttered into her soft, bare skin, and then words faded into the strong rasp of his breath. His hands tightened on her hips, lifting her higher as he felt the contractions of her body around his. As the rapture spun itself out, she moaned and held onto him weakly, and the sound was all that it took to send him over the edge. He buried himself in the clasping softness of her and sighed deeply; his hands clenched convulsively in the warm chestnut flow of her hair.

They were still for a long time afterwards. Quietly Lucy lay underneath him, trapped by his arms and the pleasant heaviness of his leg across hers. Though her eyes were closed, she could tell that he was staring at her, and she was mortified by how easily he had gained her surrender. Oh, why was it destined to be this way with him? Why did he seem to understand her so well? He would hold her to the promises she had made, and they both knew that she would not refute them.

Heath soothed the deepening indentation between her eyebrows with his thumb, and then his lips pressed against the tiny spot until the frown was smoothed out. As his hand slid down to her breast, she made a small gesture of protest, attempting to turn away from him. "I'm tired," she said sullenly, "or does playing the part of Mrs. Rayne include having to pretend that I'm not?"

"Dammit all!" He was exasperated by her stubbornness, and he stifled her words with his mouth until her lips parted and her arms crept around his neck. Then he lifted his head and sighed. "I know it won't be easy for you to leave here. But you're going to have to trust me and swallow your pride long enough to give this a chance."

"You haven't given me any alternatives. You just like to hand out your decisions as if—"

"There isn't an alternative. Everything's been set in motion. I couldn't back out even if I wanted to."

Lucy was silent. *The choice,* she thought. *I can stand by him . . . or leave him for good.*

No choice. There wasn't anything she could do except back down. She could not leave him, and in her heart she knew she didn't want to. Not after what they had shared, not after what they had been through. Still, that didn't make his bullying any easier to tolerate! As Heath interpreted her silence as continuing obstinacy, his mouth hardened in determination and he pulled her closer, intending to subdue any remaining resistance. "Heath!" she protested, making an effort to evade him, "I told you I'm tired, and—"

"Remember," he said against the corner of her mouth, "what I said before . . . Mrs. Rayne."

Lucy did remember, and her temper was sparked by his arrogant reminder of the role she was to assume from now on. Then an idea came to her that caused a pleased smile to spread across her face. She would turn everything around to her own advantage. If she had to move to Boston and make the best of things, then she would do it without one more word of protest. Heath expected her to concede to him grudgingly. Well, she would do more than that—she would bewilder him by playing her role to perfection. He wanted her to be sweet, docile and obedient. Well, she would be so sugary and forbearing and *saintly* that he wouldn't know his right hand from his left, and eventually she would have him wrapped around her finger. Then she would find some way to make him swallow *his* pride. The thought was a balm to her bruised ego, and she held onto it with no little satisfaction until the touch of his hands and his lips drove away all thought.

She could hear the distant pounding of a door, and someone was calling her name with annoying persistence. "Lucy . . . Lucy? . . . Lucy! . . ."

"Heath," she mumbled sleepily, her hand venturing across the mattress to find his arm, "get the door . . . tell whoever it is not to—" She stopped speaking as her fingertips encountered nothing but empty space. Heath was not there.

"Lucy!" came the voice from outside, and she realized that it belonged to her father. Rolling over and mumbling a heartfelt curse, she staggered out of the warm bed and went to the window. Yes, the caller was definitely her father. His hair shone white in the bright sunshine of a crisp autumn day, while the cool wind scattered yellow leaves across the ground. She could hear the rustle of the trees through the half-open window. Shivering slightly, she wandered to the closet, pulled out a thick robe and went downstairs in her bare feet. As she opened the front door and let Lucas in, she was the recipient of an appalled stare. Disapproval

was plainly and clearly written all over his face. He
looked her over from head to toe and clicked his tongue
slowly at her appearance.

Even without having glanced in a mirror, Lucy
knew what she looked like. She could feel the puffiness of a sleepless night underneath her eyes, and the
mass of tangles in her long hair, and the tender, swollen curves of her lips. She looked, in fact, like a
woman who had spent the whole night making love.
Lucy was aware of several small aches and twinges in
her body, and she was tired and relaxed—and strangely
contented. She felt a slight smile coming to her lips,
a private, secret smile that she couldn't have explained
to anyone, least of all herself.

"Father, please . . . I just got up, and I haven't
had any coffee—"

"It's eleven o'clock in the morning, and you
just got up? I've never known you to sleep until this
hour, unless you were ill or—"

"I stayed up late last night," Lucy said, turning and going to the kitchen, rubbing her eyes and
yawning. All totaled, she couldn't have had more than
two or three hours of rest. Heath had been insatiable.
"Please sit down while I make the coffee," she said
over her shoulder while Lucas followed her into the
kitchen. "Would you care for a cup?"

"I would," he replied, sitting down at the table, fingering his mustache as he watched her. "I heard
that you have a couple of maids to do your work."
There was unmistakable censure in his tone. "Glad to
see you haven't forgotten how to find your way around
a kitchen."

Lucy kept her back to him, making an effort
to smooth the wild locks of her hair with her hands.
"They don't come in until early in the afternoon. What

about the woman you hired? Is she proving to be a help?"

"She keeps things clean enough, but her cooking isn't as good as yours."

"Thank you," Lucy said, smiling at his gruff admission. As she set the coffee pot on a burner, she noticed a tiny red mark on the inside of her arm—a whisker burn, she surmised—and raised her fingertips to the base of her throat, where she felt more of the telltale marks. A vision flashed through her mind, of Heath's head bending over her body as he had kissed her intimately, and she blushed lightly, aware of an exciting pang of pleasure inside. Perhaps if he had not left so early this morning, he would have gathered her in his arms and given her a lazy grin. He might have murmured something in her ear about last night, maybe teased her a little.

"A shame that you have to leave Concord," Lucas said abruptly. "Heath stopped by last night to tell me. But . . . possibly it's better for you to have a new start."

"Maybe it is. I don't think anyone here will ever quite recover from my disgrace—Concordians have long memories, don't they?" She turned and threw him a quick grin. "I can picture myself fifty years from now, walking down Main Street, and someone whispering as I pass by, 'That's Lucy Rayne—remember what she did in sixty-eight?' By then I'll be old enough to enjoy having a scandalous reputation."

"It's not appropriate to find humor in that."

"Heath says I should learn to laugh at myself more."

"You were brought up to be a thoughtful and serious—"

"I was brought up to think that a good wife

should try to please her husband." As she went to the cabinet and pulled out two sets of cups and saucers, she realized that the idea of leaving Concord wasn't half as distasteful as she had first thought. Maybe Heath had been right. When it came right down to it, she wasn't certain she wanted to live her whole life in one town.

"Lucy," her father said with a severe frown, "I've done my best to raise you properly. I didn't expect you to toss all those values away when you married this man . . . no matter how he treats you, even if he is taking you away from where you belong—"

"He treats me well," she said swiftly, her amusement fading. The defense of her husband came quickly to her lips. "He does. And although I'm a little apprehensive about moving away from here, I married him, and . . . and that's that. I belong with him, wherever he goes." Lucy knew as she spoke that she was not simply mouthing a meaningless sentiment. She meant every word.

Lucas sighed, shaking his head as he looked at her. "I can hardly believe you're going away. I always thought you'd stay in Concord." A trace of accusation edged his voice as he added, "I always thought that you and Daniel would—"

"So did I," Lucy interrupted, and her hand trembled as she poured the coffee. Her father's disapproval would never fail to upset her. He had seen her betrayal of Daniel as a betrayal of himself as well, and he felt that she had gone against all the values he had tried to instill in her. She wondered if it would always stand between them. Yes, it was likely that he would never live down the fact that she had smudged the name and the reputation he had worked so hard to establish. "But maybe things worked out for the best," she said softly.

"The best? You can't tell me that instead of marrying into the Collier family and living in Concord, you would rather end up married to a . . . a . . ."

"There's no use in thinking about that anymore. Why say anything against Heath now? His background certainly didn't make a difference to you when you were trying to get me off of your hands—"

"I've never allowed you to talk back to me," Lucas said, startled by her sharpness. "Married or not, I still won't tolerate it from you."

"I'm sorry." Lucy met his eyes without flinching. "But I won't listen to any criticism of him."

"I didn't say anything against him."

"You implied that he is a step down from Daniel . . . which isn't true at all. Why, I wouldn't give two cents to be in Sally's place, with Daniel as a husband and Abigail as a sister-in-law. I'd be miserable! Daniel never understood me, and he wouldn't have—"

"It doesn't matter," her father said, looking glumly into his coffee. "It's all water under the bridge." It was obvious that he would have liked to put his foot down and lecture her, but for some reason he decided not to. "I'd say more, but it wouldn't do any good."

"No, father," she replied firmly. "What's done is done . . . and we all have to stick with our decisions."

With the help of the Flannerys, Lucy scoured the house for two days, packing clothes, dishes and various odds and ends that would make the residence on Beacon Hill seem like home. Most of the furniture was left behind to be sold with the house. As Heath had requested, Lucas helped pack the heaviest items and left his store in the hands of a newly employed assistant in order to take Lucy to Boston personally.

During the two nights that Heath was gone, Lucy slept on his side of the bed, burying her face in his pillow and inhaling the masculine fragrance of it. She was surprised at how much she missed him, and she took her mind off his absence by giving all her attention to the considerable amount of work to be done. Clearing out the little house was even more difficult than she had expected. For the first time she was leaving the town she had grown up in, a town that, despite everything, she was still strongly attached to. She was heading towards a new home and a life that seemed frighteningly undefined, indistinct. The only thing she was certain of was that she wanted to be where Heath was. Without him, Concord seemed empty, and so did the house, and she spent all of her spare time wondering what he was doing.

Her father hired a closed carriage from the livery to take her to the city, and all the boxes and parcels were loaded into a wagon that one of the Hosmer boys was being paid a dollar to drive behind them. Lucy did not look back as they left Concord. Focusing on the tiny lace-trimmed handkerchief she held in her lap, she dabbed at her eyes occasionally, suppressing any tears that threatened to escape. She felt as if she were leaving her childhood behind, and she was heartsore as the wheels of the carriage turned round and round, taking her away from everything familiar.

As they neared Boston, Lucy began to fuss needlessly with her dress, wanting not even one ribbon to be askew when she stepped out of the carriage. Heath almost always noticed what she wore, and since she hadn't seen him in two days, she wanted to look especially nice. The upper skirt of her dress was made of fancy silver-gray wool, trimmed with matching fringe and looped up to reveal a darker underskirt, while the long sleeves fit tightly to her wrist and puffed out at the shoulders. Her saucy hat, called a *béarnais*, was low-crowned and trimmed with velvet ribbon. The glazed straw brim matched the color of her dress perfectly, and it dipped over her forehead coyly.

Peering out the window as the carriage went by Boston Common, Lucy had a perfect view of Beacon Hill, named for the old beacon that had been built there in the seventeenth century to warn the earliest settlers in case of invasion. Certain sections of Beacon Hill, such as Louisburg Square, were the dominion of the "first families" of Boston. These families, who were occasionally referred to as "cold-roast" Bostonians, inhabited a separate world within Boston. Their names—Lodge, Cabot, and Peabody, to name a few— were synonymous with the names of royalty. Each family possessed a fortune and a reputation founded in earlier years by a revered ancestor. Some, like the Forbeses and the Gardners, had made their money through shipping or railroad investments, while others, such as the Winthrops, the Lowells and the Redmonds, had made it in textiles or banking.

Contrary to the opinions of the First Families, however, there was another, equally important sector of Boston, a class that had the money but not the snobbery of the oldest families. It was a class of entrepreneurs, the businessmen who constantly pushed and prodded the city to develop at a pace it would not have otherwise been inclined to maintain. They made Boston into a showcase for development, and they traveled by train between New York and Boston to conduct their elaborate business transactions with the aplomb of pirates. Their money was new money, and they spent it lavishly, throwing spectacular parties, filling the theaters, frequenting the shops and department stores, and monopolizing the best restaurants. First families abhorred publicity, but the entrepreneurs adored it. They were filled with unselfconscious pride at their own achievements. They were hearty, thriving, occasionally vulgar, and secure in the knowledge that there was little they could not buy. Frequently the Forbeses, the Redmonds, and all of the other first families married their daughters and sons off to the heirs of the entrepreneurs, linking elite names to impressive fortunes.

It occurred to Lucy as the carriage passed the straight facades of the row houses between Louisburg Square and Mt. Vernon Place that she was married to an entrepreneur. What an odd combination they were, a liberal-minded war veteran from Virginia and a conservative Bay Stater who had rarely ventured out of the town of Concord. And stranger still was the combination of Heath and Damon Redmond as business partners. How in the world was Heath going to mix with a proper Bostonian? If Redmond had one-tenth the arrogance, the *elitism,* that could reasonably be expected from a member of a first family, there was stormy weather ahead at the offices of the *Examiner.* Wouldn't it have been easier to find someone other than a Redmond to deal with?

The carriage stopped in front of a large house with a mansard roof and a yard bordered with an elaborate wrought-iron fence. It was much bigger than she had expected, more than twice the size of the house in Concord. Lucy stared at it dumbly as her father helped her from the carriage. She found it hard to believe that she would be living here. Heath hadn't led her to expect anything like this.

Even her father did not bother to hide the fact that he was impressed. "Look," he said, tapping his foot on the paved border of the street. In front of the house the brick had been arranged in an elaborate pat-

tern and glazed. "It's called a 'rich man's sidewalk'."
He glanced at Lucy speculatively, and it was almost
possible to see the numbers clicking through his
mind. "Seems he's been keeping a thing or two under
his hat. What kind of investments did he make? Was
it—"

"Something about the railroad," Lucy replied, tucking stray wisps of hair behind her ears and
blotting the shine of her nose with a corner of her
handkerchief. "And if the way you're looking at me
means that you're wondering if I knew anything about
his money before we were married, the answer is no."

"I wasn't thinking that at all," her father said,
looking affronted.

"Good," she said pertly. "I would hate to
think that you believed me capable of being so mer-
cenary that I would set out to entrap him just because
he has a little more money than Daniel—"

"A great deal more than Daniel."

"Yes . . . well . . ."

"Mr. Caldwell?" came a voice from behind
Lucas. It was the Hosmer boy, who had stopped the
wagon behind the carriage. "Should I start unloading
things?"

"Where is your husband?" Lucas demanded
of his daughter without expecting an answer. "He
should be out here."

"I'm sure he's busy. I'll go in the house and
find him," Lucy said quickly, and she went up the
front steps as her father and the boy discussed which
boxes to unload first.

The house was spectacular, even in its present
state. Scattered here and there were a few elegant
pieces of imported walnut furniture, most of which
would have to be reupholstered. The hardwood floors
were almost crying out to be polished, but they were

free of scars and pockmarks, and the high ceilings were adorned with twinkling chandeliers. Huge windows let in a flood of sunlight. She could picture them framed with fringed draperies. There were glossy marble fireplaces and empty walls that needed to be filled with pictures. Everything needed to be washed, dusted, and cleaned, but it was going to be a beautiful house. How could she help but love it?

As she walked past the first few rooms on the ground floor, she saw men working industriously, tearing old brocade off the walls, replacing chipped tiles, taking measurements, climbing ladders, wielding hammers. There was no sign of Heath, and uncertainly she paused in a doorway long enough to catch the attention of one of the workers.

"Miss?" he questioned, tearing off his hat hastily as she approached him.

"Mrs. Rayne," she corrected with a smile. "I'm looking for my husband. Would you happen to know where he is?"

"Yes, Mrs. Rayne." Respectfully he indicated the steps leading up to the second floor. Upstairs, the sound of heavy scraping came from one of the rooms. Lucy went to investigate, standing just inside the door and smiling as she caught sight of her husband. Unnoticed by either of them, she watched as Heath and a stocky workman lifted a heavy, bulky chest of drawers and carried it away from the corner. The powerful muscles of Heath's shoulders and back flexed underneath the thin white shirt, while fawn trousers molded to his taut buttocks and thighs. Sometimes Lucy's heart skipped a beat when she realized how handsome he was. As she looked at him, she was aware of a certain sense of feminine appreciation, perhaps even smugness. He could be infuriating at times, but there were some things about him that she wouldn't change for anything. And of all the women that had undoubtedly wanted him in the past—and those who would want him in the future—she was the only one with any rightful claim to him.

Breathing deeply from exertion, the men set the stocky article of furniture down in the center of the room and regarded it with disgust. "I can see why it was left behind," Heath remarked, rolling up a sleeve that had fallen down his forearm.

"Too heavy?" the other man asked.

"Too ugly."

"We'll need a few more pairs of hands if we're going to carry it down the stairs, through the front hall and down to the street."

"It might be easier to carry it to the window and drop it," Heath replied, causing the other man to chuckle.

"Not on that sidewalk, you won't," Lucy said with a smile, and Heath turned around, his turquoise eyes sweeping over her in a fraction of a second. There was a sudden silence, and then the air was almost crackling with awareness.

"You're here already."

"I'm a little early."

Heath tore his gaze away from her and glanced at the man nearby. "Mr. Flannigan . . . my wife, Mrs. Rayne."

After exchanging a friendly nod with Lucy, Flannigan cleared his throat selfconsciously. "I . . . ah . . . should check on the boys downstairs." As he left the room, Lucy walked over to Heath hesitantly, wondering why he was staring at her so intently.

"All the men in the house—," she started to say.

"They'll be gone after tomorrow. There are some repairs and alterations that had to be done."

"From what I've seen so far, the house is lovely."

"We don't have much yet as far as furniture goes, except for a bed, some tables, a few chairs and this . . ." He tore his hungry gaze away from her and looked ruefully at the chest of drawers. "This—"

"Monstrosity?"

"That's putting it kindly."

"Eyesore?" she offered, taking a step closer to him.

"Better."

Would it be inappropriate to kiss him before he made a move towards her? She decided it wouldn't be. Impulsively she put her hands on his chest, stood on her toes and pressed her lips against his clean-shaven cheek. "How has everything gone for the last two days? Have you been dreadfully busy?" she asked. His arms went automatically around her waist. It was the first time she had ever approached him without having been coerced. As Heath stared into her up-turned face, the memory of his own words interfered with his enjoyment of the small ritual.

You're going to play the part of Mrs. Rayne for me as well as for everyone else . . .

Heath regretted those words more than anything else he had ever said. He knew she remembered them just as well as he did. But as he looked into her soft hazel eyes, he saw nothing but sweet guileless-ness. He would have liked to allow himself to believe in it. What game was she playing? Apparently the one he had demanded of her.

You'll act the part of Mrs. Rayne for me . . .

Frowning, he bent his head and sought her lips hungrily, searching the depths of her mouth with his tongue until he was absolutely certain that her response was genuine. A magic sweetness stirred be-

tween them, more intoxicating than wine, and Heath's
tension eased as he felt Lucy relax in his arms. Her
face was flushed and her eyes were dazed as their lips
separated. "My . . . my father is downstairs . . . ,"
she said, "with the dishes, and the boxes, and . . .
the wagon—"

"He can wait five more minutes."

"But—"

"He's not going anywhere." Heath ducked his
head under the brim of her hat and found her mouth
again. Sliding her hands around his waist and over his
back, Lucy molded every inch of her body to his, returning his passion measure for measure until Heath
pulled away with a groan. "It's so good to hold you,"
he muttered, framing her face with his hands and
stealing light kisses from her lips. "Dammit. It's going
to be a while before we'll have any privacy. After getting rid of your father and everyone else around here,
there's dinner—"

"We could forget about dinner."

"Why, Mrs. Rayne . . . ," he drawled, af-
fecting shock, and she blushed as he gave her a beguiling, riverboat-gambler smile. "I wish we could.
But I mentioned to Damon that we'll be eating out for
the next few days until we can organize a household
staff, and he insisted that we meet him for dinner tonight at the Parker House."

Sighing heavily, Lucy felt genuine regret as
she pictured the long evening ahead of them. It would
be hours and hours before they would be alone together, and she discovered that she desperately wanted
to be alone with him. She was anxious to find out
exactly how far this new beginning was going to go.

"We'll have to go," he said, tapping her under the chin with a gentle forefinger, his eyes gleaming

with a teasing light. "But I'll make it up to you later—
I stake my word on it."

"Your word as a gentleman?"

"Of course."

"I'd prefer something more reliable," she replied, giving him a flirtatious glance that elicited a
delighted smile from him.

"Later," he murmured, and let go of her reluctantly.

Damon Redmond was more or less what Lucy
had expected. She got her first good look at him as
she and Heath were brought to a discreet, well-placed
table in the Parker House dining room. Parker's was
the meeting place for people of means and influence,
one of the few places in the country that served à la
carte at any hour of the day, on the premise that its
customers had the right to eat their meals at times
other than the regularly scheduled hours.

Damon took her hand, lifted it to his lips in a
practiced gesture and politely uttered all of the appropriate remarks. His breeding and arrogant self-confidence, carefully developed through several generations
of Redmonds, would have been evident even if he had
been dressed in sackcloth. Clad as he was in perfectly
tailored clothes, immaculately shined shoes and a narrow necktie, he possessed a certain glamour that held
its own against Heath's polished charm. He was tall—
another two inches and he would have matched Heath's
height—and his coal black hair and hard-featured face
gave him an aloof but handsome appearance. When he
smiled, he was doubly attractive, but not once during
the entire meal did his smile ever seem to reach his
snapping black eyes. Although he had an appealing
sense of humor, there was something calculating about
his manner, as if he were constantly weighing, judg-

ing, and assessing, which, Lucy decided, was an un-
settling quality in a dinner companion, but not a bad
quality in a newspaper editor.

After they had exchanged small talk about
Boston and ordered from the menu, Damon turned to
Lucy. "I hope that moving from Concord and estab-
lishing residence in Boston has not been overly taxing
for you, Mrs. Rayne."

"Not at all. It has been very easy, as a matter
of fact." Throwing Heath a teasing smile, she added,
"I only hope the two of you will be able to put the
Examiner in order as quickly as I intend to put the
house in order."

"Unfortunately it's going to take some time,"
Damon said dismissively, taking a sip of wine and
casting a disinterested glance around the room. Lucy
realized that he had no intention of discussing business
matters in front of her or talking about anything at all
concerning the newspaper. Belatedly she remembered
Heath's earlier warning on the way to Parker's, that
Damon had a tendency to regard women as empty-
headed creatures. She turned to Heath, who gave her
an almost unnoticeable shrug and an "I-tried-to-tell-
you" look.

"Has it been necessary to fire many of the
former employees so far?" she asked, now determined
to pursue the subject of the *Examiner.*

Heath smiled slowly before replying, aware of
what she was attempting to show Damon. "Mostly on
the editorial staff. And we've had to let several of the
reporters go. We need to find new ones, who won't be
afraid to take a few risks."

"Where are you going to get them?"

Damon seemed uncomfortable with her questions. "Here and there," he said evasively.

Heath was amused. "There's no need to keep

anything from my wife, Damon.'' His gaze slid to
Lucy's expectant face. ''Reporters are usually dug up
from backroom printing shops, Cin. But I have a feeling we'll have more luck finding the kind we want if
we look in other places.'' He lowered his voice con-
spiratorially and winked at her. ''If we're lucky, we'll
manage to steal a few from the *Journal* and the *Herald*.''

''Really? Isn't that unethical?''

''Very. But cheaper and less trouble than
training someone ourselves. There's no such thing as
formal training for reporters . . . just experience. The
more we can get who already have experience, the further ahead we are.''

''What are you going to offer them to leave the
newspapers they're already working for? More
money?''

''That and reasonable working conditions.
And also a few challenges.''

''What kinds of challenges?''

Damon cut in smoothly. ''It's a long list, Mrs.
Rayne. I'm certain that you don't wish to be bored
with it.''

''On the contrary, Mr. Redmond.'' She met
his dark eyes squarely. ''I am interested in everything
pertaining to my husband's business—''

''An interest,'' Heath said dryly, ''which I
have apparently done little to discourage.''

''Apparently,'' Damon murmured, and withdrew into a cool silence.

''About the reporters . . . ?'' Lucy asked
Heath, who grinned in approval of her unabashed
questions.

''The first thing we're going to do is to outlaw
all this ridiculously elaborate prose that somebody decided to make fashionable. I don't want anything to be

fancy or elevated . . . I'm just after something that the average reader won't have trouble understanding. And reporters in general aren't skeptical enough—they take down notes on what they hear and see without asking questions, digging deeper, analyzing. There are a lot of readers who don't know how to interpret what they read, and part of a newspaper's responsibility is to help them understand the news.''

"But how do you know that you're interpreting it the right way?''

"Well, that will always be a matter of opinion. Theoretically, we're supposed to be objective and non-partisan—but few papers are. The *Examiner* is going to set new standards in that respect. And we'll either be a stunning success or go bankrupt in a few weeks.''

Lucy laughed. "Such optimism. It's only my first night in Boston and already you're warning me of bankruptcy.'' She looked at Damon. "Do you agree with these new policies, Mr. Redmond?''

He inclined his head in a short nod. "Insofar as it will be profitable to produce a paper more directed towards the common masses.''

"I'm sure the common masses will be very grateful,'' she replied, just a little too sweetly, and closed her mouth as she felt the warning nudge of Heath's foot underneath the table.

Chapter Eight

"**WHAT A SNOB** Damon Redmond is!" Lucy exclaimed, climbing into bed and folding her arms across her chest in a disgruntled attitude. "I'm surprised he didn't insist that I ask permission every time I wanted to speak! Do you think you're going to be able to work with him? He'll drive all of the employees away in a week, with that insufferable attitude—"

"He won't be dealing with them as much as I will." Heath turned the lamp down and unbuttoned his shirt. "I'll be able to work with him. He does have his good points—"

"Such as?"

"Damon's got a sharp mind, and he'll keep a cool head in an emergency. His editorials are what I need for the paper—clear, analytical, thought-provoking. And to be blunt, he has a circle of friends and acquaintances which might come in handy sooner or later."

"Why is he bothering with all of this, anyway? If he's a Redmond, he doesn't need to worry about money."

"That's kind of a sensitive point." Heath discarded his shirt and sat down on the edge of the bed to remove his boots. His weight caused the sheet to pull tighter over her hips, causing Lucy to shiver lightly at the snug, tucked-in feeling, the coziness of the dimly-lit room, the comforting presence of the man beside her. "The real reason he's bothering with all of this is that he and his family are—as he put it— 'financially embarrassed.' If the paper can't be made into a money-making venture, the Redmonds won't have enough financial resources to keep their high standing in Boston. Not many people know about it, so—"

"I won't mention it to anyone, of course." Thoughtfully Lucy plucked at the sleeve of her nightgown. "I guess if he weren't so arrogant, I'd feel a little sorry for him. His whole family's depending on him to save their fortune? That would be difficult for him to deal with all the time." Eyeing her husband mischievously, she made a clicking sound with her tongue. "And to think . . . his success or failure depends entirely on some radical Southerner and his crazy ideas about the newspaper business—"

"I'll get you for that, girl!"

Suddenly Lucy was pinned flat on her back, and she squirmed and giggled as he reached under the covers and extracted his revenge. "Don't! Don't! I can't stand being tickled!" She shrieked with laughter and protest. "Heath . . . if you don't quit . . ."

"You'll what?" he asked, rolling onto his side as he grinned down at her.

His smile was beautiful. She caught her breath as she met his warm blue eyes, and then she chuckled throatily. "I'll tickle you back."

"It won't work on me."

"I bet it will!" Experimentally she pattered her fingers lightly over his tawny-skinned side, near his armpit. He didn't flinch.

"See? My hide's been toughened up with too many battle scars—now I can't be tickled any more."

Her face fell. "Is that true?"

He laughed softly. "No, honey. I was joking. I wasn't ticklish before the war, either."

"I don't like to joke about that." Her gaze swept over the marks that battle and combat had left on his skin. Long-ago hurts, too late for her to tend and soothe them. The thought of him wounded, bleeding, made her stomach wobble and her heart ache. Tentatively she looked over him, cataloging the healed-over marks on his body, finding that there weren't quite as many as she had thought before. There was a long, thin scar that trailed from his neck down to his collarbone, and much smaller ones across his muscle-patterned midriff, and a line that extended from the side of his abdomen down into the waistband of his trousers. Slowly Lucy reached out and touched his shoulder, first stroking over the faded evidence of a bullet wound, then gliding her fingertips to the scar over his collarbone. Her hand was small and white against the burnt-in tan of his chest.

"Why are there so many?" she wondered aloud.

Heath remained still under her ministrations, his eyes half-closing as she followed the pattern of faint ridges down to his abdomen. "That's what happens when men are put on a battlefield, honey. They all try to . . ." He paused as he felt her unbuttoning his trousers, and when he continued, his voice was slightly unsteady. "They all try to stick each other full of holes. Cinda, what the hell are you . . . oh, God, that feels—"

"Well, I know a few wounds are only to be expected," she said, leaning forward and kissing the base of his throat. Her tongue darted into the hollow, while her hand delved deeper into his trousers. She felt the ripple of his hard swallow against her lips, the·

rapid awakening of his masculinity under her palm.
"But you look like you were one of the prime tar-
gets."

"They . . . they fire at whoever they see first.
I was just a bigger target than most—"

"Much bigger," Lucy agreed demurely, and
he gave a strangled laugh, taking hold of her wrist and
pulling her inquisitive fingers away.

"Little devil. You're full of pepper tonight,
aren't you?"

"I was comforting you and your wounds—"

"They're well healed by now, thank you
ma'am. I'm just glad you weren't around at the time
to tend me—your brand of comfort would have finished me off. Near the end of the war, just the thought
of a pretty woman made stars dance in front of my
eyes."

"Ah . . . so you missed the company of all
those beautiful Virginia belles." Lucy's slight smile
disappeared as a new thought struck her. "Was there
. . . was there one in particular that you missed?"

There was a brief hesitation before he answered. "Never a special one."

Her curiosity sharpened. "Heath . . . about
the women you knew before you married me . . . did
they ever—"

"I don't remember."

"What?"

"I don't remember anything about them."

"You mean you don't want to tell me. But I
really want to know if they ever—"

"Honey, don't bother asking anything about
women from my past. A gentleman doesn't talk about
that with his wife."

"But you're not a gentleman anymore. You
told me so."

"We're not going to talk about it."

"Heath . . ." she said in a wheedling tone.

"You'd feel the same way if I started asking you about what you did with Daniel. You'd say you didn't remember—"

"I do too remember!"

He gave her a mock scowl, raising himself up on one elbow and looking down at her. "Oh? And what do you remember? A moonlit stroll down Main Street and a kiss or two? It couldn't have been much more than that."

"Well . . ." she said, peering up at him through her lashes, "I have to admit, no one's ever kissed me the way you do."

Slightly pacified, Heath began to toy with the ribbons of Lucy's gown. "That's because all you knew were cold-blooded Yankees."

"Heavens, you do like to generalize. I'm a Yankee, and I'm not cold-blooded!" She pronounced the last words *coal-bludded,* imitating his drawl perfectly, and then she grinned at him. "Or do you give yourself credit for that?"

"You're getting mighty sassy, Lucy Rayne."

"Guess you'll have to take me down a peg."

"Damned if I won't."

Over the next few weeks, their new beginning fulfilled some of Lucy's wildest hopes. They both had their own worlds to conquer, and they each plunged enthusiastically into the work that lay ahead. The days were short and busy, the nights were filled with passion. In some ways, it all seemed perfect.

But there were still walls between them, and the walls were all the worse because they were never spoken of. They were always there, undefined, unmentioned, and Lucy would find herself running into

one when she least expected it. Whenever she tried to
find out more about Heath's life before the war, he
would use dozens of different ways to avoid answering;
teasing her, making love to her, sometimes even starting an argument in order to change the subject. The
same thing happened when she asked him questions
that were too personal and probing. He would give her
meaningless answers, or he would not answer at all.
She was hurt by the realization that he didn't intend to
let her into his innermost heart, to share his secrets,
share his pain. Yes, he would allow himself to enjoy
her, comfort and protect her, but it was clear that he
didn't want to love her.

She didn't know why, and there was no one to
help her understand him.

In sheer self-protection, Lucy put up her own
walls. If he wouldn't yield any part of his heart to her,
she would keep him outside of hers as well. She was
sweet and affectionate, laughed and talked with him,
responded to his lovemaking without reservation. But
she never mentioned her secret thoughts and her private longings. She never let him get too close.

Love did not—would not—exist for either of
them. Love waited outside the walls; denied admit-
tance, it was feared and unwelcome. And so, their
moments together were occasionally empty. Sometimes laughter wasn't enough. Sometimes pleasure, or
even affection, wasn't enough.

Heath had given Lucy complete responsibility
for redecorating and furnishing the house as well as
choosing and training the staff. He had established
charge accounts for her at Jordan, Marsh and Company, C. F. Hovey Company, and other large department stores where she became a well-known figure.
After having purchased dizzying quantities of mer-

chandise at each place, Lucy had only to walk through
the door before she heard pleased exclamations from
the doorman and all the store attendants. "Oh, *Mrs.
Rayne,* good morning to you!" "Hello, Mrs. Rayne!"
"Mrs. Rayne, how *nice* to have you back so *soon!*"
Yes, it was quite a feat to have earned such a high
standing with them in such a short amount of time,
considering the famous reserve of Boston retailers. She
amused Heath to no end with her tales of being fawned
over by store clerks and managers.

Many times she agonized privately over the
decisions she had to make. She had not been brought
up to spend money casually, and she had never been
entrusted with such a magnitude of responsibility before. Choosing a sofa or picking out a china pattern
was one thing, but decorating a whole house was entirely different. Especially when that house was so
large, and worse, when she wanted the result of her
efforts to be something that would please her husband
as well as herself. It was terrifying to order thousands
of dollars worth of furniture and carpeting, worrying
all the while that she might not have chosen the right
colors and styles. The house had to be sedate enough
to suit the taste of the conservative Bostonians who
would come to visit, but Heath had made it clear that
he wouldn't live in a typically funereal New England
home. His taste was decidedly modern. Compromises
between the two styles had to be made, and compromises were difficult to find. Most of the time Lucy was
walking on unfamiliar ground, but since there was no
one around to criticize her efforts, she began to rely
on her own taste and her own instincts.

She wasn't especially fond of the elaborate
styles that were so fashionable, and so she used solid
colors and quiet patterns. To frame the windows, Lucy
chose simple velvet panels that would be replaced in

warmer weather by light curtains of crisp muslin. Wool
portieres drawn back with soft tassels, framed the
doorways to each room. In colder weather, they would
be released to stop drafts from seeping in.

The family sitting room was done in shades of
blue and rose, ornamented with lace curtains and an
exotic brocade called Château Sur Mer. The background of the brocade was pale cream, the print a lav-
ish pattern of full-blossomed roses, curling green
leaves, and delicate orchids. The colors of the parlor
were much brighter—royal blue, deep red and emerald
green, a rich background for the gleaming walnut furniture.

The bedroom had taken the most time to finish. Lucy had decided on a color scheme of ivory,
dusky blue, and soft peach. The old-fashioned, high-
poster bedstead was hung with fluttering draperies that
matched the window hangings. She bought a selection
of embroidery silks and several needlework patterns
for cushions, laprugs and lambrequins. It would take
time, but eventually she would fill the bedroom with
handmade ornaments to make it even more inviting.
The figurine that had once belonged to her mother occupied a place of honor on the mantel. As she walked
through the house, Lucy felt immense satisfaction with
every detail. It felt like home to her already; she felt
the promise of the future here, amidst the gracious
rooms and quiet sense of welcome they exuded.

After settling into his office at the *Examiner,*
Heath found out quickly that the path he had chosen
to tread was trickier and even more twisted than he
had anticipated. Most Bostonians regarded new ideas
and new approaches with suspicion, which meant that
Heath had to be sensitive to the fine line between in-
novation and going a step too far. What he considered

to be liberal, others thought of as radical, a fact he became well aware of. He learned to rely on Damon's judgment.

Damon, with his innate understanding of the New Englanders' temperament, was willing to be creative, but he also knew just how much was *too* much. Damon knew the lay of the land, and his editorials were unfailingly brilliant; relevant, straightforward, and sensible. He was a proficient editor on a technical level, almost faultless. Unfortunately, he was not popular with the employees of the paper. It took a certain talent to inspire excellence in others, a talent that Damon didn't have. He was too reserved, too impatient with others' slowness, too unbending. Heath had been brought up to think of that as typical New England haughtiness, but whatever it was called, it did not exactly endear Damon to others.

Heath, on the other hand, had been raised in a society where charm was as necessary as breathing, eating, and sleeping, and he knew exactly how to smooth over ruffled feathers and soothe bruised egos. It was up to him to use all the wiles of a con-artist to get the kind of work he wanted out of the employees of the *Examiner*. He spent countless hours talking to his most promising reporters, discussing their writing and their ideas, leading them from one point to the next until they made the conclusions that he wanted them to make. Knowing the value of praise, he took care to be fair but sparing with his approval.

Strong, accurate reporting was what would make the *Examiner* successful, and once a strong foundation was established, they would build on that. Heath intended to add a Sunday edition to the *Examiner* and restructure the paper so that the advertising would be on the inside pages and not the front page. And maybe bigger headlines, not just the width of one or two columns, but twice that size—maybe even three times that size. He would make it showier than the *Herald* and the *Journal,* so that when the three papers were side by side, the *Examiner* would be the first one to catch the eye. It would take months before the real results of his efforts would show, but at least the circulation held. It even edged upwards every now and then, and under Heath's influence, they were all slowly but surely learning how to work with each other. Even Damon, who had started out as mettlesome and independent as a thoroughbred stallion, was beginning to mellow.

"Come in," Heath said, recognizing Damon's businesslike rap on his office door. Heath occupied the only private room on the whole floor, while Damon worked in the room that the rest of the editorial staff used. There, the walls were papered with maps, the corners were filled with bookshelves, and everyone sat at small green desks. Although working so near the others served the purpose of making Damon seem marginally more approachable, it also allowed him to keep an eye on everything that went on. Having a fondness for stretching his legs every half hour, Damon would saunter through the counting room, the editorial room, and the composing room, his alert black eyes taking notice of countless details of work in progress. "Anything new to report?" Heath asked, without looking up from the story in front of him.

"Still more backlash about the ratification of the Fourteenth Amendment. Something's coming in on the wire about an earthquake in San Francisco . . . supposedly a big one. And the water pail in the corner of the editorial room has a new dent."

"You know, Damon, I'd feel a sight better

about your sense of perspective if you didn't mention the water pail in the same breath as the earthquake.''

One of Damon's rare smiles appeared. ''I know which one is going to have more immediate consequences for me.''

''It's beyond me where you got so much compassion.''

''It's possible my temper would improve if I didn't have to stay up until three so many mornings, getting the paper to press.''

''When you have a wife to get home to, I'll start feeling guilty about that.''

''Then I'll let you know as soon as I find a woman worth marrying.''

''I'm sure one's waiting for you somewhere,'' Heath replied dryly. ''But you'd find her a lot quicker if you stopped looking at a woman's genealogy before giving a thought to the rest of her attributes.''

''I've been brought up to have a healthy respect for bloodlines. Bad blood will always tell, you know.''

''No offense intended . . . but it doesn't matter who her great-grandfather was. It's not *him* you'll be climbing into bed with every night.''

''I suppose not,'' Damon replied without conviction.

Abruptly Heath changed the subject. ''What was it you came here to talk about?''

''Transportation. There's only one hack parked outside that the reporters can use for special assignments. Most of the time Ransom uses it to cover the police department, which means that whenever the others need it, it's not there. We keep on telling them to go out and discover the news, to be there as it's happening instead of waiting to hear it secondhand, but if a story's not within walking distance, we can't begin to—''

"I understand. We'll get another hack.''

"One other thing," Damon said blandly. "I've been approached by several parties—who prefer to remain nameless—to talk to you about something that everyone on Newspaper Row has. Everyone but the *Examiner.*''

"What in the hell would that be?"

"A doorman.''

"A *doorman?*" Heath repeated incredulously.

"To take cards from visitors.''

"Hell's afire!''

"It's a matter of prestige—''

"You tell them," Heath said with ominous softness, "that we'll get a doorman when they start producing a paper that will have more than one good use in an outhouse.''

Lucy had her own struggles to deal with. She stood in the front hallway as furniture was being carried in and rolls of wallpaper being unfurled, and she turned circles as she became the target for a bombardment of questions.

"Mrs. Rayne, where should we put this table?''

"Mrs. Rayne, was this paper supposed to go in the first room on the second floor, or the second room on the first floor?''

"Mrs. Rayne, pardon me, but did you want the sofa against the wall or in the center of the room?''

"Mrs. Rayne. . . did you want me to paint the trimmings in the dining room blue or cream?''

"Stop!" Lucy cried suddenly, holding up her hands as if to ward them all off. Taking a deep breath, she looked from face to face and spoke rapidly. "That table should go between the two velvet chairs in the parlor. The wallpaper—first room, second floor. Sofa against the wall. The trimmings should be cream."

As the little crowd dispersed, two more deliverymen came through the hallway, bearing more packages.

"Mrs. Rayne . . ."

"Mrs. Rayne . . ."

If anyone said her name one more time today, she would scream!

"Mr. Rayne, you wanted to see me?"

"I did," Heath said, setting his pen down and folding his forearms as he rested them on his desktop. "Have a seat, Bartlett."

"Yes, sir."

"Do you recall the discussion we had the other day about doing personal interviews?"

"Yes, sir."

"Because it's a relatively new field in this business, no one can do them really well—except the Chicago *Sun*—and maybe the New York *Tribune*. But interviews are going to become very important for the *Examiner*, Bartlett. People like to read about other people."

"I remember you telling me—"

"And when you apply yourself, your work is quite . . . satisfactory. Which is why I gave you that assignment to interview Mayor Shurtleff."

The younger man shifted uneasily in his seat as Heath's blue eyes pinned him with a fierce stare. As Heath continued to develop his own executive style, the combination of that stare and that soft, drawling voice was increasingly able to reduce the most audacious reporter to a pile of wood pulp.

"Sir, I can explain about that—"

"What you might not have remembered, Bartlett, is something else I told you."

"What is that?"

"People don't like to read old news." Heath paused and then slammed his palm down on the table for effect, causing Bartlett to jump in his seat. Heath was not above using theatrics to get his point across. "Dammit, *everyone* knows Shurtleff went to Harvard. Everyone knows he's caused a few streets to be built here and there. Everyone knows he belongs to practically every historical society in the state. What is the goddamn *point* of writing about all of that? After reading this interview you handed in, it is damned obvious that you didn't ask him whey he spends more time worrying about history than he does worrying about organizing a decent fire department! Why doesn't he do something about the public parks? What does he think about the Morrill Tariff Act and what it's done to the poor? What does he think about the Bostonians' attitude towards Reconstruction legislation? You didn't ask him any of those questions!"

"But sir . . . there were other men present in the room."

"What," Heath asked with ominous patience, "does that have to do with anything?"

"A gentleman would not think of embarrassing another in front of his peers."

"Bartlett," Heath groaned. "Good Lord! It's your job to do that. Don't you understand? . . . no, you don't." He sighed, thought for several seconds, and then looked back at the sheepish reporter. "Alright. *This* is something you'll understand. Go back to Shurtleff—tell him there were one or two things you wanted to clarify—"

"But—"

"If you have to, remind him outright that he

doesn't want bad publicity. And when you talk to him, ask him about the fire department, or the Tariff Act, or something equally controversial. If you can come back to me with an answer to one embarrassing question—*just one*—I'll raise your salary by ten percent. That clear enough?''

"Yes, sir!''

"Now, go. And for ten percent, it better be a hell of a question you ask.''

Now that the house was nearly finished and a complete staff had been hired, including a coachman, a cook, two maids, and a butler, Lucy had hours of free time on her hands. From a woman she had met during one of her shopping expeditions, she accepted an invitation to attend a Friday lecture and luncheon sponsored by the New England Women's Club. Enjoying herself immensely, she made many acquaintances and tentatively began to attend other social engagements and salon discussions. Oh, how different it was from the club meetings she had gone to in Concord! Fashion, small-town scandals and love affairs were never mentioned in the salons in Boston. Here, the women talked about literature and politics, they listened to lectures from celebrated social figures and educators, and they argued—politely, of course—over rights and wrongs, and changes that would occur in the future. Lucy would listen raptly, entranced by the debate between two Harvard professors or the monologue by a foreign statesman, which would go on for several minutes while all of them ate slices of sponge cake and sipped tea out of cups as fragile as sea shells.

Thirstily Lucy drank in ideas and information, finding to her delight that she sometimes managed to surprise Heath with her understanding of the current issues that his and other papers were grappling with.

Occasionally Heath would invite Damon to dine with them, usually after they had worked until late evening. After the first time that Heath had appeared with the unexpected dinner guest, Lucy had privately objected, telling Heath that she hadn't appreciated the lack of advance warning, and besides that, she wasn't especially fond of Damon Redmond's company. Heath had countered with the explanation that Damon had no wife to take care of him, and that since he had missed the regular meal with the Redmond clan, he would have either had to dine out alone or skip dinner. That had made Lucy feel a little sorry for Damon, and a little guilty that she hadn't wanted him there, and she always made a special effort to be hospitable to him after that.

The occasional dinners with Damon were much more pleasant than the first one at the Parker House had been. Since he had become accustomed to Lucy's uninhibited manner with her husband and her lively interest in the newspaper, Damon had learned to join in her discussions with Heath. Relating scraps of news that would amuse her, Damon made her laugh with his sly humor. He became much more relaxed around her, less cautious, freer with his smile. And then, there were times when she was telling Heath about what had been said that day at a lecture she had gone to, or what events were taking place in connection with one of her clubs, and she would glance over at Damon to find that his coal black eyes were fixed on her with disturbing attentiveness. Lucy was puzzled by him. Despite his impressive heritage and his distinguished name, he seemed to have no home, no family; he was a loner, just as Heath had been before their marriage. And because she sensed that in him, Lucy unconsciously offered him a timid sympathy that went far in softening his heart towards her.

It was due to Damon's influence—though he made light of it and would not accept Lucy's thanks—that she and Heath had been invited to one of the supper dances given to celebrate the election of a new street commissioner for the city. Officially it took a year to "arrive" in Boston, which meant that ordinarily such an exclusive invitation would not have been offered to newcomers. Damon appeared for dinner one night with two of the universally sought-after invitations tucked inside his coat, giving them to Lucy as they sat down to the table.

"Oh, Mr. Redmond!" she exclaimed, beaming at him and then staring down at the invitations in wonder. "How kind of you . . . how sweet and thoughtful, and . . . well, I didn't even know these were transferable! How did you manage to—"

"I did it for selfish reasons," Damon admitted with a shrug, matter-of-fact as always. "I've had enough experience with these kinds of evenings to know when one promises to be especially dull. I plan to rely on the two of you to alleviate my boredom."

Lucy looked at Heath with a wry smile and handed him the invitations. "Should we accept a gift when he's admitted to giving it with ulterior motives in mind?" she asked, and Heath's eyes twinkled as he replied.

"Don't know about you, honey, but I've never been one to look a gift horse in the mouth."

In order to have enough time to dress and arrange her hair for the supper dance, Lucy had not gone to the weekly lecture she usually attended on Fridays. With the help of one of the maids, she washed her hair and rinsed it with lemon juice and water. It took many pins and more than a few frustrated exclamations in order to arrange the fine silken strands of it in the current fashion, pinning it off the forehead into rolls and letting it fall down the back of her neck in long curls. Her dress was an elaborate creation of black brocaded satin embroidered with gold and silver leaves. The train-shaped skirt was trimmed with a fifteen-inch deep flounce that rustled softly as it swept over the floor, while the low, round bodice revealed the pale, perfect curves of her bosom and the tops of her shoulders. Her waist, made especially tiny with vigorous lacing, was accentuated with a wide embroidered sash, while the material of the skirt was pulled tightly to reveal the gentle flare of her hips. As Lucy looked at herself in the mirror, she smoothed the dark arches of her eyebrows with the moistened tip of her forefinger and bit her lips to make them red.

"Don't. I'll take care of that," came Heath's voice from the doorway, and she turned her head to smile at him. He was breathtaking in a formal scheme of black and white, which emphasized the blue-green of his eyes and the dark antique gold of his hair.

"You'll take care of what?" she asked.

For answer, he walked over to her, covered her bare shoulders with his hands and lowered his mouth to hers, kissing her so firmly that her lips were forced apart. The tip of his tongue feathered across the roof of her mouth, finding the most sensitive spot and lingering there until Lucy struggled away from him with a shaky laugh and a gasp.

"Heath! If I'd w-wanted your help, I would have asked for it." Hastily she turned back to the mirror, silently berating herself for letting him ruffle her so easily. Her cheeks were flaming, and her lips were now soft and rosy.

"I thought you wanted a little color in your face."

"I did! But I didn't want to look like I'd just tumbled out of bed with you."

He chuckled and walked up behind her, settling his hands on either side of her waist. "If I had
the time—"

"Yes, I know," Lucy said, swatting at his
hands in feigned annoyance and reaching for the powder puff on the dressing table. "Now leave me alone
for five more minutes so I can finish getting ready."

With mock obedience Heath sat on the ridiculously small gilded chair nearby and lounged there
indolently, watching every move she made. "Don't
you have something to do?" Lucy demanded, pausing
in the midst of brushing one of her curls. "You're just
sitting there like a lazy tomcat." As he kept silent,
she dusted her nose lightly with powder and cast a
sidelong glance at him. "You look very handsome,"
she said, her voice softer than before. He smiled
slightly, standing up and wandering to the window as
if he were uncomfortable with her scrutiny.

So sleek and polished and perfect, Lucy
thought, giving him one last look before returning her
gaze to the mirror. But just when she thought he was
too handsome to be real, the scar on his temple reminded her that although he had the looks of an angel,
he was far from perfect. That scar served as a visible
reminder to her that he had been hurt in ways it was
not possible to see. Some time in his past he had developed an impenetrable defense to protect himself,
and he had not relinquished it, even though it was no
longer necessary. Occasionally she felt that he kept
himself separate from her even in their most intimate
moments. If only he would trust her enough to let
himself be vulnerable to her. If only he were capable
of showing her that he wanted her for something more
than amusement or physical pleasure.

Perhaps some would think they had a perfect
marriage. Lucy knew that many people would proba-

bly envy them for what they had, a close friendship enhanced by passion. There was freedom in their relationship, a willingness to let each other grow, and a certain amount of honesty. Maybe it was wrong of her to want more than that. Oh, why was she bothered by a growing feeling of discontentment that showed no signs of abating?

Because she cared about him, to the point that she was frightened to admit just how much, even to herself.

After putting on long onyx earrings that dangled halfway down to her shoulders and swung jauntily against her neck, Lucy gave a short sigh. "I'm ready to leave now."

"Cinda." Heath's eyes were dark and serious as he looked at her. He walked over to her slowly, and her pulse quickened as she heard the hesitance in his tone. "Before we go, there's something I want to take care of. I thought about it a few weeks ago, and . . . it's something I should have done right after we were married."

"I can't imagine what you're talking about," she said with a wavering smile.

"I guess I'm trying to apologize for overlooking . . ." Heath's voice faded away as their eyes met.

"What?" she whispered.

Stillness. Seconds linked together in the silence, one following another rapidly.

His thumb moved over the blunt softness of her jawline; the backs of his knuckles skimmed over her throat. What was he trying to tell her with that gentle caress? He reached down and took her hand, which was light and unresisting in his. His eyes were still locked with hers as he kissed her palm, and his smooth-shaven skin caused her fingers to tingle.

Don't be tender with me . . . , she wanted to cry out. *I have no defense against your tenderness.*

Something cool and smooth slipped over her finger, catching gently at the knuckle, sliding completely to the base. Lucy looked at her hand, still clasped in his, and saw the flash of a large, brilliant diamond, pear-shaped and glittering with a thousand sparkles. An engagement ring. A symbol of what they had never pretended to feel for each other.

"You . . . ," she tried to say, and her voice was nothing but a breath of sound. "You didn't need to—"

"I should have given it to you long ago—"

"But I didn't even think about—"

"I know. It was a short engagement, and there was no time—"

"Heath . . . I don't know what to—"

"Do you like it?"

"Yes. Yes, of course—"

"If you'd prefer something different, we could—"

"No. It's beautiful. It's . . ." Her eyes glittered more brightly than the diamond. She didn't ask why he had thought of it, or why he had given it to her now, in case the reason he gave her was not the one she wanted it to be. "Th-thank you." A tear fell down her cheek, and he stopped it halfway down with his lips.

"I didn't mean to make you cry," he murmured.

"What did you think I was going to do?" she demanded, choking on a laugh and fumbling in his coat pocket for a handkerchief. But before she could dry her eyes, their mouths were clinging together in a kiss of bewildering desperation. Her tearful confusion vanished in an instant, disintegrated by the insistent fire of his kiss. Desire, rich and burning, spread upwards from the depths of her body. Heath bent his head more deeply over hers and pulled her against the hard strength of his chest. Something warm and tender blossomed inside her, unfurling layer after layer, leaving her open and painfully vulnerable.

When he lifted his mouth from hers and drew his head back an inch or two, she saw that a tawny lock of hair had fallen onto his forehead, and she reached up to smooth it back with trembling fingers. "Heath," she whispered, made dizzy by the blueness of his eyes.

She couldn't finish. Staring at him mutely, she read the question in his eyes. Ahh, for once he didn't understand her silence. She was thankful for that.

"We'd better get going," he said quietly, and she nodded slowly.

The evening was not at all the boring affair that Damon had predicted it would be. Among the guests were the most prominent businessmen, merchants, bankers, and politicians in the city. The supper conversation was constrained by the presence of the women; the real discussions of politics and current events would take place later among the men. Still, the company was fascinating. Lucy talked alternately to the woman on her left and the gentleman on her right. Heath was seated further down the table, while Damon and a blond woman with a singular air of sophistication carried on a conversation almost directly across from her. Yes, Damon appeared to be his usual reserved self. Determined to rouse him out of his habitual aloofness, Lucy made a few sly remarks to him until he responded with the kind of friendly bickering that she had been hoping for. When the dancing began later, Damon claimed the second waltz with her, informing Heath that he was demanding reparation for Lucy's teasing during dinner.

"What an accomplished dancer you are," Lucy said during the waltz, grinning impishly at him. No one could quite match Heath for smoothness, but Damon's steps were almost as flawless. "Is it a common Redmond forte?"

Damon's polite facade dissolved into a smile as he succumbed to the charm of her merry hazel eyes. Lucy wished he would smile more often; whenever he did, it transformed him from a merely attractive man into a breathtakingly handsome one. "We've all learned from the same instructor. The last three generations of Redmonds have been forced as children to take lessons from Signor Papanti, an Italian count who established a dance academy on Tremont Street—"

"I've heard of him."

"I'm not surprised. He has quite a reputation."

"I've heard that he is very, very strict—"

"He is. I remember that whenever we entered the ballroom, we would have to give him a waist-deep bow, while he stood over us with a fiddle bow raised in the air, like this . . . and if he wasn't satisfied, he'd rap us across the shoulders."

Lucy couldn't help laughing at his rueful expression. "Poor Mr. Redmond. Did you get rapped often?"

"Every time."

"You should have gone to your father and told him—"

"My father was a disciplinarian," Damon said lightly, and grinned. "He would have rapped me for complaining."

Suddenly filled with sympathy, Lucy did not answer his smile, and some unfathomable emotion flickered in Damon's dark eyes. The tempo of the waltz increased, and the gloved tips of his fingers exerted more pressure on her back to accommodate the faster turns.

"Who is that woman you were talking with at the table?" Lucy asked.

"Alicia Redmond."

"Redmond?"

"A distant cousin. Since I'm the only unmarried son left, the family has indicated to me that a match between us wouldn't be a bad proposition. What do you think of the idea?"

"Terrible," she said instantly, her decisiveness causing him to smile.

"Why?"

"I don't think I should tell you. I'm not certain you take well to personal comments."

"On the contrary, I do. It's just that they're so seldom made to me, I never have the opportunity to prove how well I receive them."

"Well, then . . ." Lucy lowered her voice a few degrees. "I think you need a different type of woman than that. She doesn't seem to be a very engaging person. Wouldn't you prefer someone who's more cheerful? She doesn't seem to make you smile."

"No, she doesn't," Damon replied thoughtfully. "But I've never been brought up to think that cheerfulness is a necessary quality in a wife. And it's not really important for me to smile in order to fulfill my duties as—"

"Oh, but that's not true!" Lucy said earnestly. "I insist that you marry someone who . . . who is natural and cheerful, and makes you laugh, and isn't af . . ."

Damon grinned. "What were you going to say? Someone who isn't afraid of me?"

She blushed. "I didn't mean—"

"But whoever would be afraid of me?" he asked, gently mocking.

"You do have a way of . . . looking at people."

"A way that makes them afraid?"

"Not exactly *afraid* . . . ," Lucy said, and stopped as she saw that the laughter had left his eyes.

"Tell me," he said. Suddenly it seemed as if he were asking her for help, for a secret that only she could tell him. Spellbound by the dark entreaty in his voice, she stared at him silently. "Please," he added, very slowly, as if he were unaccustomed to using the word.

"The way you look at people—," she murmured, "it makes them aware of their faults. It makes them think that . . . in order to impress you, they should be something other than themselves. But I don't think you intend for them to feel that way."

"No." The light played over his raven hair as he shook his head.

"That is why you should wait for someone who isn't afraid of you. It might be the only kind of woman that . . . that you'll ever come to know completely. As a husband should know his wife."

How strangely intimate and personal the conversation had become. Lucy felt her cheeks turning red, and she wondered if she had let her mouth run away from her.

"Thank you," Damon said quietly. "I appreciate your honesty."

The rest of the dance passed in silence, and it was only near the end that Lucy looked up and met his eyes again. "Mr. Redmond . . . I have one more personal remark to make."

"Fire away."

"I would prefer it if you called me Lucy when we are among friends. I know Heath wouldn't mind."

For just a second she saw a look in his eyes, a stricken look, yearning—no, was it . . . loneliness? Quickly it was concealed. "You are very kind to extend your friendship to me," he said softly. "And I will accept it, if I may—with the hope that you will accept mine in return. But I would prefer not to use your given name."

"As you wish," Lucy said with a smile, unaware of how difficult it was to attain Damon Redmond's friendship, and of how many had failed in their attempts to win it—unaware that once he had given such a pledge, he would honor it for a lifetime. For men like him, friendship was a more lasting bond than love. Lucy had no idea of how much she would need Damon's friendship in the future.

Damon stayed conspicuously far away from her for the rest of the evening, but Lucy hardly noticed, for as soon as Heath regained possession of her, he demanded all of her attention. He swept her around the ballroom with such velvet smoothness that she was barely conscious of her toes touching the floor. When she danced with Heath, the music and the movement somehow turned into magic, and everything seemed to glitter. Their hands were separated by gloves, and yet she knew the warm clasp of his skin by heart. His eyes, the warm blue-green of a tropical sea, caressed her slowly, while his white teeth flashed often in a dazzling smile. Lost in giddy enchantment, Lucy did her best to tease him unmercifully, glancing at him through coyly lowered eyelashes and letting the full softness of her breasts brush against his chest on the pretext of leaning closer to whisper to him.

To all the eyes that observed the handsome couple, their conversation was circumspect, but had it been heard, it would have caused more than one pair of ears to burn. Lucy crooned to Heath in a faked Southern drawl, making wicked observations, whispering bits of nonsense and entertaining him with veiled hints about the black silk pantalets she assured him she was wearing.

"You don't even own black silk pantalets," Heath said, his eyes dancing with amusement at her antics.

"I most certainly do. I had them made for me. You said you didn't like plain old white. And I have on a matching corset—"

"I'll be damned. I almost believe you."

"You'll believe me later," she purred, and he laughed outright.

"What's gotten into you tonight?"

"Nothing. It's just that I've finally decided something."

"Oh? What have you decided?"

"Something private. I can't tell you."

"Ah. Then your decision must involve me, or you wouldn't keep it a secret."

"In every way," she said, and smiled at him in a way that made his breath catch.

Chapter Nine

HUMMING A CHRISTMAS carol, Lucy struggled with an armload of holly and balanced some of it on top of the banister. "Bess," she said to the maid who hovered near the top of the stairs, "if you can just fasten it at the top with one of those big red bows . . . yes, and we'll do it like that all the way down . . ."

"Don't fall backwards," Bess cautioned, too concerned about Lucy's precarious balance on the edge of the steps to pay close attention to the decorations.

"Of course I won't," Lucy said encouragingly. "Oh, that bow looks just right."

"You're walking backwards."

"I won't fall. I've got my hand on the railing."

"Mrs. Rayne, why don't *I* drape the holly and *you* can tie the bows?"

"Bess, there's no need to worry."

Their conversation was interrupted by the slam of the front door, and they both looked down the stairs. Heath shook the snow off his knee-length overcoat and sailed his brown woolen hat into the corner with a vicious flick of his wrist. As he looked up and saw his audience poised on the staircase, he gave a curt nod that barely passed for a greeting.

"Well," Lucy said, "it looks as if your Christmas spirit has undergone a beating."

Heath said something under his breath and went up the stairs, passing her without another word. He paused as he neared Bess, who shrank away from him and regarded him with round gray eyes. "I want a bottle of Old Forester and a glass," he snapped. "Now."

The maid's mouth quivered, and she fled downstairs.

"Heath, what is the *matter?*" Lucy demanded, upset and annoyed by his brusque manner. "Whatever's wrong, there's no need to ignore me and frighten the . . . Heath, where are you going?" She followed him to the bedroom, unable to imagine what had happened to put him in such a mood. "Did you have trouble at the paper today?"

He gave a dry, humorless laugh. "You could say that."

"You're home early—"

"I don't want to talk, and I don't want to answer questions. Where the hell is that maid? Dammit, did you manage to hire anyone who doesn't drag his or her feet?"

"Did you have an argument with Damon?" Lucy asked patiently, knowing that he did want to talk, or he wouldn't have put on such a performance when he came in. Heath's door slamming was always an announcement that a conversation was in order.

"Damon," Heath said in tones of purest disgust, "Goddamn right I had an argument with him."

"You don't have to use that language," she reproved.

"I thought he understood what I was trying to do. But today I realized he's not the man I thought he was. After months of working on the same side, for the same purpose, he stood in that office, talking like a stranger—get the door, she's here with the whiskey.''

"Would you mind talking to me about this first?'' Her only answer was a steady blue-green glare. Lucy sighed and went to the door. "Thank you, Bess.''

"Mrs. Rayne . . . ,'' the maid whispered, regarding Heath's tall lithe form as he paced back and forth like an agitated panther, "are you going to be alright? Should I—''

"Everything's just fine,'' Lucy said, pasting on a reassuring smile, taking the small silver tray from the other woman. "Why don't you finish the decorations while Mr. Rayne and I have our discussion?'' As Bess nodded apprehensively, Lucy closed the door with her foot and set the tray down on her dressing table. "She's only been working here a week, Heath. She's not used to your temper, and it frightens her, so if you'd try to control—''

"She'd better learn to get used to it, or she can go to work for someone else.'' Heath poured himself a drink and interrupted his sneer long enough to take a healthy swallow.

"What has Damon done to make you so angry?''

"Damon doesn't give a damn one way or another about the issues we're struggling with. It's all a mental exercise with him. He looks at something, picks out the points for and against it, and he goes with the side that has the highest score. Right and wrong—just a mathematical equation to him. I'll be damned if I can work with that!''

"I'm sure that's not true. I'm sure he has integrity and honor—''

"Like hell he does!'' Heath finished the whiskey and poured another with a careless tilt of the bottle. Lucy had never seen him drink so much in such a short amount of time.

"What did you argue about?"

Suddenly all the fight and anger in him seemed to ebb, and he shook his head, taking another swallow of the biting liquor. His fingers were wrapped tightly around the glass. Lucy remained silent, sitting down on the edge of the bed and watching him as he drank the rest of the second glass of whiskey. He was in pain. She was helpless to do anything for him until he let down some of the walls. *Ask me to hold you . . . here are my arms, ready to wrap around you. Here is my heart . . . just ask.*

Heath stood by the window, silent in his self-imposed isolation. He took a deep breath and shook his head again, lifting his shoulders in a helpless shrug. "Today . . . ," he started, and the rest of his words just dried up, unwilling to be voiced. He strode over to the whiskey bottle, but Lucy made it there before him and laid her fingers across his outstretched hand.

"Don't have any more," she said, looking up at him. He saw something in her eyes that made him release his hold on the bottle. Slowly he withdrew his hand and went back to the window, but not before she had seen the flash of misery in his expression. She was shaken by the urgency of her need to comfort him. "What happened today?"

"Bad news."

"Reconstruction?" She couldn't think of anything else that could have affected him so strongly.

"What else?"

"Heath, don't make me guess. Tell me."

"We had finally made some progress. Until today, the federal government was loosening its control over the South. They decided to start with Georgia . . ."

"Yes," she hurried in to fill the silence, "I know a little about it. Georgia and a few other states were readmitted to Congress."

"And the military rule was lifted. At last. And I thought the rest of the South would be allowed to follow. And then the war would really be over. No more soldiers in the streets. No more arbitrary rules and military commissions . . . no more scalawags. We would be given back our land. We would get our rights back as citizens . . . rights we're *entitled* to." Heath sighed and leaned his forehead against the window frame.

"But now that Georgia is free of federal control, all of that will happen."

"No," he replied tersely. "Today Georgia dismissed all the blacks from the state legislature. The government took it as an open act of rebellion."

"Oh, Heath . . . oh, no." She stared at him in disbelief. "They'll come down so hard on the state—"

"They already have. Georgia's been thrown out of Congress, and it won't be readmitted until it ratifies the Fifteenth Amendment. And it's been put under military control again. Do you know how far back that puts the whole South?"

"I know that the Georgia State Legislature must have had some idea of what would happen if they dismissed all those people."

"Cin, they've had all these changes rammed down their throats too fast to swallow! They need to be eased into it . . . they . . . they're trying to hold onto their pride. For years they've had no voice, no control over what's happened to them. I'm not excusing what they did, but they need to have some kind of say about the decisions that affect them. Georgia is just as much a part of this country as Massachusetts

or New York, and Georgians deserve the same rights.
And they'll never get them. Every time the federal
troops withdraw, something like this is going to happen, and they'll be put back under the national government's thumb. It'll never be over.''

"Heath—"

"I left because I couldn't stand to see it," he
continued, ignoring her attempt to break in. "The
frustration . . . I could feel it wherever I went. It was
in the air we breathed; there was no way to get away
from it. We were beaten . . . but there were a few
hopes . . . maybe it would be alright. Maybe we could
get on with rebuilding our lives . . . maybe all that
your damned Mr. Lincoln said about lending a helping
hand to the South was going to be true—"

"If he had lived—"

"But he didn't, and we got Johnson, an in-
competent fool, and Grant, who doesn't give a damn
about anything so long as no one bothers him about
his stock manipulations. The minute the war was over,
thousands of Northerners came down to the South to
loot and scavenge, and they've done it for years, over
and over again. We're the only Americans who've ever
lost a war and been occupied by the enemy. There's
only so long you can hold still for that before you start
to fight back in the only way you know how. And it
doesn't matter if it's a good way or not, just as long
as you're doing *something*—"

"I know," Lucy said quietly. "I know that
you want to speak in defense of your people, and that
you want to help each side understand the other. But
you can't expect Damon to be a voice for the South."

"I didn't ask that of him. I only wanted a
moderate editorial. Nothing radical—"

"And he refused to write it?"

"Oh, he wrote it alright. He couldn't be more

in agreement with the federal government, and he damn well said so.''

"Did you try to reason with him?"

"It would be less painful to butt my head against a brick wall. He wasn't about to budge."

"And you exploded," Lucy said ruefully.

Heath went over to the whiskey and poured himself another drink, his sideways glance silently daring her to offer a word of protest. Wisely Lucy kept silent. "I told him I'd write the editorial myself. He said he'd leave the paper if I did."

"Heath.'' Lucy felt sick at the thought of all his plans, all his hopes, disappearing so quickly.

"I can't run this editorial the way it is now, Cin," he said thickly, tossing down the third drink. "I'd be betraying everything I believe in. And I can't ignore the whole thing. That's what the paper is for, to take on issues like this. *That's what I wanted the paper for.''*

She folded her hands in her lap and looked down at them, her mind and heart in turmoil. What could she do? What could she say to him?

A sharp, explosive sound startled her as Heath threw his glass into the fireplace. It shattered into hundreds of glittering shards, causing a whirl of sparks to fly up from the crumbling log. Flinching, half-frightened by his anger, she returned her gaze to her lap.

"Tell me how to help you," she said in a low voice. "I don't know how." She was aware of him walking towards her, she felt the coolness of his shadow cast over her, saw the dark shine of his boots as he stood in front of her.

"I don't know either," he said huskily, his accent intensified by the liquor. "All I know is that I'm sick of all of it. I'm tired of fighting to gain an inch of headway, when nothing's going to stop the tide.

I'm tired of making decisions. I left the South . . . because I was tired of being defeated . . . oh, God, Cinda, there are things . . . I haven't told you . . .'' With a sigh he dropped to his knees and buried his head in her lap, his hands tangling in the scented silk of her skirts. Lucy froze. She heard a quiet, broken sound, and she looked down at his golden head with panic and astonishment. Careless, taunting, hot-tempered Heath Rayne, with his head in her lap and his fingers clutched in the folds of her dress.

Suddenly she didn't have to worry anymore about what to say to him, because the words were tumbling out of her mouth too fast to keep them in. She bent over him, stroking his hair, murmuring to him softly, urgently. ''Of course you're tired . . . you've been working so hard . . . of course you are. I know you haven't told me everything . . . it doesn't matter.''

''I left because it won't stop . . . until their spirit is broken . . . I couldn't stay to watch it.''

''No . . . no, of course not,'' she soothed, making no effort to argue or reason with him. Later would be the time for reasoning and making sense out of it all. Now he was tired and defeated, and he just wanted a few hours in which he didn't have to think about anything. She remembered how that felt, how it had been that night after she had run to him after Daniel had rejected her. Heath had been there to help her, letting her draw from his strength. Did she have enough strength to sustain him in the same way?

''I couldn't help . . .''

''Shhhh . . . everything will be fine.''

''You don't understand what it was like—''

''Yes, I do. I understand,'' she said, resting her cool fingers on the back of his neck.

''No . . . I went back, I *saw* . . . they were all there . . . Raine . . . Raine was there too. Clay had been wounded—his back just . . . gave out. They needed me. I could have helped. I would have taken care of all of them . . . I wouldn't have touched her. I wouldn't have.''

''Heath?'' Lucy asked, her breath disturbing his tawny hair as she bent over him. ''Who is Raine? Who are you talking about?''

He only shook his head, catching at her small hand and pressing the back of it against his scarred temple.

Frowning sharply, Lucy wondered what had gone on between him and Raine, whoever she was. Love? Hate? She struggled to accept the fact that in the past he might have loved another woman deeply, given her all that he had not given Lucy. Maybe it had been Raine. Lucy had not known until now how deeply jealousy could be felt.

''She wouldn't admit . . . she needed me . . .'' He wiped his sleeve across his eyes in a gesture that caught at her heart, and then he dropped his head back into the comfortable hollow of her lap. She was silent as she listened to him, torn between hoping that he would go on and not wanting to hear any more. ''She never did. Never.''

Lucy rubbed her knuckles across his temple in a hesitant caress.

''I wanted you,'' he said, his voice soft and singed, ''the first time I saw you. Did I tell you that?''

''No, you didn't.''

''It was raining. You were crossing the street. You took longer than everyone else, because . . . because you were picking your way around all the little . . . puddles. I wanted you.''

''Heath—''

''After I found you at the river, you kept call-

ing me Daniel . . . but it was me. It was me holding
you—''

"I knew it was."

"But you kept . . ." He sighed and then fell
silent, his head and arms becoming heavier in her lap
as he relaxed. Lucy knew that if he passed out, she
would never be able to get him up onto the bed. The
thought of having to call someone else to help her
galvanized her into action.

"Heath, sit up here and let me help you off
with your boots."

"No . . . you don't have to—''

"Yes I do, because you'll never get them off
by yourself."

Mumbling a curse, Heath relinquished the
warm softness of her lap and pulled himself up onto
the bed, holding one foot out for her to take hold of.
She grasped the boot firmly and tried to work it off,
finding that Heath's effort to help by wiggling his toes
hindered her progress considerably. After struggling
for a few minutes, one boot came off, and then the
other.

"You probably haven't eaten anything all
day," she fretted, watching as Heath allowed himself
to sprawl on the mattress with outflung arms.

"No."

"So this is what happens when you fill an
empty stomach with a pint of corn whiskey." She
crawled up beside him and undid his necktie. "I've
never seen anyone drink that like it was water. I *told*
you not to have any more." As she scolded him gently, she went through the laborious process of undressing him. "Here, pull your arm out of that sleeve—''

"I can't."

"Heath, if you would just try—''

"I can't. You didn't unbutton it."

"I'm glad you don't drink very often, because I wouldn't like having to do this for you all the time—"

"You're not very good at it," he said, clinging possessively to a lock of her hair as she tugged the hem of his shirt out of his pants.

"Well, I'm hardly going to apologize for my lack of experience at undressing men. My goodness, you're heavy." It was only with determination and a great deal of effort that Lucy finished stripping his clothes off, pausing only briefly to admire the muscled slope of his torso before reaching for a pillow. "Now, if we can just get you under the covers—"

"Cinda," he said unsteadily, "I told you . . . to act like my wife . . . before . . . but I meant only if you . . . you know I didn't mean—"

"I know," she murmured, vaguely startled by his concern. Had he really been worrying about that, wondering if her responses to him were manufactured out of a sense of duty? *You impossible man,* she thought with a sudden rush of warmth, *how can you know me so well in some ways and so little in others?*

Her gaze was caught and trapped by his. His eyes were brilliant with an azure smolder, the heat of a summer sky, and she felt a tender throbbing of response deep inside. He rolled over and pulled her underneath him with surprising ease.

"You need to sleep." She put her hands against his hard, bare chest.

"No."

His mouth crushed hers in a hot, whiskey-flavored kiss, allowing her no chance to speak. She felt the violent pounding of his heart underneath her palm, and the tentative words of refusal she had meant to say vanished like a wisp of smoke. The ragged bonds of restraint snapped. His lips, demanding and plunder-

ing, took hers. His body straddled hers as he cradled
her head in his hands, and he was rough in his desperation. He held her with bruising force, kissing her
as if he were drinking of life itself, like a battered
survivor, clinging to the only truth he knew.

She admitted to herself at last that she loved
him. Love welled through her body, filling her breasts,
seeping through her throat, swirling through her head
until she was dizzy. Love seemed to pour out of her
fingertips as she slid her hands across his shoulders.
Surely he could taste it on her lips, feel it thrilling
inside her body. She was stunned at how much time it
had taken to recognize it. Her entire life had been a
prelude to this moment.

"I need you, Cin," he groaned, and his mouth
dragged over hers again and again, in intense, punishing kisses that robbed her of breath. Her lungs fought
to accommodate a deep gulp of air, but her corset was
as tight as a band of steel. Defenseless in his forceful
grip, she offered her mouth and body freely, in an
effort to show him that she was his. She would not
deny him. But his desire was too savage, too elemental
to pacify. She tried to unfasten the row of tiny buttons
at her midriff, fumbling helplessly, but suddenly his
hands were there, and he ripped the front of her dress
open with a simple, savage tug. For once, her corset
laces came undone easily.

Lucy twisted free of the remnants of her bodice and the binding stays, shivering as her naked
breasts pressed against his hard, tanned flesh. His
hands claimed her greedily, his touch lusty and sure
as he rubbed her nipples into hard, delicate buds. His
uneven breath feathered against her neck, and she
turned her face to his, nuzzling his lean cheek with
her lips, clumsily seeking his mouth. She gave a half-
stifled moan as he kissed her, the sound low and res-

onant against his lips. They had known each other intimately, as husband and wife, countless times. He
had held her with tenderness and passion, but never
with such rampant wildness.

The lower half of her body was swathed heavily in mounds of clothes. Impatiently he ripped and
tugged until she was freed from the burdensome mass,
and her pale skin gleamed in the early evening light.
She stretched the full length of her body along his,
pressing her loins against the burning, turgid swell of
his manhood. "I want you," she whispered against
his shoulder. "I want to give you whatever you need
. . . whatever you want . . ."

His hand glided over her hip to the soft,
pulsing ache between her legs, and he slipped the tip
of his finger inside her, stroking the sleek heat of her.
Lucy whimpered, moving her trembling thighs apart,
burying her face in his throat in unconscious pleading.
She slid her damp palms over the hard-textured surface
of his back, digging the heels of her hands into the
flexing muscles as his fingertip explored the secret hollow of her body. Always before, he had been aware of
the exquisite fragility of her flesh, and there had been
an element of self-restraint in his touch, as if he had
been afraid he would hurt her. Now all constraints
were gone, all deliberation had vanished. He lowered
his hips to her and thrust into her violently, sending
shocks of pleasure through her as their flesh merged.
She groaned and shifted against him, her body expanding to hold him in a firm, hungry grasp. Sub-
merged in a wave of unending sweetness, they tangled
together more intimately, chaining each other with
kisses and seeking caresses. Heath hooked his hands
around the backs of her knees, lifting them and urging
her legs to wrap around his hips. He whispered her
name as if it were a love-word, and his mouth drifted

through the tear tracks on her face. They would not yield their secrets. Oh, but love . . .

Love was unvoiced and undenied. As they fitted together into one being, each movement was a new discovery, each second an eternity of emotion. *Let it last*, her heart beseeched the darkness silently. *Let it last forever.*

A soft voice broke through his cloud of slumber, persisting despite his best efforts to ignore it. "It's seven o'clock, Heath . . . *wake up* . . . I won't let you sleep any longer, so open your eyes. Breakfast will be ready soon."

Oh, God. At the thought of getting up, facing a day of complicated tasks, unappetizing decisions, raised voices, and the nauseating prospect of breakfast, something inside him shrank back in distaste. He felt Lucy's gentle kiss on his cheek, and he rolled onto his stomach, making a grumpy noise. She snatched away the extra pillow before he could pull it over his tousled head, and just what she was saying he couldn't make out, but it sounded sympathetic.

Lucy sat down by his side and traced a line down the length of his spine; she planted a kiss in the center of his back and began to massage his shoulders. "Don't be difficult," she coaxed, plying her hands to his taut muscles with deep, rhythmic movements. "You know how much worse it would be if I didn't wake you up and you were off-schedule the whole day. You have to get to the *Examiner* early this morning. You have mountains to move, and many things to—"

"If you're trying to get me out of bed," Heath growled, the thought of the newspaper wrenching him awake in the space of two seconds, "you'd better use different tactics then telling me how much I've got to do." He sighed as she found the aching muscles right

between his shoulder blades. "Ahh . . . lower . . .
mmmm."

"I've drawn a hot bath for you. You'll feel so
much better after soaking in it for a few minutes. And
I brought up some fresh coffee. It's right on the bed
table for you to—"

"Uggh."

"Why don't you try taking a few sips of it
while you're having your bath? I'll bring it in to you."

He nodded reluctantly, winced at the pain that
shot through his skull, and sat up with a groan. Silently Lucy handed him a silk robe patterned with subdued burgundy and blue stripes. He pulled it on and
stood up, looking down at her as she tied the belt
around his lean waist. When she was done, he pulled
her against his body, buried his face in the curve of
her neck and thought that the greatest gift he could be
given was to be allowed to fall asleep standing up,
with his head resting on her soft shoulder.

"I'm not going anywhere today," he said in a
muffled voice.

"Why not?"

He opened his eyes and squinted at the window. Lucy had pulled back the cream-colored velvet
panels to let the morning light in. "It's too sunny."

She chuckled, letting go of him as he headed
to the bathroom. Having already dressed and fixed her
hair, she had nothing to do this morning except take
care of Heath. Despite the troubles at the *Examiner*—
which could surely be resolved in a way that would
allow both Heath and Damon to keep their pride intact—she was wonderfully, deliriously happy. It was
hard not to shower Heath with an overabundance of
love. She wanted to burst through his defenses with it,
she wanted to surround him with it. But even mentioning the word *love* would be making a demand that

he was not ready for. She would rein in her feelings as much as she could, waiting patiently until he could bring himself to tell her what was in his heart. After all that he had said and done last night, she knew that he cared for her. He had told her he needed her. How incredibly good it had been to hear him say that!

She subdued her exuberant expression into something approaching normal and picked up the cup of steaming black coffee, being careful not to slosh the brew into the saucer. As she carried it into the bathroom, she saw Heath's head resting on the rolled rim of the enameled bath tub, his eyes closed as if he had fallen asleep again. Gingerly she sat down on the lid of the water closet. Heath opened one eye and reached out for the coffee.

Silently she handed it to him, resisting the urge to reach out and sift her fingers through the damp, slightly curling strands of hair that had fallen on his forehead. Heath took an experimental swallow and then another before he gave the cup back to her. "It's not bad," he said grudgingly, taking hold of a cake of soap and working up a lather.

"Maybe in a few minutes you'll feel like having breakfast—"

"I wouldn't lay odds on it."

Her smile was filled with sympathy as she looked at him.

He looked away from her, devoting his attention to the soap. "I . . . hope I didn't talk too much last night," he said casually. "I don't remember much about it."

Lucy pushed the nagging thoughts about Raine—whoever she was—right out of her mind. She didn't want to think about her. And besides, it didn't matter who Raine was, because she was part of Heath's past, while Lucy was his wife. Lucy was his present and his future, and she would not allow anyone or anything to disrupt this satisfactory state of affairs.

"No," she replied with equal casualness. "You didn't say much of anything."

"Oh." His relief was poorly concealed as he proceeded with his bath. Discreetly Lucy enjoyed the sight of his lithe body as he lathered his chest with foamy white soap and rinsed off. After a few minutes, he paused for a swallow of coffee and smiled wryly.

"Remember when you told me it was crazy for a Southerner to try to run a Boston newspaper? You might have been—"

"I was wrong."

"Oh?"

"Absolutely wrong."

He eyed her skeptically. "I seem to have missed a step somewhere along the way. When did you decide that?"

"After I started reading the paper. I . . . I like your ideas. I like the way the newspaper is turning out, and other people will start to feel the same way. I know you'll start making a profit when you lure in a few more advertisers."

The corners of his eyes crinkled with the promise of a smile. "I appreciate your faith in me. Unfortunately the paper's going to be finished off by a second civil war."

"Then you'll have to find some way to compromise. It didn't seem as if you and Damon were having any serious disagreements before—"

"We were. And they've all stemmed from the fact that our political, social, and moral leanings are entirely different."

"Surely you're exaggerating—"

"You don't know Damon as I do," Heath said darkly. "And if you did, you'd agree that the conflict over this editorial is going to happen again, because it's not really about what happened in Georgia yesterday. It's about his beliefs as opposed to mine, and they're never going to mesh—''

"You can find some common ground to meet on. Neither of you wants to try to fight the war over again, and you've got to remind him of that. You're one of the most persuasive people I've ever met. I know you can talk him into taking a more moderate stand.''

"Now who's being persuasive?'' He pulled the plug and reached for a towel as the bathwater gurgled down the drain. Roughly he toweled his hair dry and stepped out of the tub, wrapping the towel around his hips. "What if I can't talk him into changing the editorial? If I write it the way I want it, he'll leave.''

"Then he leaves.''

"We might lose the paper without him.''

"Then it's everyone's loss. But the only one I'm concerned about is you. You've got to do whatever it takes to keep your pride and self-respect. You would never forgive yourself if you felt that you betrayed your beliefs and your people. It's your paper. Run it the way you want, for as long as you have it.''

He caressed the side of her jaw with his fingertips, sending a light shiver down her spine. "I should warn you that if we lose the paper, we'll have to sell the house.''

"That's fine.''

"And the furniture.''

"I don't care.''

"And—''

"We can pawn, sell, and trade off everything we own . . . but if you dare say one thing about my diamond, you'll regret it for the rest of your married life. This ring is mine, and it's not leaving my finger.''

He grinned at her vehemence. "I wasn't going to say anything about your ring, honey." Bending down to kiss her, he left wet handprints on the waist and bodice of her gown, but Lucy was too enthralled by his hearty kiss to protest.

"You taste like coffee," she whispered when his lips left hers.

"I could do with more."

"Coffee or kisses?"

"Always more kisses . . ." He dropped a light one on the corner of her mouth. "But I was referring to coffee. Have you had breakfast yet?"

"I was waiting for you."

"Then why don't you go downstairs while I get dressed? I'll join you in a few minutes."

"Don't be long," she said, and paused in the doorway to look up and down his scantily covered body in a way that caused his blood to stir. She quirked the side of her mouth suggestively. "The . . . muffins will get cold."

As she left, Heath wondered bemusedly how she had learned to infuse such a simple statement with such a variety of innuendos. He also wondered how it was physically possible for him to want her so much again, when he had just spent the entire night satiating himself with her.

Just when Lucy reached the bottom of the stairs, someone knocked on the front door with a demanding staccato. The butler came into the front entranceway to greet the visitor; he looked so uncustomarily harried that Lucy knew he hadn't yet finished his own breakfast.

"I'll answer the door, Sowers," she said.

"But Mrs. Rayne—"

"I have an idea of who it might be. You may go back to the kitchen." The grateful butler disappeared without hesitation, and Lucy went to the door, opening it in the middle of another flurry of knocking. As her intuition had led her to hope, the visitor was Damon Redmond. He was as immaculately groomed as always, but his eyes were bloodshot and there were tired lines on his face. He was leaning against the doorframe as if its support was necessary to keep him upright. "Good morning," she said.

"We all have our own opinions about that, Mrs. Rayne."

"Oh, dear," she said, and smiled as she opened the door to let him in. "Please join us for some breakfast."

"Thank you, but—"

"At least some coffee," she coaxed, and he smiled wearily.

"Have you ever met anyone who could refuse you anything? I doubt it." Damon surrendered his coat to her without another word and followed her to the breakfast room. Lucy thought compassionately that he must be just as perturbed as Heath about the editorial; he looked as though he hadn't gotten more than an hour or two of sleep. Quickly she handed the coat to Bess with a murmur about needing another place setting, then allowed Damon to seat her at the table.

"Heath will be down here in just a minute," she said as Damon settled into a chair across from hers. "As soon as he's finished washing up and dressing . . ." Her voice trailed off into silence as she noticed that his dark eyes had flickered to the bodice of her dress. Looking down at herself, Lucy realized that one of Heath's wet handprints was still clearly visible, right underneath her breast. She could feel her cheeks turning crimson. "He required a little assistance with his bath," she said lamely.

"Of course," Damon replied, unfailingly polite, though she saw a dark twinkle in his eyes.

"He's in remarkably good temper, considering . . . everything." She would not make any further revelations until she found out if Damon was there to decide on a compromise or abandon ship.

Damon sobered instantly. "I couldn't just meet him at the paper. I thought if we talked here beforehand—"

"I think that's a very good idea."

"I would like to believe that there's a good chance of reconciling our differences."

"He is a very reasonable person, Mr. Redmond. I know for a fact that he would like to find a suitable compromise between your position and his."

"With all due respect, Mrs. Rayne," Damon said stiffly, "I didn't have that impression yesterday."

"I am certain that many people think of him as being very . . . progressive—"

"Very tactfully put—"

"Perhaps too progressive. But he believes very strongly in what he is doing, and he feels a great sense of responsibility to his people. Surely you can understand that."

"I didn't come here to debate with you—"

"What I'm trying to tell you," Lucy insisted softly, "is that if he feels you are approaching him with some understanding of his position, he will be much more inclined to listen to what you have to say. And, as you already know, if you try to best him in an outright confrontation, he will dig his heels in even deeper."

"Thank you for the advice," Damon murmured. "I'll try to remember it."

Tacitly they decided to change the subject as Bess came in with extra dishes and silverware. The maid fumbled slightly as she arranged a place setting before Damon, glancing at his dark, attractive face so often that Lucy nearly admonished her for being so clumsy about her work. Damon didn't appear to notice the maid's interest; his attention was completely focused on Lucy in a manner that was both flattering and disconcerting. Lucy passed him a basket of freshly baked muffins, admonishing him to take one of the larger ones. She smiled with pleasure as he put two of them on his plate. "I'm glad someone besides me has an appetite this morning," she said.

"Just because I'm in the midst of a personal crisis and potential financial disaster doesn't mean I should starve to death as well." Damon broke open a steaming muffin and spread it with butter.

"How very practical."

"Of course. Nothing else is to be expected from a Redmond. The Cabots are blunt, the Forbeses are perverse, the Lawrences are tight-fisted, the Lowells are cold. The Redmonds are practical."

How ridiculous. Lucy smiled at him while thinking privately that most of the first family traditions were pure nonsense. How could any one person belonging to a first family ever have a life of his own? Everything had been mapped out for Damon from the day he was born until the day he died, including his education, his friends, his business, his future wife— even his personality. She knew that many people had been shocked by his decision to buy a newspaper instead of following his older brothers' footsteps in the world of banking. Lucy hoped he would continue to break away from the Redmond mold, for she had a feeling that quite a different Damon Redmond existed inside the somber young man his family had intended him to be.

"I was also brought up to be practical," she

confided, pouring a generous splash of cream into her coffee and stirring it slowly. "For me, everything was always very organized and predictable. Decisions were easy to make. Problems were easily solved." She shook her head reminiscently and chuckled. "And then I met Heath, and nothing has been the same since then. Nothing is simple anymore. It's difficult to be practical around someone who can make the most sensible things seem absurd."

"He does like to approach things on a different level than the rest of us," Damon admitted wryly. "A very complicated level. By now I should have figured out a way to avoid problems like this one. But so far I haven't had much success at coming to understand him."

Lucy was saved from having to reply by Bess's reappearance with a tray of food. Thoughtfully she lifted the coffee cup to her lips. It was so hot that she could only let a few drops of the dark liquid graze the tip of her tongue. She found it interesting that she and Damon would both have the same difficulties in dealing with Heath. Overly practical people would always think of him as someone beyond comprehension. There was a time when she, also, had considered it important to try to understand him. But there was no category Heath would fit in. There were too many pieces to the puzzle. It was better just to accept him as he was, ambiguities and all, and to be content with the knowledge that he needed someone like her, constant and unchanging, in order to keep his world in balance.

Heath entered the room just then, stopping in the doorway as he laid eyes on the unexpected visitor. Lucy looked from his face to Damon's, unconsciously holding her breath.

"I'm not surprised you're here," Heath said

dryly. "I haven't yet heard of a Yankee hesitating to venture into enemy territory."

Damon held his white napkin up by the corner and dangled it as if it were a flag of surrender. "I came to inquire, General, if there's any hope of a negotiated peace."

Heath smiled slightly, pulling out the chair next to Lucy and sitting down. "Possibly. You might start by passing the muffins."

"Yes, sir."

Lucy let out her breath and smiled as the negotiations proceeded and compromises were discussed. Neither of the two men at the table was so inflexible that he would sacrifice ambition for the sake of pride. And in Lucy's opinion, neither of them would seriously consider giving up the newspaper. The *Examiner* meant more than money to them; more than ink and paper, words and columns. It had given two worldly men their only chance to be idealists, and they were not ready to relinquish that.

It took hours of dedicated persuasion for Lucy to coax Heath into taking her to the Hosmers' Christmas Eve party in Concord instead of attending the magnificent annual Redmond gala. But Christmas in a small town was different from Christmas in the city. There was less glamour and pageantry, certainly, but a Concord Christmas was old-fashioned and special. Every home was decorated with pine cones and holly; each room was fragrant with cinnamon-dusted pomander balls. The doorways were garnished with large bows and tiny round potatoes that had been covered with sprigs of mistletoe and long ribbon streamers. By long-established custom, anyone caught underneath one of them had to surrender a kiss.

People in Concord celebrated the holidays with

well-planned parties, where long-familiar friends gathered to eat, drink, and converse. The tables were burdened with rounds of Christmas Irish bread, filled with raisins, frosted and topped with a cherry, bowls of cranberry punch, berry turnovers, candied fruit peel, and delicate cups of eggnog sprinkled with nutmeg.

Knowing that she would see old acquaintances, many of whom she hadn't visited with in months, Lucy dressed with care. She wore a green velvet dress with sleeves cut in long leaf-like points, and a sash richly embroidered with gold thread. Her crinoline was unusually narrow, only half the width of ordinary hoop skirts, and the excess material was gathered in back to fall in a train. Heath had approved of the new style wholeheartedly. More conventional crinolines were so wide that they took up all the room on a sofa, besides preventing a man from standing any closer to a woman than arms' distance.

As Heath escorted Lucy to the front door of the small Concord home, the Hosmers received them with a surprising degree of warmth. Mrs. Hosmer exclaimed over Lucy's velvet dress and commanded one of her three sons to fetch cups of eggnog for the Raynes, while Mr. Hosmer pulled Heath aside and introduced him to other guests.

"Lucy," Mrs. Hosmer said, her piercing eyes softer than usual, "we haven't heard a thing about you since you disappeared to Boston. How do you like living in the city?"

"My husband and I find it busy, but quite agreeable," Lucy replied, watching covertly as Mr. Hosmer led Heath into the next room.

"I imagine you must. Especially considering your husband's livelihood . . . a newspaper, of all

things . . . frankly none of us expected such a potential . . . you understand . . ."

"I understand," Lucy said with a faint smile.
"His acquisition of the paper was a surprise to me as
well."

"Oh, really?" Mrs. Hosmer inquired, and the
dubious tilt of her voice made it clear that she didn't
believe that at all. "Well, it appears that he's becoming quite an influential man in Boston, in spite of his
background."

"Is he?" Lucy parried, accepting a cup of
eggnog. "How nice of you to say so."

"You've done better for yourself than you led
us all to believe at first."

The statement caught Lucy off-guard. "It was
not my intention to deceive anyone," she said carefully, and the other woman had the grace to blush.

"I'm certain it wasn't, my dear." She looked
past Lucy's shoulder at a new couple that had just entered the house. "My goodness," she chattered, "if
it isn't the most handsome young couple in Concord!
Sally, why don't you . . . oh . . ." Mrs. Hosmer
flushed deeply in distress as she looked from Lucy to
Daniel and Sally. Lucy turned around and faced them
with composure, finding that the sight of Daniel after
so many months was not the shock that she had anticipated.

"Merry Christmas," she said, her lips curving slightly. "You do make a handsome couple."

"Lucy!" Sally exclaimed, her radiant golden
curls bobbing as she took a few steps forward and
hugged her quickly. "How stylish you are! I can
hardly believe how fashionable your dress is, and
your hair—"

"Don't babble, Sally," Daniel said absently,
his dark, searching eyes meeting with Lucy's.

Lucy could not repress a smile. Daniel had not changed. "You both look well," she said, her gaze flickering from Sally's blond prettiness to Daniel's set face. He looked handsome and well kept, having let his mustache grow from a crescent into a distinguished bullet-head, full and curled at the tips. Although the style would have been too old for most men his age, it suited him perfectly. His lean, slim form was clad in a "ditto suit," the coat, vest and trousers all made of matching material. Calm and self-assured as always, he gave her a reserved smile even as his eyes noted every change in her. Though she no longer felt anything for him but a distant fondness, Lucy was still glad that she looked her best and that there could be no fault found in her appearance.

She wondered if he still remembered the terrible scene between them, when she had been in a position of disgrace and had begged him not to turn her away. *"I don't want the woman you've become . . ."* he had said. At the time she had not understood what he had meant; now she did.

How long ago that had been! Lucy was so profoundly grateful not to be married to Daniel that she felt weak in the knees. He was a good man, a gentle one. His emotions were quiet and steady, and his character utterly civilized. But if she had ended up as Daniel's wife, she would never have experienced all that she cherished about Heath: his passion, violent, stormy and sweet; his rough affection and tender concern; his barbs, and gentle teasing; his demands; his ambitions; even his secrets.

Daniel's expression altered subtly as he stared at her, as if he were remembering days long past. It felt strange to Lucy, standing before him and realizing that she had once loved him, while now the distance between them could never be traversed except in memories.

"Your wedding will be soon?" she asked him.

"Later this year, in the spring," he replied quietly.

"Ahhh," she breathed, nodding slowly. Always. Always later this year, always later on. He had strung Lucy out for three years with such promises. She felt a quick stab of pity as she turned to Sally. "Better hold him to it," she said, and the blond laughed lightly, unaware of the implications and the subtle warning that were lodged in the simple words. Daniel, however, did not miss her meaning, and he flushed slightly.

"Of course I intend to hold him to it," Sally said, giggling, and Lucy smiled before turning away and leaving them, suddenly needing to find Heath.

As she looked around the corner into a small yellow and light green parlor, someone came up behind her, hooked a firm arm around her waist and whisked her neatly into the empty room. A soft, jeering voice touched the inside of her ear in an intimate stroke.

"Love renewed by absence. How touching."

Lucy relaxed as she identified her captor. "You startled me."

Heath let her twist around in his arms to face him, and she saw that there was self-mockery and something akin to irritation in his expression. She was quick to guess at the cause. "Did you by any chance happen to see me talking to Sally and Daniel?"

"Was that Daniel? It was difficult to tell through that soup-strainer on his face."

"There's no need to make fun of his mustache."

Heath let go of her abruptly. "I beg your pardon. I forgot that you've always had a fondness for it."

"What in heaven's name is bothering you?" Without waiting for an answer, she started for the half-open door. "People are going to notice we're gone, and I don't want them to think—"

He caught her upper arm in a light, unyielding grip and spun her around. "I want to know what the two of you were talking about."

Her eyes rounded with surprise. "I don't understand why you seem so angry."

"Don't tell me you weren't aware of the way he was looking at you."

"I couldn't help the way he was looking at me," she protested, making an unsuccessful attempt to tug her arm free from his tightening grasp.

"And you . . . staring up at him, all starry-eyed and breathless—"

"I wasn't!"

"The picture was too perfect. A New England Christmas. Two childhood sweethearts sharing old memories—"

"You're being unreasonable!"

"You would have been a handsome couple. You do suit each other quite well."

"I don't think so," she said quickly, placing a small, restraining hand on his chest as he towered over her.

"Oh?" The bright flare of jealousy in his gaze showed no signs of diminishing.

"No—I don't prefer that kind of man at all. He's . . . he's too short, for one thing. I never realized before how short he was. And his hair . . . well, it's much too dark. I prefer lighter hair much, *much* more." Heath's grip loosened marginally, a sign that encouraged Lucy to continue. "He's too quiet, too predictable . . . too straight-laced. I would die of boredom if I had to spend more than five minutes with him. He doesn't like to argue or swear, and he doesn't drink too much or lose his temper. He's not the kind who would appreciate black silk pantalets.''

"He has a respectable family that everyone approves of.''

"I don't care about what anyone else thinks.''

Heath yanked her closer to him, his savage mood barely concealed. His fingers bit into the backs of her shoulders, but not harshly enough to leave bruises. Thick gold-tipped lashes lowered over azure eyes as he stared down at her mouth.

"You've wanted him ever since you were a child,'' he pointed out gruffly.

"Until my taste matured.''

"He's a gentleman.''

"Yes. That's the worst thing of all.''

Heedless of the half-open door and the possibility of stray glances, he pulled her upwards, forcing her to rise on her toes as he kissed her. The slow, smooth pressure of his lips on hers increased until she parted them with a muffled exclamation, yielding the tender heat of her mouth to his demand. Dark fire danced through her veins, its burning sweetness filtering to the surface of her skin in a spreading flush. The force of her response to him swept away every coherent thought, every barrier she had constructed for her own protection. His mouth traveled in a warm velvet slide down her throat, the edge of his teeth grazed the thinly veiled nerves just below her skin. Her knees nearly buckled beneath her as his hand ventured beneath the soft material of her dress, cupping around the nakedness of her breast. The tingling peak came to life in his palm, drawing into an aching bud at his touch. "Heath," she whispered, "you're all I want. No one else . . . no one . . ."

"I only brought you here tonight because you wanted it." His voice was soft and harsh at the same time. "I wouldn't care if I never set foot in Concord again."

"But I grew up here. I'll need to visit occasionally." As his mouth concentrated on a particularly sensitive area of her neck, her head dropped to his shoulder, too heavy to support any longer. "It's not a bad little town—"

"You were the best thing about it. You were the only reason I stayed here so long."

She smiled tremulously. "Is that true?"

"After what happened at the river and the two days we spent together, I decided to wait and see just how attached you were to Daniel."

"You did more than just 'wait and see.' "

"I couldn't seem to leave you alone."

"Your lack of self-control is no excuse for ruining my long-standing engagement."

He brushed feather-light kisses across her lips, lingering at the corners. "Ever have regrets?"

She arched her breast into his hand, straining to be closer to him. "You wouldn't have asked that unless you knew I didn't."

Heath smiled against her skin, reluctantly withdrawing his hand from her bodice. "Answer me anyway."

With a sudden burst of energy, she twisted away from him and laughed as she eluded his swift attempt to recapture her. Fleeing to a position of precarious safety behind a small, round table, she braced her hands lightly on the edge and threw him a taunting look. "You do like to give orders, don't you?"

"And I like you to follow them." He made a

feint towards one side of the table and then reached out an arm to catch her as she darted around the other side. Though he could have stopped her easily, he let her wriggle away, and his mouth quirked in amusement as he watched her flee triumphantly to the other side of the room.

"I only follow your orders when I want to," she informed him, backing into the corner as he approached.

"Answer the question I asked you before," he commanded, adopting a threatening scowl. "Do you ever have regrets about marrying me instead of Daniel?" She backed up against the wall, her eyes sparkling with laughter as she refused to say a word. "The longer you take to answer, Mrs. Rayne, the more imminent the danger of your backside being paddled."

Lucy grinned impudently. "I can just picture you trying to get past all these petticoats and my bustle—"

"Honey, of all the things that have ever presented a challenge to me, getting past your bustle has never been one of them."

"How dare you say something like that to your wife," she exclaimed, dodging past him and giving a smothered laugh as he caught her at the waist and whirled her around.

Abruptly their private amusement was cut short by a voice from the doorway. "Lucy?" Mrs. Hosmer eyed them both with obvious disapproval. She had never taken well to such goings-on in her home. It provided a bad example for her three sons to follow, besides offending her own sense of propriety. "Lucy, your father has just arrived. He is looking for you. I am certain he would be quite dismayed if you failed to give him your Christmas greetings right away."

"I'm sure he'd be devastated," Heath murmured in Lucy's ear, and it was all she could do to keep from giggling.

"Thank you, Mrs. Hosmer," she said, slipping out of her husband's grasp and sending him a properly reproving glance. "We'll go to him this very minute."

"We certainly will," Heath echoed, smiling blandly until Mrs. Hosmer fixed him with a suspicious stare and left the room. Then his expression became disgruntled. "By all means, let's show your father what a bad influence I've been on his little girl."

"He won't think that at all. He's always adored you for having rescued his fallen daughter."

"And his daughter? What does she think about it?"

"She thinks that . . ." Lucy paused and cast a swift glance over her head, "that you have been very remiss in failing to notice that she is standing right underneath a sprig of mistletoe."

His laughter was soft and lazy, eliciting a delicious chill from the pit of her stomach. While he stared into her eyes, he reached up, plucked the mistletoe from the top of the doorframe, and slipped the small green sprig into his pocket. "For later," he said, and smiled at her.

Chapter Ten

HEATH WAS STILL unused to the harshness of the climate, and he was fond of cursing the weather each time he stepped outside. The cold of a Northern winter sank deep into the bones, and the wind blew easily through several layers of clothing. Since Lucy had lived in Massachusetts all her life, she was accustomed to the harshness of winter and thought nothing of it. To Heath, it was almost intolerable. As the season advanced well into the month of January, the cold worsened until it was impossible to go outside for longer than a few minutes at a time. Heath insisted on having every room in the house warm and all the stoves filled with fuel, which pained Lucy; she had been raised on a strict tradition of thriftiness, especially in the matter of heating the house. However, for the sake of keeping him content and even tempered, she forced herself to learn to squander coal and wood without flinching.

During a week of especially bad weather, the graying heaps of snow that lined the narrow Boston streets melted partially, resulting in several inches of ice when the temperatures dropped again. Traveling was difficult and unpleasant at best, while in some sections of the city it was impossible. Heath arrived home from the newspaper office thoroughly chilled, his hair darkened by the wetness of sleet and rain.

"You're not wearing a hat," Lucy said, frowning and helping him off with his coat.

"I forgot it today," he said ruefully, his teeth chattering. "Bad mistake."

"Very bad," she agreed, snatching off his scarf and regarding him worriedly. "Why are you so wet?"

"Washington Street . . . too iced-over for . . . the carriage to go through. Had to walk down to the corner. Cold as . . . a welldigger's ass."

"Your hands and your face are frozen," she exclaimed, trying to warm them with the friction of her small palms, and her futile efforts caused him to grin briefly.

"Not just the hands and face."

She was too concerned to laugh. Impatiently she ushered him upstairs, insisting that he take off his wet clothes and put on a warm robe immediately. Heath stood in front of the fire a long time, basking in the warmth of it like a shivering tomcat.

They had dinner in their bedroom at a small table before the fireplace while the golden light of the flames forced the shadows to retreat to the edges of the room. Lucy entertained Heath with an account of the lecture she had gone to that day. As he sipped brandy and listened quietly, Heath looked particularly thoughtful this evening. His long fingers curved around the brandy glass; his thumb rubbed gently across the rim. At times like this there was a languid grace about his movements that Lucy could watch for hours.

"And then Representative Gowen said . . . Heath, are you listening to me?"

"I'm listening," he assured her lazily, settling back further and propping his bare foot on the edge of her chair. With great difficulty, he took his attention away from the contemplation of her face in the candlelight and concentrated on the conversation. "What did Representative Gowen say?"

"He talked about protecting the country's shipping industry and making the navy strong again."

"Good. It's been neglected ever since the war ended."

"And he said that we had the advantage in shipbuilding all through the fifties while ships were being made out of wood, but now that they're being made out of iron, the British have gone far ahead of us. Representative Gowen thinks we should give higher subsidies to American shipping and tax all the things we import for our shipbuilding."

"Go on," he said softly, resting his chin in his hand and staring at her.

"If you're interested in the rest of what he said, I . . . took a few notes on his lecture that you could read." She shrugged with overdone carelessness. "Or I can tell you about it. It doesn't matter."

"Notes," Heath repeated, instantly curious. He wondered what she was up to, and he bent all of his effort towards suppressing a smile at her display of elaborate unconcern. "Yes, I'd like to see them." Evidently that was the response Lucy had wanted, for she stood up without hesitation and went to her dressing table.

"They're right here." She opened the top drawer and pulled out a thin sheaf of paper. "Just a few scribbles."

As she handed her work to him, Lucy was assailed with a multitude of regrets. She wanted to snatch it back before he could read it. She didn't know what had possessed her to write about the lecture. It seemed like such a good idea this morning, but suddenly she was very sorry that she had followed through with it. It was just that Heath was always talking about his reporters, about their accomplishments and the mistakes they made, and she had wanted to see if she could write an article. Lucy wondered miserably if her efforts would embarrass him. Only the fear of seeming even more foolish than she felt at the moment kept her from saying anything. She wrung her hands behind her back, too agitated to sit down.

Halfway through the first page, Heath glanced up at her sharply. "This is hardly what I'd call a few scribbles, Cin."

She shrugged casually and looked away from him as he continued to read. When he was finished, Heath set the article on the table carefully. There was an odd expression on his face, one which she couldn't decipher. "It's perfect. I couldn't suggest a single improvement. How long did it take you to write this?"

"Oh, just an hour or two." It had taken all afternoon, but there was no need for him to know that.

"The structure, the length, the style . . . it's all just the way . . ." He broke off and gave her a quizzical half-smile. "Do you know how hard Damon and I have to prod our reporters to get something like this?"

Feeling a glow of pleasure at his praise, she fought hard to keep an idiotic smile off her face. "I just wanted to try my hand at it."

"I'd like to give it to Damon."

"Do you mean for the *Examiner?*"

"Yes, that's what I mean."

"I don't think it's good enough," she hedged.

"This isn't a time for modesty," he said flatly. "It's good enough."

"Do you think so?" She beamed at him. "If you want to, then take it to Damon, but don't tell him who wrote it. Just sign it with some made-up initials, and if he doesn't like it, no one will have to know."

"I won't tell him who wrote it," he assured her. "But he'll probably suspect."

"Are you just trying to humor me and spare my feelings, or do you really like the article?"

"I'm not trying to spare your feelings." Heath glanced down at the article and ran his fingertips over the top page, still amazed by the clear preciseness of her writing. A sensation of pride crept through his chest as he realized what she had done. "In fact, I'm ashamed to admit that I'm surprised."

"Ashamed?"

"I shouldn't be surprised by something like this. Not from you." He stood up and went over to her, nudging her chin with his forefinger and tipping her face upwards. Did she know how different she was from the girl he had married? A year ago, she had possessed something, a hint of something special, that had attracted him against his will. Now that unnameable hint of magic had developed into something far more potent. God help him when she finally learned to use it. "What a marvel you are." He smiled slowly. "Do something for me, Lucy."

"What?"

"Don't ever let me start to think of you as merely my . . . playmate."

"Is there a danger of that?"

He cast a roguish glance towards the bed. "I'm afraid that in my appreciation for some of your talents, I might tend to overlook some of the others."

"Can I think of you as *my* playmate?"

A smile tugged at the corners of his mouth. "Always." He slipped her robe off her shoulders and stroked the upper rise of her breasts with his thumbs, aware of the faint, breathy sound she made in response. "Are you tired of talking?" he whispered, catching delicately at her earlobe with his teeth. "Then come to bed and play, Cinda. I've got a new game for you tonight.'' And she followed him willingly, entranced by the beguiling wickedness of his smile.

Lucy's article was printed in the paper, and it was not long before Heath encouraged her to write another one. The second was much more difficult to write than the first, but as she discovered how readily Heath responded to her hesitant questions, she became less shy about asking for his help. He sat down with her and made suggestions about how her work could be improved, while she managed to swallow her indignation about having her favorite paragraph removed. And she realized how good he was at what he did, and how he could make the prospect of rewriting an article seem like a pleasure instead of a chore. No wonder Damon had complimented his editorial abilities so highly.

Heath had a gift for putting things plainly, and that was a valuable talent. Most writers were never quite able to say exactly what they meant. Not Heath. He knew exactly what he meant and he wanted everyone else to know, too. The *Examiner,* as he saw it, would have to reflect that same attitude, audacious and a little brassy. He wanted his reporters to be daring. And he demanded that they report on things that ''the other reporters at the other papers'' hadn't even heard about. His conception of news was radical compared to the standards of the day. Most papers were merely showcases for an editorial voice. But the *Examiner* placed unheard-of importance on the efforts of its reporters: don't wait for news to happen, go out and find it, make it, *define* it. Only a few of the reporters understood what Heath wanted of them, and they worked hard to satisfy his expectations.

Living with Heath had given Lucy an advantage over all of them—she understood more about him, his feelings for language and his work than any of them would ever be able to grasp. A newspaperman was traditionally a witness of the times he lived in. But she knew that Heath wanted to be more than that, though he hadn't said as much out loud. He wanted to be able to influence events, people, and decisions through the simple power of words on paper. The causes he believed in wouldn't be solved any other way. Therefore, the first objective was to make the *Examiner* the most informed and powerful newspaper in Boston. Lucy believed it was possible, and she was going to lend her efforts toward bringing it about. She had her own talent with words and a growing self-confidence that would help her to choose them well. And more significantly, she had connections with influential people in Boston that neither Heath nor Damon had access to—not the bigwigs themselves, but their wives.

Time and time again she proved her worth as a source of information, as she had on the day when no one could pry a word out of a state senator concerning the proposed takeover of the East Boston ferries by the city. Lucy found out every detail about the ferry proposal from the senator's wife as they sipped tea at a club meeting. Through the women she associated with, she found out who was planning what and who was going where, and she discreetly passed on the information to her husband. *Examiner* reporters began to pop up in unexpected places, just in time to catch the latest stories, and their reports were gaining the reputation of being more updated than anyone else's. The choicest stories, however, Lucy reserved for herself to write, and her skills improved steadily.

She loved being able to share in Heath's work. It was gratifying to find that sometimes they could communicate on a purely intellectual level. In Lucy's past experience, she had discovered that most men didn't like to see a woman's intellectual side. But Heath wasn't threatened by her intelligence: he enjoyed trading ideas with her. In fact, he seemed to enjoy everything about her, even her occasional moments of contrariness or bad temper. Sometimes he went out of his way to rouse her out of her primness and good manners, provoking her into an argument. He loved to argue with her, tease and charm her. He held the keys to all of her passions, and he made certain that she lived and experienced each one of them as lustily as he did. Her memories of life before her marriage seemed like a pale reflection of this. What had she known of happiness then? What had she known about anything?

On the twenty-sixth of January, Virginia, having accepted the Fifteenth Amendment, was readmitted to the Union. The news spurred a giant flurry of activity in the offices of every newspaper on Washington Street; everyone was talking about the controversial test-oaths of loyalty that the senate demanded of all public officials, as well as the numerous provisos concerning voting rights, holding elected offices, and public schools. Then in February, Mississippi ratified the amendment, and the state seemed to turn upside down as dozens of incidents of violence against blacks followed. There was a great deal of news to cover.

Heath began the practice of working extra hours and coming home exhausted every night. None of Lucy's pleas to slow down and rest had any effect on him. Seemingly tireless, he pushed everyone nearly as hard as he did himself, adding a Sunday edition of the paper and an extra two pages to the daily issues. As a result, everyone at the *Examiner* had the satisfaction of seeing the subscription rate jump by five thousand readers, putting it on a level with the *Journal*.

Heath and Damon were exuberant at the progress the paper had made. Now they were no longer just surviving. They were *competitive*. And there were jokes around town that the owners of the *Herald* were beginning to look over their shoulders in fear of "Examination."

Lucy was delighted by Heath's success, but at the same time she was worried by his ceaseless activity. He worked every waking hour of the day, took her to social events during the weekend, and discarded sleep as if it were an easily expendable commodity. Even Damon had admitted the last time he visited that he couldn't keep up with Heath's pace. Gradually the punishing schedule began to take its toll. Heath's temper became much shorter than before. He developed a slight but persistent hoarseness from being outside in the cold weather so often, and the smooth drawl of his voice was replaced by a husky rasping that wouldn't seem to go away. Upon noticing the new honed look about his cheekbones and realizing that he had lost weight, Lucy put her foot down.

"Cin," Heath said, striding into the bedroom and straightening his necktie, "are you almost ready? We're going to be . . ." He stopped short as he saw that she was still dressed in her robe, sitting on the edge of the bed.

"I'm not going tonight," she said stubbornly.

His mouth hardened with impatience. "Honey, I already explained to you that we don't have a choice. This is an Associated Press dinner, and there are some people I have to talk with—"

"You also said that Damon would be there. He can talk to them."

"There's no time to argue—"

"Then let's not." She looked at him and couldn't control the moisture that welled up in the corners of her eyes. He was as handsome and immaculately dressed as ever, but the distinctive glow of vitality he had always possessed had been drained by overwork, and there were faint shadows underneath his blue eyes. His expression was harsh and tired. What was making him so discontented that he would try to work himself to death? Was it some inadequacy of hers? Was it some nagging worry that he couldn't bring himself to talk about? "I don't like going out every weekend," she said, her voice becoming wobbly. "We haven't had time to sit down and just . . . just *be together*."

"It won't be like this forever," Heath said quietly. "There are just a lot of things to take care of right now, and—"

"But you don't have to do it all by yourself!" she cried. "You never trust anyone to take care of some of that work . . . and . . . and that's just arrogance, to think that you're the only one who can do it!"

"Lucy . . ." As he saw the tears that dropped from her eyes, he sighed and rubbed his temples. "Alright. In another few weeks I'll start looking for ways to delegate responsibility."

That didn't satisfy her. In fact, it only made her want to cry harder. "I don't know how much longer you can go on like this, but I c-can't!"

Muttering a curse, he took off his shoes, coat, and necktie, picked her up, and sat down on the bed with her in his lap. Lucy huddled against his chest, burying her wet face into his neck. He was warm and solid, his heartbeat steady underneath her hand. "Shhhh . . . it's alright," he said into her hair, cradling her tightly. "We're not going tonight. We'll stay here."

"I'm not as h-happy as I used to be—"

"I know. I know, honey. I'll make it right. Everything's going to be fine from now on."

"You don't l-laugh as much as you used to."

"I will. Starting tomorrow."

"You spend all your energy on that *paper* . . . a-and I only get you when you're all t-tired out."

"God." He smiled and nuzzled through her hair, kissing the soft hollow behind her earlobe. "I'm sorry. Don't cry so hard, sweet . . . shhhh . . ."

He murmured to her and cradled her, stroking her hair until her tears stopped. A tentative, eagerly welcomed relief stole over Lucy as they eased back together on the bed. Nothing was wrong as long as he was with her and his arms were around her. "Stay with me," she said, tightening her hold on him as she felt his weight shift. "Don't go. Let's just . . . let's just rest a little while. And we'll eat dinner up here later."

Since it was still early evening, Lucy expected him to refuse. There were always papers and articles for Heath to look through before he went to bed each night. But at the moment he was surprisingly tractable, making no protest as she left him and dimmed the lights. When she returned to the bed, he made a sleepy sound and gathered her close, resting his head on her bosom. Lucy welcomed the weight of him, letting her fingers drift through his tawny hair as she stared blindly into the fireplace. His body took on a relaxed heaviness as he slept. But this sleep was different from his usual, peaceful, contented slumber. This was ominously still. This sleep was deep and exhausted, a hungry sleep that had consumed him far too quickly. He did not even stir at the gentle tapping on the bedroom door.

"Yes?" Lucy responded in a low tone, looking at the doorway. "What is it?"

Bess peered around the corner cautiously. "Mrs. Rayne, the coachman—"

"Thank him for his trouble and tell him that he won't be needed tonight," Lucy said, unsmiling. "Tell him to put the carriage away. And then make certain that we are not disturbed again tonight." She knew that her manner was unnecessarily brusque, but the maid did not seem to take offense.

"Yes, Mrs. Rayne."

The door closed again, and the room was enshrouded in darkness except for the soft red glow of the coals on the grate. There was little sound, just the occasional crackle of the coals and the deep, slow rhythm of Heath's breathing. Lucy stayed awake beyond midnight, as if her watchfulness were the only thing that would guarantee her husband's slumber. Perhaps someday she would find amusement in the memory of how tense and uncertain these hours had been, at how she had given in to unreasoning fear and curved her arms around him as if to protect him from the world that waited outside. Perhaps someday she would remember this and laugh. But not now. Not now.

"You have a fever," she insisted, following him back and forth as he dressed and prepared to leave.

"Maybe I do," Heath said matter-of-factly. He dried his freshly shaven face with a towel and strode back into the bedroom. "It's winter. Everyone has a little temperature now and then. It's damn well not going to stop me from working."

Lucy made an exasperated sound. "If I'd known how stubborn you were going to be, I would have tied you to the bed while you were sleeping!"

He grinned at her and stretched, feeling more energetic than he had in weeks. "I'm glad we stayed home last night. A little extra rest is just what I needed.''

"You still need it. You obviously think one night's sleep is going to undo weeks of self-abuse. Well, it's not!'' As Lucy noticed how carefree he looked, she became so irritated that snapping at him was all she could think of to do. Was there any other way to get through to him? "And if you don't come home early tonight, and keep all the promises you made to me about—''

"Don't nag, honey.'' He dropped a kiss on her nose and left the room to head downstairs.

Lucy's fists balled as she struggled to keep her voice from becoming as shrill as a fishwife's. "What about breakfast?'' she managed to ask in a reasonably controlled manner.

His raspy voice floated to her from the hallway. "No time, Cin. I'll see you tonight.''

Despite the auspicious beginning to his day, Heath's good mood disappeared an hour after he walked into his office. He sat down at his desk to read. A minor headache that he hadn't been aware of before blossomed into a full-fledged, skull-cracking throbbing. A headache that seemed to be connected to every bone in his body, right down to his heels. He ignored it and concentrated on the words in front of him until they shifted back and forth across the page. Doggedly he worked until it was almost noon, and Damon's familiar knock sounded at the door. With every rap on the door, there was a corresponding vibration in Heath's head.

"You don't have to hammer,'' he said, scowling, and Damon entered the office with a mock display of timidity.

"Excuse me. I can see that you aren't eager

for interruptions this morning. I just wanted to check with you on the ideas for the editorial.''

"I can't remember finding any problems with it . . . it was . . .'' Heath paused and rubbed his eyes. "What the hell was it about . . . Hiram Revels?''

"No. That was yesterday.'' Damon regarded him with those cool, curious black eyes, causing Heath to feel an inexplicable surge of annoyance. "This is about the Cuban Rebellion,'' Damon continued more slowly, "praising Secretary Fish for keeping the president from proclaiming the Cubans belligerents. And I thought we'd include a paragraph about the bastards who are running Spain. That should excite a certain amount of sympathy for the Cubans.''

"Good. Good. Go with it.''

"Alright.'' Damon paused before leaving, his voice becoming quiet. "Wife managed to keep you home last night?''

"Obviously,'' Heath replied hoarsely.

"Good for her. You haven't given yourself much of a breather lately. Don't worry, you didn't miss much at the AP supper. I'm capable of handling things, you know. If you'll just loosen the reins, I can take up the slack.''

Heath looked up as if he hadn't heard him correctly. The brightness of fever had lent a shining heat to his eyes, making them such a startling, unholy shade of blue that Damon froze with a sharply indrawn breath.

"God almighty.'' For someone as consistently unruffled as Damon, the soft exclamation was the equivalent of another man's shout of alarm. "You're not well. I'll have someone take you home in the hack.''

"Don't be a fool. I just need some . . . water.'' Heath let his head fall to his arms, slumping on the desk.

''He's calling me a fool,'' Damon muttered. ''Wonderful.'' He left the small office and returned in less than five minutes. As Heath rested his cheek on the cool surface of the desk and concentrated on regaining his strength, he would have sworn on a stack of Bibles that at least an hour had passed. ''The hack's right outside,'' Damon said. ''It will probably take two or three of us to get you out of here, so I'll—''

''I walk out alone,'' Heath said, lifting his head and staring at Damon with eerily blue eyes.

''You need help.''

''Not . . . in front of them.''

Damon knew that Heath was referring to the staff of the *Examiner*. Heath didn't want to appear less than invincible in front of them. Damon was tempted to argue, correctly deducing that Heath's resistance would crumble if he prolonged the debate a little longer. It would be foolhardy to let him walk out on his own. But Damon was beginning to understand the nature of a Southerner's pride, and he had a strange admiration for the gallant foolishness of it. He also knew that Heath would forever bear a grudge towards him if he didn't accede to this particular demand.

''Alright. You can try to make it out of here without help,'' Damon said reluctantly. ''But I'm walking beside you, in case you fall. And if you fall on me, you'll do me significant damage, in which case I'll sue you up to your ears.''

Heath muttered something uncomplimentary about Yankees and stood up in one fluid move, grasping the edge of the desk as the room swayed around him.

''Stubborn Reb,'' Damon couldn't keep from whispering. ''What have you done to yourself?''

* * *

Alerted by the imperious pounding of a fist on the door, Lucy rushed to the front hallway just as Sowers received the caller. "Heath!" she cried, sick with panic as she saw her husband leaning heavily against the doorframe, his face pale underneath the tan of his skin. Damon was on his other side, holding him up by an arm.

"I'm fine," Heath croaked.

"He's ill," Damon said shortly, motioning to the butler to help him move Heath inside the house. "I've sent for the physician that has attended my family for years. He ought to be here in a few minutes."

"I just need to rest—"

"Damned Southerners," Damon said. "They never know when to surrender." Though the statement was uttered in his typically cool manner, there was something almost like rough affection underlining his voice.

It took the three of them to get Heath up to the bedroom and onto the bed, and then Sowers went downstairs to wait for the physician. Normally Lucy would have gone crimson with embarrassment at the thought of partially undressing her husband in someone else's presence, but she stripped off his coat and pulled off his shoes without hesitation, barely aware of Damon's watchful ebony gaze. Heath was shivering. Anxiously Lucy murmured to him and pulled the covers up to his neck, her hands smoothing repeatedly over the outline of his shoulders.

"Mrs. Rayne?"

She recognized Bess's voice and replied without looking up. "Bring quilts."

"What about hot bricks wrapped in flannel—"

"Yes. Yes, but hurry," Lucy said, biting her

lip. The maid left the room and flew downstairs, and Heath turned his cheek into the palm of Lucy's hand, closing his eyes and falling asleep with dreadful ease. She felt like weeping. His skin was burning. How could he possibly be shaking with cold? She glanced at Damon; her hazel eyes were dark with guilt and misery. "He's been working too hard," she whispered. "I should have stopped him."

"You couldn't have," Damon said quietly. "We all tried. But there's a demon riding on his back—there has been for a long time. You couldn't have stopped him."

Startled, Lucy gave him a searching stare. What did he mean? Had Heath confided something to Damon that he had not told her? Or was Damon merely guessing at some undisclosed reason for Heath's relentless labor? She was never to find out the answer, because the physician arrived before Damon could reply.

No matter how kindly and trustworthy they might appear, doctors always frightened Lucy. Their very presence was an indication that something was seriously wrong. They always seemed to be needlessly callous, and in Lucy's mind, the fact that they had looked so often on the face of pain and death set them apart from ordinary people. Dr. Evans, the man Damon had sent for, was more bearable than most. He had an appropriately grandfatherly manner, and he seemed to understand Lucy's fears, assuring her that there was nothing wrong with Heath except a fever and exhaustion. Tonics and undisturbed rest were prescribed, and then the elderly doctor left with encouraging promptness. Lucy walked with him to the front door and saw him out.

"How is he?" came Damon's voice from behind her, and she turned to find that he had been waiting in the parlor.

"Much better than I had feared," she replied slowly. "He just needs rest. I can't tell you how relieved I am, and how grateful to you for—"

"It was nothing."

Lucy was undeceived by his indifferent tone of voice. Damon might try to hide his feelings, but she had witnessed his concern as they had brought Heath upstairs, and she had been aware of his gentleness with her. "I am grateful," she repeated, wanting to say more but fearing the possibility of embarrassing him.

"I must be getting back to the paper."

"Could I offer you something to eat or drink before you leave?" she asked, realizing that he had missed his lunch hour. "Some tea?"

"Thank you, but no. There are many things I have to do."

"That sounds like something my husband would say."

Her remark drew a smile out of Damon. "His fondness for overwork must be contagious."

She chuckled ruefully. "Then be careful. We don't want you to be ill, too."

"No." The dark smile in his eyes turned bittersweet as he looked down at her. "Please tell your husband something for me, Mrs. Rayne. Tell him not to worry about the *Examiner*. I'll keep everything in order for him."

"I know that he trusts you to take care of everything."

"And you?" Damon's expression hardened with self-mockery as soon as the question had left his lips. Lucy wasn't certain why he had asked, and she had the feeling that he wasn't certain, either.

"I also trust you," she said softly. "Excuse me. I must go up to Heath. Sowers will see you out."

Curious and confused, Lucy went upstairs without looking back at him. Her instincts told her that she had nothing to fear from Damon Redmond, but he treated her with such careful politeness, as if he were afraid she might discover a jealously guarded secret. He did not seem to want her gratitude, yet he had been here today like an unobtrusive shadow, taking care of everything and staying until he was certain that he was no longer needed.

She slept lightly that night, sensitive to Heath's every movement, waking several times to coax him to swallow more tonic, and tucking the quilts more tightly around him as he shivered with cold. Weary from anxiety and lack of sleep, she allowed herself to take a short nap as morning drew near. She woke up to the horrifying discovery that the sheets were clammy and drenched with perspiration, and that Heath's hair was wet from the roots to the ends. Her gown clung to her damply, infused with the coolness of early morning.

"Heath?" She pulled the covers up around him, trying to keep him warm until the bedding could be changed. His head moved on the pillow, and his thick lashes lifted to reveal a bright, slitted gaze.

"No, don't," he muttered, making an effort to push away the blankets. "Hot . . . it's hot . . ."

"I know it is," she said gently, placing her hand on his forehead. His skin seemed to radiate the heat of a coal. "Be still . . . *please* be still. For me." He said something indistinct and closed his eyes, turning his face away from her.

Fortunately Bess, having once been married, was not squeamish about personal matters. She had an invaluable combination of efficiency and pragmatism. Lucy was grateful for her help in seeing to Heath's comfort and changing the sheets to clean, dry ones. "The doctor said this would only last a day or two," she said to the maid as they walked with armloads of fresh linen into the room.

"That's good," Bess replied, looking doubtfully at the still figure on the bed. Heath's earlier restlessness had vanished with startling speed. Now he slept as if he had been knocked unconscious.

"Did you ever have to nurse your husband through something like this?" Lucy asked, pale and upset, and somehow terribly calm.

"Yes, Mrs. Rayne."

"I suppose the fever is always this bad on the second day?"

"Not always." As their eyes met, Lucy read the truth on the maid's face, that Heath's fever was worse than any Bess had seen before.

"I . . . I think we'll try to tempt him with a little soup later on. One with a very clear broth," Lucy said slowly, ignoring the inner voice that suggested the doctor had been wrong and Heath was seriously ill. No, he would be sick for a day or two, and then he would start to get better.

But the next day the fever had not abated. It was worse than before, and Heath was no longer coherent. Caught in an unceasing delirium, he was drenched with sweat one moment, shaking with chills the next, and Lucy endlessly repeated the cycle of sponging him down, changing the sheets and giving him medicine. She sent for Dr. Evans again, who stayed much longer this time than the first. He wore a grave expression as he led Lucy away from the bedside and spoke to her quietly.

"If it doesn't break soon, we'll have to pack him in ice. It's dangerous for his temperature to be this high."

They draped the mattress with vulcanized waterproof cloth, and packed snow and ice around him. But nothing they tried could break the fever.

Lucy sat alone with Heath in a darkened room, staring at a stranger whose mind wandered aimlessly in a delirium, whose lips formed names she did not recognize, who spoke with a touch of madness in his voice. This man who suffered and shivered so violently was not Heath, her golden-haired, laughing-eyed husband. Only during small fractions of time was he recognizable to her, and those moments were painfully few and far between. She spoke to him and he did not hear her. He asked questions but did not seem to understand the answers. He seemed to have gone back to a time when he had not known her, and it hurt to realize that he never uttered her name.

Damon had sent over one of the women in the Redmonds' employ to help Lucy nurse Heath. Lucy rarely left the bedside, however: she was unwilling to leave him long in the company of a stranger. She had to be bullied into eating and sleeping, but how could she sleep knowing that hour by hour her husband was slipping away from her?

Often he seemed to think that he was back at the prison camp on Governor's Island during the war. The first time it happened, Lucy was in the middle of wringing out a cloth for his forehead. She looked down and saw him staring at her, his eyes glazed. Her heart jumped, because it seemed that he recognized her.

"Water," he whispered. She slipped a trembling hand behind his head, bringing a cup to his lips. Heath drank thirstily and made a sound of disgust, choking as if she had given him poison. "We deserve more than . . . this filth," he gasped. "No matter what side . . . we're not . . . animals." Dazedly she took the cup away and backed away from the hatred in his voice. Heath shuddered uncontrollably. "No blankets . . . can't you see . . . these m-men are dying. Cold-assed Yankee . . . you t-take the best of our food, and . . . sell it to line your own pockets . . . leave us only f-fat and gristle . . ."

He thought she was a Union prison guard.

"Paper . . . ," he breathed. "Paper."

"What about the paper?" she asked, thinking that he meant the *Examiner.*

"More. Rations for it. I'll . . . bargain."

He was asking for paper to write on. To keep the record he had written during the war. As he continued to rant, Lucy started to sob openly. "Heath," she said, tears streaming down her face, "it's me . . . it's Lucy. I love you. Don't you see me? Don't you know me?"

The sound of her crying reached his ears, and he quieted for several seconds, confused, turning restlessly. "Don't," he said. "Don't cry."

"I can't help it—"

"Please, Raine. I'll do anything for you. Don't go. Raine . . . you know how I need you. Don't do it . . ."

Lucy blanched, feeling as if she had been kicked in the stomach. Raine again. The pain in Heath's voice cut deeply into her heart. She fumbled for a dry rag and mopped her face, pressing the cloth into the corners of her eyes to absorb her tears.

"Mama, I'm seventeen . . . ," he muttered softly. "I'm a man now. I know what you think . . . Mama . . . but I love her." Suddenly there was the dry ghost of his laugh. "She's so beautiful. You can't argue against that . . . can you . . ."

Lucy's back ached as she bent over him and spread a wet cloth over his hot forehead.

"Raine . . ." He swiped off the cloth and gripped her wrist. "Damn you. You don't love him . . . oh, *God* . . ." His fingers tightened until she flinched and twisted her wrist away, rubbing it to ease the ache. Heath's whole body jumped, and he cried out, his hand lifting slowly to his temple. "I didn't come here to hurt you. I would never hurt you."

Dear God, Lucy thought dazedly, *help me to bear this*.

"Mrs. Rayne, Mr. Redmond is here to see you."

Lucy paused in the middle of splashing her face with water and reached for a towel. The nurse Damon had sent over had just taken over the vigil at Heath's side.

"I should change my dress," Lucy murmured, looking down at herself. She was sticky and tired, and she could feel the straggles of hair that clung to her neck and face.

"He said that he only intends to pay a quick call," Bess said. "About the newspaper."

"Then I suppose there's no time to change. Find a comb for me, quickly."

Numbly Lucy made an effort to tidy her hair and make herself more presentable; then, she walked downstairs to the parlor. Damon stood up as soon as she entered the room. He was dressed in a crisp, dark suit, and he was polished and well-groomed. Lucy felt a strange sense of comfort in the mere sight of him. He was so sane and levelheaded that his presence seemed to diminish the nightmarish aura that hung over the house. His face registered no shock or dismay at her appearance, only calmness.

"I'm sorry to disturb you."

She nodded jerkily.

"Is there any change?" he asked quietly.

"No. No change."

"You need someone from your family to be with you. Should I send for someone?"

"There's no one but my father. And he wouldn't be able to help. He would only . . . feel uncomfortable, and I . . . don't want to see him right now." Lucy wondered if she should have phrased her refusal differently. Maybe it was a sin that she did not want her father with her, and in that case she shouldn't have admitted to Damon how she felt. She thought of Lucas, so content and absorbed in the business of running his general store, his silver-white head bent over his bookkeeping. Her father had never liked to deal with deep emotions, whether they were his or anyone else's. He had never known what to do when she cried. He had always liked the practical part of parenting the best, giving advice to her and occasionally lecturing, giving her pennies and letting her fish around in the candy jar when she had behaved well. He wouldn't know how to help her in a situation like this.

She cleared her throat awkwardly. "Bess mentioned something about the newspaper."

"Yes. There was an article about the State Bureau of Labor that Heath had brought home to look over. Would you have an idea of where he might have put it?"

"It would be in his desk. If you'll wait here, I'll see if I can find it."

"I would appreciate that."

The sight of Heath's desk in the library, with its neat stacks of paper, deftly slitted envelopes and haphazardly stacked reference books, caused Lucy to smile wistfully. The last time she had seen him sitting there, she had gone in to scold him for staying up so late, and he had interrupted her lecture by pulling her onto his lap and quieting her with a thorough kiss. She would give anything for one of his kisses right now. What wouldn't she do, for him to look at her and call her by name, knowing who she was?

Opening and shutting drawers, she looked for the article, glad of the small task and the opportunity it gave her to think about something besides her frustration and weariness. In the second drawer on the right side was a stack of tiny envelopes, tied with a string and wedged in the back corner. The top one was addressed to Heath in a curling feminine script.

Feeling guilty, for she had never gone through his desk, Lucy stared at the letters. The right thing to do would be to ignore the packet and pretend that she had never seen it. She flushed and then went white, casting a furtive glance around the room before she picked up the tempting stack of letters and slipped it into the pocket of her dress. She would just look through them quickly, just to find out who had written them. *I'm his wife,* she told herself. *I have the right to know about these. There should be no secrets between us. And he certainly knows everything about me!* Nevertheless, her conscience bothered her as she closed the drawer and resumed her search for the article. When she found it, she went back to the parlor and gave it to Damon, terribly aware of the bulge of letters in her pocket.

"Thank you," Damon said, looking at her differently from before. Did he see the guilt on her face? Could he tell that she had discovered something in Heath's desk? Perhaps his expression wasn't different from before. It could have been that she was just imagining things. "If there is anything you need or anything I can do," he said, "please ask."

"I will," Lucy replied, suddenly impatient to have him out of the house. It was shameless. But now that she had done something wrong, the least she was entitled to was the knowledge of what she had discovered. She could hardly wait to be alone and examine the letters in private.

When Damon had left and Lucy was alone, she pulled the curtain across the doorway of the parlor and sat down in a plump upholstered chair. Resting her head against the back of it, she sighed and closed her eyes for a second to ease their dry burning. She could hardly believe what she was doing. While her husband was helpless and ill upstairs, she was down here going through his private correspondence. *I shouldn't . . . I shouldn't. But I have to know.* Untying the string rapidly, she began to flip through the envelopes. All written by the same hand. All written by the same woman. Was it Raine?

No. Her shoulders sagged with relief as she pulled out the top letter and looked at the name at the bottom. Amy. That was the name of Heath's half-sister. The lines slanted up and down, penned in a careful, childish script that betrayed the writer's youth. The first letter was dated more than a year ago, in June 1868. As Lucy scanned it, she discovered it was filled with Amy's remarks and observations about the condition of the Price plantation and its residents. The name Clay—Heath's half-brother—was mentioned most often, and there was a brief reference to Raine, but nothing that described who Raine was. Impatiently Lucy slid the letter back into the envelope and reached for the next. She read letter after letter, her eyes lingering on certain phrases and sentences that jumped out at her.

Today Mother said that we couldn't mention your name anymore. But Raine and I still talk about you in secret. Raine says she misses you, even after what happened between you.

Clay's back hurts him a lot. He is sickly.

Mother is angry all the time. She says she should never have left England to marry Daddy. Now that he is gone, she wants to move back there. Poor Clay knows that she has to stay here because of him. Dr. Collins said Clay has to live where it's warm.

Raine showed me the first flower you ever gave her. She pressed it in her Bible . . .

Raine and Clay had another fight . . .

I like Raine sometimes, but she gets angry so quick. She wants nothing to do with Clay now. I think Mother is right about one thing. Raine's not a good wife to him.

Lucy's breath stopped as she reread the last sentence. Raine was Clay's wife? Then she must have married him knowing that Heath loved her. But why would she have chosen Clay over Heath? For the plantation? For money? Perhaps because Heath was illegitimate. Yes, that must have been the reason.

I told Clay and Raine about your letter. Clay laughed when he found out you're married to a Yankee woman. He said it was what you deserve. Raine was upset for a while, then she got mad. I think she still loves you. Why did you marry a Yankee woman? Does she have lots of money? There are lots of girls here who need husbands. I think you'd have been better off with one of them.

* * *

Raine doesn't share a room with Clay any-more. She sleeps in the room you used whenever you came to visit.

I think Clay is dying . . .

Lucy's absorbed silence was broken by the sound of Bess's voice.

"Mrs. Rayne?"

"What is it?" Lucy asked, instantly ashamed to hear how sharp her voice was. But she felt like a thief who had been caught in the middle of a robbery, and irritation was the only way she could mask her guilt.

"Mr. Rayne is calling for you."

Lucy shot up immediately. The letters fell from her lap to the floor in a rustling cascade. She threw them a harried glance.

"I'll pick them up," Bess said.

"No. No, I'll do it later. Leave them there, please." Pressing trembling fingertips to her mouth, Lucy hesitated, her eyes flickering to the staircase. Abruptly she was afraid. Why was he calling for her now? Was God giving her one more chance to hear Heath speak her name before—wildly she shook off the thought.

Bess's expectant gaze spurred her into action. Lucy gritted her teeth, taking one step forward, and then another, and she found as she made her way up the steps that she had left her fear behind. A calm sort of blankness settled over her. Her heart had stopped in midbeat, suspended in the middle of her chest like a frozen pendulum.

The nurse, her expression solemn and com-passionate, met Lucy at the bedroom door. "It's worse now," she said.

"I'll see to him. Leave us alone, please."

Heath stirred faintly and moaned as she approached the bed. "Lucy . . . I want Lucy . . ."

Tenderly she laid her palm against his bristled cheek. "I'm here."

But he didn't seem to know her touch, and he kept repeating her name. Lucy bent down low and spoke to him quietly, interrupting his litany with endearments and soothing words until he quieted. She kept her hand on his face, leaning over him until the muscles in her neck and back were screaming in protest. She was tired of everything, of running on nerves and being drained of hope. She was tired of being alone, and she wanted her husband back, and she was sick of enduring the ceaseless fear that she would never have him back.

Gradually Lucy lowered her head until it was cradled in her other arm. She closed her eyes to face a darkness splotched with multicolored lights. Remnants of the past floated by her as she slept and dreamed . . . Heath, laughing at her transparent wiles . . . making love to her . . . burying his head in her lap and uttering a drunken confession . . . smiling at her in the glow of candlelight . . . holding her when she cried. His arms seemed to fade away from her, and she fought to stay near him, but as he drifted deeper into the darkness she couldn't find him. Alone, she whirled around in the blackness, sifting through the shadows in a futile effort to touch him. But he was gone. She had lost him. And she had never told him that she loved him . . .

Lucy opened her eyes with a gasp, her heart pounding. A nightmare. Blinking, she raised her head from her arm and looked at Heath. His lashes lay like dark fans on his pale skin. Reflexively, her hand curved more firmly against the side of his face. The pulse underneath his jaw beat steadily under her thumb. His skin felt cool.

Was she still dreaming? Was the fever really gone? She was shaking all over, unable to believe what was before her eyes. Checking him again, Lucy felt his quiet pulse, and the softness of breath against her fingertips, and the miraculous disappearance of the fever. She forgot her weariness and aching muscles as joy rushed through her. He was hers again.

Chapter Eleven

"**H**EATH, WHAT ARE you doing?" Lucy stopped short in the middle of the bedroom. She had gone to check on him as soon as she got home. It was a shock to see him out of bed and almost fully dressed for the first time in weeks. He turned to her as he buttoned his cuffs, casting a sardonic glance at her.

"Looks like I'm putting my clothes on, doesn't it?"

"You're not supposed to be out of bed."

"I've been in that bed for two weeks. I've swallowed bottles of tonic, slept more than fourteen hours a day, and eaten every spoonful of the sickroom swill that's been put before me. I think I deserve a few hours out of bed."

Their eyes met, his glinting with cool determination, hers soft with cautious entreaty. Lucy saw that no amount of chiding, pleading, or persuasion would have any effect on him, and she lifted her hands in a gesture of helplessness.

"You always choose to test your limits. But this time it's too soon—"

"This time the choice isn't mine. I can't play the invalid any longer. There are problems at the paper."

"Mr. Redmond can take care of—"

"Damon came to visit yesterday while you were at your club meeting. He's been having some difficulties lately . . ." Heath's mouth twisted with self-disgust as he added, "mainly because he's had to pull my weight as well as his. He'll be here again today, for some suggestions on how he should work things out until I'm back."

"I didn't know he had visited yesterday," she said, suddenly feeling the sting of exclusion.

"You didn't have to," Heath said softly.

She drew in a quiet, short breath of air. "Oh," she said, and laughed shakily, trying to cover up the stab of hurt his words had caused. "You mean it's your business. I didn't mean to pry . . . You must feel as if I've been trying to keep you under my thumb."

"I didn't say that."

But they both knew it was true. Slowly Lucy walked to the dressing table and sat down on the pretense of straightening her hair. Her eyebrows were nearly drawn together by the pucker that had formed between them. *He must be nearly wild with his lack of freedom, of privacy. But could I have done anything differently the last few weeks? Could I have kept myself from being intrusive, worried, nagging?* Only if she had loved him less. She had nearly lost him, and that had made her afraid to leave him alone for very long. It made her want to grab each moment she could with him, know his every thought, keep him all to herself. Unfettered, her possessiveness might someday turn her into a jealous shrew. She had to give him room, or risk turning him away from her.

Heath had once told her that the demands she made would be too overwhelming for some people to handle. She loved strongly. She needed strongly. Lucy couldn't deny that it would be a long time before she felt secure enough to be comfortable with their relationship as it was. Her instinct was to take every opportunity she had to reinforce her hold over Heath, constantly searching for ways to strengthen their bond, when she should merely relax and allow him the freedom he needed.

She turned and looked at Heath, forcing herself to smile lightly. "Should I have another place set for dinner?"

He returned her smile, though it didn't reach his eyes. "Please do."

After he left the room, Lucy continued staring at the spot where he had stood. Heath Rayne, the Northeastern newspaper tycoon, looked and sounded very different from the man she had married. He was less playful now, more authoritative. The carefree air had been replaced by a formidable aura of power and responsibility. Even the sunny gold of his hair had darkened in the winter months to ash brown, making him look older than his twenty-seven years. The air of mystery around him had intensified. He was more compelling, more baffling, less accessible than ever.

Lucy sighed in frustration, acknowledging for the first time that there were differences in him, both outward and inward, that she would have to start accepting. Why had no one told her that men changed after courtship was over and the marriage had begun?

She had expected that Heath would have enjoyed being fussed over and cosseted while he recovered from his illness. The fact that her assumption was completely wrong served to prove once again how little she knew him. He had barely tolerated her coddling and her sympathy. There were times that she had to touch him or press a kiss to his cheek, just to reassure herself that he was alright, but he was outwardly unresponsive to her gestures of affection. Pale, quiet, and controlled, he had accepted his confinement to the bed with a surprising lack of argument, until now.

In response to Lucy's private questions, Dr. Evans had said that Heath's behavior was nothing out of the ordinary, and that it would take him several weeks to recover the health he had enjoyed before the illness. However, Lucy felt certain that the changes she saw in Heath, his enigmatic moods, his uncustomary quietness, were only partly a result of his physical condition. The other cause was something far more troubling. It seemed that he had come to some realization during his struggle with the fever, some self-recognition that bothered him exceedingly. He did not speak of it to her. Indeed, he seemed at times to be guarding against the possibility of mentioning it.

Raine. Though neither of them had ever mentioned her name to the other, her name hung in the silence between them, preventing the free exchanges they had once shared. Lucy didn't know if Heath remembered anything about the delirium in which he had been trapped for so long. Did he know that he had mentioned Raine so often? Did he even suspect it of himself?

The suspicions that plagued Lucy were not eased by his apparent lack of interest in her. They occupied separate rooms, slept in separate beds each night, and though the time was long past when they could have resumed their former habit of sleeping together, Heath gave no indication that he would prefer a change in the current arrangements. All of the half-formed plans in Lucy's mind for casually moving back into the master bedroom had dissolved over the past several days. She had let it go on for too long; now it would be difficult and awkward to return to Heath's bed. Was there truly any need for her to have to seduce her way into the position that was already rightfully

hers? Surely not. But why, then, was she half-afraid
that she would be refused? She wasn't certain. It was
the coward's way out, to wait until he mentioned
something about wanting her again, but her confidence
was bruised, and she didn't want to risk greater damage.

Damon visited the house often to consult with
Heath about the *Examiner*. If he noticed that things
were not right between Lucy and Heath, he didn't say
a word. His concern was the newspaper, and currently
that took precedence over everything else. Without
Heath to keep them directed and motivated, the employees of the paper tended to be fractious and less
careful about their work. Damon was a hard taskmas-
ter, demanding, sarcastic, and impatient with others'
weaknesses. He freely admitted that he didn't have
Heath's patience, nor his ability to play reporters off
one another in order to extract their best efforts.

It was with great relief that everyone welcomed Heath back to the offices of the *Examiner*. As
his familiar footsteps sounded on the floor of the editorial room, there was a chorus of greetings and a
deluge of questions, which he fended off with raised
hands and a familiar, confident grin.

"In my office. I'll talk to you one at a time.
Starting with the *A's* and through to the *Z's* . . . that
is, if anyone around here has learned how to alpha-
betize yet."

Damon raised a dark eyebrow as Heath passed
by his desk. "I had expected a more ceremonious return."

Heath stopped and looked down at him, his
smile broadening marginally. "You think I should have
made a speech?"

"Hardly. I'm just glad you decided to get your

indolent self out of bed and get back to the business of publishing a newspaper. You haven't exactly earned your keep the last few weeks.''

"After reading yesterday's issue and seeing how you've been handling things in my absence, I decided it was time to come back.''

"You think you could have improved upon yesterday's issue?'' Damon inquired, with a condescending expression that would have made the rest of the Redmond clan proud.

"I damn well could have. I suffered from eye strain after trying to find a mention of the Cincinnati Red Stockings anywhere in the paper.''

"I couldn't see anything newsworthy in the fact that some ball club is going professional—''

"And going on an eight-month tour from New York to the West Coast. I read all about it in the *Journal—they're* starting a weekly baseball column.''

"Baseball's going nowhere.''

"The hell it is. Baseball's *American*. I'm going to have Bartlett write a page-one feature on the Red Stockings.''

"Next week it'll be roller skating,'' Damon grumbled.

"No matter what your highbrow opinions are, people like to read about sports.''

"Yet another theory on what people like to read. If you're going to write about sports, let's do something on cricket. The game of gentlemen.''

Heath grimaced in mock outrage. "Typical. Typical Bostonian for you. I don't know how you kept the paper going without me.''

"If you want the truth, I enjoyed the peace and quiet while you were gone,'' Damon informed him, and they scowled at each other, delighted that things were back to normal. The rest of the editorial room fairly crackled with new energy. Rayne and Red-mond—there was nothing like working for the pair of them. Separately, either one of them would have taken the paper to an undesirable extreme. Without Damon's influence, Heath would have been inclined to leap into creative disasters, and without Heath, Damon would have made it an unimaginative washout. But together, they ran a paper like no one else on Newspaper Row, with daring innovative leaps and plenty of crispness and starch.

Exhausted by a long day and a drawn-out current events discussion, Lucy was unusually quiet during dinner. Heath, in turn, was preoccupied with matters concerning the *Examiner*. The result was a short and businesslike meal, after which Lucy retired to the parlor to read and Heath went to the library to work.

When the lacquered brass clock on the mantel struck twelve, Heath finally set his pen down and organized the materials on top of his desk. Passing the doorway of the parlor, he caught a glimpse of Lucy's wine-colored dress. On impulse, he ducked his head in to check on her. A smile touched his mouth as he saw that she had fallen asleep, curled up on the small sofa. Her magazine had fallen to the floor, while her hands were lax in her lap. She looked young and very vulnerable in sleep. He walked over to her, his smile disappearing as he stared at her.

It had been a long time since he had held her. Suddenly Heath wanted her so badly he could taste it, wanted to crush her in his arms. He knew she hadn't understood why he had felt the need to put the distance between them for the last several weeks. Because of his own damnable pride, he hadn't wanted to be dependent on her, and the fact that she had dominated

his every waking moment during his illness had been
hard to swallow. In order to keep from using her as a
target for his frustration, he had drawn away from her.
Perhaps that had hurt her, but it had been kinder than
subjecting her to his abuse.

His blue eyes were shadowed with regret as he
stood over her. His fingers rifled absently through the
stray locks of hair that had fallen from her chignon. It
testified of her strength, that during the last weeks she
had been able to see to his needs as well as her own.
And he liked her newfound assertiveness, though many
men would call him insane for encouraging it. However, there were times when he had doubts about the
responsibilities he had forced her to accept. Had he
been right to take away the cotton wool she had been
wrapped in all her life? Was she truly happier with
things as they were instead of as they might have been?

"Lucy, girl . . . I haven't made things easy
for you, have I?"

Slumbering deeply, she did not hear him.
Heath smiled ruefully, bending down and sliding his
arms under her shoulders and the backs of her knees.
Her body was relaxed and incredibly warm. She made
a grumbling sound of awakening and blinked a few
times.

"S'alright, Cin . . . I'm taking you upstairs."
Only half-comprehending what he had said, she laid
her head on his shoulder and went back to sleep, tucking her face against his neck with a tired sigh. Heath
carried her upstairs and into the bedroom, enduring
her mumbling complaints with gentle indulgence as he
stood her on her feet and unfastened her dress. Lucy
hung her head and rubbed her eyes with her knuckles,
yawning. Her childish gesture wrung Heath's heart,
quelling the biting immediacy of his desire.

They had the rest of their lives. He could wait

one more night for her. After unfastening her corset
and tossing the unholy contraption to the floor, he
lifted her meagerly clad body into his arms and settled
her on the bed, smiling as she burrowed under the
covers and went still.

    And his eyes did not move from her as he un-
dressed, for the sight of her in his bed was so natural
and fitting that he called himself a fool for not having
brought her back here sooner. Naked, he slipped into
bed beside her and pulled her close, one hand riding
low on her abdomen and the other buried beneath the
pillow on which her head lay. The warmth of their
bodies mingled beneath the covers, causing him to sigh
in supreme comfort; a man should get married for this
if nothing else. Sleeping with the same woman every
night, becoming familiar with her scent, her body, the
pattern of her breathing, was addictive. He, who had
never been inclined to form habits before, was devel-
oping quite a number of them, and all of them were
centered around Lucy.

    He had become used to her meeting him at the
front door when he came home from the newspaper,
and on the occasions when she wasn't there, he was
both annoyed and disconcerted, as if some important
task had been neglected. He liked the routines she had
established around the house, the apple pie they had
for dessert every Sunday, the candles that were always
lit for dinner, the patient way she listened when he
unburdened himself about the paper and the news. He
liked to tease her about being a ''manners-mender.''
Her concern for etiquette was a sterling New England
trait that she would never lose. Someday they would
raise children here, and he would enjoy watching as
she corrected their language and taught them how to
sit straight in their chairs. And he in turn would go
behind her back to give his daughters extra money for

hair ribbons and fripperies, and teach his boys how to cuss like a Southerner.

Holding her closer, he buried his face in the fragrant softness of her hair. Sweet Lucy, prim, practical, and passionate, still so unaware of how tempting she was, and how much he needed her. His hand moved possessively over her body, and he found reassurance in the familiar feel of her.

Lucy rolled over and stretched, wriggling in the thrall of contentment that had begun the moment she had discovered where she was. She had only vague memories of the night before, of falling asleep downstairs, and Heath carrying her up here. If only he hadn't left this morning before she had woken up! But she was *here*, back in the right bed, with the recollection of her husband's tenderness fresh in her memory. She had no doubt that tonight their physical relationship would begin again. Flushing, she turned on her stomach and smiled into the pillow, imagining the things they would do to make up for the long period of abstinence. She wanted to do everything, *everything* with him. The only question was what they would begin with. Shameless thoughts. She lay there for several minutes more, breathing in the masculine scent of his pillow, wishing that tonight were already here.

The first half of her day went by at a leisurely pace. She had an odd feeling, however, that something out of the ordinary was going to happen, and the sense of anticipation—almost like dread—would not leave her, even though it had no rational basis. Why was it that everything seemed a little bit different today? Lucy's uneasiness was justified a little after noon, when Bess came rushing into the parlor to tell her that Heath had just set foot on the front steps. She set down her needlework and flew to the door, knowing that

Heath would not be home at this hour unless some kind of emergency had arisen.

"Cin, I just got a telegram at the office," he said without preamble. "I don't have much time to explain things . . . I have to leave in a few minutes."

"Leave? Leave for where?"

"Virginia." He cast a harried glance around the hallway and took her arm, urging her upstairs. "Let's go to the bedroom—you can help me pack while we talk."

"Why? What's happened?" Lucy asked breathlessly, fighting to keep up with his long strides as they went up the steps.

"Things are in a godawful mess down there. My half-brother Clay . . . well, yesterday he finally . . . he's gone."

"Oh, Heath . . . I'm sorry. When is the funeral going to be held?"

"It's already been held this morning."

"So quickly? That's hardly enough time to make the proper arrangements."

"I imagine they didn't arrange much of a ceremony," Heath said darkly, letting go of her arm as they went into the bedroom. "Dammit, where do we keep the brown traveling bag?"

Lucy hurried to the door and called to Bess. "Bess, would you find the brown leather bag with Mr. Rayne's initials on it? It's under the stairs with the trunks." She turned to Heath. "No, don't fold your shirts that way—they'll be all wrinkled. Let me. And please stop swearing. Goodness, how many shirts are you taking? You aren't planning on staying there for very long, are you?"

"I don't know how long," Heath replied, sounding grim as he sorted through his neckties. "The telegram was from my half-sister Amy. It seems that

Victoria, my stepmother, has decided to dump everything in her lap and leave for England immediately.''

"The day after her son dies? Leaving without
her daughter? That hardly sounds rational.''

"Exactly. There you have Victoria, in a nut-
shell. She's never been rational. And she never has
given a d . . . she never has cared anything about anyone, even her own daughter. The only one she ever
cared about was Clay, and now that he's gone, there's
nothing to keep her here. Her family's in England, and
they'll probably take her in.'' His mouth twisted wryly.
"No need to worry about Victoria. She'll always land
on her feet. In the meanwhile, Amy's alone, with a
broken-down plantation to sell and a hundred decisions that need to be made.''

"Alone? What about Raine?''

Heath froze, and there was complete silence
in the room. He stared at her, his gaze penetrating and
sharp, as if he were trying to see past the guileless
hazel of her eyes. Bess bustled into the room, lugging
the brown suit bag with both hands.

"Put it down on the bed, please,'' Lucy said
very softly, meeting Heath's gaze without flinching,
knowing that he was trying to figure out how much
she might be aware of.

"What do you know about Raine?'' Heath
asked bluntly, when Bess had left the room. Apparently he didn't have the time for subtlety.

"You mentioned her in your sleep a time or
two.'' *How can you? How can you try to keep what
was between the two of you a secret from me?* she
wanted to scream at him, suddenly furious. *Why aren't
you being honest with me?* She could hardly believe
that was her voice she heard, so calm and mildly curious. "I gather she is your sister-in-law? Or is that
some deep, dark secret you don't want to disclose?''

"She is my sister-in-law," Heath replied curtly, redirecting his attention to the neckties.

"What about my question? Isn't she with Amy now?"

"Probably. Here, would you fold these trousers? Yes, Raine's with Amy, but most likely she'll go to live with whatever kin she has left in the country. So it's just Amy that we have to worry about."

"I didn't intend to worry about anyone but Amy," Lucy said coolly, aware as she looked down at the trousers and folded them neatly that Heath was giving her another long, searching look. "What do you intend to do? Sell the plantation and then . . . ?"

"She's young, Cin. And she's never had anything resembling a mother. Victoria was a worthless parent. I guess I could ask some of the Prices in Raleigh to take Amy in. But my father was the outcast of the family, and times being what they are, his daughter won't exactly be welcomed with open arms. Maybe I should find some school to put her in—"

"Down there?" Lucy asked, reluctantly experiencing a twinge of sympathy for Amy. Heath didn't know it, but she had read every one of Amy's letters, had come to know the girl through that careful, childish handwriting, and she felt pity for her. It would be frightening to be alone at such a young age. "But who will she spend the holidays with? Is there anyone for her in the South, or is she completely alone?"

"What's the alternative?" Heath asked, his face expressionless, and Lucy sighed, folding another pair of trousers, her forehead indented with vexation.

"You ask that as if you didn't know what the alternative is. You know perfectly well that it would be more practical to find a boarding school for her up here. Somewhere accessible, so that you could keep an eye on her. She's your sister—I won't offer any objection if you want to let her visit us during school vacations.''

It would be extra trouble and worry, and Lucy knew that she would have preferred not to have someone else around to intrude on her time with Heath. But how could she refuse to allow Amy a tiny corner of his life? Did Lucy have any right to stand in the way between the two of them? Of course not. And if she didn't give in to this gracefully, he might come to resent her unwillingness to be flexible as far as his half-sister was concerned.

"Why don't you bring her up here?" she said quietly, and she knew by the sudden glow in his eyes that that was what he had wanted.

"Thank you."

Lucy shrugged, looking away from him, glad that he had enough sensitivity to be matter-of-fact about her concession. At the moment she couldn't bear gratitude from him. Not when she was so frustrated and upset.

"I won't be gone more than a week, Cinda."

"I wouldn't mind going with you." Knowing that he would refuse her offer, she said the words more out of a wish to be difficult than a real desire to accompany him. But the words would have choked her if she had not let them out. Oh, why couldn't she be kind, gracious, and understanding? Why was she allowing herself to be angry with him instead of offering him comfort?

"It's bad enough with one of us going. You've got to stay here and keep everything running smoothly."

"What about the newspaper?"

"I hate to leave it." He groaned in frustration. "Damn, I hate this. But I'll have to rely on Damon to take care of it again."

"You'll need to take a night shirt," she said in a monotone, looking through the contents of the leather bag. "I know you don't like to wear anything when you're sleeping, but since you're traveling—"

"I don't know if I have any night shirts."

"You do," she said flatly. "One. Somewhere. I saw it once as I was looking for some handkerchiefs." Pausing, she added delicately, "I'm often surprised by the things I find around the house."

Silence. Lucy rearranged the contents of the leather bag with meticulous care, knowing that she was the target of a suspicious stare. Then she looked up and raised her eyebrows a fraction of an inch, in an expression of inquiry. The cat-and-mouse game was a novelty; they had never resorted to it before. Heath looked as though he were about ready to end her inexpert taunting with a few hard questions, but instead he reached into the chest of drawers and tossed a few pairs of socks to the bed.

"If you need anything while I'm gone," he said, "the Markhams are right down the street, and David owes me a favor or two. Go to them if you have any problems."

"Why not the Redmonds?"

"Damon's going to be busy enough with the paper."

"But before when you were ill, he told me that if I ever needed—"

"Don't," he interrupted sharply. "Don't argue. Don't bother Damon. And don't cross me on this."

Lucy was infuriated by his high-handed manner. Anger sustained her through the process of packing, the last-minute instructions he gave, through everything that had to be done up to the point of saying goodbye. And then, as the carriage waited outside and they both stood inside the front door, and the servants coughed uncomfortably and left the hallway, Lucy felt all of her anger disappear in an instant. She kept her eyes on the lapels of Heath's coat, miserably aware of the silence between them. She knew that she must break it, that he must not be allowed to leave with no words spoken between them.

"It's been a long time since you were in Virginia," she said stiffly.

"Three years."

"How do I know you won't want to stay there?" She spoke dryly, but there was a thread of real worry in her tone.

"Because they don't know how to make New England apple pie."

She smiled half-heartedly. "That's not a good reason."

"The real reason," he said huskily. "Because I made a choice when I married you, and I made sure it was what I wanted."

"So did I."

They both thought back on last night, and on what tonight might have brought, had they been able to spend it together.

"The timing on all of this could have been better," Heath remarked grimly.

"You never left me before." She was unable to look at him. "Not for this long."

"I wouldn't now, if I had a choice."

"Come back soon."

"Yes, ma'am." His hands curved around her shoulders, and he bent his head to kiss her. It had been intended as a light, affectionate kiss, but as her lips trembled beneath his, there was a low, soft sound from deep in his throat, and hungrily he enfolded her in his arms. Startled by the sudden blaze of heat between

them, she made a move to pull away, but he held her
more tightly, his mouth forcing hers open. Insidious
pleasure trickled through her, sweet and irresistible.
Her hands fluttered over the hard surface of his back
before resting on his shoulders, and her breasts pressed
against his chest as she strained closer. His lips moved
roughly on hers, a warm velvet friction that seemed to
last forever. She swallowed convulsively and took a
quick, abbreviated breath, and her lungs seemed to be
filled not with air, but fire. Her whole body was light
and hot, weightless in his arms, shaking with the need
to be closer to him. Even when he let her go, it seemed
that their bodies were joined with an invisible current;
she could feel its pull as he stepped back from her.

Heath muttered something in baffled frustration and left swiftly, closing the door with unnatural
quietness. Shivering, Lucy went to the window and
stared after him as the carriage headed down the street.

He was gone for nearly two weeks. During
that time, she didn't see Damon, though she received
a brief card expressing sympathy and the hope that she
would let him know if she needed anything. Lucy
didn't know why Heath had been so adamant about
wanting her to refrain from speaking with Damon.
Could it be that he was jealous? Surely he knew that
there was nothing between her and Damon except
friendship, but he had been so abrupt with her on the
matter that she couldn't help wondering.

Industriously Lucy made preparations for
Heath's return with Amy, seeing to it that the house
was cleaned thoroughly and extra rooms prepared so
that the girl would have a choice of where she wanted
to sleep. However, no matter how much work there
was to be done, Lucy still found herself daydreaming
wistfully and giving in to occasional depression.

Loneliness was a constant ache in her chest. Each day and night went by at a faltering pace, giving her ample time to reflect on the past month and all the things she might have done differently. It gave her the opportunity to come to certain conclusions about herself and her marriage. From now on, she would be more honest with Heath. She would tell him she loved him. There was no reason to wait for him to say the words, since he could probably go on for the next fifty years without needing to confess his love out loud.

He had to love her. They had shared too many firsts together. They had been too intimate with each other, both physically and emotionally, for him not to love her. Why, the morning he had left her, he had admitted that he didn't want to leave her! That and all the other signs pointed to the fact that his feelings must be as deep as hers. Lucy wanted to have the freedom to tell him how she felt about him, and when he returned from Virginia, she was going to change things.

Heath sent word that they would arrive in Boston around noon on Saturday, and Lucy spent the entire morning preparing herself. She was so nervous and excited that her hands were shaking, and Bess had to help her dress and arrange her hair. Her velveteen dress was a beautiful new shade of deep pink called Aurora, made with fancy scalloped sleeves and a tight-fitting basque. Her dark hair was neatly confined in shining braids that were twisted and pinned at the nape of her neck, and she smoothed back the wisps at her forehead and temples with cologne. Lucy pinched her cheeks until they were the same deep pink as her dress, and she walked back and forth to the mirror several times as she waited, too agitated to do any reading or needlework. Finally one of the maids, a girl who was barely out of her teens, knocked on the bedroom door, jumping back as Lucy flung it open.

"Are they here?"

"The carriage has just arrived, Mrs. Rayne."

"Then let's go downstairs. Remember to take Miss Price's coat first, then Mr. Rayne's."

Lucy could feel her heart thundering as she descended, and Sowers waited until she reached the last step before he opened the door. For the first few seconds, all she registered was a small flurry of skirts and capes, and then her attention was completely focused on Heath as he walked through the doorway.

"Cinda." He stopped as he looked at her, his mouth curving with a slow half-smile.

The time spent in the South seemed to have wrought miracles. Once again he was the dashing rascal she had remembered from the early months in Concord, with vitality in his step and laughter in his eyes. The sun had darkened his skin to copper and infused his hair with a sheen of light gold. Ah, she had forgotten how handsome he was. What was it about the South that had such a magical effect on him? The people? The sun, the climate?

"Welcome home," she managed to say.

"How have you been?" His accent was much heavier than before, making his voice smooth and drawling. She loved the sound of it. *I missed you,* his gaze seemed to tell her, and the silent message caused her pulse to rise in an uneven surge.

"I've been fine." She started to smile at him, when a nearby movement caught her eye, and she turned with words of welcome poised on her lips. There was a tall blond girl, slender, attractive, and unassuming. Amy. Her face was much softer than Heath's, but there were similarities in the shape of the eyes and mouth. She was looking at Lucy with shyness and uncertainty.

There was also another woman. Lucy knew immediately who she was.

But how could it be? How could it be?

Helpless fury, hurt, outrage—that would all come later. For now, Lucy was too stunned to feel anything. She could feel her face turn pale, clean, and stark as she succumbed to numbness. That was better than anger, and far better than fear. The less Raine could see on her face, the better.

"I apologize for the lack of advance warning," Heath said with studied casualness. "We had a last-minute addition to our entourage. Lucy, I would like you to meet Amy, my sister, and my sister-in-law, Mrs. Laraine Price."

"Amy . . . Mrs. Price . . . I'm pleased to meet you. I am sorry for your loss," Lucy murmured automatically, and Raine moved forward to her, her steps so smooth that the hem of her skirts seemed to glide over the floor. Slim, extraordinarily beautiful, Raine had the kind of looks and grace that made all other women feel clumsy and awkward. Her eyes were misty gray, framed with long, curling lashes that cast shadows over the gleaming purity of her skin. Light brown hair was arranged in long ringlets that brushed her shoulders. She was of medium height, but her willowy slenderness made her seem much taller.

"Heath's wife . . ." She took Lucy's hand in her own cool, pale one and pressed it gently. "He didn't tell us how pretty you are. Please call me Raine, won't you?" Lucy was surprised to feel that the other woman's hand was trembling. Apparently Raine was nervous, or upset, or both; but she showed no other sign of it except that betraying tremor. Her face was untroubled, her smile sweet and lovely. She didn't look anything like the woman that Amy had described in those letters to Heath. "Amy," Raine continued, letting go of Lucy's hand and turning to the silent girl behind her, "don't be afraid of your new sister. Come here and thank her for her hospitality."

Obediently Amy approached Lucy, her eyes downcast, her hands twisted together in front of her. It seemed that she was afraid of strangers, or perhaps just of Lucy. It was also obvious that she was debating on how friendly she had to be to her brother's Yankee wife.

Suddenly Lucy forgot all about Raine, and Heath, and her own jealousy as she looked at the tall, shy girl. She felt immense sympathy for her. Amy had just gone through the loss of her brother and the desertion of her mother, and she was in a land of strangers—of Northerners. *She looks very lonely. She looks afraid. I wouldn't want to have to coo and simper over a stranger, if I were her.*

"I imagine you must be very tired," Lucy said matter-of-factly, and Amy looked up with a wary glance. Her eyes were the same shade of blue-green as Heath's, not quite as deep-set or darkly lashed as his, but striking in their own way.

"Yes. I don't like to travel."

"I don't either," Lucy replied, while Amy's eyes encompassed every detail of her stylish clothes. Lucy couldn't help but notice that both Amy and Raine wore dresses that were clean and well kept, but had the look of being turned.

"Heath said you were a little thing," Amy commented. "He said you wear slippers with heels on them all the time."

"Amy!" The personal remark earned a reprimand from Raine.

"I do wear heeled slippers." Lucy smiled. "All the time."

"She is little," Amy said to Heath, and he grinned at her.

"I told you."

"I'm sorry," Raine apologized to Lucy, her gray eyes touched with something akin to embarrassment. "She's such a child."

"I wouldn't dare call anyone who is taller than me a child," Lucy said, conscious of Amy's tentative smile.

Lucy's mind was in such turmoil that she never quite remembered what happened during the next several minutes. She remained calm and polite, and even managed another smile or two as the guests were settled in their rooms. Heath disappeared to wash up and change his clothes, and Lucy tried desperately to collect her thoughts before going to their room to talk with him. As she passed by Amy's room, she saw through the open doorway that the girl was sitting on the edge of the bed, staring blindly at the Rosebank print on the walls.

"Amy?" Lucy was struck by her perfect stillness. "Would you like something? Some hot tea or—"

"No. Thank you." The girl looked at her guardedly. "This is a pretty room." It was done in a shade of soft, pale yellow, ornamented with pastel flowers.

"I'm glad it pleases you." Slowly Lucy walked into the room and over to the window, wondering if Amy welcomed her company or thought of it as an intrusion. "I hope it isn't too warm in here for you . . . Heath prefers every room in the house over-heated and stuffy. If you'd like some fresh air, the window—"

"No. This is fine," Amy said with a little shiver. "It's cold in Massachusetts."

"You'll like it more in the springtime."

"Heath says he's going to find a school for me up here."

"Are you . . . unhappy about the idea?"

Amy regarded her with unblinking turquoise eyes. "I don't mind it. I like to read. I'd like to take classes."

That was encouraging. "Some of the best young ladies' academies in the country are in Massachusetts," Lucy said warmly. "They've even founded a female seminary in Wellesley . . . in a few years, if you wanted to continue your education, you could go to college just like men do."

The last four words seemed to attract Amy's close attention. "Are you a feminist?" she asked, clearly intrigued by the idea.

"In some ways, maybe," Lucy admitted. "I certainly think that women should be allowed to study and learn things. I don't think we should be treated as if our minds are inferior."

"Mama and Raine say that a man won't marry a woman if he thinks she's smarter than he is."

"That certainly indicates something about your brother," Lucy muttered.

"What?"

"Oh, nothing. Nothing, Amy. I was just thinking of going to talk with Heath."

"About Raine?"

The perception in those steady blue-green eyes reminded Lucy uncannily of the way Heath looked at her sometimes. "About many things," she replied. "I haven't talked to him in two weeks. We have catching up to do."

"He didn't know Raine was coming along,"

Amy said, undeceived by Lucy's evasiveness. "Neither of us did. On the morning we were to leave, she said that her people in Goochland County wouldn't take her in. And she doesn't have any kin left in Henrico County."

And now she's right where she wants to be, Lucy thought with a stab of fury. How easily men were taken in by women! A few tears, some sweet Southern helplessness. Oh, it must have been ridiculously easy for Raine. And here she, Lucy, was, harboring the woman under her own roof! It had the makings of a fine farce.

"Why don't you take a little nap?" Lucy suggested calmly, noticing the faint gray shadows underneath the girl's eyes. "I'll come and wake you in time to freshen up for dinner."

Amy nodded gravely, watching Lucy's every movement as she left the room and closed the door.

Heath was waiting in the bedroom for her, dressed in clean clothes, his freshly washed hair shining and damp. The new bronzed darkness of his skin was startling against the whiteness of his shirt. They stared at each other, unsmiling, and invisible signals seemed to race back and forth between them. He was tense. She was furious. He was prepared to be stubborn, and so was she. Underlying everything was an overwhelming surfeit of frustration. They hadn't made love in weeks, and all the channels of communication that had once been open were now sealed shut. Want and anger combined to form a boundary between them.

"I would like to talk downstairs in the library." Lucy's voice was taut. "There is less chance that we'll be overheard there."

"You must be planning to shout," he said dryly.

"I hope it doesn't come to that. But if you

won't listen to me any other way, then I will shout. And if you decide to treat this lightly and laugh at me, then I will walk out that door, and I wouldn't come back until she is gone from this house.''

All humor left his expression. ''I'll tread lightly on your temper, Mrs. Rayne . . . if you'll do the same for mine. Shall we move the discussion down to the library?''

The beginnings of sunset filled the library with a pinkish light that mingled with the glow of the lamps. Heath poured himself a drink, noticed Lucy's extended hand, and with a quirk of his mouth, he handed her a watered-down version of the same. Lucy welcomed the warm, steadying effect of the spirits, and she took one sip after another until her teeth no longer chattered against the rim of the glass. She closed her eyes and waited for the drink to sear its way down to her stomach, and then she looked at him with an indescribable mixture of emotions gleaming in her eyes.

''How could you bring her here?''

''I would have warned you that she was coming with us if I'd had a chance. But the morning we were leaving—''

''I heard about her problems with her family from Amy,'' Lucy said. ''It's just too bad. I have a lot in common with Raine's relatives—I don't want her living with me, either.''

Heath tilted his head back and downed the last swallow of whiskey, the movement replete with masculine grace. Then his eyes locked with hers in an intense stare. ''She's not going to be staying with us for long. When Victoria left for England, she wanted Amy and Raine to go with her. Victoria has family there that would take them in. But they both refused. Amy knew that I'd come and get her. And Raine . . .

well, I guess she just didn't want to move to another country, but she didn't give it much thought beyond that.''

Lucy could have strangled him. *She gave it plenty of thought. Raine knew exactly what she was doing—she knew she'd see you again. She wants to see if she can get you back, you idiot!*

"But now," Heath continued, "Raine is thinking seriously about England. She's going to stay a few days until we get Amy settled somewhere, and then she'll leave to join Victoria.''

"Why didn't Raine just stay in the South until she made up her mind?''

"She had no place to stay. And I thought it was better for Amy's sake that she accompany us up here. You and I are strangers to Amy, and Raine's the only familiar—''

"Oh, spare me this," Lucy interrupted, whirling around and going to the window. "It wasn't for Amy's good that you brought Raine here. And you could have seen that Raine had the means to stay in a hotel for a few days.''

"Ah, that would certainly be the gentlemanly thing to do. Leave a young, recently bereaved widow alone in a hotel—''

"And we both know you didn't bring her here because you're such a damned gentleman, either.''

"Then tell me why we think I brought her here," he said, in tones dripping with sweetness.

Lucy pressed her forehead against the cool frostiness of the window pane, swallowing against the tightness in her throat. "When you were ill with fever . . .'' she began, and the room became deadly quiet, "you seemed to think you were living in the past, in the times just before the war and during it. You talked on and off about the fighting, about your parents, your friends . . . but most of all . . . you talked about her. Raine.'' She gave a strangled laugh. ''I'm sick of that name, I've heard it so much. You begged her not to marry Clay. You talked about how beautiful she was . . . you said . . . that you . . . loved her.'' Slowly she turned around. Heath's face was carefully blank, like that of a statue. ''Why didn't you ever mention her to me before that?'' she asked in a soft, thin voice.

''It wasn't necessary.''

''What happened? Why did she marry Clay?''

''Because he was a Price. A legitimate Price. The Prices were a large and influential family before the war. I was nothing but a by-blow. Raine and I came to care for each other, but I made the mistake of introducing her to my half-brother . . . it didn't take long for them to become engaged.''

Oh, God. If he could forgive Raine for that, he must care for her deeply. Lucy writhed inwardly at the injustice of it. How could he still want Raine after the way she had treated him?

''You don't seem to blame her for choosing Clay over you,'' she said sharply.

''At the time I did blame her.'' A ghost of a smile curved his mouth. ''Hell, yes, I blamed her, cursed her, thought up hundreds of ways to get back at her. But the feelings have changed over time. I understand why she did it now. I never realized how powerless, how dependent women are . . . Raine made the only decision she could have. She didn't have the freedom to choose any other way. It was obvious that Clay, with his money and his name, was able to provide for her in a way that I couldn't have.''

''You're making excuses for her. She didn't have to choose Clay. His name, his money, his family, shouldn't have made any difference—''

''I didn't think you'd be the kind to blame her

for what she did. You would have married Daniel for the very same reasons she married Clay.''

"That's not true!'' Lucy gasped in surprise. "There's a big difference. I loved Daniel.''

"Did you?'' Heath shook his head slowly and smiled in a tired way. "It doesn't matter anymore. I finally understood everything while I was in prison camp. I learned a lot of things on Governor's Island, especially about what it's like to be helpless. I had no control over what happened to me. I accepted what was given to me, took as much advantage as I could out of every situation, but ultimately I was helpless. For the first time in my life. Well, so was Raine. So were you.''

"I'm not helpless anymore!''

"No, you're not. You've changed. But Raine hasn't. She'll always be helpless.''

"Why are you the one who has to protect her? Are you planning to provide for her the rest of her life?''

"No. She'll find someone to take care of her soon. It's what she's best at. All I'm asking is that you put up with her for the next few days. It's not forever.''

"I assume that you'll be going to work as usual?'' As Heath nodded curtly, Lucy couldn't help the sneer that rose to her lips. "That's what I thought. Tell me, what am I supposed to do with Amy and Raine? What should I say to Raine? How can I look at her and carry on a civil conversation when all I can remember is how you raved in a delirium about her for two days straight?''

"Remember this,'' he said with stinging softness. "There is nothing between Raine and me. There hasn't been for years. Remember that she's been through hell during the last few years. Remember that while you were sitting next to the candy jar in your father's store and flirting with the customers, she was afraid of Yankees burning the house down over her head, of being raped, of being killed, of starving. She's been through the death of her husband, and she's seen her friends and neighbors nearly kill each other over the Reconstruction issues that you like to discuss over coffee and dessert now and then. When you start feeling sorry for yourself, remember *that.*"

"How lucky she is," Lucy replied, her eyes cold, "to have you to defend her from me."

Heath swore and raked his hand through his hair. He turned abruptly and poured himself another drink.

"Maybe it won't be difficult to find something to talk with her about. She and I have so much in common. Don't we, Heath?" She stared at him until he set his glass down and met her gaze squarely.

"Just what are you asking?"

"Raine and I have you in common, Heath." Was that really her voice, so poisonously soft? "But just how much? How well has she known you? As well as I have? Were you ever lovers?"

He looked at her as if he didn't recognize her. *"Damn* you for asking that."

"Were you lovers?"

"If that makes a difference to you, then you can go to hell!"

"Were you?" she whispered.

"No," he said, breathing hard, looking more outraged than she had ever seen him. "No. Not then, not now."

"You can stop glaring at me like that. You invited all of this by bringing her here. You brought it on your own head, so don't blame me for asking questions."

"You're unbelievable," he said in a low voice,

and it wasn't a compliment. "It amazes me that there was ever a time I thought you needed toughening up."

"Would you prefer someone more . . . helpless?"

Even Lucy had to admit that she had pushed him too far. Heath turned away from her and clenched his fists, so angry that he couldn't see straight. A little bit afraid of him, Lucy walked past him and paused at the door, glancing at his rigid back.

"I don't want this situation to continue indefinitely, Heath. I can tolerate having her here for a few days, but that's all. If this turns into a contest of who can stay here the longest, I guarantee she'll outlast me, because I can't take too much of this."

"What the hell have you turned into?"

A woman who loves you. A woman who is afraid she'll lose you.

"I'm trying to be honest with you," she said.

"Like hell you're trying to be honest. Why don't you just admit that this is all because of petty jealousy? And if you're really this insecure, and you don't have any more trust in me than this, then I don't know you as well as I thought I did. I thought I understood enough about you to make this marriage work."

"This marriage was working just fine before you brought her here. Do you think it's reasonable to make this kind of demand of me? Do you think it's fair?"

"No," he said tersely, "I don't."

She was disconcerted by his admission. "Then . . . I don't understand why you're asking me to put up with this."

Heath paused for a long time. When he spoke, he was so quiet and matter-of-fact that Lucy suddenly felt like an overemotional child.

"I won't always be able to give you a reason for everything I do. But I don't ask you to justify everything *you* do. Who said that things between us are always going to be fair? Marriage doesn't work that way. There are no contracts between us. The only guarantees are those I gave you when I put that ring on your finger."

Chapter Twelve

UNDER THE CIRCUMSTANCES, Lucy thought she did well at playing the gracious hostess. She did her best to insure that no one could find fault with her household or her hospitality, and outwardly there were no signs of disharmony between any of the four of them. The conversations were conducted with exquisite politeness—at times, they were so careful that it seemed like a mockery of ordinary courtesy. It was a week in her life that she would forever look back on with distaste, but it was a highly instructive time. She learned about many new things, including the considerable differences between Southern women and Northern ones.

Amy and Raine possessed an artfulness and a charm that Lucy could only marvel at in a half-disparaging, half-envious way. In addition to their other talents, they had the ability to invite compliments and flattery with every breath they took. It was an art that even Amy, who was barely in her teens, seemed to have mastered. No matter how a conversation began, it always wound its way back to them. No Northern woman would ever attempt to give a man a wide-eyed look and say, "Oh, what a goose I am," or "I just don't know anything about anything," but Raine did. It annoyed Lucy to distraction, but she had to admit that Raine was appealing when she put on such airs.

Though she wouldn't begin to claim that she knew a great deal about the workings of men's minds, Lucy was certain that any man, no matter who he was, would find Raine attractive. Did Heath admire that kind of behavior in a woman? Lucy was disheartened by the thought. Why had Heath encouraged her to use her mind if he wanted a woman who didn't like to talk about important things? Why did he encourage her to argue with him if he wanted someone who would smile and agree with everything he said? Had it all been some kind of test that she had failed?

Heath had never been so puzzling to her. Everything she had come to associate with him—his attitudes, his sense of humor, his beliefs—all of that went slightly askew when the two Southern women were present. He was different around them. Ordinarily he was irritated by pointless chattering. Why, then, did he tolerate this nonsense?

Gone were the fascinating dinnertime conversations about politics and the *Examiner*. Raine and Amy didn't want to talk about the news and popular debates; they talked about local gossip, as if the world revolved around their tiny county in Virginia. Heath didn't seem to mind. He listened indulgently to them, laughed at their clever mimicking of people he had once known, and handed out compliments whenever they were called for. Lucy thought little of such automatic and meaningless flattery, and she was glad that Heath didn't attempt to direct any of it her way. It would have been an insult to her intelligence. Silently she sat through these witless conversations and occupied herself with wondering about what thoughts lurked behind Raine's silvery eyes.

Lucy knew that sooner or later, she and Raine would find themselves in a situation in which they would have the opportunity to speak privately. She

wondered all through Saturday and Sunday about what
the other woman would be like when Heath wasn't
around. Would Raine continue to play the game of
Southern belle, or would she choose to reveal something about why she was really here? On Monday
morning, Heath left early and went to the offices on
Washington Street, and Amy excused herself from the
table, leaving Lucy and Raine alone in the breakfast
room.

Adding more sugar to her coffee and stirring
it carefully, Lucy looked at the other woman with a
measuring glance. Raine was lovely in a faded pink
gown. A velvet ribbon had been woven through those
astoundingly perfect ringlets of hair, called "kiss
curls." Raine stared back at her with a faint smile.

For the first time, they would talk to each other
without an audience.

"Well, it appears that we've been deserted,"
Lucy said, setting down her spoon and taking a sip
of coffee.

"I'm glad we're alone. I would like to thank
you again, privately, for your kindness to Amy and
me. We certainly don't wish to be the cause of any
trouble in your home."

Lucy smiled in response to the delicate insin-
uation. "Please don't worry. You haven't caused any
trouble at all."

"There's not a word of truth in that," Raine
said with a mellifluous laugh. "Unexpected company's always trouble. But I'll be leaving for England
soon, and then you'll have your home and your husband all to yourself again."

Lucy's spine stiffened at the implication that
Raine had somehow undermined her position as
Heath's wife. "You're welcome in my home. And I
don't mind any of the time that my husband wishes to

spend with either of his sisters.'' Lucy emphasized the
last word lightly. After giving Raine a few seconds to
digest *that,* she continued in a casual tone. "How exciting the prospect of living in England must be.''

"I wish I felt that way. But a transplanted
Southerner is always a sorry sight. In fact, knowing
Heath as I do, I just can't understand what he is doing
up here." Her clear gray eyes took in every nuance of
Lucy's alert expression. "You should have seen him
when he set foot on the plantation . . . he just looked
around and took a deep breath, and talked about how
good it was to feel the sun on his face again. Poor
thing, I've never seen him so blue. Downright peaked.
But a week or two in Virginia, and he was nearly himself again. It reminds me of what my Mama always
said—Southerners just aren't meant to live anywhere
but in the South. I don't know what Heath was thinking of when he moved to the North. People here don't
understand men like him. Not that you don't know
how to please him . . . why, he's just crazy about you.
If anyone could keep him happy living up North, I
know it'd be you.''

"So far it's worked out quite well." It was a
struggle for Lucy to keep from sounding defensive.
"He's carving out a unique place for himself here. His
accomplishments with the *Examiner* have been ex-
traordinary.''

"Oh . . . that newspaper. Well, he certainly
is living out his Daddy's dream. But someday I hope
he'll decide to follow his own dreams.''

"He seems to be quite happy with what he is
doing.''

"Oh . . ." Raine cast her eyes down con-
tritely. "I didn't mean to imply that he wasn't. Of
course he's happy. Of course.''

There was a note in her voice that irritated

Lucy beyond reason, as if Raine were speaking to a distraught child that required soothing. Some of her annoyance must have been evident, for Raine gave her an appealing smile that was colored with more than a hint of satisfaction.

Lucy's mind raced as she searched for the right words to say, words that would somehow show Raine that she, Lucy, was married to him and intended to stay that way. *I'm his wife. You can't change that, much as you'd like to. And if you had ever known him as well I do, you would never have given him up to marry Clay.* The thought returned a measure of her confidence. "It's only right that you're concerned about Heath's happiness," she said. "You're his sister-in-law—"

"And I've known him for years."

"But you don't know much about the way things are for him now. His life is exactly the way he wants it. He is following his own dreams, not anyone else's. New dreams. His old ones died long ago."

Raine's smile faltered. "Some things never change."

Now the line was drawn. Lucy had never thought that one of the fiercest battles of her life would be fought over a breakfast table, with quiet words carefully chosen. "Many things about Heath have changed."

"He'll always be a Southerner," Raine insisted gently.

"But not strictly so. He has been successful here because of his ability to change. Now there's some New England in him, too." Despite the seriousness of the conversation, Lucy almost wanted to smile as she heard herself. Heath would have died, had he been witness to this conversation.

"It might make you happy to think that." Now

Raine was visibly trembling. "Maybe it's even true. But you don't know what he wants. If he's between two worlds right now, then I know which one he belongs in, and someday he'll come back to it."

"And I'll be right by his side." Lucy stared at her without blinking. "I'll follow him wherever he goes."

"You couldn't fit in where he belongs. Not if you stayed there a hundred years." Suddenly Raine's control broke and contempt edged her voice, making her sound curiously young. "How did you get him to marry you? You're nothing like the women he was brought up with. He never showed any interest at all in your kind—"

"Until he decided he wanted to get married."

Raine was speechless. She looked at Lucy's small, set face for a long time, and then her expression went blank, as if a shutter had been drawn closed. "You must accept my apology, Lucinda. I didn't mean to fly off the handle . . . I didn't know what I was saying. I have been . . . upset since Clay's death. I have not been myself." Lucy nodded warily, pushing her chair back and standing up. Slowly Raine did the same. "Let's forget all about our talk this morning. You won't mention it to anyone, I hope."

"Not unless I see the need to."

Raine bit her lip, looking defenseless and lost. "Forgive me for what I said. Any fool could see that you're a good wife to Heath."

"There's nothing to forgive," Lucy said, finding to her disgust that there was nothing she could do but be courteous in the face of Raine's distress. Oh, if only she could say what she really thought! "You have been through a difficult time. I can only imagine what it would be like to lose a husband." She paused deliberately before adding, ''In fact, just thinking about it makes me appreciate what I have all the more.''

''I'm glad to hear that you appreciate Heath. He is a very special man. I've always thought so.''

''According to Amy, you were married to a very special man yourself.''

''Yes. Clay was quite something.'' There was little sign of emotion on Raine's face. ''At one time you could have said that Clay and Heath favored each other. But the war changed them both. Clay went in one direction, and Heath in the other. They both surprised us all.''

Feeling chilled by the odd silver gleam in the other woman's eyes, Lucy nodded and turned away. She would have been even more disturbed had she seen the smile that curved Raine's soft mouth as she left the room.

That night Lucy acknowledged privately that the situation was going to be even more of a strain than she had anticipated. She was desperate to be alone with Heath, but they didn't have the time or the opportunity for that. Their guests seemed to have a monopoly on his attention, and she had barely exchanged ten words with him since he had gotten home. When they all retired for the evening, Lucy emerged from her bath, slipped on a robe and went to the bedroom with the intention of talking with him. She was just in time to see Raine's slim silhouette in the semidarkness of the hallway. The muffled sound of drawers sliding open and shut came from inside the room as Heath prepared for bed. Unaware of her astounded audience, Raine opened the door quietly.

Pure outrage swept over Lucy. What did Raine think she was doing? What did she intend to accomplish? This was too much! Never in her life had Lucy felt the urge to attack someone physically, but at the

moment she longed to put her hands on the dangling
nut brown ringlets that adorned Raine's head and pull
them out one by one.

"Raine," Lucy said, and the quiet, crisp snap
of her voice caused the other woman to freeze in the
middle of stepping through the doorway. "Is there
something I can help you with?"

"Oh . . . ," Raine said, and blushed brightly,
looking around in confusion. "Goodness, I . . . well,
I just can't find my way around here. There are so
many rooms, and . . . I must have gotten myself turned
around the wrong way. I'm so sorry—"

The door swung open all the way, and Heath
stood there in trousers and bare feet, his unbuttoned
shirt hanging open to reveal his chest and the trim
expanse of his abdomen. Surprise flickered in his eyes
as he saw Raine, and then his glance moved to Lucy.
"What's going on?"

"Raine forgot that her room is at the other end
of the hallway," she said softly. "But then, it must be
confusing, with all these doors. And it's such a big
house." She looked at the other woman. "Your room
is in that direction, Raine. Next time just remember
to turn right at the top of the stairs."

Raine flushed and murmured an apology,
walking to her own room with rustling skirts. A delicate fragrance of flowers floated in her wake. Lucy
waited until the graceful feminine figure had disappeared before she fixed Heath with an accusing stare.

He sighed tautly. "Don't start."

She swept past him into the bedroom, heading
for her dressing table with her chin thrust high.
Snatching up a heavy silver brush, she dragged it
through the wild chestnut torrent of her hair so roughly
that she could feel the scratch of the bristles on her
scalp. Heath sat on the bed and watched her silently,

his eyes wandering freely over her silk-draped body before returning to her face.

"I suppose you're going to tell me that she has a rotten sense of direction," Lucy said through gritted teeth. After slamming down the brush, she separated her hair into locks and began the nightly ritual of braiding it. "This whole situation is ridiculous. I'm a fool for putting up with it." As Heath said something under his breath, she glared at him. "What did you say?"

After staring her down with cool blue eyes, he spoke in a chilling tone. "They'll be gone in a few days. I've narrowed down the choices for Amy's school, and next week she'll be starting classes at one or the other of them—"

"Amy's not the problem. Amy's not the one I want out of this house."

"Raine will leave for England the day after Amy is settled in school."

"Why not now?"

"Because Raine's mind is not going to be put at ease until she knows that Amy is safely settled—"

"I would appreciate it," Lucy interrupted hotly, "if you worried as much about my peace of mind as you do about hers."

"I never realized your peace of mind was so damned fragile."

"I just want to know what's going on between you and her, and why you insist on keeping her here when you know how I feel about it!"

"Nothing is going on between us!" Heath's temper exploded. "For God's sake, why do you keep on pushing her at me? It's like you're daring me to . . ."

"Daring you to what?"

"Lucy," he said, concentrating all his effort

to rein in his frustration, "I don't know what's happened. You're obviously miserable, and you're making life hell for both of us. I know you pretty well and this isn't you. You're one of the few women I know with some common sense . . . and here you are, completely rattled over nothing."

"Nothing!" she exclaimed bitterly. "How can you sit there and say this is nothing?"

"Alright, then," he said gently. "Help me to understand."

"You would understand a lot more if you could have heard the conversation I had with her this morning."

His gaze sharpened. "What did you talk about?"

"You, of course." Lucy laughed shortly. "All about you. About where . . . and with whom . . . you belong."

"What did she say?"

Lucy was suddenly overwhelmed with the fear that what Raine had said that morning was the truth. And on the chance that it had been, she couldn't sit here and say it to his face. Oh, what if Raine was right? What if Heath found that he couldn't let go of his past dreams, now that they were within his reach? What if he decided that he would never be happy anywhere but the South? Lucy had visible proof of the effect his former home had on him. He had left Boston pale and worn, and he had come back from Virginia looking like a different man. Perhaps it was true, that he did belong there with his own kind of people, living in the world he had been born to live in.

"What did she say?" Heath repeated tersely.

Lucy couldn't face his questions or her doubts any longer. She needed to retreat and find time to think. "Ask her yourself. I'm tired. I need to get some rest.'' Standing up from the dressing table, she went to the door, unable to be in the same room with him any longer.

Heath moved so swiftly that she didn't even hear him, whirling her around and catching her by the shoulders. ''Stop it.'' He gave her a quick shake. ''Talk to me.''

''No more. Don't touch me! I'm going to bed.''

''You're going to bed, Mrs. Rayne, but it's going to be here. In this room.''

''I won't!'' Violently she tried to twist away from his imprisoning hands, gasping with fury.

He gave her another brief, hard shake, his fingers biting into her flesh. ''Calm down, you little hornet, and stop trying to work yourself up into a tantrum. It won't take much more for me to turn you over my knee.''

''Oh! That will solve everything,'' she choked. Acid seemed to rise in her throat. ''Let go of me!'' She was blinded by a haze of red, and with a sick feeling of despair she knew she had lost her control. Shaking wildly, she tried to strike him, but she was as helpless as a child against him. The weight of humiliation and smoldering anger settled on her chest, making it difficult to breathe. ''You bring her here, and . . . you expect me to be happy about it. Well, I won't! I don't have to put up with it . . . I don't have to. This is my home, and I'm your wife, and I don't want her here! Are you listening to me?'' Her voice became shrill. ''You get her out of here. I want her *out!*'' Through her rage, there was a faint awareness that Heath was startled by her white-faced vehemence.

What is he thinking? she wondered, and stared at him dumbly, suddenly exhausted. *That I've lost my*

*wits. I'm pushing him away—I don't know how to stop
myself. What should I do? What next?*

His eyes were dark and troubled. It was fear
that he saw on her face, fear that to him was incom-
prehensible, but he sought to ease it without hesitation. Swiftly he pulled her close and wrapped his arms
around her, as if sheltering her from a rough wind.
She tried to struggle against him, but he only pulled
her further inside his shirt, holding her against the
comforting hardness of his chest. Lucy shuddered and
let herself relax, breathing in the scent of warm male
skin. It was only now that she realized how much she
had needed this simple contact with him, the protection of his body. No one else in the world could give
her such a haven.

"Heath—"

"Hush up. Be still," he said, and she felt the
pleasant abrasion of his unshaven face against her temple. As she was hugged against the boundless strength
of his body, her panic began to melt away. Wordlessly
she leaned on him, realizing that he wasn't going to
let her go until she gave him some of her burdens to
shoulder. It was a relief to let him take control of
everything, to be taken care of for just a little while.

When he sensed that she was ready to talk,
Heath loosened his arms a little. "You were strong for
me when I needed you." His voice was quiet and
steady. "Let me be strong for you now. Tell me why
you're afraid, and I'll tell you why you have no reason
to be."

She hardly knew how to begin. "I don't even
know you when you're around them. You change into
this . . . this patronizing creature, and they look up at
you and hang on to your words as if . . . as if you
know everything—"

"I'm sorry," he said, and smiled ruefully at

her indignancy and bewilderment. He should have expected that his behavior with Raine and Amy would seem strange to Lucy . . . Lucy, who had no experience with the rituals of flattery and condescension they had all been raised on. Back in the days in Virginia before the war, he had been unaware that there was any other way for men and women to relate to each other. A man naturally had to maintain the pretense that he knew everything, and a woman naturally pretended that she believed him. A Southern woman would never think of puncturing a man's vanity, no matter what she thought of him. It had all been pleasant and comfortable, and very easy.

He wondered how he could make Lucy understand that his values had changed. There had come a time when he began to desire honesty from a woman. There had come a time when he had lost Raine, the woman he had imagined himself to be in love with. And after all had been said and done, and he had had time to think, he had decided that he did not want a woman whom he had to treat like a child. Neither had he wanted to be worshipped. He had wanted a woman who could be a partner.

"It's hard to explain," he said slowly. "It's the way they talk to each other in Henrico County. There's a role that a man is expected to play, and the role that women play. It's a matter of habit. Theirs and mine."

"You seem to be enjoying it too much."

Heath laughed huskily. "Are you afraid I'll want you to pander to my ego from now on? No. I'm starting to find it a nuisance, as a matter of fact."

"It doesn't look like that to me."

His hands wandered up and down her back in a soothing caress. "It's true. In the past year I've gotten used to being cut down to size whenever I start acting too high-and-mighty. If you didn't keep me in line, I'd be damn well unmanageable. As it is, you're going to have a lot of work to do once they leave.''

"I've . . . heard that Southerners don't belong anywhere except in the South.''

"I belong here.''

"Don't you miss your own kind of people—''

"My own kind?'' he repeated, and laughed softly for a reason she didn't understand. "No, I don't miss the people in the South. You're the kind of woman I want. Damon's the kind of business partner I like to work with. We have good friends and neighbors who like to mind their own business. I don't see room for improvement in any of that.''

"But you came back from Virginia so much happier and stronger than when you had left here . . .''

"If you'll remember, when I left Boston I was still getting over a previous illness. A little time in the sunshine makes anyone look better.''

"It wasn't just the sunshine. When you walked in the front door, you were smiling and . . . you were practically glowing, and I knew it was because you had been with—''

"I was happy to be coming home to *you*, you little numbskull. I couldn't wait to get back to you, even though I knew you'd have a fit when you found out Raine was here with us.''

"I still don't want her here.''

"I swear to you I'll get her out as soon as possible. And you'll never have to see her again. In the meantime, would you just keep reminding yourself that there's nothing you have to fear from her?''

She gave a small nod and tried to pull away from him. "Wait,'' he said, catching his hands under her elbows, keeping hold of her, even though he let her take a step back. "Where are you planning on going?"

"To the other bedroom. Please don't argue."

He was nettled by her stubbornness. "Sleep in here."

"No . . . I know what would happen if I slept here, and I don't want that. Not tonight."

"Cin, it's been weeks. Months."

"It's not my fault! You were sick, and then—"

"Simmer down. I'm not accusing you of anything. We've had a bad time of it for the last month or two, and it's no one's fault. Circumstances have gotten between us, time and again. But there's no reason for being apart now, and I don't want to put up with it any longer." His voice became softer, cajoling. "You've forgotten what it was like between us. Let me take care of you tonight. Let me remind you. Afterwards you're going to feel better about everything. I promise."

"I can't," she said miserably. "I feel . . . empty . . . drained. There's nothing in me to give tonight. I don't want our first time after so long to be like that. It wouldn't be good. It wouldn't be right."

"Lucy—"

"Please, just let me be by myself for tonight."

Reluctantly he let go of her. "I'll be damned if I'm going to beg."

"I don't want you to beg. I just want to be alone."

He followed her to the door and braced his hand on the doorjamb, momentarily preventing her exit. She looked up into his turquoise eyes and wrapped her arms around her middle, embarrassed about the scene she had made and vaguely anxious that he wasn't going to let her go.

"Remember the months right after we moved to Boston?" His gaze seemed to strip away her pretensions and pierce through to her heart. "For a while it was good between us. Very good."

"Y-yes, it was," she stammered, mesmerized by the intent expression in his turquoise eyes.

"No matter what our differences were, you never withheld yourself in order to get back at me for something I had done or said."

"No! Of c-course not—"

"I wouldn't let you go right now, Cin, if I thought that this was some kind of punishment." He read his answer in her stricken face, and he nodded slightly, appearing to be satisfied. Lowering his arm from the doorframe, he turned the knob for her and held the door open. "Go on. You've bought yourself a little time."

Thankfully she fled, wrapping her robe more tightly around herself and heading into the adjoining bedroom.

"Oh, there you are," Lucy said, walking into the library and smiling as she saw Amy rifling industriously through the bookshelves. Amy paused as she saw her, abashedly holding a precariously balanced stack of books in her left arm. "I saw that Raine is taking a nap, and I couldn't find you."

"I thought I'd look in here for some books—" Amy began.

"You really do like to read, don't you?"

"Novels," Amy said, and Lucy laughed in delight.

"Let me see what you have . . . mmmn, some

of my favorites. *Snow Bound* . . . *The Hidden Hand*
. . . *Wuthering Heights*—''

"That's my favorite."

"Have you ever read *St. Elmo?* No? I'll find
it for you—you must read it. It's about a long, passionate love affair, and a poor girl who becomes rich
and successful . . . I see you've only looked through
the books on these shelves—''

"The ones on the other side of the room look
dull.''

"Yes," Lucy said, wrinkling her nose briefly.
"Those are Heath's shelves. These are mine."

"You have so many new books," Amy said,
her blue eyes reverent as she looked at the neat rows
of well-bound volumes.

"When I was younger, my father used to scold
me for spending so much money on books instead of
more practical things." Lucy grinned reminiscently
and sat down in Heath's chair. "Thank goodness Heath
never says a word, no matter how many I buy.''

"Clay fussed at me for reading too much. We
couldn't afford books, not when we needed the money
for . . . other things.''

"Doctors' bills?" Lucy asked softly, thinking
about the letters that had detailed Clay's back problems and constant illnesses.

"And hired help—we couldn't get along without it," Amy said, setting the books on Heath's desk
and leaning on the edge of it. "It was only Clay,
Raine, Mother, and me on the plantation. None of us
were very good at that kind of work. We paid one of
the neighbor's boys to help—he was lazy, but when he
was pushed he did a good job.''

"I'm sorry." Impulsively Lucy reached over
and patted the girl's hand.

"Sorry for what?"

"I'm sorry that things were so hard for you . . . and that you didn't have books or—"

"It didn't seem that bad at the time—you never realize how bad something really was until you look back on it. Course, it all could have been much easier if Heath had been there to help . . . but he wasn't."

That must have been when Heath moved up here. Lucy felt compelled to defend his absence. "It's not like him to turn his back on someone who needs help," she said. "Maybe if someone had just tried to make him understand—"

"It wasn't his fault. He wanted to help. Heath came to the plantation after the war, but they wouldn't let him stay." Amy regarded her with surprise. "He never told you about that?"

"Not really," Lucy admitted, her mind scheming on how she could extract further revelations from Amy. If she could get her to talk, Amy might prove to be a windfall of information. "I do know that there were a few problems between Heath, Clay, and Raine—"

"And Mother too. She never liked him. You know why, don't you?"

"Because he was . . . he was . . . another woman's son?" Lucy asked tentatively.

"That's right. Clay and I were born Prices. Mother always said that we were the real children. And . . ." Amy looked around and lowered her voice, "she said Heath was just a mistake. She said it to his face, too, lots of times."

"What did Heath do?"

"He just smiled. He had this smile that would make her hopping mad . . . oh, she just couldn't stand to be around him. It would take days to calm her down after Daddy had brought Heath to visit."

"How did you and Clay feel about him?"

"I always liked him. Clay didn't seem to, but the two of them never fought. Not ever, until Raine."

"Who was she?" Lucy asked, taking care not to sound too eager or impatient. "A neighbor of yours?"

"Not exactly. But her family lived in the county. She was a Stanton—one of four sisters, the next to oldest one. Raine was the prettiest one. Everyone said so. She liked to flirt and tease, but she wasn't ever interested in the county boys."

Lucy leaned forward, listening intently. Encouraged by her interest, Amy began to talk freely. "And then Heath's mama died, and he came to live with us when he was seventeen. Mother would have liked to die herself, having to put up with him under the same roof, but Daddy wouldn't listen to her. He was crazy about Heath. So Mother had to put up with Heath being there. But it helped that all of her friends understood and felt sorry for her, and she really didn't have to see him much. He was always running around the county with his friends."

"Misbehaving?"

"I guess he was," Amy conceded. "Heath was just . . . wild. He was always in trouble, charming his way out of it one day and getting back into it the next. Everyone seemed to like him, but no one wanted him to court their daughters . . . you understand why. Raine says that Heath would have been the most popular boy in the county if he'd come from the right kind of background. He could ride, cuss, and shoot better than anyone, and he was as smart as a whip. From what I hear, all the girls made eyes at him—Raine says he was the handsomest thing that had ever set foot over the county line—but they were all scared to be seen with him too often. It would have ruined their reputations."

Lucy absorbed the information silently. Heath had always been an outsider, even in Virginia. Never again would she be surprised at the recollection of how fearlessly he had taken on the challenge of making a place for himself up here. It was no wonder that he had never expressed a desire to go back to the South. He had never really belonged anywhere.

"How did Heath and Raine . . ." Lucy started to ask and found that she could not finish the question because the phrase *Heath and Raine* stuck in her throat. She hated the idea of them together, but it was imperative that she find out just what had gone on between them. Amy seemed to understand exactly what she wanted to know.

"From the minute Heath laid eyes on her, he wouldn't leave her alone. The Stantons didn't like him paying court to her, but they had four girls to marry off, and he did have a nice inheritance coming to him. Raine went buggy-riding with him on a dare from one of her sisters. She won't tell what happened, but she said that at the beginning of the afternoon he could barely get a 'how do you do' out of her, and by the end he had talked her into marrying him. Then she met Clay—and really, they were a lot alike, except that Clay was a Price and Heath was . . ."

"Illegitimate," Lucy said flatly. "Clay must have seemed like a better bargain."

"She loved Clay," Amy replied defensively. "He was handsome and nice, and—"

"I'm sure he was." Hastily Lucy attempted to smooth over her mistake. "I'm sorry. That came out differently than I had intended. Please go on . . . you were about to tell me what happened after Raine met Clay."

"They got married. Heath tried to stop them, but he couldn't. He fought with Clay, and said something to him. Whatever it was, they were never on friendly terms again. And after the wedding, Heath got so bad that no one could do anything with him—drinking and doing wild things—and finally, Daddy sent him abroad, hoping it would make a gentleman out of him. And then the war started.''

"What about after the war? Why wouldn't they let him stay at the plantation?''

"It was mostly Clay. Clay's back was hurt, and he was always sickly after the war. He thought that if Heath came back to live with them, Heath would take his place as head of the plantation and then take Raine away from him. And Mother didn't want Heath there . . . and Raine . . . she stood on the front porch and argued with Heath, and she called him all kinds of names. He got mad, and he . . .''

"What?'' Lucy prompted, appalled and fascinated. Amy's face went red.

"He laughed at her because she had married Clay for his money and the plantation—the money was all in worthless bluebacks, and the plantation was falling apart. He just laughed at her. Raine grabbed a riding whip that someone had left on the porch railing, and hit him with it—that's where he got that scar on his temple, near his eye—''

"Oh, dear lord,'' Lucy whispered, raising her fingertips to her mouth and covering it. All her jealousy of Raine was drowned in a flood of sympathy for Heath. It was the kind of thoroughly unselfish sympathy that caused her to flinch at the image Amy's words had created. To be hurt so badly by someone you loved—and especially if you had as much stubborn pride as Heath. Why, it was something you might never get over. Raine had left her mark on him. If only Lucy could be certain that the scar was merely skin-deep.

Or was it a deeper mark left on the soul, still un-healed? She was afraid that she would never find out.

"Amy seemed to be happy after the talk you had with her after dinner," Lucy said, pausing in the act of proofreading a letter Heath had penned in his scrawling, decisive hand. Together they sat at his desk, while the gentle ticking of a clock reminded them that midnight was approaching. The fires had been banked for the night; the darkened house was becoming cooler, and yet Lucy had a cozy feeling as she and Heath worked by the light of the brightly burning lamp.

"She's going to like Winthrop Academy. It's well recommended, both academically and . . . every other way. I've been assured that it's the kind of place where someone like Amy will do very well."

"By 'someone like Amy,' do you mean a re-located Southerner?"

He grinned and reached over to tug one of her curls, unable to resist the temptation. "Yes, that's what I mean."

"Do you think she has any doubts about stay-ing here instead of joining her mother?"

"No. Not a chance."

Lucy put down the letter, smoothing her knuckles over it absently. "When you take her to the academy, make certain that she understands she is welcome here whenever she wants to come back."

"I will. And I'll make a bargain with you . . . if you'll take her shopping tomorrow and get her what-ever she needs, then I'll have her tucked safely away at the academy the day after. Then everyone will be out by the end of the week, and . . . God, I'm almost afraid to say it . . . everything will be back to nor-mal."

Lucy rapped her knuckles three times on the wooden desk and crossed her fingers.

"In the meantime," Heath said, standing up and pulling her with him, "the night is young—"

"Actually," Lucy replied with a nervous laugh, trying to shake her hands free of his, "the night is quite, *quite* mature, and I'm falling asleep standing up—"

"I know how to wake you." He bent his head, and she turned away abruptly.

"Heath, not now." She couldn't. She *couldn't*, not with Raine under the same roof. It would seem tainted. She had to know that Raine was gone completely, so that there would be no danger of lingering thoughts of Raine—his or hers—interfering with their lovemaking.

Heath went still, his good humor dropping away visibly, his expression becoming moody and distinctly resentful. "Just how long is this going to go on?" he asked softly. "Until I'm half-crazed?"

"I don't feel like—"

"I'm well aware of what you don't feel like doing . . . but I damn well do feel like it, and that's as much your problem as it is mine."

Angered by his high-handed manner, she folded her arms across her chest and glared at him. Her temper was so short these days. Why was self-restraint so impossible? "I can't force what I don't feel, Heath."

"Then try pretending you feel it," he sneered. "Or isn't that what you've always done?"

Lucy was stunned by the quick flash of cruelty. She could see that Heath was immediately sorry for what he had said; regret was written all over his face, but before he could say anything else, she replied coldly.

"If you're so anxious, then by all means, let's get it over with. How about right here? Please, go ahead, but be quick about it."

They exchanged a heated stare for a long minute, neither of them backing down.

"I won't ask again," Heath finally said, his voice cutting. "I won't bother you again. When you decide you feel like it, or you're ready, or the moon is full, or whatever the hell it is you're waiting for, then let me know." He started to leave the room, paused, and added, "And then maybe I'll think about it."

She resisted the urge to stamp her foot at him as he left. But if he thought that she would make the first move after what he had said, then he had a long wait ahead of him!

Lucy realized as she looked out the window that the first signs of spring would be here in a matter of weeks. Spring always arrived reluctantly and never stayed long; you had to use your intuition to know it was here. Just when you realized there would be no more snowfall or freezing rain for the rest of the year, the weather blossomed into a hot, steaming summer—time to flock to the beaches of Cape Cod and wade in the icy water, dig in the cool black silt for clams, find creative uses for clumps of seaweed. She smiled and pictured Heath at the seashore. His eyes would be dazzlingly blue against the backdrop of the ocean. When summer came, she would think of some way to lure him away from work to take her to Cape Cod for several days. They had yet to take a wedding trip anywhere, and it would be the perfect place. Flushed with the pleasure of making plans for the future, she looked towards the doorway as she heard Raine's soft steps across the polished floor of the breakfast room.

"I hope you'll have some breakfast before you

leave," Lucy said, discovering that it took little effort to be nice to Raine, since she knew that Raine would be gone from her life in less than a half hour.

"Perhaps some coffee," Raine said, serenely seating herself at the table. "I don't like to travel on a full stomach."

"You certainly have a long journey ahead of you."

Raine said nothing; she merely watched Lucy through the dark screen of her lashes.

"I'm certain," Lucy continued lightly, pouring coffee from a silver service, "that Heath regrets having been forced to leave without seeing you off this morning. But he has to make up for the time he missed while taking Amy to the academy yesterday."

"I knew he would have to leave early this morning. We exchanged our farewells last night." The way Raine spoke conjured up visions of long, tender goodbyes. Irritated, Lucy had to remind herself once again that Raine would be gone soon. Had the hands of the clock frozen in place, or was time really moving that slowly?

"We both wish you well in England—"

"And I wish you well," Raine said, her cool gray eyes shining with a mysterious light as she took a cup of coffee from Lucy's outstretched hand. "I do like you, Lucinda. You may find that hard to believe, but I do. You're difficult not to like. Before I met you, I knew that to have caught Heath, you had to be as slick as goose grease. I was wrong. Heath married you because you're a cheerful little thing, and you have a sweet smile . . . the only warm thing Heath saw in a cold place, among very cold people. You caught him at the right time and the right place, and that was a stroke of luck for you. But I still pity you. The two of you are a mismatch, and that won't ever change."

"He married me for one reason. Because I make him happy. That won't ever change."

"I guess time will prove me right or wrong—"

"It will prove you wrong."

"It might." Raine stood up from the table, leaving her coffee untouched. "All the same, I wish you luck, Lucinda. I am sorry for you. Because I understand more than anyone how you feel about him."

Frozen, Lucy fastened her gaze on the scene through the window, ignoring Raine until she left quietly.

The day after Raine left, Lucy began to feel that it wouldn't take long at all to put their marriage back on the right track. As had been their habit in the months before Heath's illness, they went to church on Sunday and visited with friends and acquaintances they hadn't seen for a long time. Although Heath's religious background had been scandalously undisciplined and it took dedicated effort to drag him to church, Lucy always found some way to coax him to accompany her. As the congregation poured out of the Arlington Street Church, the air in Boston was permeated with the appetizing scents of hundreds of Sunday roasts, kept hot in the ovens during church services so they could be eaten between two and three o'clock.

"Thank God *that* is over," Heath muttered. The sermon had been long and vigorous that morning, full of spine-tingling fire and brimstone. To Heath it seemed to have lasted for hours. He had spent an entire morning wrestling with the pleasure and pain of having Lucy tucked by his side. Acutely aware of her sweet fragrance, her softness, he had found his mind occupied with thoughts that had nothing to do with the service. He felt like more of a sinner coming out of the church than he had going in.

Scandalized, Lucy glanced around to make certain no one had overheard him as they filed out between the two white columns of the freestone church with the rest of the crowd. "Do be quiet—someone's bound to overhear you!"

"I don't like to be preached to as if I'm one of a bunch of schoolchildren who need to be taken to task for—"

"I don't know about everyone else, but there's plenty you and I should be taken to task for," Lucy whispered sharply. "We haven't been here in months."

"Which has been just—"

"Oh, don't say it," she implored, and assumed a quick smile as they passed by the Treadwells and the Nicholsons. They stopped and exchanged pleasantries. "Good morning. Lovely Sunday afternoon, isn't it? Yes, it was a fine sermon." As soon as they resumed their walk to the carriage, Heath dropped his affable expression.

"I don't know why they always have to comment on how long it's been since the last Sunday we were here—"

"We can fix that by attending every week regularly."

"Or not at all."

He sounded so shamelessly unrepentant as he made the suggestion that Lucy groaned in a mixture of laughter and exasperation, and let go of his arm.

"I'm beginning to think your name is short for *heathen.*"

He looked down at her and smiled, his appearance nothing short of angelic, with his sun-washed hair and bright blue eyes. "Don't look at me like that," she said, giving him a severe frown even though she wanted to laugh. "I'm already concerned about the bad example you'll set for our children."

"Forgive me if I don't seem too concerned about our children." There was a faintly mocking curve to his lower lip. "I don't think we'll have to worry about them for a while, unless you're planning on some method of conception I don't know about."

"I can't believe you'd be crude enough to say something like that on a Sunday," she said with frosty dignity, causing him to laugh.

"Are you worried about my salvation?" He looked down at her with a teasing smile and lethal charm.

"Someone has to, and it's obviously not going to be you. Oh, stop laughing—I'm being serious!"

"I'm always charmed by the pious airs you put on every Sunday," he remarked, a half-smile tugging at his mouth. "Alright. If you want to go to church every week, we'll go every week. But it's doubtful that I'll get anything out of it."

His concession mollified her a little. "That's fine. I don't expect any miracles. At the very least, it won't do you any harm."

Heath helped her into the carriage, his eyes glinting as they rested on her small, beautifully turned figure. He hadn't planned on making any promises to her, but then she had mentioned the word *children*, and his heart had skipped a few beats. The thought of having sons and daughters with Lucy filled him with pleasure and anticipation. In a way, he would be sorry to lose Lucy's undivided attention. He liked having her all to himself; there was no doubt about it. He could spend a whole lifetime like this, perfectly happy with just the two of them together. But the two of them with sons and daughters—what a family they would have!

* * *

"Monday," Damon said grimly, making it sound like a curse, "should be struck off the calendar." He and Bartlett, one of the youngest reporters the paper employed, looked around the dispirited editorial room. A few reporters were scribbling languidly at their desks, while others thumbed through reference books and waited for the office hack to come back so they could go out and search for some news.

Bartlett sighed under the oppressive weight of boredom. "Even bad news would be welcome right now."

"In this business, bad news is good news . . . but do you ever get material for a good story on Monday? Of course not. Would it be too much to ask for a natural disaster? A small hurricane? God knows in a state like Massachusetts there should at least be a political scandal." He turned to Bartlett. "What about your personal interview? Did Mrs. Lowell consent to talk to you about her charity auction?"

"No, sir—"

"I knew she wouldn't," Damon said with glum satisfaction. "No matter what Heath said, I knew she wouldn't. The Lowells hate publicity of any kind. My mother used to tell me that a lady is only in the paper three times in her whole life; when she's born, when she's married, and when she dies. And when you think about it, that really does cover the major points."

Bartlett had no idea how to reply. "I suppose so, sir."

"Mr. Redmond!" Joseph Davis, the city editor's young assistant, nearly tripped over a reporter's desk as he made his way over to Damon. "Mr. Redmond—"

"Yes? What are you so excited about? Don't tell me you've found some news to report."

"The doorman told me to tell you that someone is here for Mr. Rayne."

"Tell him that Mr. Rayne isn't available, but
if he'll leave his card—"

"It isn't a 'him,' " Davis said breathlessly.
"It's Mrs. Rayne."

Damon's ebony eyes flashed with interest.
Without a word, he left Bartlett and Davis standing
there as he strode rapidly through the editorial room
to the door. The doorman, gilt-buttoned and rigid-
backed with dignity, stood aside to reveal Lucy, then
closed the door to allow the two of them the privacy
of the hallway. Wearing an emerald green dress and a
tiny velvet hat that perched coquettishly on her head,
Lucy looked like a small, exotic bird against the businesslike gloom of the walls. Damon knew as soon as
he saw her that something was wrong. Although she
smiled at him, there was tension in her face.

"Mr. Redmond, I am sorry to interrupt your
workday."

He took her slender hand in his and pressed a
light kiss on the back of it. "I couldn't think of a more
pleasant interruption. You've never been here before,
have you? Tell me, are you beginning the practice of
delivering your articles in person?"

"Well, no, I . . ." She looked up at him and
laughed. "You weren't supposed to know I was the
one writing them. Did Heath tell you?"

"Of course not. But I knew right away—I
could almost hear your voice out loud as I read them.
You have a marvelous talent with words. Now, before
I begin to shower you with further compliments, tell
me how I can help you."

"I would like to speak with my husband."

"Unfortunately, he's not in the office at the
moment."

"Where is he?"

"Out and around, tying up loose ends, keeping an eye out for news . . ." Damon's voice trailed off into silence as Lucy bent her head and gripped her tiny handbag tightly. "Is there trouble?" he asked softly.

She lifted her head and smiled uncomfortably. "No, I don't think so. I'm probably upset over nothing. I'm certain it's nothing, but . . . but I heard a rumor at my current events club today, and I had to ask my husband about it. Do you know when he'll be back? I know this is all probably very silly, but I felt I had to find him immediately. To me it's very important—"

"What rumor?" Damon cut through her nervous chatter patiently. She hesitated, opening her mouth and then closing it abruptly. "Mrs. Rayne . . . if it bothered you enough to cause you to come here, then it's something that needs to be addressed immediately. It might be something I can clear up right away."

"You'll think it's ridiculous—"

"Nothing that disturbs you is ridiculous. Please tell me about it."

"It was so surprising—I didn't know what to say when someone told me—I think I must have made a fool of myself, because I mumbled something, I don't even know what, and then I left, right in the middle of the meeting—"

"What did this 'someone' tell you?"

"You must be aware that Heath's sister-in-law, Mrs. Laraine Price, was staying with us a few days last week—"

"Yes," Damon said dryly, "I heard a little about it."

"She left for England two days ago. She's not

in Boston any longer. But Mrs. Cummings, one of the women in my club, said that someone had seen Raine yesterday—''

''But that doesn't make sense. No one knows Mrs. Price. How would someone be able to recognize her?''

''There was a day last week when she went shopping with Heath's younger sister and me. I introduced them to a few people—you know how you always see a familiar face at C. F. Hovey? So whoever it was that thought she saw Raine yesterday must have been one of those people . . . oh, it's all ridiculous, just like I said. There's no reason for Raine to be here, and I don't believe a word of it, because Heath wouldn't lie to me, but . . . but . . .''

''But you thought you'd come here to ask him about it anyway?''

''Yes.''

Something about the way Damon was behaving . . . so carefully, so politely, gave Lucy the sense that he was keeping something from her.

''I have a suggestion,'' he was saying, with a charming smile—a little too forced, that smile—''why don't you go home and wait for Heath there? I'll make certain he leaves the office early tonight, and you can work everything out—''

''He isn't usually out of the office at this time, is he?'' Lucy interrupted.

''It depends on—''

''Is he?'' she demanded, and his black eyes locked with hers before he answered reluctantly.

''He's taking care of some business.''

A terrible suspicion flared in her mind, burning like a newly struck match. ''Where is he?''

Chapter Thirteen

SHE HAD NEVER seen Damon look so ill at ease. "I don't know."

"Damon," she said, deliberately using his first name. Her voice was low and insistent, fraught with tension. "You gave your friendship to me. I thought I could depend on it. I'm not asking for your help or your advice . . . I'm just asking for you not to stand in my way. You know where he is. If you won't tell me, I'll find him somehow. I'll walk every street of this city—"

"You can't. That's dangerous—"

"And I'll find him on my own. But it's not your right as my friend to keep this from me."

"It's not fair to bargain with friendship."

"I'm fighting to keep my husband. Rules don't apply. Maybe when you're married, you'll have a better idea of what desperate lengths you'll go to . . . for your sake, I hope not. Now, where is Heath?"

"Mrs. Rayne . . . I can't tell you."

"I understand," she said evenly, her eyes shining with determination. "I'm going, then. Could you at least suggest where I should start looking? Near the Long Wharf? The Marketplace? The—"

"God, no. Lucy, don't. The most godawful things could happen to you, and I'd never forgive myself for—"

"If anything does happen to me, I certainly wouldn't blame you. And I suppose Heath wouldn't either. Well, I have a great deal of territory to cover, and I must be starting. Goodbye."

"Wait." Damon looked at her with a mixture of wonder and outrage, never having dreamed that she was capable of manipulating him so deftly or exerting such unfair pressure on him. They both knew that he would feel responsible if she went out alone and was harmed. He had been reared to be a gentleman in everything he did, brought up so perfectly that he was never at a loss in any situation—but Good God, what was a gentleman supposed to do when faced with something like *this?* "He's at Parker's," he finally said, looking as if he hated himself. "Having lunch."

Lucy nodded slowly, with a bitter smile. "Of course. À la carte at any time. I should have guessed."

He caught her wrist lightly as she turned away. "Stop, Lu . . . I mean, Mrs.—"

"I'm going to Parker's. There's no use in trying to stop me."

"There's nothing you can accomplish by going there."

"I have to see with my own eyes if he's with her."

"Wait for his explanation. Don't try to corner him."

"It's no longer your concern."

He let go of her wrist and combed his fingers through his raven hair, trying frantically to think of what to do. "Wait. Wait right here. I'm going to put the city editor in charge, and I'll be back in a few seconds. I'm going with you. Don't move. Don't go anywhere." He disappeared through the office door and plowed through the editorial room, snapped out a few hasty commands and charged back to the hallway.

No one was there except the doorman, who had resumed his post. "Where is she?" Damon asked a little wildly.

"I'm afraid I don't know, Mr. Redmond. She left right after you went through the door."

Swearing violently, Damon went out to the street, where the office hack had just arrived. After yanking a hapless reporter out of the small vehicle, he informed the driver that they were going to the Parker House, and that he'd better snap to it.

Heath arched a dark brow as he stared at Raine, his eyes cool and blue-green. She returned his gaze without shame or pleading, while the perfect oval of her face glowed pale and clean against the muted burgundy background of the restaurant. The waiter moved quietly around the table, refilling their water glasses without spilling a drop on the smooth white tablecloth. As soon as the waiter left, Heath spoke quietly.

"If it were just up to me, you could live in Boston. You could live right down the street and it wouldn't make a difference to me. I don't care. It probably doesn't say much for my sense of compassion . . . but I don't care."

"You can't convince me that there's nothing in your heart for me."

"Truthfully? . . . maybe a scar or two. But nothing more."

"Not even anger?" she asked, watching him intently. "I find that hard to believe."

"I was angry for a long time. And then I began to understand why you did it—why you married Clay, why you didn't want me there after the war—"

"But I wanted you! I did!" The hard note of desperation entered her voice. "For so long I've

wanted to take back that day and live it all over again.
I'd take back everything I said—I didn't mean any of
it. I wouldn't have hurt you. I never meant to hurt you,
but I already had too much to think about without having to worry about your feelings as well. We all had
to be selfish . . . you were selfish, too!''

''I was selfish, too,'' Heath repeated softly.

''Then you do understand—''

''I understood and forgave you a long time
ago.''

''Then what's stopping us from being together
now?'' she asked, bewildered.

''To begin with, I'm married.''

''I'm not asking you to break up your marriage. I'm not after a wedding ring . . . I just want
you. I'll stay here, and welcome you whenever you
need me. My arms will always be open—''

''I don't need them. After I let go of all the
anger, I stopped wanting you.'' Heath paused, disliking the necessity of being blunt and callous. But Raine
had left him no alternative. ''I stopped thinking about
you.''

''I won't believe that.''

''I doesn't matter what you believe, as long as
you leave Boston within the next twenty-four hours.''

''But if you don't care whether I leave or
not—''

''My wife does, and that's all that matters. If
I have to personally load you onto the next ship that
sails out of the harbor or the next train that pulls out
of the station, then I will. You have the rest of the
world to live in . . . anywhere but Massachusetts.''

''What about you? Lucinda won't always be
able to keep you happy. Soon you're going to want
someone who understands you, someone from the
place where you were brought up, someone who can

talk about the old days with you. You don't have a past with her. You have a past with me.''

There were a hundred different ways Heath could have answered her. There were so many things he could have tried to make her understand—how little the old days meant to him, how well Lucy understood him, and how easy it was for her to make him happy. He could have told her how much his life up here pleased him, and about the sense of purpose and fulfillment it brought him, but there was only one thing truly necessary for Raine to understand, and only one way he knew how to say it.

''I love her, Raine.''

''Once you loved me.''

''I was attracted to you. I cared for you. But that wasn't love. It wasn't real.''

''Nothing else has ever been as real for me.''

''Then I'm sorry for you. And I hope that one day you'll find someone. But there's no hope for you and me. Raine . . . I've been looking for her all my life. Now that I have her, no one else could ever be anything but second-best.''

''S-second-best? To *her?*''

''Yes. Don't ever doubt that.''

''Heath . . . Heath, I don't understand.'' Her stubbornness began to falter, and her heavy lashes fluttered with confusion. ''What do you see in her? What has she done to trap you? Is she . . .'' Raine floundered vainly for words. ''Is she prettier than I am? Is that what you think? Is it that she likes to talk about that newspaper with you?''

The pity in his eyes was genuine as he looked at her. ''I don't know if I can explain something to you that you can't see, or touch, or feel. You wouldn't understand. It's nothing that she's done or said . . . it's not the way she looks—though God knows I couldn't find fault with that. Sometimes people don't have to do anything to make you love them . . . you just do, and there's no help for it.''

She looked down at the tablecloth, refusing to answer. But he read her silence accurately, and he knew that tomorrow morning she would be leaving Boston.

The hack made it to the Parker House just as Lucy's carriage did. Damon leapt onto the curb and was at the door of the carriage in the blink of an eye.

"Lucy, let me in there—let me talk to you for just a minute. Please."

At Lucy's reluctant assent, the disapproving coachman opened the door for Damon, who slid inside immediately. Closed in the dark quietness of the carriage, Damon sat next to her and rapidly sorted through his options. What could he say to her?

"Don't go in there," he said finally, feeling like a tongue-tied idiot as he read the deep misery in her eyes.

"I don't want to," she replied, her voice cracking. "I'm afraid that I'll see Heath and Raine together, and then I won't have any choice but—"

"They *are* in there together . . . take my word for it. So there's no need to go in there and make a scene."

"Damon . . . why is he with her?" she whispered. "Why didn't he tell me? I don't know what to do." She searched clumsily in her handbag for a handkerchief as she started to cry. Her tears were too much for him. After pulling out a handkerchief from his pocket and handing it to her, Damon listened to her muffled weeping for a few seconds, feeling more helpless than he had in years. Carefully he took her into his arms, in a loose, brotherly embrace that communicated no hint of passion. As her weeping continued, his hand moved over the back of her head in a light, protective caress, and his eyes closed for a split second as he gave in to the painful luxury of pretending.

It was too dangerous a game to be playing. He regretted his offer of comfort as soon as he felt her sobbing against his shoulder, but he could no sooner turn away from Lucy's tears than he could stop his heart from beating. He thought of what Heath's friendship meant to him. He thought of his own honor. He thought about Lucy's happiness. There was only one path before him.

"Here's something for you to think about," he said, his voice deliberately light. "At the moment, it would appear to an objective bystander that the two of us are in a far more incriminating situation than Heath and Raine." Startled, she pulled away from him, her eyes wide. "Which should remind us," Damon continued evenly, "not to judge by appearances."

"What are you saying?"

"That nothing's ever exactly what it seems. And instead of jumping to conclusions, you should let your husband explain his actions. He deserves that chance. He doesn't deserve to be put through hell because of some misunderstanding."

"There's one thing I understand very well," Lucy said, wiping her wet cheeks with a corner of the handkerchief. "He lied to me. Every minute that he was with me and didn't tell me that she was still in Boston, he was lying."

"So would I, if I thought I'd lose you."

Coming from Damon, that was the response Lucy had least expected. "You wouldn't really. You're a gentleman. I don't believe you would lie . . . would you?"

He sighed. "The problem with having such high expectations of people, Lucy, is that those standards aren't always easy to live up to. We're all bound to make mistakes . . . and from where I'm standing, I'd say that Heath makes less mistakes than most."

"Are you saying I should excuse him for lying to me?"

"Look at it this way: why would Heath risk telling you that Raine was still in Boston when he had every reason to believe you wouldn't find out? What you didn't know wouldn't have hurt you."

"You're trying to justify his dishonesty!"

"I'm trying to explain why he didn't tell you. He thought he could take care of the problem himself and protect you from ever knowing—"

"I don't need that kind of protection."

"Then tell him. He'll listen."

"How do you know?" she asked suddenly, blowing her nose with a vigorous gust.

"I've never seen a man who listens to his wife the way he listens to you."

"He just humors me."

"No. No, that's not it at all. Lucy . . ." Damon broke off with a rueful laugh. "God, he'll kill me if he ever finds out I told you. But you need to know it, and it's not right to keep it from you. Lucy, Heath never planned to stay in Massachusetts for more than a few months. It was all because of you that he stayed. You're the reason he bought the house in Concord and eventually the *Examiner*. You're the reason he decided to live in New England instead of going back to the South."

"W-what? That can't be true."

"I'll swear it on a stack of Bibles. He came to visit me before leaving New England. He said he was leaving here for good, that he hadn't found what he was looking for, and I thought that was the last I'd ever see of him. He had the look of a man who'd lost his roots. A lot of the veterans turn out like that—they start to wander. Some start walking the rails and jumping boxcars for the rest of their lives—''

''Heath would never have been reduced to that.''

''No, but there was something in his expression . . . something unsettled . . . homeless . . . I can't explain. You'd have to see it to understand what I'm talking about. It was gone the next time I saw him. He came back a month later and told me he'd bought a place in Concord. Heath said he'd decided on the girl he was going to marry, and he had this ridiculous idea about him and me buying the *Examiner,* which was sinking like a stone at the time.'' Damon laughed softly. ''I'm no fool when it comes to money, Lucy. And I didn't have too much at the time, so I intended to be careful about what I did with it. But I'm damned if Heath didn't eventually talk me into buying the paper, and then he showed up with you as his wife.''

''Wait a minute . . . did you say that he had decided on the girl he was going to marry right after he bought the place in Concord?''

''It was in late May. He even told me your name.''

''But . . . but that was before he even met me,'' Lucy said, astounded. Her mind flew back to that January when he had pulled her out of the frozen river. Heath had bought the house in Concord the summer before that. ''He'd only seen me crossing the street, and through the window of my father's store . . . and you say that he had already decided—''

''What he saw, he must have liked.'' Slowly Damon smiled. ''What I'm trying to tell you is that it was all for you. You're the reason for everything he's done. For that matter, you're the reason I'm the managing editor of the *Examiner*. If it weren't for you, Heath would never have talked me into buying the paper.'' Damon regarded her quizzically. ''Do you feel better about everything now? No? Then I'll tell you one more thing . . . no matter what appearances are, only a fool would think that Heath would choose someone else over you. As far as he's concerned, no woman alive could compete with you. He's branded for life.''

''Why do you seem so convinced of that?''

Damon appeared to choose his next words with great care. ''He's changed since he met you. When I knew him before, Heath was a different man.''

''Different in what way?''

''He lived very . . . loosely. He drank hard, all the time. And . . .'' Damon paused and looked at her with dark, unfathomable eyes. ''He used and discarded women with no more thought than if he were going through a box of King Bee cigarettes.''

Lucy's cheeks colored. ''King Bees—''

''Twenty for a nickel. Preferred by men who choose quantity over quality. One after another. I see I've embarrassed you. But you understand what I'm saying . . . have you ever seen him even look at another woman?''

''Not while I'm around, but—''

''He doesn't when you're not around, either. I'd stake my life on the fact that he's completely faithful to you. I've been with him when beautiful women have passed by, and he's never spared any of them a glance. You're the reason why.''

''You're trying to pacify me, but—''

''I'm not trying to pacify you. I'm trying to tell you that I've never seen a man so in . . . well, I'll let him tell you that. I've already overstepped the boundaries too far. Tell me . . . what's your decision going to be? Are you going in there or heading home?''

''I'm not sure.''

''If you go home, I'll talk to him when he gets back to the *Examiner*. I'll tell him that you know Raine is in town. You should be able to handle things from then on.''

She nodded and raised her eyes to his, seeing nothing but quiet friendliness in his gaze, never suspecting what lay beneath it. ''Damon . . . I'm sorry for the things I've said to you today. I held our friendship over your head like a whip—''

''Whatever works,'' he replied, and shrugged.

''Well, if nothing else, today has accomplished one thing . . .''

''What's that?''

''We're finally on a first-name basis.''

Her innocent smile brought him both pleasure and pain. For her sake, he would never treat her with anything but brotherly affection. And, in love with Heath as she was, she would never recognize Damon's real feelings for her. He was relieved that she didn't suspect, despite the deeply buried desire to unburden his heart.

''Aren't we, Damon?'' she prompted, and his mouth curled with a self-mocking smile.

''That we are, Lucy.'' He opened the door of the carriage and gave her a brief salute before swinging lightly onto the pavement.

The hour was late, and still Heath had not returned home. Lucy ate dinner in dispirited silence and went upstairs to take a bath. Sinking into the hot water until she was immersed up to her shoulders, she half-closed her eyes and let her mind drift from one thought to another. No matter what condition Heath arrived in or what hour he walked in the front door, she was determined to talk to him. They would have to come to an understanding; she couldn't live with this uncertainly any longer. If she had to force his hand, then she would, but after tonight she would know the truth about his feelings, and he would know the truth about hers.

She washed her hair and wrapped a towel around it, stepping carefully out of the bathtub. Unable to find her robe, she secured another towel around her chest, tucking the corner of it between the firm swells of her bosom. Walking into the bedroom, Lucy found that it was comfortably warm, and she knelt before the fireplace to dry her hair. The heat of the fire felt good on her face, enticing her to inch closer to the fireguard. She worked at the damp tangles of her hair with light strokes of a brush, pausing often to pry fine strands apart with her fingers.

Dropping one smooth lock and reaching for another, Lucy discovered that some of her hair was caught in the fancy wrought-iron edges of the fireguard. With an impatient exclamation, she tugged at the entire screen to move it further away from the fire, and then she pulled again at the obstinate lock of hair. It was firmly caught. She was effectively trapped, kneeling on the floor. Yanking harder, she accidentally pulled a few hairs right out of her scalp, and the sharp sting of it caused her to swear. It was so infuriating that after a few minutes she almost found it funny, and a frustrated giggle escaped her. Rubbing her sore scalp and tilting her head to the side, she called for help.

"Bess! Bess, can you hear me? Is anyone . . . oh, I don't believe this . . . Bess!"

"Cin? What in the hell are you doing?"

Lucy twisted around in response to the low masculine voice and sighed in resignation. Heath was home. She had planned to have a dignified conversation with him about their differences. She had pictured herself, regal, calm, and forgiving as she talked to him, and instead, she was on the floor, half-naked and sitting in a wet heap of towels.

"I was drying my hair. It got caught," she said, feeling so foolish and wry that she started to giggle helplessly. Heath did not seem to share her amusement in the situation. His face was hard and expressionless as he closed the door and walked over to her in three strides. Swiftly he dropped to his haunches and brushed her hands away from the fire-guard.

"Let go. I'll do it."

"I think it's beyond saving," Lucy informed him, her voice trembling with laughter. "It's really not that much hair . . . if you have something to cut it with—"

"Hush."

With a great effort, she swallowed her amusement and assumed a serious expression as she watched him free her hair, two and three strands at a time. "My back is hurting," she said. "I've been kneeling here for the last ten minutes, and this wet hair is very heavy." When she saw that there was no reply, she fell silent, observing his tedious progress until her back really did begin to hurt. "Heath, I'm getting sore."

"Lean on me."

"I'll get you all wet."

Ignoring her half-hearted protest, he sat down beside her and reached his arms around her to the fireplace screen. There was nothing she could do but settle her back against his chest. Slowly she allowed her head to rest on his shoulder. Occasionally she felt the firmness of his jaw brush against her temple as he worked at her hair with infinite care. Around him lingered the fragrance of shaving soap and expensive linen, the after-work scent of printers' ink, the warm, masculine smell of his skin. The combination of scents was something she associated only with Heath, and it was comforting and pleasant.

"I talked with Damon," Heath said.

Her eyes were alert, but because of their position she couldn't see his face. "He told you everything?"

"Knowing him, probably not everything. But enough."

"Heath, I have some questions—"

"I'm certain you do. But I have one to ask you first."

"Ask me whatever you want. I want us to be open and truthful with each other."

"I want that too. I've never lied to you."

"You kept something from me that I should have been told, which . . . isn't a lie, but it's not being truthful, either."

"The truth," Heath said quietly, "is that I couldn't tell you. For all I knew, you'd fall to pieces if you found out Raine hadn't left Boston. I'm usually on the mark when it comes to guessing what your reactions are going to be . . . but not where Raine is concerned. So when I received her message, and found out that she wouldn't leave until she and I had a chance to talk privately, I thought the best thing to do was take care of everything myself. Cin, I know what it must look like, but you don't really believe that Raine and I . . ." He stopped abruptly. Lucy knew what he was asking.

"No," she said simply, and she felt his body relax as if in relief. "I don't believe you would ever be unfaithful to me, even if you were in love with another woman. You have too much honor. You have too much—''

"I'm not in love with her."

"I . . . I didn't think you were."

"I never was."

"All the same, you shouldn't have avoided telling me that she was still here."

"At the time it seemed like the best way to handle it."

"I understand that," she said carefully. "But when I found out she was in Boston after I thought she had left, I was afraid for a few minutes that I couldn't trust you. If we're afraid to be honest with each other . . . then this marriage is nothing but a sham."

"Don't say that." Heath let go of the skeins of hair in his hands and settled his hands just below her breasts, almost causing them to spill out of the towel as he pulled her back against him. "You have to trust me. I'm the only one in the world who cares more for your happiness than for his own."

She covered his hands with hers, her heart beginning to pound as she heard the gentle obstinacy in his voice. "I want you to be able to trust me in the same way," she said. "More than anything else, that's what I wanted to tell you tonight. And if you're willing, let's just forget about the past few weeks and start off tomorrow with a clean slate."

"And . . . that's it? No arguments or—''

"You'd prefer to have an argument?"

"I'd expected a minor battle, at least."

"Not over this. There's nothing to argue about. We both want the same thing, don't we?'' She caressed the backs of his hands with her palms, and her whole body tingled with pleasure at being near him.

"Apparently so," he said, sounding faintly bemused.

"I just want to know one thing . . . why did Raine stay? I told her before she left the house that I wouldn't let you go."

"She wanted to see if the old days still meant anything to me."

"And what did you say?"

"That they didn't."

"I hope she believed you."

"I know she did. Because I told her one other thing."

"What?"

"I told her that I love you." He felt the quiver that ran through her, and he rubbed his cheek against the softness of her hair. "Lucy, my beautiful girl . . . I thought you'd known it for a long time. But I should have told you out loud, long before now. I fell in love with you a year ago, the first time I held you in my arms."

Lucy licked at a tear that had suddenly trickled down to the corner of her mouth. "There's something you don't know about me."

"What is that?"

"I'm the kind of woman that needs to hear those words often."

"I love you," he repeated, and there was a smile in his voice.

"Every day, and every night. Say it again . . . please."

He repeated the words behind her ear, and against her throat, and in the tender hollows of her body as he bent his head and began to unwrap the clinging towel.

"Ouch!" Lucy's hand flew to her head as her hair was pulled sharply. Immediately Heath shifted her and cursed, turning his attention back to the remaining strands of hair tangled in the wrought-iron fireguard. Despite her own frustrated passion and Heath's hungry impatience, Lucy began to snicker. "If you don't hurry, I'm going to have a bald spot."

"I'm in no mood for laughing, Cin."

His scowl only aggravated her giggling. "I can't h-help it . . . for so long we've wanted to . . . and now that everything is fine, we have to wait . . . so you can—"

He smothered her words with his lips, kissing her as he had wanted to for weeks, until her laughter had dissolved in a flood of wanting. She made a slight noise, soft and imploring, and he increased the seeking pressure of his mouth. His fingers worked busily at her hair until it came free, and a purr of satisfaction vibrated low in his throat. Staggering to his feet with Lucy in his arms, Heath kissed her as he carried her to the bed, miraculously managing to keep from stumbling or dropping her.

Lucy pulled him down to her as soon as her back touched the mattress, her slender arms clasped around his broad shoulders, her slim body arching up to his. Desperately she pulled at the tenacious buttons of his shirt, wanting to feel the strong, naked slide of his body over hers. Together they tore at his clothing, both of them intent on stripping away the layers of cloth that separated them. Suddenly Heath gave a ragged laugh at her impatience and anchored her head to the pillow with his hands, interrupting her progress with his shirt in order to kiss her roughly. Their tongues mated in hot, smooth strokes, lips sealed more tightly together, bodies entwined in a snug embrace.

"I'll never take this for granted," Lucy whispered, turning her head away and refocusing her attention on his clothes. "Being close to you . . . being able to love you . . ."

His mouth traveled down her neck in a moist, wanton caress. "This was never making love before . . . not before you. I knew how different it was going to be with you the first time we kissed."

"You knew that . . . just from a kiss?"

"I'll have to remind you about that kiss."

Somehow Heath shed the rest of his clothes, and he gathered her to him, whispering words that caused her to flush all over. And then, unexpectedly, their movements became slower, languid, reverent. With the knowledge that there would never again be walls between them, all cause for desperation was gone. Trembling, Lucy wound her fingers in his gleaming golden hair as his head moved over her breasts. His mouth captured a soft rose peak and aroused it with a gentle pull. The sleek texture of his tongue soothed her awakening flesh and readied it for another excruciatingly tender tug of his mouth. Her body was filled with a sweet, heavy ache—slumberous and yet aware of every light touch of his hands, every brush of his hair-roughened legs against hers, every short, burning puff of his breath on her skin.

She wanted to tell him how good it was, but words fluttered beyond her reach, eluding the pursuit of her lips and tongue. Instead, she drew her fingertips down his back in a light, scraping touch, causing him to shiver and catch his breath. And then she saw the bright flash of his smile before his mouth wandered to the fragile skin below her breast, the fragrant under-curve where she felt the teasing flicker of his tongue. Her knees were urged apart by the weight of his body, and she opened to him willingly, tensed and eager to feel him inside her.

"Not yet . . . not yet," he said softly, slipping his hands underneath her. Smoothly he rolled over onto his back, taking her with him. Lucy found herself straddling his thigh, her pliant curves flattened on top of his hard-muscled frame. As she read the invitation in his glowing turquoise eyes, she clambered gamely over him, inching upwards until their mouths were even and the tips of their noses were touching. Her hair flowed over him in a shining deluge, and he smoothed it away from her face. He held her hair back until their lips met, and then he let it drop to form a silken curtain around his face as their kiss deepened. Lucy writhed on top of him, against the masculine hardness of him pressing between her legs, until his hands clamped over her buttocks to keep her still.

"Don't move," he said hoarsely, his fingers flexing gently into the sleek roundness of her flesh. "After all the waiting you put me through, I'm going to be the one that decides how, when, and where."

She smiled and offered her mouth to his with sweet generosity. "Then all you have to do is tell me," she breathed against his lips. Her eyes danced with an impish light. "Don't be shy." She pressed a kiss on the corner of his mouth. "How?" Another kiss, on the firm line of his jaw. "When?" A last, soft kiss on the side of his neck. "And where?"

Deftly he flipped her onto her back, his mouth taking a fleeting taste of hers before he lifted himself away from her, and she was bereft of his touch. "Heath?" she asked, suddenly bewildered, and her eyes flew open to find him. She could only see the dark silhouette of him against the bright firelight. "Heath—"

"Shhh. I'll answer all your questions at once."

She felt the warm palms of his hands curve over her bent knees, prying them open and spreading them wide, sliding over her inner thighs until she fell back against the pillow helplessly, her mind reeling at the burning touch of his fingertips. His head settled between her thighs, his hands suppressed the sudden flinch of her body, and then his mouth was opening over the softest, most private part of her. Her legs flexed involuntarily as she instinctively sought to protect herself from this utter vulnerability, but her ankles were pinned underneath him. His tongue stole out to stroke her trembling flesh, and his hand slid over her hipbones in a slow, circular massage. Subsiding back against the pillows, she said his name weakly, her voice a shadow of sound. She sensed the depths of the pleasure it gave him to hold her helpless and trusting in his hands, knowing her as no other man ever would. Her blood surged with startling force, so that all she could hear was its pounding in her ears, and then ecstasy convulsed her with a violent caress.

Slowly Heath raised his mouth, nuzzling the damp triangle of curls at the top of her thighs, and despite what they had just shared, Lucy went scarlet at the sight. His eyes twinkled as he saw her discomfiture, and he eased back up to kiss the side of her neck. How intimate he was with her, as if no part of her should remain secret from him. She had never dreamed that any man would want to know her so well; she had never imagined when she first met this man that someday he would possess her thoughts, her heart, and her body so completely. And yet, perhaps she had known. Who was to say when love began? The first glance, the first kiss, the first promise—it didn't matter. She looked at him with her heart in her eyes, and the gentle suggestion of a smile lurked in the corners of her mouth.

"I love you, Heath. I love you."

He rose above her, and the dispersed light

from the fireplace played over the scarred sleekness of his skin. Fire and gold, sinew and strength—he was a marvel to her, and she reveled in the knowledge that he had given himself to her. Filling her slowly, he waited with unsteady gasps as he felt the delicate inner stretch of her body, and then she lifted her hips to accept him more deeply. Endless moments were theirs as their flesh was joined. She answered his long, heavy strokes with the same perfect rhythm, with the tender strength of her love. His muscles tightened, and he thrust into her one last time, the heat of him spreading through her in a searing flow. They held each other tightly, reluctant to allow any separation between their bodies. Splaying her fingers through his hair, she kissed the salty dampness of his temples, his cheeks, his lips. He smiled and rolled over lazily as he was suffused with pure masculine contentment, pulling her on top of him so that she could continue the rain of kisses undisturbed.

She cuddled closer against him while their warmth combined under the covers. "Now I'm even sorrier for all those nights we didn't spend together." Her hand wandered across the ridged flatness of his midriff.

"I'm not. We both had some learning to do, some thinking to do."

"Are you saying you didn't miss me?" she demanded in mock outrage.

"Settle down," he said, and chuckled, pulling her closer against his side. "Hell, yes, I missed you . . . I spent most of those nights staring up at the ceiling or pacing the floor. But I needed that time alone in order to figure out what a stubborn fool I had been for letting my pride come between us."

"Your pride?"

"Those weeks after I was sick . . . I realized how much I depended on you . . . and it was hard on my ego." A touch of sheepishness entered his voice. "I was raised to think a man should take care of everything and be in control at all times. And then all of a sudden I was at everyone's mercy, especially yours. I shouldn't have taken it out on you, but I felt I had to put some distance between us, until I felt more . . . in control again."

"Maybe I was a little bossy. But I was frightened for you. I've never been so afraid about anything—"

"You weren't bossy. You were exactly the way you should have been. I know all about what you went through, and what you did, and God knows I wasn't so much of a fool that I didn't appreciate what a woman you turned out to be. On the other hand, a man's pride is easily bruised, Cin."

"I'll take care to remember that," she said with exaggerated solemnity, and yelped as he made a move as if to tickle her.

"Sass. I try to talk to you about something serious, and all I get is sass."

"Heath . . ." She crawled on top of him and lay her head on his chest, "I wish it could have been like this in the beginning. Now I can hardly believe there was so much anger between us, and that I was actually afraid of being . . . intimate with you—"

"We didn't know each other then. And I should have been more patient with you. After all, I'd taken you away from Daniel—"

"You were doing me a favor."

"True, but you didn't know that at the time."

"Conceited thing." She made the words sound like an endearment as she strung kisses along his collarbone.

"But I'll always have a little guilt about the way I got you away from Daniel. I should have done it another way. That morning after Emerson's fire . . . I knew if I could get you in a compromising position, someone was bound to see us. It was just a coincidence that it happened to be Daniel and Sally."

"Don't feel guilty about it."

"But to do that to you after you came to see if I was alright . . . and it was no accident that I seduced you, Cin—it was deliberate—and you didn't even know what you were doing—"

"I knew what I was doing," she said calmly, surprising him into silence. "No one forced me to go out there alone to see you. And as for what happened after that . . . I wasn't fighting you. I wanted you. If it hadn't happened then, it would have happened some other time."

"You're making me regret not having compromised you during those two days after we first met. I would have, with any encouragement at all."

"Rascal. I never knew when you were going to sneak around the corner and surprise me in my pantalets."

"I thought about how you looked in those pantalets and my shirt every time I saw you after that."

"I could tell." Lucy smiled in the darkness. "Afterwards you always looked at me in a way that made me blush, and I couldn't help remembering the time we'd spent alone together. But even if I'd never seen you again, I would never have forgotten those two days. And I think I would have always wondered what it might have been like with you. Would you have wondered, too?"

"It would have haunted me for the rest of my life."

Lucy slid her arms around his neck and whispered against his mouth. "Isn't it strange, how fate brought us together?"

"Don't give fate too much credit for us being together, honey. I wanted you from the beginning. And some men always find a way to get what they want—even if fate doesn't lend them a hand."

She believed him. Heath Rayne was that kind of man.

Author's Note

The burning of Ralph Waldo Emerson's home occurred in 1872, three years after the date used in *Love, Come to Me*. By Emerson's own accounting, all of his books and manuscripts were saved by the men of Concord, who ran into the smoke-filled house to retrieve his work, despite the danger of falling timbers. After taking a trip abroad with his daughter, Emerson returned to Concord to find that his friends had rebuilt the house for him exactly as it had once been.

Although the Boston *Examiner* is a fictitious newspaper, a Boston newspaper was created in 1872 that eventually did challenge the long-established supremacy of the Boston *Herald*. Under the innovative direction of the young Chas. H. Taylor, the Boston *Globe* became a paper noted for its progressiveness and the contributions it made to the development of modern journalism.

The Era of Reconstruction was largely considered to be closed with the election of Rutherford B. Hayes in 1876 and the withdrawal of the last federal troops from the South.

PASSION RIDES THE PAST

☐ **GREEN DRAGON, WHITE TIGER by Annette Motley.** From her barren Asian homeland to the opulent splendor of the seventh century Tang Court, lovely, indomitable Black Jade pursues passion and power with two generations of emperors, and finds her ultimate glory on the Dragon Throne. (400615—$4.95)

☐ **TO LOVE A ROGUE by Valerie Sherwood.** Raile Cameron, a renegade gunrunner, lovingly rescues the sensuous and charming Lorraine London from indentured servitude in Revolutionary America. Lorraine fights his wild and teasing embraces, as they sail the stormy Caribbean seas, until finally she surrenders to fiery passion. (400518—$4.50)

☐ **WINDS OF BETRAYAL by June Lund Shiplett.** She was caught between two passionate men—and her own wild desire. Beautiful Lizette Kolter deeply loves her husband Bain Kolter, but the strong and virile freebooter, Sancho de Cordoba, seeks revenge on Bain by making her his prisoner of love. She was one man's lawful wife, but another's lawless desire. (150376—$3.95)

☐ **HIGHLAND SUNSET by Joan Wolf.** She surrendered to the power of his passion . . . and her own undeniable desire. When beautiful, dark-haired Vanessa Maclan met Edward Romney, Earl of Linton, she told herself she should hate this strong and handsome English lord. But it was not hate but hunger that this man of so much power and passion woke within the Highland beauty. (400488—$3.95)

Buy them at your local bookstore or use this convenient coupon for ordering.

NEW AMERICAN LIBRARY
P.O. Box 999, Bergenfield, New Jersey 07621

Please send me the books I have checked above. I am enclosing $_____
(please add $1.00 to this order to cover postage and handling). Send check or money order—no cash or C.O.D.'s. Prices and numbers are subject to change without notice.

Name_____

Address_____

City _____ State _____ Zip Code _____

Allow 4-6 weeks for delivery.
This offer is subject to withdrawal without notice.

From Onyx—
Tantalizing Historical Romance

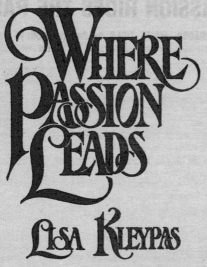

WHERE PASSION LEADS

Lisa Kleypas

*Only the fire of love could melt the barriers
between a governess' daughter and a rakish lord . . .*

When beautiful young Rosalie Belleau first fell prey to
the passion of handsome Lord Randall Berkeley, he
believed she was any man's for the taking. Before he
realized his mistake, he had branded her with his
desire—and she had stolen his heart! But Rosalie's
path was strewn with unknown enemies, and only the
flames of passion could light the lovers' way through a
labyrinth of danger . . . and on to the dazzling heights
of ecstasy. . . .

There's an epidemic with 27 million victims. And no visible symptoms.

It's an epidemic of people who can't read.

Believe it or not, 27 million Americans are functionally illiterate, about one adult in five.

The solution to this problem is you... when you join the fight against illiteracy. So call the Coalition for Literacy at toll-free **1-800-228-8813** and volunteer.

Volunteer Against Illiteracy. The only degree you need is a degree of caring.